The Seafror

By the same author

Fiction

A Seaside Mourning
A Christmas Malice
Balmoral Kill
The Shadow of William Quest
Deadly Quest
Loxley
Wolfshead

The Seafront Corpse was first published in Great Britain in 2016 by Gaslight Crime

ISBN-13: 978-1519788986

ISBN-10: 1519788983

The Seafront Corpse

An Inspector Chance Mystery

John Bainbridge

GASLIGHT CRIME

One

Sussex 1931

There were always ways to make money if you had the nous.

Despite the Depression, he had nothing but contempt for those who didn't. The newspaper he'd found on the train had been full of the usual whining from disgruntled miners. All it took was a visit from the Prince of Wales and they'd trot off happily to the Labour Exchange, thinking someone cared. What fools people were.

He'd passed on the station buffet for the best tea-room Tennysham had on offer. Upstairs in Grove's department store, it had still been Grove's Drapery Bazaar when he'd first known it. The ground floor stank of good perfume and greasy cosmetics. Blank-faced assistants faking an interest in old women in furs. One was rubbing cream on the back of a brown blotched hand, veins heavier than the rings. She caught his eye and smiled, the mask real for an instant. He winked.

The tea-room was fairly full at that time of the afternoon and Leslie Warrender took a seat in the window where two rigidly corseted matrons had just left. The table was still to be cleared. He moved a saucer and pocketed the threepenny bit underneath as he consulted the menu. The waitress came up to him, looking flustered.

'I'm really sorry, sir, I'll straighten this for you. We're short-staffed today and the lunch-time rush isn't long over.'

'That's quite all right. Not too early for afternoon tea, am I?'

She hesitated, glancing at the large rectangular clock. He bestowed a boyish smile that made her forget her aching feet.

'Oh no, not at all, sir. We've just started. Are you ready to order?'

'I rather think I'll try the set tea.'

'Very good, sir.'

He tucked into his food as soon as it came. Looked down at the passers-by, blurred beneath the long glass verandah. Across the street he watched a blind man standing patiently with a tray of shoe-laces. His head turned, following the sound of footsteps going past. Sorry chum, the world's moved on. Nobody wanted to see the maimed haunting street corners, reminding them.

It amused him to think how well-heeled he must look when all he had was a pound note in his pocket. When he'd finished eating, he took out a match-book and a finely tooled silver case. It was inscribed with initials that had happened to be his. Tapping an expensive Sullivan, he lit up and sat back, blowing smoke elegantly.

A third-rate pianist had started tinkling softly in the background and he watched the other customers from his vantage point by a fern on a wooden stand. You could learn a lot from watching people, especially women and he was out of practice. A shaft of bitterness fell like a shadow across the table.

Forget that. The past was over and done with. What mattered now was a bright future. What a provincial dump Tennysham was. A few months ago he'd never intended to see it again. Then fate had handed him an unexpected reminder. He wasn't one for looking back and his time working here seemed like a lifetime ago.

The waitress broke into his thoughts, tucking the bill by a plate and removing the cake stand. Her eager, shiny face left him cold. Decent legs though.

There'd been a girl in Tennysham who'd had good legs. No money to speak of but very pretty. She'd been eager. If women only knew how that brought out the worst in a man. He went for women who looked indifferent. Sleek hair, perfectly groomed, their perfume wafting money.

Carrying his small case, he walked out into the High Street. A weak sun was breaking through the clouds. In the window a sign suggested *Pastels For Spring* before a display of hats and light gloves draped across hand-bags.

A unwanted memory stirred of the downs in springtime. Nature walks from infant school, the mournful bleating of lambs and a feeling of freedom. High on the green ramparts overlooking the Channel, as the Romans had when they marched along the dirty cream tracks.

He'd lie in bed, reading about the smugglers who used those ways by night. No hidden coves in Sussex. Long pebble beaches and perilous paths, steeper than trench ladders up the chalk clefts. He'd fall asleep to the sound of boys' voices drifting from the chapel. Long before the war when the world was different.

Only a fool was sentimental about childhood. He'd had far too much time to think. Revisiting old stamping grounds never did anyone any good. He supposed it was because his old ma was dead. Women never stopped believing in him. Well, he was about to collect a fresh start. Who needed a pallid English spring when the parasols would be out on the Riviera?

The rows of streets behind the sea-front all looked the same. Starchy, scrubbed, wearing their facades like uniforms. Down at heel but fighting a rear-guard action. The ugly bulk of a gas-works rose above the chimney pots and gulls circled like vultures.

Pearl-street, chosen at random had several houses with *Room To Let* propped in their bay window. On a whim he stopped at number nineteen, his birthday. Clean nets, a red geranium and *Aberfeldy* on the glass over the door.

The woman who answered his knock was holding a tea cloth. He flicked on the charm, as instant as electric lighting. Her other hand touched her inexpertly-styled hair. The sum she named was the going rate, he supposed. Her expression was sympathetic as she looked at his case.

'Salesman are you?'

'Insurance agent.' It was the first thing that came into his head. He believed in thinking on his feet. Say brushes or cloths and she might want to see some samples.

'Would you be wanting an evening meal?'

'Better not. I'd be coming and going. I've an old friend to look up while I'm in the area.'

'That's nice for you. It's the room at the front so there's a sea view of a sort.'

She smiled in a defeated kind of way as she held the door wider. Flattening herself against the wallpaper so he could climb the stairs first. A nice woman with hope in her eyes. She needed the money. Wedding ring worn thin, a widow, he'd bet.

'It's the first on the left.'

There was a brief moment when he wondered if the house was paid off. She couldn't be more than late forties. In another life she'd be pathetically grateful for someone like him to take an interest. He'd be doing her a favour, take her out of herself.

He had bigger fish to fry.

Two

Four days later

'That man's still there.'

Ivy Betts paused in the window of number three, her arms full of clean bed-linen. Across The Esplanade sea and sky were merged in dull grey, the colour her dad called *feldgrau*. He was a bit of a card, her dad, throwing in the odd French word, which made her ma's lips tighten and singing snatches of French songs while he worked on his bike.

It looked as though it might rain. She watched as an elderly couple came in view with a small white dog. As they passed the sea-front shelter where the man sat in a corner, they slowed as though considering joining him. Ivy knew she should get on but couldn't resist watching the small tableau.

They would exchange good mornings 'cause that was what you said. Then they'd laugh and have a word about the weather, *could be worse*, as they settled themselves.

Only it didn't happen. The dog started to turn in. The old couple stuck their heads in and thought better of it, the woman tugging at the dog's leash in a dumb show of disapproval.

'Come away, Ivy. The beds won't make themselves.'

'Yes, Miss Aldridge, sorry.' She'd better look lively. Ivy began to flatten the under-blanket over the mattress, averting her eyes from a small irregular stain on the ticking. Her dad would say it was the shape of Belgium.

Her employer watched her work. 'It's a wicked waste after two nights, the price the laundry charges.'

Ivy framed an understanding expression but made no comment as she moved to each corner.

'What was so interesting outside?'

'Only a man in the shelter over the way. He's been there a long time and he doesn't seem to move. I saw him on my way to work. I wondered if he's poorly or unhappy.'

Miss Aldridge sniffed. She had a language of them and she, Mrs Thompson and Eric, the boot boy all knew what each one meant.

'You shouldn't be wasting your time wondering about things that don't concern you.'

'A couple did look in the shelter. I suppose he can't be ill.'

'There you are then.' Taking up her pince-nez, she focused on the scene across The Esplanade. The cord dangled against her flat chest. 'Hmm, looks respectable enough from the back. He's probably asleep. Now, Ivy, don't you forget to save the soap this time. There's plenty of girls would be glad of your position, you know.'

'Yes, Miss, I won't.'

She didn't risk pulling a face behind her back. Her employer had eyes in the back of her head and she needed this job.

Finishing the bed, Ivy wiped a row of stubble from the basin before reaching for the drum of Dawn and shaking out a meagre amount. The remaining sliver of soap held a curly dark hair like a question mark.

She'd got in terrible trouble last week when she'd thrown away the tiny heel of a bar, which Miss Aldridge had retrieved from the kitchen bin. They were to be softened, coaxed together and worked into a new bar for one of the cheaper rooms.

The Belvedere wasn't one of the best hotels along the sea-front, whatever Miss Aldridge thought. Situated at the less favoured end of town where the buildings started to peter out, you had a fair walk to the pier and the rooms at the back overlooked the roof-top of the bus depot.

It was a commercial-hotel with a few winter residents. They catered for holidaying families though it was too early in the year for those. The beach did have a stretch of sand between the grey pebbles but that was down the other end too.

It occurred to her that Miss Aldridge was more hard up than she let on. When she first came, her employer had always worn a large sapphire ring. Ugly with an old-fashioned claw setting, she'd once mentioned it had belonged to her mother. Come to think of it, she hadn't noticed it for a while.

What's more, Miss Aldridge hadn't found a replacement for Meg which meant twice as much work fell on her shoulders. And only that morning Mrs Thompson complained the meat order had to be cheaper every week.

Her dad always said she thought too much. *No sense worrying over strangers, girl. They wouldn't do the same for you.* Bundling the used linen into the basket on the landing, Ivy decided she'd think about something cheerful while she did the brass. Rushed off her feet serving the breakfasts, she'd earned a sit-down.

*

Raindrops ran down the window panes, blurring the view of slate roofs and heavy sky. Inside a comfortable fug was building, the wisp of smoke from the ash-tray overlaid by the strong sweet hay coming from his sergeant's pipe. The gas fire popped as it began to throw out heat and his wet mackintosh gave off a hint of wet dog. Friday afternoon, on a good day to be inside.

'Sorry, Wilf, wool-gathering. What was that?'

'I said..' Pause... 'Aren't you glad to be back somewhere civilised?'

The words came like Morse Code, punctuated by alternate drawing and examining his tobacco. Who needs Morse when you can send smoke signals?

'Oh, Brighton? No, I liked it well enough but I'm not sorry to be gone. Too much work.'

They'd been chewing over the difference between the two towns. Or rather Bishop had while he finished scanning the last report and scrawling his initials. Chucking the thin folder on his out-tray, Eddie Chance yawned and tipped his chair back on two legs.

Tennysham-on-sea might be considered dull but he rather liked that in a place. It was all of a muchness.

Brighton was like an experienced whore with different tricks for different customers. The glamour set sweeping up to The Metropole in their fur collars were a world apart from the shabby streets behind the grand squares.

'Their crime's much worse than ours,' Bishop said complacently.

They'd had their share of London villains who fancied some sea air and a little business up at the race-course. Nothing that rattled him but he was enjoying the quiet life.

'Cup of tea wouldn't go amiss. Shall I give Phyllis a shout?' His pipe behaving itself at last, Bishop's face was deadpan, his eyes twinkling.

'Why not?'

If the young woman who entered a few minutes later, thought she had more about her than tea-making duty, she gave no visible sign of resentment as she parked the tray.

'Biscuits, sir?'

Hesitating, Chance considered the slight paunch he meant to see off before it settled down for life. The week-end loomed and he was off duty. Good. There were still shelves to put up. His mother-in-law was sure to be round. Resolve collapsed. Grunting in acknowledgement, he helped himself to three digestives and dunked one immediately. Bliss.

'Sarge?'

'Ta. All quiet out the front?'

'One dog licence, a lost umbrella, an empty wallet handed in and an old lady's just been enquiring about the bus times. That's all.'

She sounded disappointed, Chance thought.

Bishop raised his eyes to the yellowed ceiling. 'Does she think a blue lamp means Southdown?'

'It's not the first time.' Phyllis picked up the full ash-tray on the desk and was turning to leave when someone knocked on the office door.

'Get that, will you?'

The tips of the detective-constable's ears were red. Whether cold or embarrassment at being the centre of attention, Chance couldn't decide. Clearing his throat, Godwin hesitated as the three occupants looked at him.

'Spit it out, man.'

'A call's just come in about a body being found on the beach, sir.'

'What sort of body? Heart attack? Drowning? Don't give half a report, Constable. What about sex?'

The colour deepened. 'It's a male, sir. Cause of death not known. Found by a young woman. Sergeant Lelliott said he wondered if you'd mind going in the circumstances?'

'Could be a fall, I suppose. Anywhere near the pier?'

'No, sir. It's in a shelter on the prom.'

Chance blinked. 'Where is this woman now and is anyone with the corpse?'

'She's waiting at The Belvedere Hotel, sir. Seems she found the body and ran back to her place of work. It's her employer who telephoned.'

'And the corpse?'

'Don't know, sir.' Godwin looked miserable, shuffling his feet.

Chance flicked a look at his sergeant, leaning against the filing cabinet. 'Probably nothing for us but we'd better get down there.'

'Has the doc been sent for, lad?'

'I'm not sure, Sarge.'

Sighing, Chance took pity on him, aware of the suppressed excitement radiating across his desk. In contrast to Godwin, Phyllis had the air of a bloodhound quivering on the scent.

'Get back to the desk. Ask Sergeant Lelliott to locate Dr. Wheeler and request him to attend the scene urgently and get a car brought round. You'd better grab your gear and come with us, just in case. I take it you know where it is?'

'Yes, sir. It's the last one before Eastcliff. That's at..'

'All right, Godwin. I know where the cliffs start. I grew up here.'

'Sorry, sir, I forgot.'

'No,' Chance said, pleasantly, as his constable shut the door. 'Absolutely not.'

Taking a deep breath, Phyllis spoke rapidly. 'Sir, I thought if a young woman's involved, she might be glad of a female officer present.'

'I'm sure you have some filing to do, Constable Marden.'

She looked at Sergeant Bishop as he passed the inspector his mac from the back of a chair.

'On your way, love. You can read all about it later when you type the reports.'

Chance sighed again and picked up his hat, waving the young woman before them. 'I knew it was too good to last.' The remaining biscuits lay discarded in his saucer.

They were silent in the car. The pavements were empty of people as they passed the building site on the corner. The new picture-house was rising above the bright wrinkled advertisements on the hoardings. A woman was shaking her umbrella beneath the ornate glass arcade in the High Street and they were changing a window display in the town's only department store.

Bishop clutched the door-strap as the car swerved into a short street with the sea at its end.

'Steady on, Constable.'

'Sorry, sir. Took it a bit wide to avoid the water.'

Chance sat back. A great puddle had already collected on the corner where the road surface dipped.

'The drain's blocked,' Bishop said. 'Those Victorian sewers have had it. What do we pay rates for?'

'The Mayor's New Year Ball,' Chance murmured, next to him. They'd just passed a tattered poster, still up two months later. As the head of C.I.D. he'd received an invitation, along with Superintendent Hayes and Bob Forrest, his opposite number in uniform. He'd declined, citing a long-standing family engagement. Fingers crossed Stella would never find out or his life wouldn't be worth living.

At this time of year the white stucco hotels looked like wedding cake left out for the birds. Here and there the run was broken with buff brick and flint or someone had been daring with blue paint. The twin booths at the entrance to the pier were shuttered and the iron gate padlocked across the public urinal. The air stung with salt as he wound down his window.

'The one at the end.' Godwin pointed along the promenade and Constable Richards steered the police car into the kerb.

'Looks like we're expected,' Bishop said.

A pinched-faced youth stood waiting. Inadequately dressed for the weather, hair plastered to his head, he watched them apprehensively.

The three detectives got out. Chance turned up his collar and looked back at the driver.

'And you, Richards. If I have to get wet again, so can you. Wait there and keep an eye out for the doctor.'

'Will do, sir.'

'Are you from the hotel, son?'

The youth nodded. 'Miss Aldridge said I was to stand here and wait for you and stop anyone from coming by.'

'Your name is?'

'Eric Leigh, sir. I do the shoes and the luggage. And the bins,' he added, 'and all the ..'

'All right, lad. We get the picture. Take your hands out of your pockets when you're speaking to the Inspector.'

Bishop's severe voice still sounded kind. Chance repressed a grin.

'Has anyone come past here since you were posted, Eric?'

The boy shook his head vigorously. 'No, sir. No one with any sense would be out in this.' His pimples stood to attention.

The poor kid's face was like a join the dots puzzle, Chance thought. I'm surrounded by blushing youths. At least Godwin had a skill and prospects. This one would be on his first job since school. No Certificate probably, no prospects and out the door if he didn't keep his nose clean. And the shoes clean.

'I'm sure you couldn't resist taking a look. Ever seen him before?'

'No, sir. Not that I know of.'

'Did you touch anything?'

Another vigorous shake. 'Miss Aldridge said not to go inside. I only had a quick see from the path.'

'Cut along back to the hotel now. Tell Miss Aldridge we'll be along as soon as we can to see the young lady who found the body.'

'Ivy, sir. She's proper shook up.'

He was on the edge of the two steps down to the road when Chance spoke again.

'And thanks, Eric. You've done well.'

The boy grinned, jumped down nimbly and dashed diagonally across the road. They watched as he disappeared round the side of a hotel on the end of a terrace.

'To work then.' Chance led the way to the front of the shelter, halting with Bishop on the open threshold.

Behind them Godwin flinched as rain ran down the steeply pitched roof, landing on his neck. Shifting, he managed to see round the inspector's broad shoulder.

Ignoring the stifled exclamation, Chance picked up the trilby lying upside down at his feet. He examined the inner band before tossing it on the slatted bench. The sound of boots on shingle made him turn. Godwin had moved a few feet away with his back to them.

'First time?'

'On our side of the fence. He came to us from uniform not long before you returned.'

'He can have this one but he'll have to toughen up. He'd see a sight worse than this in traffic.'

'Fair enough.'

The body sat propped in the corner, dull eyes not gazing out to sea. Chance considered dispassionately. Early forties at a guess. His own age. The type that women would consider good-looking, though he'd been going off. Hammocks slung below the eyes and pasty skin even before death?

'Poor devil.' Bishop pulled a face at the odour of morning pub. 'He doesn't have the look of a tramp though.'

'No. That's brandy and plenty of it. I can't see a gent of the road affording that.' Chance looked in the corner behind the stiff outstretched legs. 'No bottle. Decent shoes, good coat and he's clean. Too clean for a wash and brush up in a public toilet. Let's see if there's any identification.' He undid the buttons of the overcoat, revealing a sleeveless pullover.

Bishop gave a low whistle. They both stared at the rusty brown bloodstain worn like a school badge on the fawn wool.

'Looks like we're in business. What d'you make of it, Wilf?'

'Stabbed through the heart or lung maybe. Then the murderer did up the coat to delay the alarm being raised? A cool customer.'

'Weren't they just? With the hat tilted forward, he'd have passed for asleep if no one looked too closely. We'd better wait for the expert to look at the wound.'

'What about his pockets?'

Chance felt inside the coat. 'Nothing. How about the trousers?' Holding out his hand he showed some loose change before returning the coins and wriggling his hand in the other pocket. 2s 9d and a clean handkerchief. The coat pockets are empty. That's it. No wallet or door key.'

'He must have been killed here. No one could move a sitting body without it being obvious. So he'd had a few, he's on his way home from the pub. Decides to sit here for a bit, minding his own business?'

'But why? No cigarettes on him. Was he meeting someone?'

'Could be. Maybe he felt rough. Thing is, it's a long way home if you go via the promenade.' Bishop looked through the window in the rear of the shelter. 'Perhaps he was staying somewhere over the road?'

'It would account for his not having a key. Hang on.' Chance stepped out of the open shelter, raising his voice slightly. 'Godwin, your big moment. Come and earn your pay.'

'Sir.' Looking pale, the constable picked up the tripod he'd left against the pillar. Then he unfolded his camera. 'Are you going to close his eyes, sir?'

Chance decided Godwin hadn't actually thrown up. 'He was knifed. We're waiting for the doctor to uncover the wound. He'll close the eyes in due course. You're going to have to get used to these things.'

'He's wearing a wrist-watch.' Bishop had pushed back a coat sleeve. 'That doesn't look like robbery even if the wallet's missing. Still perhaps the killer was disturbed.'

Joining him, Chance turned over the hand, then the other. 'Are you thinking what I'm thinking, Wilf?'

'I am.' Catching Godwin's eye, Bishop beckoned him closer.

'Take a look. What do you see?'

'Er, he's not wearing a wedding ring.'

'True but look closer. What about the palms?'

Godwin looked up triumphantly. 'His hands are rough so he was some kind of workman?'

'You're on the right lines. These are long-standing.' Bishop indicated the ridge of thick, hard skin below the fingers. 'The Inspector and I have seen these before, together with the washed-out skin. That's what they call prison pallor. He's been a guest of His Majesty. Pound to a penny he earned those callouses breaking rocks. They're the marks of hard labour.'

'When you're ready, Godwin. Start with close shots of the entry site here.'

'Right, sir.'

They stood outside as he bent and squatted, taking photographs from several angles. Whatever his shortcomings Godwin seemed at home with his equipment.

'He's a dab hand at fingerprints too,' Bishop muttered in Chance's ear.

'I wish him joy of it. Think how many people have been in there.'

'At least it isn't summer. You'll have to get this place dusted after the body's been taken away, Godwin. The edge of this pillar's a likely spot. People often rest their hand on something.'

'Yes, Sarge.'

'They probably wore gloves. No footprints besides ours. Couple of spent matches but they could have been there for weeks. They'll need to be bagged up, just in case.'

'Here comes Wheeler.' A Morris was pulling up with a plain van stopping behind it. Chance raised a hand as a short figure got out. A word to Richards and he strode towards them. 'He's brought the blood-wagon with him.'

'Afternoon Eddie, Wilf. Nice day for it.' The usual cigarette wedged in the side of his mouth, the doctor busied himself brushing ash off his tweeds. 'What do you have for me?'

'In there, Lionel. A knife wound. He's all yours.'

'Not a very cheerful chappie. He went with a sea view though. People pay good money for that.' Straightening up, Dr. Wheeler peered towards the horizon. 'There are worse places to die if your time's up.'

'What can you tell us?'

'Hold your horses.' Stooping again, Wheeler lifted the pullover, his finger probing the small rust-edged rip in the shirt. 'Keep that out of the way, will you?'

Glancing at Godwin, Bishop stepped forward and seated himself next to the corpse. Holding the pullover up to the armpits, he watched as the doctor unbuttoned the shirt and teased the cloth away from the wound.

'Thought so. Bullseye. Stabbed right in the region of the heart.' He smacked his lips, possibly in admiration for a job well done.

'There isn't much blood.' Godwin's voice was diffident.

'That, Constable, is an interesting phenomenon. With a single knife thrust that penetrates the heart, it's not uncommon for there to be little blood visible on the surface. It stops pumping immediately and all the damage is contained within. See? The entry site almost seals the bleeding. Funnily enough, a slashing knife wound which produces copious amounts of blood will often do less damage. It's all in the depth and angle of thrust.'

'So it's unlikely the killer had blood on him?' Frowning, Chance studied the fatal cut in the middle of what looked like a smudged fingerprint beneath the skin. The colour resembled gentian violet.

'I'd say probably not. A smear on a cuff at most.'

'A single thrust. From a thin blade?'

'Probably. I'll know more when I get him on the slab.'

'Would death have been instantaneous?' Bishop said.

'Virtually. Judging by the smell of alcohol, I doubt he saw it coming. Someone he knew, I'd say.'

'Or someone he didn't view as a threat,' Chance said. 'What about the strength required? Could a woman have done it?'

'You know what they say about the female of the species. It wouldn't have taken great strength.'

'Was it someone with medical knowledge?'

'Can't help you there. Might have been. On the other hand it could have been luck.'

'Care to speculate on the time of death?'

'If I must. Help me turn him over, will you? Rummaging in his bag, the doctor extracted a thermometer. Godwin stared at the beach.

'Where are we?' A glance at his wrist-watch. 'Almost twenty past four. The body being outside doesn't help, as you know. At a rough guess, call it sometime last evening between about seven o'clock to midnight.'

Chance looked at Bishop and groaned. 'That's quite a margin. I hope you'll be able to narrow it down.'

'We'll see. I can fit him in straight after breakfast as it's Saturday. Shall I expect you there?'

'We'll both come. Sorry, Wilf.'

'That's all right. Glad's been muttering about spring-cleaning. She'll be pleased to have me out from under her feet.'

'He was definitely killed in situ by the way.'

'Take a look, Godwin.'

'Yes, sir.'

'Hypostasis, Constable.' Dr. Wheeler jabbed a yellow stained finger at the exposed skin. 'Otherwise known as lividity. In layman's terms the pooling of blood in the immediate hours after death. It collects at the lowest parts free from pressure. For instance not the buttocks on a prone body but the backs of the knees. The pattern tells us whether a corpse has been moved. The colour of a fine port, I always think. Ruby rather than tawny.'

'All right, Godwin, we're done here. Sergeant Bishop and I will be at the hotel.' Chance eyed their driver who was slouching by the van, jawing with the mortuary assistant. 'Ask Constable Richards if he could possibly spare the time to lend you a hand.'

'Sir.' Godwin gave him an uncertain smile. The inspector's face gave nothing away.

'I shall see you both at nine thirty. Tea will be provided after the show. Unless you'll need something stronger?' Drawing on his gloves, Wheeler took his bag from Bishop and stepped out on to the promenade. 'Wretched rain's stopping at last.'

Chance watched him go, thinking he could relish a pint later. Nothing to do with the doctor's parting shot. The war had made half the men in England unemotional about sliced open bodies. When you'd seen your best pal's brains blown out, sat up and wiped the bits out of your hair.. The body in the shelter was like a tailor's shop dummy in comparison. Which wasn't to say he didn't care.

He dismissed his thoughts as the three men approached, Godwin and the other chap carrying a stretcher. He gave them a few crisp instructions and turned to Bishop.

'We'll have a word with the young woman who found the body. Then I'll get on to the coroner and see Superintendent Hayes and Bob Forrest. Bob can organise a search for the weapon.'

'Better hunt for a brandy bottle while they're at it.'

Chance and his sergeant crossed the road. The Belvedere looked depressingly like the place where he and Stella had spent their honeymoon. Including the severe female watching them at the entrance. Modest hotels were much the same everywhere.

Funny how even when you lived by the sea, the coast was where you went to begin married life. It hadn't been a disaster. Everything had worked itself out by the last night. It hadn't been a rip-roaring success either.

They'd gone along the coast to Kent. Broadstairs, on the grounds that Stella's mother reckoned it was refined. Her family and his ma had clubbed together for three nights away. Stella's father had been alive then.

The day had passed in a haze. His chief memory was excruciating embarrassment and his stiff collar rubbing his neck. The thing was they'd never spent that much time alone together. The days stretched emptily. All normal sources of conversation vanished. How did you talk to someone for all those hours when you weren't interested in furnishing your new home?

Much later he'd worked out that routine and mild boredom set the tone for most marriages. These days people looked to him for a lead and nothing embarrassed him.

'You're the officer in charge?' The waiting woman stood to one side as he reached the entrance. 'I'm Dorothy Aldridge. It was I who telephoned the police. I am the owner of The Belvedere.'

A refined type with wiry, dark greying hair. The gratification in her voice made it sound as though she owned The Ritz. Chance didn't miss the look at their shoes.

'Afternoon, madam.' He lifted his hat. 'Detective-Inspector Chance and this is Sergeant Bishop.'

'In here if you please.'

An appetite-deadening odour of boiled cabbage wafted from the back regions. The flap of Bishop's mac brushed the stand of an ugly gong as he swept past.

In here was a large dining-room. The only occupant was a slight young woman with damp hair. Hardly more than a girl, she was seated on a chair turned away from a table. Her face anxious, she stood as they entered.

'This is Ivy Betts. It was she who found the body.'

She made it sound as though the girl had committed a breach of good taste.

'Good afternoon, Miss Betts. My name's Inspector Chance.' Without asking he pulled out a chair and positioned it to one side. Bishop followed, seating himself at the table and producing his note-book.

The girl murmured a reply, giving them a tentative smile. She sank on to the chair and waited. One hand clasped a handkerchief.

'I'm sorry you've had a rotten experience. I have to ask you about it now while it's fresh in your mind. Better to get it over and done with. Sergeant Bishop here is going to write down everything you tell us. You won't get home for a while yet as we'll need you to wait at the police station to sign a typed statement.' He paused to check she was taking it in.

'I understand.'

'In a few days you'll be required to give evidence at the inquest, as you discovered the body. That simply means answering a few questions. The coroner's a nice man and it won't take long. There's nothing for you to worry about. All clear?'

'Yes, sir.'

'Inspector will do. First off, you did well to call us. I know it's public duty and all that but believe me, plenty would have carried on walking. It must have been a nasty shock for you?'

She nodded. 'It was a shock to come upon the poor man. But somehow I knew something wasn't right. It'd been nagging at me all day.'

Chance raised his eyebrows at Bishop. 'Go on.'

'It's the second time I've seen a dead body so it wasn't *quite* so bad. I saw my gran. Helped my mum and aunty to lay her out.' Embarrassed, she stopped abruptly.

'I'm sure the inspector doesn't want to hear about that, Ivy.' Miss Aldridge had remained standing by the window nearest the door. A hand on the curtain, she divided her attention between the room and the activity on the promenade.

'I understand what you mean,' Chance said gently. 'It's never quite as tough after the first one. You know the person's not there.'

'Yes, that's it. They've gone.'

'It isn't necessary for you to remain, Miss Aldridge.' He spoke over his shoulder.

'I do feel responsible for Ivy as her employer, Inspector. After all I am *in loco parentis* as it were.' She fixed him with a lofty look. 'Taking the place of Ivy's parents.'

Thank you, Chance thought. True he'd heartily loathed old Virgil and his Latin primer but the odd tag had sunk in.

'Besides Ivy's very young and she wishes me to stay. Don't you, dear?'

'Yes, Miss Aldridge.' Her voice lacked conviction.

Perhaps Constable Marden had a point. 'Right, Miss Betts. Can you tell us exactly how you came to find the body? Don't miss anything out. We like lots of detail and take it slowly so Sergeant Bishop can keep up. He doesn't write very fast.' He flashed her an encouraging smile. 'Begin with your nagging feeling.'

'I first saw the man on my way to work, you see.'

'What time was that?'

'I start at six thirty to help Mrs Thompson with the breakfasts. She's the cook.'

'Right. So your job is..?'

'Chamber-maid.'

'In a busy establishment like this, we all have to pull together, Inspector. Unfortunately nowhere can be run on the same basis as they were before the war.' Miss Aldridge had clamped her pince-nez on her nose and was peering over her *Vacancies* sign.

'Go on, Miss Betts.'

'I walked along The Esplanade on my way to work. Staff aren't supposed to use the front entrance so it's a slightly longer way round. There isn't much in it and I like to look at the sea. I don't cross over to the prom though, there isn't time.' Pausing, she glanced at the sergeant. 'When I drew nearly opposite the shelter I could see a man was sitting in there.'

'Tell me exactly what you saw.'

'Not much. The back of his head and shoulders through the glass. His hat and a bit of his coat collar. I'd no reason to look more closely and I was keeping an eye on the time.'

'Of course. Was he alone, do you think?'

'Yes. You can see all along the shelter. Unless a child was sitting in one, I suppose, below the line of the window.'

'Anyone else about?'

She screwed up her face as she concentrated. 'No one on foot except me. A chap cycled past, coming the other way.'

'Carry on.'

'After the breakfasts were over, I did my work in the kitchen then I went upstairs to start the bedrooms. While I was in a room at the front, I looked out of the window and noticed the man was still there.'

'About what time was this?'

Ivy looked at Miss Aldridge for confirmation. Chance looked up, following her gaze.

'I came upstairs to speak to Ivy, Inspector. It was about five and twenty past ten.'

'Thank you, Miss Aldridge.' She looked like a spinster to him. Evidently his guess was right as she didn't correct her title.

'I felt sorry for him. I thought he looked lonely and perhaps he was a widower. We see a few lonely people here.'

A disparaging sort of sound came from the corner. Miss Aldridge lowered herself to the window seat. 'That's ridiculous, Ivy. I've told you before, it's foolish to go making up stories about people. It's a way of making yourself look important. You'd better disregard that, Inspector.'

Ivy took a deep breath. 'That's not what I'm trying to do. Really it's not. You can't help wondering about people. That's all I meant.'

It sounded like a worn plea. 'I'm sure Miss Aldridge didn't mean you were making things up.'

'It was kind of you to take an interest, Miss.' Bishop smiled at her. 'Shame more people don't. It would make our work easier.'

You could always rely on Bishop to say the right thing. 'Tell me about this feeling you had.'

'It sounds fanciful when you say it aloud. While I was sweeping the stairs and fetching the linen, I kept getting a feeling something was wrong. Almost as if something was lying in wait for me. I kept telling myself that the man was all right. Those people had spoken to him.'

'Which people?'

'Sorry, I'm getting muddled.' Ivy fingered a pulled thread on her skirt.

'Take your time, Miss. You're being a big help.'

She gave Bishop another grateful glance. 'When I was looking out of the window in number three, a couple came along with their little dog. They stopped at the shelter.

That's to say, not really stopped. They paused for a second and looked in at the man. I couldn't tell if they spoke. Then they wandered on.'

'Ever seen the couple before?'

She shook her head. 'I don't think so.'

'Pity. Could you describe them at all?'

'Not very well. In their sixties, I should think. The man had on a grey mackintosh and tweed cap. The lady wore a brown coat and a blue felt hat.'

'That's very good. What was the dog like?'

'Small and white. I don't know what kind.'

'Not to worry. Would you happen to know anyone who fits that description, Miss Aldridge? People tend to walk their dog in the same place.'

'I'm afraid I'm unable to assist you, Inspector. A great many people exercise their dog on the beach, more's the pity. I really don't have time to stand and watch them.'

Chance's face remained perfectly serious as he studied the young woman. 'Was that all you saw, Miss Betts?'

'Yes. Then I finished work at half-past three. When I came out, the man was still there in the same position. I thought maybe he had nowhere else to go but he could have been taken queer. So it wouldn't hurt to cross over and walk past the shelter, just in case he needed help.'

'Decent of you, especially as it was raining.'

She hesitated, 'When I got there his hat was tilted forward. You know the way men do when they're taking a nap in the sunshine?'

Chance nodded. He and Bishop exchanged a look.

'Except like you said, it was wet and miserable. Something was terribly wrong but I didn't know what to do. I didn't like to walk on, so I coughed. He didn't stir so I spoke to him and put my hand on his sleeve and his hat fell off.' She sat back, giving a nervous giggle that was half-way to a sob. 'His eyes were open. That's when I knew. They had this awful yellowish tinge.. like jaundice. There was no light in them.'

'Would you like a cup of tea?'

Chance leant forward, uncrossing his legs. He turned to Miss Aldridge. 'Or maybe a nip of brandy?'

'Cook offered to make Ivy a cup of tea with plenty of sugar. That's the best remedy for shock. She didn't want one. Pull yourself together, Ivy. The officers need you to speak clearly.'

'Brandy.. the poor soul had had ever such a lot to drink. The smell poured off him. I recognised it. My dad has a bottle every Christmas. It always makes me feel queasy.'

It will always be the smell of death to you now, Chance thought. He wondered if the father acquired a taste for it in France. From what he recalled, the cheap stuff tasted much like vinegar. Stung as harshly on a wound.

'All right, Miss Betts. We won't keep you much longer and we'll see about getting you home afterwards. Did you notice anything lying around in the shelter?'

'You mean like a bag or something?'

'That's right. Something on the seat beside him or dropped on the floor for instance?'

She shook her head. 'No, sir. All I saw were his eyes. I knew he was dead then.'

'Was anyone else around?'

'Not that I saw. It was raining cats and dogs. I ran back here as fast as I could.'

'Is there anything else you can think of?'

'I know who he was. I wasn't sure when I fled but while we were waiting for you, it came to me.'

'You recognised him? What was his name?'

'Mr. Lynch. I don't know his Christian name. He stayed with us before Christmas. You remember him, I expect, Miss Aldridge?'

Her employer removed her pince-nez. 'Not in the slightest, Ivy. Are you sure he was a guest here? You've probably mistaken the.. him for someone else.'

Chance looked at them both. 'What month was this, Miss Betts?'

'Early in December. It was the same week Miss Aldridge sent Eric up to the attic to get the decorations down.'

'Still not ringing any bells, Madam?'

'We see a great many guests, Inspector. I suppose he could have been a commercial traveller. We do get some in winter. Not in summer as we're full with holidaying families. We have several elderly gentlefolk with us on a long-stay arrangement and of course some people do like to winter on the south coast with our mild climate. So you see I'm unlikely to remember a single man.'

'We don't know he wasn't accompanied,' Bishop said. 'Can you recall if he did stay on his own, Miss?'

'Yes, he did. He had number seven. That's a single at the back.'

'You obviously have a good memory, Miss Betts. Was there any special reason for you to remember this Mr. Lynch?'

'No, sir, except he was very pleasant. Not all guests are.'

'You talked to him then. Do you remember what was said?'

'Sorry, he only passed the time of day when I served his breakfast. Mentioned the weather, that kind of thing. I think he could have been a salesman though. He had ever such a nice way with him and I don't think he stayed long.'

'We'll take a look at your visitors' book if we may?' Chance turned to Miss Aldridge.

'Certainly, Inspector. It's kept behind the reception desk. I'd prefer it not to be taken away.'

Chance nodded absently. 'I'll get someone to copy the details. Did you see Mr. Lynch speak to anyone while he was here, Miss Betts? That includes the other guests.'

Ivy looked at her employer. 'I wouldn't know, sir. I only really see the guests at breakfast and I have to get on with my work.' Another glance. 'If you chat to the guests, someone else's food gets cold.'

Miss Aldridge nodded in approval.

'Thank you, Miss Betts. You've been a great help. We'll take you with us now. That's the hard part done. We'll get you a hot drink while you wait.'

Ivy Betts thanked him, her expression relieved.

Standing, Chance looked out of the window. Godwin and Richards were packing up. 'My men will need a word with the rest of your staff, madam. Someone else might recall speaking to the deceased.'

Miss Aldridge looked pointedly at her wrist-watch. 'It isn't convenient at present. Mrs Thompson, my cook will be busy in the kitchen. I realise you have to identify the unfortunate man but aren't you being needlessly thorough?'

Chance glanced round the chilly room. The row of cruets on the sideboard had a forlorn look about them. They spoke of lonely diners chewing tough meat, exchanging stilted remarks with strangers. He was glad he had a home to go to.

'We don't waste time unnecessarily, Miss Aldridge. Mr. Lynch didn't die of natural causes. He was murdered.'

Three

He'd overheard Inspector Forrest complain to Chance that it was distracting to have a woman about the place. The inspector had agreed that the *murkier aspects of the job* as he put it, were no place for a woman. But she was keen and anyway the whole thing was the old man's pet project and she was here to stay.

Forrest had grumbled something about if she saw out her probation. Then Chance had noticed him in the corridor and kicked shut Inspector Forrest's door.

It was true, Sidney Godwin thought, that he was aware of her all the time. Though he'd rather die than have her know. Phyllis treated him like she was a really decent sister, the sort who'd back you up and advise you how to treat girls without making you feel a fool.

His sister was all right but she wasn't above undermining him. Her friends all seemed to giggle when they met him. He knew Phyllis was twenty-one but she seemed older.

Sometimes he wondered when you acquired assurance.

How did you start to become the sort of chap with a hard, no nonsense manner for villains and a ready word for the canteen ladies?

Though the feeling in C.I.D. was that Chance had had an easy ride since he'd been back and they didn't know what he was made of yet.

Impossible to imagine him feeling sick when he lit up. He wondered if Inspector Chance had practised flipping his trilby on the hat stand without missing. Maybe he'd been a bowler in his younger days. They always had a useful team at the Grammar.

'What's up, Sid?'

He hadn't realised he'd sighed aloud. 'Dunno. This wretched thing.' He could feel a red tide mark rising across his face as he mumbled.

'Want a hand?' Leaning over the machine, Phyllis released two letters that kept crossing over. 'That isn't straight.'

He sat well back, rigid with embarrassment as she deftly adjusted the paper and carbon. She didn't get ink on her fingers the way he always did.

'Thanks.'

'It does look a bit of a mess.'

'I know.'

'What are you typing?'

'Notes on the investigation so far. The inspector calls it the day-book. He wants me to keep a record of progress. Who said what, what action we've taken, all the statements. We've only got one so far from the girl who found the body. The other staff at the Belvedere couldn't remember the victim staying there. There's only four of them, the owner, cook, chamber-maid and boot-boy.'

'Sounds interesting work.'

'It's all got to go in order and any of us can look at it, if we want to check on something. If I don't keep up with it every day, it's going to be a right old muddle.'

'Cheer up, you'll manage. You aren't the only one who's fed up with being stuck in here.'

'You're off this afternoon, aren't you?'

'Oh I didn't mean I can't wait to leave work. It's having to stay here and wait for something to happen. I wish I was properly on the investigation. I never get given anything interesting to do.'

To say she was on the case at all was stretching it. He had enough sense not to say that. A murder had to qualify as one of the murkier aspects of the job.

'You did get sent along with P.C Payne to interview someone last week.'

'Only because I'm female and some underwear was pinched from a washing-line. George Payne didn't know where to look when he had to list the missing items. He went and asked the woman if he could take down her particulars. She said the thief already had.'

Shifting her folders, Phyllis sat on the edge of the next desk. 'You were at the scene of the crime. What was it like? No soft-soap, I want to learn.'

His parents used to take him and his sister on a day trip to London once a year. It was the highlight of his father's annual holiday. Every summer his mother said it wasn't worth going away when they were lucky enough to live by the sea. The truth was, young Sidney dimly knew, they couldn't afford it.

Over the years they'd gradually ticked off the sights. His favourite had been the Science Museum. One summer his father had suggested Madame Tussaud's. The memory of that long forgotten visit swam before him now.

The body lodged in the corner of the shelter had put him in mind of a waxwork. He could imagine him next to Crippen in the Chamber Of Horrors. A wave had rolled in his guts and he'd prayed he wouldn't disgrace himself in front of the inspector.

'It wasn't too bad. Not much blood.' His voice sounded strained but maybe not to anyone else. He strove for more detail that would interest her. 'It was quite interesting to watch them making deductions. A bit like Sherlock Holmes in a way.'

Phyllis chuckled.

'Only not that clever. Common sense really.' He knew that sounded lame.

She smiled at him. 'I prefer Raffles myself. Shouldn't really in our job. How did you get on at the hotels?'

'No good. No one noticed anything.'

Inspector Chance had sent him calling at the Belvedere's neighbours along the terrace opposite the sea-front. He hadn't quite stopped feeling self-conscious when he had to introduce himself to a stranger. Only now did he realise that the uniform he'd been proud to discard had been useful armour. Being so lanky didn't help. He felt he never knew what to do with his hands.

'This time of year they're half-empty. The one that's right opposite the shelter isn't even open. It changed hands recently and it's being done up.'

Phyllis nodded thoughtfully. 'It was too late for anyone arriving and none of the hotels along there are big enough to have a bar overlooking the promenade. You'd have to go nearer the pier for that. The best chance would be someone looking out from the lounge or their room. Drawing the curtains or looking at the moon.'

'I did ask about the guests.' He wished he didn't sound defensive. 'No one was coming or going after dinner. They were all playing cards and swigging cocoa.'

'What did the inspector say?'

He'd said 'Typical. Old pussies in detective yarns were always noticing things and falling over themselves to help the police'.

*

Bishop patted his pocket and Chance knew that he was wishing he could light his pipe. The disinfectant was overpowering. Any second now and they could leave for the comparative comfort of Wheeler's office. That is if he didn't footle about so much. Still no one wanted eau de corpse on their skin.

It wouldn't go down well in the bar at the golf club where he was heading. The mortuary assistant stood by with a towel while the doctor shook his hands like a shimmying chorus girl. That towel wasn't what they gave the patients either.

'I presume you both want tea and biscuits after your ordeal?'

'Why else d'you think we came?' Bishop followed him smartly.

Not for your scintillating company, Chance thought. He wasn't in the mood to play straight man to the other's ego. When they were seated, Wheeler made them wait while he scribbled a note, pursing his lips.

They always did that to look impressive while you wondered about the cost. Fortunately he rarely had to trouble the medical profession on his own behalf. He didn't intend getting the 'flu that was going around.

The assistant brought in a tray and there was another pantomime when he enquired whether they took lemon. Chance shovelled two spoons of sugar in his cup by way of answer.

'Well now, gentlemen. You'll receive my report as soon as my notes are typed up. Bearing in mind it's the weekend. The lab will telephone you with the results of the blood tests, that should be Monday. You say the fingerprints have gone on their way. There's nothing else I can add.'

'About the time of death though. You said between nine and midnight just now. Sure you can't narrow that any further?'

Dr Wheeler spoke with pained emphasis. 'If you were listening, Edgar, I said there needs to be a margin for error. An outdoor temperature slows the onset of rigor, thus making the standard scale unreliable. There's a lot to take into account. Those are the times I'm prepared to give the coroner.'

'Off the record?'

'The stomach contents suggest nearer nine than midnight. And don't quote me on that.'

'Wouldn't dream of it.' Chance helped himself from the plate of assorted biscuits. Chocolate. Milk was good for you.

'Do you have the time of the inquest fixed yet?'

'Tuesday at eleven.' Chance spoke through a mouthful of crumbs.

'Jacobs will parcel up the clothes and get them round to you later.'

A miserable-looking individual with soulful eyes. First time they'd spoken. He seemed to creep about soft-footed like he was Wheeler's batman. It wasn't a cheery sort of job of course, cleaning bloody scalpels and swilling down the floor. Chance wondered idly if Jacobs had sliced the lemon with one of his work-knives.

'I see there's a laundry mark on the handkerchief.'

We'll do the detecting, thank you. He supposed it wouldn't do to make an enemy of the police-surgeon.

'We have his name,' Bishop said. 'No one reported him missing overnight which probably means he's not married.'

'I'll get my receptionist to check on Monday but I'm fairly sure he isn't on my list.'

'Good of you but he comes from London. He may have been here for work.'

'He had a meagre supper. Your lot will be touring all the pubs presumably? A half in every one. Nice work if you can get it.'

'Not many perks in our job.' Bishop's voice was amiable.

Chance glared at Wheeler. When a constable called at a pub out of hours, the land-lord did tend to proffer a sample of their wares for goodwill. He didn't care whether they accepted or not. He did resent the implication that his men were lazy.

He interrupted by getting to his feet. 'Time we were off. Thanks for getting it done promptly.'

'Needs must when the devil drives. We aren't used to this sort of thing in Tennysham. Think you can catch the murderer?'

Stella had asked him the same thing last night. He gave Wheeler the same reply.

Leaving the mortuary they walked round the side of the building. Along the main drive they waited for an ambulance to pass, its bell ringing.

'You'll notice some changes round here,' Bishop said.

When the Queen Victoria Cottage Hospital had been built in readiness for the Diamond Jubilee, it had backed on to fields. They'd still been there when he moved away.

Now no longer quite on the edge of town, the flint and brick building was hemmed in by identical new council houses. All that remained of the fields was a green in the middle with a solitary young tree. No more rabbits, plenty of white dog dirt.

'Not bad properties though.' At least renting meant you weren't in hock for the rest of your working life.

'Do you think our murder victim was working here in December?'

'Seems likely. He only stayed two days.' Chance considered as they walked towards the town centre. 'The Betts girl thought he was probably a salesman.'

'The post-mortem didn't help much.'

'No, we're going to have our work cut out to find the weapon. The scar on his knee should help identify him though.'

'Probably from childhood,' Bishop quoted. 'Someone would have to know him very well to have seen it.'

'Maybe there's a wife tucked away somewhere.'

'Most men his age are spoken for.'

'We'll get the *Echo* to put out an appeal for witnesses who saw anyone near the sea-front after eight-thirty.'

'They'll be glad to. It's the biggest story they've had in years.' Bishop glanced sideways at Chance. 'You don't want to take any notice of Wheeler, Eddie.'

'Easy to say. Even Stella's mother only calls me Edgar when I've offended her.'

'He hasn't known you long and he's still testing the water.'

Chance pulled a face. 'You mean like two strange dogs meeting?'

Bishop laughed. 'He's a bit of a know-all. Should have been a barrister. Don't rise to the bait.'

'Fancy consulting the Duke of Sussex after?'

It was their old joke.

*

A hazy sunshine was breaking through by the time they reached Frederic Street and the puddles were beginning to steam. The air held an indefinable promise of early spring.

Inside the desk was deserted. Joe Lelliott could be heard humming tunelessly out the back. As they went through to the offices, a kettle started to whistle.

'I'm just going to have a word.'

Chance knocked perfunctorily at a door and stuck his head round. 'Can you spare a minute?'

The man behind the desk had his five o'clock shadow arriving several hours early. It suited his dark expression.

'None of my chaps have found anything so far. Not so much as a broken bottle on the beach.'

'It was a faint hope but what can you do? You have to try.'

'They'll keep at it. What did Dr. Wheeler have to say about the weapon?'

'Quite a short blade, like a pocket-knife.' Chance reeled off the dimensions he'd been given. 'Long enough to do the business. According to him if the victim had been fat he might just have survived or bled to death slowly.'

'Maybe unpremeditated then? I'll pass on the description. I hear you're on the cadge?' Forrest's untidy black brows drew together when he frowned.

'The Super said he'd have a word. You can see how we're fixed. Two are down with the 'flu, leaving me with one constable. And young Godwin's our flash and dabs chap. I gather he's not long come over to plain clothes?'

'Your predecessor took him on just before he left. He was keen to join your lot and he's a grafter.'

'Glad to hear it. He hasn't had a lot to do since I've been here.'

Forrest nodded and squashed his cigarette-end in his tin ash-tray. He smoked filter tips. 'I know how it is, Eddie. Murder takes priority. You can keep Richards as he was in on the start. He has a brain if you can galvanise it. Lazy so-and-so could do with a boot up the rear.'

'I'll do my best to oblige.'

'Your cup runneth over, as the padres say. He's in now. I'll send him through.'

'Right. Whose beat takes in the sea-front east of the pier?'

'That'll be George Payne.' Forrest replied without thinking. Leaning back he tapped his fountain pen against the large street map on the wall. The town was sectioned into areas marked by black ink.

'I'd like a word with him.'

'If he'd seen anything he'd have reported it.'

'It's not that. A witness saw a couple glance in the shelter yesterday morning. They were walking a small white dog. The victim was long dead but it's possible they noticed something that wasn't there later, by the time we turned up.'

'Pinched, you mean? And you think Payne might have an idea who they were? He's on duty but he'll be in at one for his break. I'll tell him to find you.'

'It's worth a try.'

'You might be lucky. He's not the brightest spark but he knows his patch. Tell you what though, if I were you I'd speak to Cecil Knowles as well. His beat's on the west side of the pier. Dog walkers might wander a fair way along the beach.'

'That's a good idea. I don't think I know him.'

'You will when you see him.' Forrest consulted the wall clock. 'He's off at two but he never goes straight home. Try the canteen.'

'Thanks, I will.'

'Look for an old woman in the corner. How's it going?'

'Too soon to say. We haven't even confirmed the identification yet. The inquest's set for Tuesday.' The 'phone-bell started to ring.

'Thanks Bob, I appreciate it.'

'Buy me a pint some time.' Forrest reached for the receiver and growled his name.

*

Discarding his things, Chance returned to the main office. Halting by Godwin's desk he held out his arm. He flicked through the pages handed to him.

'Your typing's improved remarkably since yesterday. Miss Betts's statement was sloppy.'

Godwin glanced at Phyllis's bent head.

'Talking of Miss Ivy Betts,' Chance swung round. 'I meant to say, when I asked if she saw Mr. Lynch speaking to anyone else, I thought she hesitated. Did I imagine it or was she evasive?'

'Can't say I noticed anything,' Bishop said. 'She looked at her employer once or twice as though checking she was saying the right thing. I put that down to Miss Aldridge being a tartar.'

'I might be making too much of it. She was trying to think three months back and she'd had a shock.'

'That poor girl was tired out. I wouldn't want a daughter of mine working for that one.'

'Nor mine. Do you know anything about Miss Dorothy Aldridge?'

'I've seen her name in the paper occasionally. You know the sort of mention, hoteliers' association, on the committee for the flower show.'

'I never read that sort of thing.'

'That's all I know. I don't think they're an old Tennysham family.'

'Well I'll bear Miss Betts in mind. We need to find out what Mr. Lynch was doing here in December. We don't know a bally thing yet.' Chance gave Phyllis a sharp look. 'If you see Richards, tell him to get in here, will you, Constable?'

'Certainly, sir.' She picked up her files and had barely left when the door opened again.

'Speak of the devil. Nice of you to join us, Richards. Inspector Forrest has kindly loaned me your services. He's assured me you'll be a great asset to the team. You're just in time. Sergeant Bishop is going to bring you and Godwin up to speed.'

'Grab a seat and pin your ears back.'

'Yes, Sarge.'

'First off, we're calling the victim Mr. R. Lynch for the moment. That's what he called himself in the hotel register but it's unconfirmed. He gave a London address which turns out not to exist. Inspector Chance and I have attended the post-mortem. You can study the full report for yourselves on Monday but this is the gist.' Bishop glanced at his note-book and flipped it shut.

'Time of death Thursday night between nine and midnight. The doc thinks nearer nine than twelve but he can't be more exact. Cause of death a single thrust from a blade piercing the heart, upper right ventricle. Would have been virtually instantaneous. It didn't need especial strength. A woman could have done it if she had the stomach. Any questions so far?'

'Did it need medical knowledge?'

'Good point, Richards. No pun intended. According to Dr. Wheeler that's open to question. Which doesn't get us very far. It could have been sheer luck or someone who knew what they were doing.'

'What about someone who didn't know anything about anatomy but mugged up a book, Sarge?'

'True, Godwin. Good to see you're both awake. I don't suppose our murderer took a book out on his library ticket though.'

'Did the victim put up a fight, Sarge? It didn't look that way to me?'

'Dr. Wheeler says not. As you saw, the body was seated and there were no defence cuts on sleeves or hands. No bruises. The position suggests he never saw it coming.'

'Taken by surprise. The person he least suspected. A beautiful blonde who leant towards him, asking for a light.' Richards spoke with all the relish of a keen reader of novelettes.

Chance raised his eyes to the ceiling. 'No light on him. Concentrate on the business in hand, Constable.'

'He was drunk, wasn't he?' Godwin said. 'So he would have been relaxed.'

'We won't know how much he'd had to drink until we hear back from the lab. They'll do it pronto. The inspector has a theory about that.'

Chance stretched his arms behind his head. 'There's something about that brandy I don't buy. It costs enough. You'd have to be really pie-eyed to spill it all over yourself. Then what happened to the bottle? I think we were treated to a carefully staged tableau.'

'I don't get it, sir.'

'Ask yourself Godwin, what did that overpowering stink of brandy achieve?'

'Made me feel sick.'

'No, not that.' Chance sounded impatient. 'What else? Reason it out.'

'It would put anyone off from sitting there?' His voice was uncertain.

'You've got it. Now follow it through. What would that do?'

'Er.. delay the body being examined, sir?'

'Yes.' Chance sat up straighter. 'Picture this. Ivy Betts said the trilby was forward over his face when she approached him. We never saw the body like that. His hat fell off when she shook his arm.'

'Those shelters are quite deep,' Bishop said.

'That's right. To all intents and purposes a man was sitting in a corner looking perfectly normal. His hat suggested he was having a nap, she thought. Say a passer-by turns up, thinking of sitting down. One whiff of alcohol and most people will walk smartly on, all disgusted. Ivy Betts actually saw that happen.'

'So the murderer arranged the body to give themselves an alibi, sir?'

'That sort of thing, Godwin. It would delay the body being found and make it harder to determine the time of death. Remember, they buttoned the overcoat over the stab wound. Mr. Lynch must have had his coat hanging open when he was attacked.'

'It's only March though.'

Chance shrugged. 'Plenty of men unbutton their coat when they sit. I do myself. Anyway the overcoat absolutely reeks of brandy. They were complaining at the mortuary.' He grinned briefly. 'Couldn't make out any stains on that dark material but I think the alcohol was sprinkled on it like vinegar on chips. We'll know more when we get the blood tests.' He looked expectantly at Bishop.

'The weapon. Dr. Wheeler says we're looking for a knife with a thin blade. Narrowing symmetrically at the point with a minimum length of four inches.'

Chance tuned out as Bishop went into detail of the dimensions. 'Could be a pocket-knife, small vegetable knife, that kind of thing.'

'Small enough to carry easily.' Richards said.

'The kind found in every home in England.' Bishop glanced at the clock. 'Right, stomach contents. Last meal approximately one to two hours before death. Slight odour of alcohol. Not possible to identify as brandy. Undigested bits of meat and what looked like pastry. In other words a pie.'

Bishop paused as Godwin exclaimed in disgust. Richards remained impassive. 'Which could mean Lynch had supper indoors or in a late-opening café but suggests a pub to me.'

Godwin wriggled on his seat. 'I was going to have a pie. Don't fancy it now.'

Bishop grinned at him. 'Go down that road, lad and you'll never eat in our job. Now then, the inquest is on Tuesday at eleven. Between now and then we need to find the weapon if possible but most of all we need someone to identify the corpse.'

Four

'We'll have a breather here and I'll get back in time to catch Payne.'

'Are you sure you don't want me along if you find out about them?' Bishop caught the eye of the barman who was opening a bottle of stout.

'It's not that I don't want you. The couple won't be able to tell us much if anything. It should only take a few minutes but I don't want to leave anything undone. The stone I don't turn over will be the one with the answers underneath.'

Bishop would understand what he didn't say. It was his first time in charge of a murder inquiry and he didn't intend to mess up. 'No, you get off and spend some time with Glad. You deserve it.'

'Fair enough. Grab a table.'

Chance sat back and looked about him. It had been an auspicious day when young Police Constable Eddie Chance had been introduced to The Duke Of Sussex. The invitation had been extended by the older and wiser Wilf Bishop.

Hard to believe he'd ever been so wet behind the ears, Chance reflected. He had though. That was why he'd go easy on young Godwin now. He'd toughen up and thank God for his generation, it wouldn't take a war to do it. He wondered why that particular phrase still stuck in his head. Habit.

He and the church had parted company for ever.

Not that his family had ever been religious. Christmas and Easter like most people, Sunday School and harvest festival. He'd even won a prize for scripture once. That was down to his effortless good memory rather than any enthusiasm for the subject.

The day would come when he'd walk Daphne up the aisle of course and Vic would follow in a few years. There'd been the odd funeral too. That was all though. He'd vowed, one foggy morning in 1916, that if he survived he was finished with God and the blasted Church of England.

'Thanks, Wilf.' Chance took an appreciative swallow. 'How many years have you been drinking in this place?'

Bishop laughed, producing his tobacco pouch. 'Nine years more than you.'

The Duke Of Sussex was on the corner of a road leading off the High Street, away from the sea. Bishop who was something of a history buff on the quiet had told him there'd only ever been one duke of that title. One of George the third's anonymous sons who'd died in 1843.

The pub had been built many years later with the shiny green-tiled frontage of a Victorian spit and sawdust. The dim interior had gleaming brass and etched mirrors. Glimpsed through cigarette smoke, it didn't appear to have been decorated since.

They sat opposite one another in the snug where no one could overhear.

'This place hasn't changed. Why is that a comfort?'

'Because you're getting older.' Bishop's eyes twinkled as he waved his spent match.

'Beattie's the same as ever. Except she insists on calling me Mr. Chance.'

The landlady was probably not many years younger than Miss Dorothy Aldridge. Not for her the unobtrusive coat and skirt and a dab of powder. Beattie sailed in like a galleon with gay flags fluttering and a magnificent figurehead.

'Take it as a compliment.'

Bishop's dentures had slightly changed his voice. A second abscess in as many months and he said he'd begged the dentist to take the whole damned lot out.

'How's the family settled in?'

'Ups and downs. Daphne's sulking. She misses working with a bunch of girls her own age. Vic seems all right at his new school.'

'Work's meant to be dull. The main thing is your girl's found something.'

Chance nodded. Yesterday's *Sketch* had led with the latest figures for the jobless. Life was getting steadily more bleak for some, especially up country. The Welsh had been having it tough for years. They were luckier in the South. 'Stella's thrilled with the house and being near her mother again.'

'I suppose you're all straight by now?' Bishop said innocently.

'Funny. Apparently I still haven't put up all the shelves and she's bought a couple of those ghastly china things that hang on the wall. A vase and a face if you can believe it. Then the beastly garden will want doing any week now.'

'The joys of being a home-owner.' Bishop wiped a trace of froth from his upper lip. 'How many knives do you have indoors?'

'What? Oh I see what you're getting at. Quite a few when you tot it up.'

'We can forget big 'uns like a carving knife and bread knife.'

'Even so. There's all the small ones in the kitchen drawer. Forget cutlery. We keep a letter-opener on the mantelpiece. Vic has a pocket-knife of course. Stella has one of those ladies' ones with a mother of pearl handle. I daresay Daphne does too.'

'I keep a pruning knife in the shed. That's the right size. And unlike you I've an old one for decorating. Same as every house in the land.'

'What odds would you give for finding it?'

'Worse than evens if the weapon was wiped and put back where it's usually kept.'

'You know what they say about the best place to hide a tree?'

'In a wood.'

'Exactly. If our murderer chucked it though, there's hope. We'll soon know if Forrest's lads find anything.'

'It's a long beach,' Bishop said.

'As you said, we need to confirm Mr. R. Lynch's identity urgently and find a next of kin. The coroner won't be happy with the say so of a chamber-maid.'

'Especially with a false address.'

'No, but that tells us something in itself. Whatever he was up to here in December, we can be sure it was something dodgy.'

'It's not as if he was accompanied.' Bishop said. 'Otherwise it could have been divorce evidence.'

Chance grinned. 'Somehow I can't see Miss Aldridge allowing that on her premises. The way I see it, a fake address is bound to mean a false name.'

'Two nights the register said. Was he meeting someone for the day? Maybe his dabs will be on record. Don't forget those callouses, Eddie.'

'Drink up and I'll get us another. I hope we're right. They could have been workman's hands'.

'We should hear from the Yard on Monday.'

*

Of course she still took a pride in her uniform. Simply putting it on made her feel more confident. As though a great mantle of responsibility lay on her shoulders. She could cope with that. Her job was to help those in trouble.

People in Tennysham still turned and stared, unused to the sight of a woman police-constable. Phyllis always pretended not to notice. Inside she felt like smiling and had to struggle to keep a dignified face.

Almost a year in and she'd gradually admitted to herself that the job wasn't what she'd expected. She couldn't make up her mind what to feel. Much of the work was dull. Filling in forms about lost canaries. Typing confessions about fiddled meters.

There'd been one chap who stuck in her mind though. A family man who'd never been in trouble before. Caught stealing coal from the yard by the station. He'd been laid off and his wife was ill. Having to keep calling the doctor back was sinking him. Bit by bit, he'd said, he'd sold anything someone would buy. Then the Assistance people demanded they get rid of the few sticks they had left.

Once she'd had to search a female under arrest. Examining the clothes, leaving the woman to cover herself with a scratchy grey blanket. It made her feel ashamed. And she was terrified of catching nits.

They didn't really have enough for her to do. It was beastly having to complete jobs slowly and invent tasks. Like the afternoons spent in the graveyard as they called the filing-room. In the early days she'd ruined a hanky dusting shelves and she'd snagged her stockings more than once. She lived in dread of them realising she was a spare part and getting rid of her.

Even the mystery of the phantom knicker-nicker, as Fred Richards dubbed him, wasn't sufficient to keep a bright young woman absorbed. She'd suggested they interview the neighbour. A hard-faced woman had been watching from her back bedroom window when they were inspecting the gate to the twitten.

Only no one would listen to her. It had been pointed out that she wasn't there to detect. Now even Richards had been loaned to C.I.D. If she'd wanted nothing more than typing and tea-making, she'd have become a secretary.

The rain seemed to have vanished. Wet pavements told yesterday's tale. Life had moved on. It was too pleasant a day to stay downhearted for long. Phyllis's spirits lifted as she reached the last shops on her way home.

'Mind your head, miss.'

The greengrocer in his long sack-coloured overall was hooking a pole and releasing his striped awning. She stopped short as a flurry of drips sprinkled the pavement.

'Nice to see the sun coming out, ain't it? Spring's on the way.'

Returning his smile, she picked up a cabbage. Seeing her hesitate, he jerked his thumb at the bucket by the door.

'King Alfreds. Best daffs going, they are. Fresh off the train from Devon.'

She'd treat them to a bunch.

A few minutes later she continued through the quiet streets, her string bag swinging as she thought over her morning. The atmosphere at work had changed completely. Usually it was fairly predictable. You could tell the time by beat constables coming and going. Sergeant Lelliott said the same things every morning, 'phone-bells ringing, tea-breaks and office banter. She could hold her own there.

They were a good-natured bunch on the whole. Everyone looking busy when Superintendent Hayes was on the move. From time to time there'd be an outbreak of noise when someone's collar was felt and a cell was occupied. Though Tennysham rarely had the worst crime.

She had the measure of Inspector Forrest. Inclined to be grumpy, a roll of indigestion tablets on his desk. Liked to throw his door open and bellow instead of asking quietly. She knew he didn't want her there but it was nothing personal. He wouldn't tolerate bullies and he had daughters himself. A good copper. Head down, she did as she was told.

Inspector Chance was an unknown quantity to everyone except a couple of older officers. He had a pithy turn of phrase for the others. An air of not suffering fools gladly but to her he was scrupulously formal. She knew he didn't take her seriously. She'd rather be treated like any other constable.

And now they had a murder. It wasn't unheard of. Not long after she'd started her probationary term, a woman had been strangled in the poorest part of town near the gas-works. It had been what she'd learnt to call a domestic.

The husband had been brought in almost at once. She'd been sent out to buy a packet of Craven A and take them in with a cup of tea. He sat wiping his knuckles across his pink-rimmed eyes like a child. Crying and sniffling. Saying over and over in a whining voice that he hadn't meant to do it. She'd asked for it. It was her fault. She'd made him.

Sergeant Lelliott had told her that most murderers were snivelling inadequate men, unable to cope with the reality of what they'd done. This investigation was different. The men were waiting to see what Inspector Chance made of it. There was always the possibility he'd fail and the Chief Constable would request help from Scotland Yard.

Phyllis found herself hoping that they would solve the case. She wondered if the murderer was in Tennysham. Perhaps even someone she'd walked past in the street. Whoever they were, somehow she didn't believe they were crying and pleading that they hadn't meant to do it.

She came in the back way in case Dad was in his workshop. As she came down the garden path she saw him moving about in the kitchen. He noticed her and his face lit up.

'Hullo, love. I got off early so I thought I'd start the potatoes.'

'Oh Dad, you needn't have. I can do them.'

'It's no trouble. You've enough to do.'

'I managed to get some chops for our tea. The butcher was almost sold out.' She emptied her bag on the table.

'Fried onions'll go a treat with those.'

'I'll just put these in water. Aren't they cheerful? Then I'll go and change. I'll be glad to get these shoes off.'

The sensible brogues were heavy. Not much use if you had to give chase. The uniform was a drawback, as unflattering as a prison warder's. The cap crushed her short brown hair but it never held a wave anyway. Slipping on a jersey and old skirt, she examined herself briefly in the dressing-table mirror. Dragged a brush through her hair and pushed it up with her fingers. *You'll do*.

She replaced the brush with its matching comb and hand-mirror. The brush and mirror had flat backs inlaid with a floral design. A birthday present suitable for a young lady, not the tree climbing tom-boy she'd been. Valued for the giver rather than the vanity set.

Charging down the stairs, Phyllis joined her father at the table.

'Kettle's boiled. I'm just making myself a doorstep. Do you want one?'

'No thanks, Dad. I'll wait.' She poured the tea while he made his sandwich, pressing the bread firmly on the layer of dripping. 'How come you got off early?'

Frank Marden finished chewing before he answered. 'Things are slow. We're up to date and I don't think Arthur has a fat lot in the order book.'

'You'll be all right though, won't you?'

'Course I will. Don't look so anxious. Phyl. Even if it stays slack, it's last in, first out. That would be Stan, sorry to say.'

Phyllis studied his hand holding his snack. A trace of printer's ink remained around his nails, however much Lifebuoy he used. Her father was the cleanest man she knew. She looked up at him. His remaining hair still had some brown among the grey. Pepper and salt. His eyes met hers and slid away.

'Times are hard. Businesses are thinking about what they can cut back on. Things will pick up though, bound to.'

She nodded. 'Of course they will.'

'How're things at the station? Are you rushed off your feet with all the to do?'

'Not really. They're very busy in C.I.D. but it doesn't make much difference to me. If I'm wanted for anything, it'll be more typing.'

'Do they know who the body was yet?'

Phyllis shook her head. 'Not for sure. It was someone who'd stayed at the Belvedere before Christmas but they don't know where he came from or if he had any family. They really need next of kin for formal identification.'

'That's bad. Someone's going to get the worst news and they don't know what's coming.'

'Sergeant Bishop and the inspector were at the post-mortem this morning. They've sent two constables enquiring round the pubs. They think the victim had a drink somewhere before he was murdered.'

Marden stood and put his plate in the sink. 'You don't expect it here.' He looked out at the empty garden.

'I don't suppose you noticed anyone on Thursday night?' She had the description off pat. 'About five foot nine, blue eyes, fairish hair, clean-shaven. He was wearing a donkey brown overcoat and a lighter brown trilby. Dad?'

'What, love?' He turned to face her. 'I was thinking how sodden everything looks.'

'You didn't see anyone of that description in the Bell?'

'I wouldn't have noticed. There were quite a few in and we were busy playing dominoes.'

'It was only a thought. Do you remember Vi Betts?'

'Your pal? Course I do. Didn't she move away?'

'That's right. We lost touch since she went to live with her auntie and uncle in St Albans. Anyway it's her sister Ivy who found the body.'

'Poor kid.'

'She was two years below us. I only knew her to say hello to.'

'She won't forget that in a hurry.'

Phyllis sipped her tea. 'No, I thought I'd look her up. It might help her to talk to someone about it. Someone of her own age.' She looked round the neat kitchen, not meeting his eyes.

Her dad was a brick. He was ready to turn his hand to anything about the house. Losing her mum young and having her to raise, he'd had no choice. The potatoes were done and the peelings wrapped in last week's newspaper. Ready to give to his pal who kept a pig on his smallholding.

'That's good of you, love.'

Now she felt guilty.

*

George Payne though anxious to help, couldn't place the couple described. After much scratching his head and suggesting every dog owner he could think of, Chance managed to send him packing.

Cecil Knowles turned out to be the overweight constable who seemed a fixture in the canteen. Usually seen hunched over a newspaper folded at the day's racing. Disgraceful that on duty. Chance didn't remember him from the old days and Knowles's accent pegged him as a Londoner.

'The wife has family here. We moved down, must be all of four year ago now. It soon goes.'

Chance grunted. Constable Payne had used up his small store of patience. He had no intention of getting sidetracked again.

'So do you recognise the description?'

Knowles rubbed his chin while he thought. 'With a small white dog. Lady wears a blue felt hat? I'd say I can help you there, sir.' He came to a standstill.

'Well? Who are they?'

'Can't tell you their surname. The dog's called Teddy, I believe.'

'I'm not interested in a statement from the mutt. So you know them by sight. Do you know where they live?'

'Yes, sir, Pearl-street. I've seen them coming and going on a number of occasions. Often with their granddaughter. She lives with them I'd say. I don't know for sure that's who she is but she's far too young to be their daughter.'

'At last,' Chance sighed heavily. 'I want you to go round there straight away. Explain to them what it's about and to expect a visit from me later this afternoon. And get their names while you're at it.'

'I've actually knocked off, sir.'

'No one's knocked off in a murder investigation, Constable. Inspector Forrest suggested I find you now.'

'It's not that I mind if it'll help. The Inspector's cleared an hour's over-time, has he?'

'I said so, didn't I?' He'd no idea and wasn't about to waste more time finding out.

'What shall I do if they're out, sir?'

'Use your initiative. Knock up a neighbour for a start. See if you can find out when they'll be back.'

Eventually Knowles had returned. Strangling the flow of another chatty conversation, Chance managed to find out that the couple had been at home. Their name was Dawson. He set off to meet them as the clock-tower was striking four.

The Dawsons lived in one of the streets behind the sea-front, west of the pier. Modest terraced houses at their end with a straight-sided bay window and small front garden. Further down the homes were larger and several were boarding-houses. The pavements were pinkish brick with a tree every few yards. Their roots were a death-trap for the unwary.

A net curtain flicked as he stepped through the gate. The door opened as he reached for the knocker.

'Mrs Dawson? Good afternoon.' He lifted his hat. 'My name's Detective-Inspector Chance.' Holding out his warrant card. 'I believe P.C. Knowles explained why I need to speak to you and your husband.'

'He did, Inspector. We've been waiting for you. Do come in.' She gave him the shadow of a smile. Her eyes remained wary and her knuckles tense on the door. The type who was alarmed by anything to do with the police. He wanted to put her at ease.

'Please don't worry, Mrs Dawson. This shouldn't take long.' A scrabbling sound was coming from the door at the end of the passage. He identified it as claws sliding on lino.

'Our dog. I shut her in the kitchen. She's friendly but liable to jump up and shed her hairs everywhere.'

Her face relaxed a little, though fine lines showed she habitually felt anxious about life. 'If you'd like to come through, my husband's in the back room.'

He was about to follow down the narrow hall when a movement made him look up. 'Hullo.'

A young girl in a knitted jersey and pleated skirt was hovering at the top of the stairs. She began to descend.

'Hullo. Are you a plain clothes policeman?'

'That's right.'

She smiled, revealing an engaging gap between her front teeth. 'An inspector's rather high up, isn't it?'

He grinned. 'So-so.'

'This is our granddaughter, Joan. You mustn't question the gentleman, dear. Will you go and calm Tessie down for me?'

'Yes, Gran.'

'Ah, here's my husband.' She sounded relieved.

'Afternoon, sir.'

'How do you do.'

The man in the doorway was stocky with a pleasant expression. He was wearing collar and tie, a smart pull-over and immaculately creased turn-ups. Possibly he'd changed into what he considered appropriate. Chance suspected he always looked that neat indoors.

Mr. Dawson stood back and gestured him to enter. 'I thought perhaps in here with the table would be best.'

It was the typical middle room of a terraced house. On the gloomy side with a sash window giving on to a tiled path and dividing wall. Fitted cupboard doors filled both sides of the fireplace and a dining-table took up most of the square of patterned carpet.

'Herbert Dawson.' He extended his hand to shake. 'Sit wherever you like, Inspector Chance.'

'Thanks.'

Taking a seat opposite, Mr. Dawson regarded Chance attentively.

'Oh, I'm forgetting my manners.' Mrs Dawson jumped up again. 'Can I get you a cup of tea, Inspector?'

'I won't, thank you.' Her face looked crestfallen. 'I've not long had one,' he added quickly. 'Now P.C. Knowles explained that the man you passed in the sea-front shelter yesterday morning was in fact dead?'

Mr. Dawson nodded. 'Yes he did.' He glanced at his wife beside him. 'My wife and I are appalled. We both feel terrible about it and rather foolish. I assure you, we had absolutely no idea. We were flabbergasted when the constable told us.'

'I still can't take it in. Murdered in broad daylight. Are we in trouble for not reporting it, Inspector? You see we didn't look properly. We didn't stop really. Only paused and it can't have been for more than a few seconds.' Mrs Dawson's face was the picture of misery as she waited for him to reply.

'Please don't distress yourself, madam. There's no question of your being in trouble.' Chance leant forward earnestly. 'Actually the victim was killed some time on Thursday evening. I'm here solely in case you can give me any information.'

'That's such a relief. I thought we might have committed an offence in the eyes of the law?'

He smiled at her. 'I can understand how you didn't realise the man was dead in the circumstances. It's surprisingly difficult for the layman to be sure without obvious signs.'

The police-surgeon had told him that when he'd first joined the force. If the eyes were shut and there was no sign of violence, even they had to look twice. The person could be in a coma. They had to check for what they call vital signs.

One of the canteen ladies had been saying her auntie had sat next to an old lady on a tram for twenty minutes before realising she wasn't asleep.

She really had been going to the terminus.

'Don't take on, Olive.' Dawson's voice was gentle as he patted his wife's hand.

They made a contrasting couple, Chance thought. Dawson, muscular still in his sixties, his wife small and painfully thin.

'Thank you for saying that, Inspector. How may we assist you?'

'I want to know exactly what you did see at the shelter. Can you remember what time you reached there?'

'I think we left here about ten o'clock.' Dawson looked at his wife for confirmation.

She nodded. 'That's right. I'd done some hand-washing and put it through the mangle but I didn't like to peg it out. It looked unsettled. Herbert takes Tessie out first thing then we usually take her for a proper walk after I've done the heavy work. We pick up anything we need on the way back.'

'How long would it take you to get almost to Eastcliff from here?'

'Oh about twenty minutes? A little more, the way Tessie meanders.' She turned to her husband. 'I said you'd have to go on your own yesterday as I didn't want to miss the butcher's boy. He was very late. I looked at the clock and it was ten to but then he knocked. So we settled on walking by the sea.'

Chance wondered why that made her sound sad. She was making a meal of it but better to let her tell it in her own way. He guessed she chattered away most of the time when she wasn't nervous. It was what women did. Dawson didn't seem to mind if his fond expression was anything to go on.

'I knew it was going to rain. Didn't I say so, dear? I did think we'd be better off going to the park but you would insist on the promenade. I beg your pardon, Inspector. I'm putting off getting to where we saw the man.' Mrs Dawson looked apologetically at him.

'I'd rather you took your time, Mrs Dawson. Now I need you both to picture the shelter carefully for me. I know it's an unpleasant thing to ask but it is important.'

He opened his note-book. 'Rotten memory,' he said cheerfully, seeing her look of alarm.

'Will we have to be witnesses at the inquest?'

'You'll certainly be summoned to attend but I shouldn't think the coroner will call you. Not unless you can add some new information. Can you describe what happened when you reached the shelter, sir?'

'Certainly. As we drew near, we could see it was occupied. A man was sitting in the corner. The dog was still on the leash or we would have realised something was badly wrong. She'd have run right up to him, you see. As it was, she was certainly interested in him but we didn't think anything of it. She's like that with everyone.'

Chance nodded. 'Did you see anyone else about?'

Mr. Dawson shook his head. 'No one. It's always quieter at that end of the beach.'

'There was plenty of room in the shelter.' Mrs Dawson broke in. 'I did think we might sit down for a spell. Tessie tried to turn in. She's such a friendly girl and will try to sniff people's shoes. I was holding the leash and had to tug her back. We thought at first the man was dozing.'

'A second later we realised he was a drunk sleeping it off,' Mr. Dawson said. 'Or that's what we thought at the time. You could smell the alcohol coming off him.'

'He looked as though he was asleep. We didn't really see his face even, only the chin. His hat was over his eyes and I feel awful now, but as soon as we saw he was drunk we went on quickly.'

'Right.' Chance doodled as he listened. 'I know you hurried off but can you think back? Did you notice anything on the bench or the ground?'

Mrs. Dawson had a habit of putting her head on one side as she thought. Wearing various shades of brown, she reminded him of a sparrow. 'I'm sorry, Inspector, I saw nothing. We didn't want any unpleasantness.'

Mr. Dawson frowned. His thick eyebrows were still dark. 'I'm certain there was nothing there. I'd remember if there'd been a bag for instance. I wish we could be of help.'

'You have been, sir,' Chance said absently. 'All information helps even if it's negative.'

'Who saw us, Inspector?' Mrs Dawson looked puzzled.

'How d'you mean, madam?'

'It's just occurred to me. The beach was empty, as my husband said, but someone described us to the police. Was someone watching to see when the body was discovered?'

'Oh I see. No, nothing like that. Not to worry. Someone in one of the hotels opposite happened to be looking out of a window.'

'That's a relief. For a moment I thought.. oh, I don't know what I thought.' She smiled weakly. 'This whole business has shaken me up. Constable Knowles was very kind. We've often seen him about and said good morning but we didn't know his name until this afternoon.'

Chance was about to stand up when she spoke again.

'There is one thing.'

'Yes, madam?'

'There was no bottle. I don't know if the poor fellow was a tramp but I didn't see the bottle he'd been drinking from. You've a good memory, Herbert. Did you see one?'

Mrs Dawson and Chance turned to her husband.

'I didn't but he could have had a half-bottle in his pocket.'

'If someone had found the man on Thursday night, could he have been saved?'

Chance shook his head. 'He died almost instantly, Mrs. Dawson. No one could have done anything.'

'You must try not to dwell on it, Olive. Though it's a dreadful thing for the town. There was nothing in the paper last night. How did he come to be there?'

'We don't know. It was too late to catch that edition. It'll be in today.' Chance spoke with feeling. The stringer for the *East Sussex Echo* had been pestering the front desk first thing. He usually slouched in, sporting a bored expression and a fleck of lavatory paper on his chin. He'd like to know who tipped him off.

'By the way were either of you out and about Thursday night?'

Mrs Dawson shook her head. 'We rarely go out for the evening. Only if there's a play on and we can take Joan.'

'I always walk Tessie,' Mr. Dawson said. 'That's about half-past eight but we never go further than the end of the street and back. Long enough for her to sniff a few lamp-posts.'

'Just a thought in case you went to the pub.'

'I'm not much of a drinker. Was the dead man robbed, Inspector? I suppose you can't say?'

'Fraid not, sir. It's early stages. We're still gathering information as you can see. Thank you both for your help. I think that about wraps it up. Unless you can think of anything else you'd like to add?' Chance stood, picking up his trilby from the table.

'Only that we're very sorry.' Dawson spread his hands in a helpless gesture. 'I feel like the Pharisee who passed on by. How did I not know?'

'There was no reason for you to examine the man,' Chance said. 'Most people would have reacted in exactly the same way. The mind sees what it expects to and drunks aren't exactly unknown.'

'I don't ever want to walk past there again,' Mrs Dawson murmured.

'That's understandable but I'm sure it will pass.'

She was looking at the mantelpiece. Chance glanced at a photograph of the granddaughter. She must be about Vic's age. The other pictures were of a young woman and a chap in uniform.

'I'll let you get back to your granddaughter. At least she wasn't with you yesterday.'

Mrs Dawson's pensive face was back. 'Yes, indeed. We feel very protective of her. We lost her mother when Joan wasn't much more than a baby. Our daughter Evelyn, that's her there.' She showed him the photograph. 'Joan's getting just like her. I hope she stays fair. My hair turned to mousy. I suppose Evelyn's would have done in time.'

It was definitely time to leave. He handed it back, hoping he looked sympathetic. It had occurred to him long ago that you went through life pinning on suitable expressions, interest, listening, sympathy and so on. Yet you never knew how they appeared to the other person.

Like any copper he'd done his share of delivering bad news. He supposed he passed muster. Most likely the other person never noticed anyway. They could only see their grief.

'I'll see you out, Inspector.'

A tweed cap and a blue felt hat hung together on the coat pegs. Side by side and overlapping. Like a metaphor for a long marriage. He wondered if they bickered like most couples.

The house was quiet as he stood on the doorstep. The girl had probably taken the dog in the garden.

'What kind of dog is Tessie?'

Dawson smiled, knocking a few years off. He had a good head of hair for his age, completely grey. Chance ran a hand over his crown. Still thick on top.

'Mongrel with a good dash of terrier.'

As he walked home Chance thought about how the daughter might have died. The Spanish 'flu was his best guess. No mention of the father. Did a rough calculation. Died of his injuries? Since the war, almost everyone was walking wounded. Only the scars didn't always show.

What had the murdered man carried with him from the past?

Five

Eddie Chance sprawled in his arm-chair with his eyes shut. Ankles crossed, head back, the *News Of The World* spread open on his lap. His stomach full of roast beef and Yorkshire pud, he felt too pleasantly stuffed to move.

A low rhythm of voices came from the kitchen where the women were washing up. Daphne had nipped off smartly as soon as dinner was over. Said she was meeting a girl she'd got talking to in the library. Vic was about somewhere, in his bedroom or outside.

They'd moved into the dining-room. Irene's voice was suddenly close, accompanied by the clink of china. Disjointed phrases reached him like a familiar riff. Peace was almost over.

'Can't be trusted .. do it thoroughly.' Something about a wet tea-spoon in the sugar bowl. That meant him. 'They never.. something properly. .. hang up .. afterwards.'

Is that too much to ask? he mouthed silently.

The doors of the dining-hatch were suddenly thrust open. Irene's head poked out like a cuckoo clock.

He was buried behind the pages when she entered. Ostentatiously stepping over his outstretched legs she collected his empty cup and saucer.

'It wouldn't hurt you to bring them out.'

An apologetic murmur.

The paper lowered when she'd gone. Chance raised his eyebrows at the other occupant of the front room. Harold Napier smiled sheepishly. He never had a lot to say. He'd probably waved the white flag long since.

Although they met at family occasions, Chance didn't feel he'd ever come to know Stella's step-father. They'd be seeing a lot more of one another now, he thought. He really should make an effort.

Harold had been quietly reading the *Sunday Pic,* which meant they hadn't had to speak. If he was as bored a visitor as Chance would be in his place, it didn't show. Previous attempts to find common ground had failed. Jazz? Harold wasn't really musical. Football? Not really his thing. Politics? He couldn't really say.

He could hardly suggest they be allies against the man's own wife. Why the heck did he marry the lovely widow Irene? Chance fantasised idly that Harold was a bigamist. Nothing so exciting.

Colourless in appearance with thinning grey hair and matching personality, he was a pen-pusher at the council offices. Chance had never enquired which department.

Harold cleared his throat. 'I could always lend a hand with the garden, you know, Eddie. If I wouldn't be treading on your toes, that is.'

Of course, Harold's one known enthusiasm. Sadly not one they could share. 'That's very decent of you. I wouldn't want to put you out.'

'I'd enjoy it. Stella was telling her mother some ideas she's had. You can't get much free time in your job.'

'Well, if you're sure?'

Ideas, what ideas? Perhaps the poor chap wanted a bolthole. Understandable but doomed. Irene was sure to accompany him to see her grandchildren and make sure she didn't miss anything.

'Thanks very much, Harold. Stella does get carried away. I blame magazines.'

'Who gets carried away? You can hear every word through that hatch.'

Stella Chance plucked the newspaper from her husband's lap and sat on the settee. She swung one shapely leg over the other. The fluffy slippers only slightly spoilt the effect.

'It's much appreciated, Harold and you'd do it far better. But you mustn't let Eddie take advantage. He needs the exercise.'

'He won't be needing any tea after all those potatoes.' Irene sat down and studied her son-in-law critically. 'Bicarb, that's all he'll be wanting.'

The 'phone-bell in the hall pinged and began to ring.

'I suppose that's for him?'

'We don't know anyone else on the 'phone, Mum.'

Chance got to his feet. 'Looks like I'll have to love you and leave you, Irene.'

His eyes met Stella's. The expression beneath the finely arched eyebrows was amused. Shutting the door he picked up the receiver of the newly installed instrument. The voice at the other end was the desk-sergeant. He listened intently.

'Has she, by Jove? Put her in my office, will you? A car's on its way? Good man. We'll pick up Wilf. Thanks Joe. I'll be waiting outside.'

Saved by the bell.

Hands in his pockets, Chance paced in front of his privet hedge. Hever Drive was empty. All the neighbours would be nodding over their Sunday papers as he had been. As the weeks went by they'd be nodding to one another as they chopped their hedges. With any luck Harold would be doing his.

Although they'd moved in just after Armistice Day, so far he'd managed not to get to know any neighbours. He hoped Daphne was making a pal. Stella had spoken to them but he let the details wash over him without sticking.

The rain had held off again although the sky was grey. From their side of the road Chance could see the Channel beyond the roof-tops of much of the town. The pier stood out like a banjolele and somewhere down there was the sea-front shelter nearly opposite the Belvedere.

A black car rounded the corner from Warwick Avenue and Richards drove towards him, rather fast.

'Have you seen this lady, Richards?' Chance took the front passenger seat.

'Yes, sir. Sergeant Lelliott came and fetched me. We've given her some tea, like you said. A Mrs Lilian Simmonds. Looks respectable, forties, very on edge.'

'You didn't tell her anything?'

'No, sir. Just that you'd get there as quickly as you could, if she didn't mind waiting.'

'Good. She didn't look the type to bolt?'

'Don't think so. I had the impression she'd made up her mind to come and wanted to get it over with.'

'You know we're collecting Sergeant Bishop?'

'Sir.'

They were making their way down the hill when Chance spoke again.

'Did you learn to drive in the war?'

'Before, sir. My old man was a chauffeur. He taught me.'

'You didn't want to be a mechanic? It's a good trade.'

Richards shook his head. 'I can do a bit. There was no way round it in France. You had to keep an engine going any way you could. But it doesn't interest me, too fiddly. I didn't fancy my head under a bonnet all day.'

Chance nodded. He wondered where Richards had served. You didn't ask.

'My brother started out as a mechanic. Came back minus an arm. Loos.' Richards indicated before slowing, his voice matter of fact.

'Rotten luck.' He thought briefly about his own brother. 'Stay put. I'll go.'

The door was opened by a woman in a Sunday frock. The apron she'd just dragged off was thrown on the hall-stand. Gladys Bishop smiled broadly and called Wilf's name over her shoulder.

'Hullo stranger. I know you haven't come to see me.'

'It's always good to see you, Glad.'

'Get away with you. I hear all about you flirting with the canteen girls, you know.'

'That's slander,' Chance protested, laughing. 'There's not one under fifty. Besides I only do it to get seconds.'

'She called again, louder. 'Have you time to step in a minute?'

'I'm afraid not. Sorry to take him away on a Sunday, Glad. It's important or I wouldn't do it.'

'Not to worry. I've been a policeman's wife long enough. Here he is.'

'Having a read?'

Bishop had appeared from the back.

'Chance'd be a fine thing. Geddit?'

Glad passed him his hat and coat.

'A woman's turned up at the station, concerned about her missing lodger.'

'What are we waiting for? See you later, love. Go and put your feet up.'

'This has to be the breakthrough we need,' Chance said when they were in the car.

'I should think so. We'll soon know when she sees a photograph.'

'Sergeant Bishop and I will talk to her,' Chance said to Richards. 'Fish out the mug-shots Godwin took and bring one in to us, will you?'

'Very good, sir. Will we be taking her to the mortuary?'

'Not today. She might not need to view the body. With any luck she can point us in the direction of next of kin. Stick around to drive us to her place though. If it's him we'll take her home and search Mr. Lynch's room.'

'Wonder if he paid in advance?' Bishop asked no one in particular.

'I should think most of them make sure of it.'

'This could be a wild goose chase, sir. Someone who's skipped.'

Chance treated Richards to a withering glare as the car pulled up.

'Your lady's all ready for you. She knows you're on your way.' Sergeant Lelliott leant across the desk as they walked in.

'Thanks, Joe. Is Constable Marden on duty?'

'Yes, she's around. Do you want her?'

'I'll have to show this witness a head and shoulders of the victim. If she makes a fuss, women are better at that sort of thing.'

'Understood. I'll make sure Phyllis is hovering.'

'She'll be doing that any way,' Chance said.

When he opened his door, the woman seated in front of his desk swung round and rose to her feet.

'Good afternoon, madam.'

She returned his greeting in a nervous voice, tinged with a Sussex accent.

'My name's Detective-Inspector Chance. No, please do sit. Sorry to have kept you waiting.'

'That's quite all right.'

'I hope you've been looked after?' He glanced at her empty cup. 'Would you like some more tea?'

'No, thank you.'

'My sergeant here is going to take notes of our conversation.'

The woman looked alarmed. 'This is much more formal than I expected. I only wanted a quick word with someone.'

'It's just the way we do things, madam. It saves time in the long run if everything's written down.' Bishop was deliberately reassuring as he settled himself in the corner.

'Yes, I see. I don't want to take up your time.'

Chance sat behind his desk. 'That's what we're here for,' he said cheerfully. 'Cigarette?' He proffered the silver-plate box kept for visitors.

She shook her head. 'I don't, thank you.'

The cleaning ladies didn't come in on Sunday. He picked up the ash-tray and emptied it in the waste-paper basket behind him.

'First of all, may I have your name?'

'Lily.. Lilian Simmonds.'

'Is that Mrs or Miss?'

'Mrs.' There had been a tiny hesitation. He put it down to nerves.

'And you're here because you're concerned about your lodger. Is that right?'

'Yes. That is, a paying-guest. I don't actually take lodgers. He hasn't been back since Thursday evening.' She had her hand-bag on her lap. Her gloved hands pressed on the clasp.

'His name is?'

'Mr. Leslie Warrender.'

'Do you have his address?'

'London, but I don't know where exactly. Most of my gentlemen come down on the train from London. They work their way along the south coast.'

'You do have a register?'

'Oh, yes. They write ever such kind comments but I don't insist on their full address. Most of them put London or somewhere like Southampton. I always say have a good look round and make sure you don't leave anything behind. Half the time I wouldn't know where to send it.'

'How long has this paying-guest been with you?'

'You might think I'm making a fuss about nothing. He only came on Monday and took a room for the week. He was planning to leave tomorrow. I'm worried he's met with an accident.'

The two men exchanged glances. Chance fiddled with his lighter.

'What makes you think he hasn't decided to leave early, Mrs Simmonds? His plans could have changed.'

'Leslie.. Mr. Warrender wouldn't do that to me. He's a gentleman and we're on friendly terms.' She leant forward. 'He wouldn't dream of leaving without saying anything.'

Bishop's head jerked up at the Christian name. He pulled a wry face. Chance knew what he was thinking. *Quick worker.*

'Has he paid for the room in advance?'

'I know what you're thinking.'

Mrs Simmonds looked at him. Her skin was a mass of freckles. Sandy hair, though where her parting disappeared beneath her brim there were faded roots. He thought of his old ma saying *only fast women dye their hair.* He didn't think Mrs Simmonds was fast. He suspected she might be lonely.

'He offered of course. I said to pay me at the end of the week. You have to trust people, don't you?'

Chance smiled faintly. 'We don't see the best of people in our line.'

'No, I suppose not. Well I've been let down in the past, believe me but you can't let life sour you. I think I'm a good judge of character.'

People always did.

'It's not an easy life being a salesman, always on the road. Most of my gentlemen are commercials. I get to hear all sorts. In fact Leslie tried quite hard to insist I take his money in advance and I know he had some. I hope I'm not wasting your time.' She dried up and looked around the drab office.

'If you're worried, Mrs Simmonds, you did the right thing coming here.'

She gave him a grateful smile. 'I've thought all week-end as to whether I should or not. I didn't like to trouble the police. I kept hoping he'd walk in with some explanation. Mr. Freeman, my other paying-guest, he's a commercial-traveller in stationery. He offered to come with me but I hadn't made up my mind.'

'What did in the end?'

'I couldn't go on wondering. He said he had someone to see here but if they'd asked him to stay, he would have come back and told me. Don't you agree?'

'In the usual run of things.'

You get to thinking by yourself and everything seems so much worse when the shops and pubs have closed. There's nowhere they could be.'

He understood what she meant. The long reaches of Sunday. Slower and more deadly than any other day. When worries magnified and there was little distraction.

'I did wonder about ringing up the hospital but what could I say? I know he hasn't up and gone though. His things are still in his room.'

'Are they?' Chance's voice was sharp.

Mrs Simmonds blushed. 'I looked. Not that he came with much. They don't as a rule. Most of them don't have more than the one suit they're wearing. His case is under the bed where he left it.'

She started as someone knocked on the door.

'Come in. Ah, Richards.'

'What you wanted, sir.'

He backed out like a butler, eyeing Mrs Simmonds as he went.

Chance dropped the brown envelope on the desk. 'Can you describe this man to us, Mrs Simmonds?'

'I'll try. I'm not very good at heights but Mr. Warrender's a little shorter than you, Inspector, and of medium build. He has light hair brushed back with a side-parting. Blue eyes, fair complexion, clean-shaven. A good voice. You know, top-drawer. Most women would say he's attractive.' She added this with a casual air.

'How old would you say he is?'

'Forty-three, forty-four or so.'

'Did you see the evening paper yesterday?'

'I've given up taking it.'

'The body of a man was discovered on the promenade on Friday afternoon. We haven't yet established his identity.'

She ran the tip of her tongue over her upper lip. The pink lipstick was all wrong for her colouring.

'It can't be him.'

'I'm afraid the body fits your description.'

Bishop looked a question at him and slipped out of the room. Chance reached for the envelope.

'I'm going to have to ask you to look at a snapshot of the deceased. It's not a pleasant thing to do but we need your help.'

'Is it ..'

'The picture shows a head and shoulders. Nothing untoward.'

She swallowed. 'I didn't expect anything like this. I suppose it's my own fault for coming here.'

'You've done the right thing.' He held out the image. 'Ready?'

Mrs Simmonds leant forward without taking it. There was an audible intake of breath. They had their answer.

'It's him.'

'You're quite certain?'

'Yes. That's Leslie Warrender.'

'Thank you, Mrs Simmonds. Sorry to put you through that.'

She nodded, her face pale beneath the freckles.

Chance shoved the photograph in his drawer. Something caught at the back. He wrenched some paper free and slammed it shut.

Bishop returned to his seat. Chance made a face at him.

'Tea's on the way.' Bishop said.

Mrs Simmonds opened her hand-bag and produced a handkerchief. 'What happened to him?'

'He was killed with a single stab wound.'

'You mean someone killed him? It wasn't something like a heart attack?'

'It was very quick. The doctor was sure he wouldn't have known much about it.'

'I can't believe it.'

Everyone said that. Nobody could stand the finality of death. The mind slammed the door. Grief slid in underneath.

She bit her lip. 'Do you have the man who did it?'

'Not yet. We're..' He broke off as the door opened. Constable Marden placed a tray on the edge of the desk. They waited while she poured. Chance indicated she should wait.

Bishop added sugar to a cup and handed it to their witness. 'Drink this, love. Good for shock, it'll make you feel better.'

Thanking him, she took a sip and grimaced. 'I don't understand. Who'd do a thing like that?'

'That's what we have to find out. Do you feel up to answering some more questions, Mrs Simmonds?'

'I suppose so.' She set down her tea. 'It's strange, this time last week we hadn't even met. He was a lovely man.' Her voice shook, 'kind and sympathetic. We had such a nice talk the other night. People don't get murdered for no reason in a respectable place like this.'

'No,' Chance said quietly.

'He listened, you know? Most people don't. You do but that's your job. He wasn't trying to find out things. Leslie cared about what makes people tick. He made me laugh.' The tears rolled silently down her cheeks.

Chance looked meaningfully at Phyllis, standing against the wall. She stepped forward.

'If you'd like to come with me, madam, I'll show you where you can powder your nose.' She placed a gentle hand on Mrs Simmonds's shoulder and guided her to stand.

'Sorry to be a trouble.'

'Take as long as you need,' Chance said insincerely as Phyllis took the other woman's hand-bag and helped her from the room.

Six

'Well, it was worth missing a Sunday afternoon snooze for,' Bishop said. 'I reckon she just saw her new fancy-man snatched away.' His voice was not without sympathy. 'They'll never learn.'

'You can never count on anything in life,' Chance said. He tested the weight of the tea-pot. 'Good old Phyllis. That young woman is in danger of making herself indispensable. She comforts weeping witnesses and she thought to bring a large pot. What's more I think she's raided the superintendent's china. More tea, vicar?'

'Ta. Leslie Warrender, eh? Or Mr. R. Lynch. Which one d'you reckon he was?'

Chance frowned. 'There's no knowing yet, possibly neither. We'll see what his belongings have to tell us.'

'Things are moving.'

'Just as well, I have to see Hayes again tomorrow. He'll want as much progress as possible before the inquest.'

'How did you get on yesterday afternoon?'

'Nothing fresh to speak of. The couple, their name's Dawson, didn't see anything different in the shelter. The wife said there was no bottle on view.'

Bishop drank his tea. 'So we're no further forward there.'

'No, but we know nothing went missing from the shelter between about ten-thirty and when Miss Betts turned up. I do wonder if the murderer removed something besides the wallet. I can't believe it was a robbery gone wrong. Not when the corpse was sitting like that and wearing a wrist-watch.'

'We know now he wouldn't have had a latch-key on him. What were the Dawsons like?'

'Decent people. They're raising an orphaned granddaughter. I saw her briefly. She's about eleven or twelve. Nice kid.'

'Quite a shock for them.'

'They were horrified, especially the wife. She was all nervy and thinking I'd come to arrest them. Anyway the coroner won't want them called. It's Miss Betts's evidence that counts.'

'You know I've just had a thought.'

'Don't keep it to yourself.'

'Friday afternoon, young Phyllis said an empty wallet had been handed in.'

Chance stared at him. 'It's a good job one of us has a brain. Well done, Wilf. I wonder if Mrs Simmonds could identify her guest's?'

'I'll fetch it from lost property. Of course it'll be covered in prints.'

*

'Sorry it's rather basic. It is clean.'

Phyllis stood to one side as Mrs Simmonds dried her hands. The thin towel hanging from a wooden rail needing throwing out. It wouldn't do for a floor-cloth in her opinion.

'That's all right. I didn't expect it to be like Grove's.' The two women smiled at one another.

'It smells lovely in there, doesn't it? Soft towels, expensive soap. No carbolic.'

'What prices though. They can afford it. Still it cheers me up just to walk round there.'

'Me too. Even their paper bags are pretty.'

'Nice to see how the other half live.' Mrs Simmonds rummaged in her bag. 'Mind you, some of those women behind the counter are snooty. The way they look down their nose at you. You'd think they were mannequins.'

'I know what you mean. They look as though they're pricing your costume.'

'I mustn't keep your inspector waiting but I look a fright.' Opening her compact, Mrs Simmonds dabbed at her cheeks.

'You look fine, really. And the inspector appreciates your coming to us. We couldn't do our job effectively without the public's help.' She felt a warm glow of pride as she spoke.

'He's nice, isn't he, your boss? Attractive with that crooked smile.'

'I've never thought. He seems so old. Sorry, I didn't mean..'

'I know, dear.' She spoke between reapplying her lipstick. 'Take my tip and make the most of being young and single. When I was your age all I thought about was being married. It isn't all a bed of roses. Not if you pick the wrong one. Then again, it isn't easy for a woman on her own.' Her voice ended on a wistful note.

'Do you know if your lodger was married?'

She couldn't resist the urge to ask.

'He was a bachelor. He said he'd never found the right woman.' She looked critically at her reflection. 'The first night he stayed, I wondered if he was meeting a woman the next day. You know, someone special. He had an air about him. As if he was expecting something exciting. More lively than a day trudging round trying to get people to take out insurance.'

'That's interesting. I'm afraid the inspector will need to ask you some more questions, Mrs Simmonds. I'm sure you understand how important your help is. Will you be able to manage now?'

She snapped shut her bag. Phyllis noticed it had seen better days.

'I'll be fine, dear. I'll have to be.' Settling her small hat on the back of her head, she eyed herself in the mirror. 'Life goes on as they say. Best get this over with.'

*

'Feeling better, Mrs Simmonds?'

'Yes, thank you.'

She'd repaired her face and seemed more composed, smoothing her skirt as she sat down. 'Your young lady was very kind.'

Chance sat back in his chair, eyeing her thoughtfully. 'We could do this tomorrow if you're feeling faint. It's just that in a murder inquiry time is of the essence. We'll run you home after and in any case we must search Mr. Warrender's room today.'

'It's quite all right, Inspector.' She spoke with a quiet dignity. 'The young lady explained you need to question me now. I want you to find whoever did this. Will I have to identify his body?'

'I hope you won't have to,' Chance said. 'Certainly not today. It depends on what we find among Mr. Warrender's effects. There should be his home or business address which will lead us to some family.'

'I know he was a bachelor. Your young lady asked me.'

'Did she indeed?'

'Leslie didn't mention any relatives.'

'The coroner requires formal evidence of identity from next of kin if possible. Or failing that someone who knew the deceased well. You will be required to attend the inquest in case the coroner has any questions. They would only be about Mr. Warrender taking a room.'

She nodded. 'I see. Well, if I must.'

'Right.' He glanced at the clock. 'I'll make this as brief as I can. I'm sure you'll be glad to get indoors.'

She gave him a tired smile. 'I can stop wondering now. I know the worst did happen.'

'Did you happen to catch sight of Mr. Warrender's wallet at all?'

She looked surprised. 'Yes, he invited me out for a drink on Wednesday night and I saw it when he paid.'

Bishop came over to where she sat.

'Take a good look at this, Mrs Simmonds if you would.' He held out a shabby brown wallet.

She put a hand to her mouth. 'That's the one.'

'You're sure, if you only saw it briefly?'

'Can you turn it over? I'm certain that's it. I noticed that mark on the leather, like an ink stain.'

'Do you know if he had much money on him?' Chance said as Bishop returned to his chair. 'You said you knew he had enough for your rent.'

Mrs Simmonds had removed her gloves while she was gone. She twisted her wedding ring.

'I couldn't help seeing he had quite a wad of notes. I thought he'd signed up some policies and been paid in cash.'

'Policies?'

'He was an insurance salesman.'

'D'you know which company employed him?'

'I'm afraid not.'

'Let's start from the beginning. I want you to tell us everything you can remember about Leslie Warrender. Start from his turning up at your house. When was that?'

Bishop's pencil made swift notes in his own short-hand as Mrs Simmonds described Warrender's appearing on her doorstep on Monday afternoon. She'd given him a cup of tea after he'd seen the room and they'd had a chat. She'd been going to take him in the front room set aside for the use of her p.gs.

Somehow they'd ended up at the kitchen table instead. She had some dishes draining on the side where she'd been baking and he'd even offered to wipe them for her. She wouldn't hear of it of course but he was ever so thoughtful. No, he didn't want evening meals.

Bishop pursed his lips as he scribbled.

'How many paying-guests do you have?'

'I've three letting rooms. At the moment it's only Mr. Freeman. He works his way along the coast every few months. He's a commercial-traveller and he always stays with me.'

'Will he be there now?'

'I daresay he will. He wasn't in when I left. I've lent him a latch-key because I know him. I'm not harsh like some land-ladies about letting them in during the day. Especially on a Sunday when there's nowhere to go.' She smiled sadly. 'It's not so bad if it's not raining but there's only so many times you can walk up and down the pier.'

Bishop coughed. 'That's decent of you, madam but you want to be careful about handing out keys to all and sundry. Even if you think you know them.'

'I will from now on. Now there's a murderer on the loose.' She looked down, twisting her ring again. 'It isn't easy without a man in the house. Knowing what to do for the best. I'd give up letting if I could but I have to make a living.'

There was an uncomfortable silence.

'Did you give Mr. Warrender a latch-key?' Chance said.

'No, there was no need.'

Her wistfulness implied he could have had one for the asking.

'We'll want a word with your other guest,' Chance said. 'Did he see much of Mr. Warrender?'

'I introduced them on Monday when Mr. Freeman arrived. They may have chatted in the evenings.'

'And they met at breakfast, presumably?'

Mrs Simmonds shook her head. 'They weren't together for long. Mr. Freeman likes his early so he can get to the station. Leslie came down later.'

'He didn't want to be off on his day's work then?'

'He said it was no use calling on people too early. After the first morning, Tuesday, I kept him company with a cup of tea while he had his bacon and egg.'

Lucky beggar, Chance thought. He was currently rationed to a fry-up on week-ends only. Stella said she was watching his waistline for him. He suspected it had more to do with boiled eggs and toast not spitting fat over the new stove.

'When Mr. Warrender did set off, did he mention anywhere specific he was going?'

'Let me see. He said he'd be covering other towns in the area. Hastings, Bexhill and Eastbourne I suppose. He did say Tennysham was an ideal base.'

'He must have talked about himself? What about when he took you for a drink? How did that come about?' Not very gallantly put but it would do.

Her skin went crimson. 'He said things were going very well for him. He'd had an unexpected bit of luck and would I like to help him celebrate? We went to The Ship and had a very nice time.'

Chance speculated exactly what form that celebration had taken. On the whole, he had Mrs Simmonds pegged as a romantic so it might have stopped at a couple of port and lemons. He didn't intend to find out.

'That's when he said he lived in London but he was more interested in finding out about me. I told him how dull my life is but he wouldn't have it.'

'You mentioned he didn't want you to provide supper. What time did he return each evening?'

'On Monday he went out again after we had a cup of tea and he'd unpacked. For a wander, he said. He came back around six. It was about the same on Tuesday and Wednesday. I should think he had something to eat in a café after he'd finished his day's calls. He said he'd be travelling around and he'd get something out.'

'What happened on Thursday?'

'He came back about the same time. Went upstairs for a wash. Then he came downstairs about half-seven and said he was off out for a drink. He didn't suggest I accompany him so I sort of assumed he was meeting someone. He didn't say so.'

'Did he say where he was going?'

'No. I was talking to Mr. Freeman in the front room and Leslie only stuck his head round the door. That's the last I saw of him.'

'Did you think he'd returned when you locked up? When did you realise Mr. Warrender was missing?'

'Next morning. I thought he'd over-slept when he didn't come down. I knocked on his door and looked in. His bed hadn't been slept in.'

'And Thursday night, when you went to bed?'

Her eyelashes were damp and she blinked rapidly.

'I was sitting in my room downstairs at the back and I dozed off. I hadn't slept well the night before. When I woke it was after midnight. I just assumed everyone was in so I bolted the front door and went to bed.'

'How did he seem earlier that evening?'

'Cheerful. As if he didn't have a care in the world. He was whistling when he came down the stairs.'

She stared fixedly at the shelf of buff-covered booklets on *Game Law* and *Modern Policing* as though they would have some answers.

Seven

'Pearl-street?'

He'd stopped listening when she'd given Bishop her details. Chance sat in the back of the car with Mrs Simmonds. Her shoulders were hunched in her top-coat, hand-bag clutched against her side.

'Do you know Mr. and Mrs Dawson?' Possibly not. It was quite a long street.

She turned to him, surprised. 'Yes, they were very good to my mother. Olive.. Mrs Dawson lets me have some of her marmalade for my guests. I can't make it like she does.'

'Did you know their daughter?'

'No. She died not long before they moved in.'

'What happened to her?'

'She drowned. A tragic accident. Their Joan was only a baby and it left her an orphan.'

'Can't be easy for them. Bringing up a child in their sixties.'

'They dote on her. She's supposed to be the image of her mother.'

'I met the Dawsons yesterday,' Chance said. 'I'd better tell you why.'

'I can't believe it,' Mrs Simmonds said again when he'd finished. 'Friday morning? I've been worrying and hoping since then and all the time Leslie was already dead. I wish they'd come and told me.'

'I asked them not to discuss it with anyone,' Chance said. 'In any case they'd no idea he was staying with you.'

'I suppose none of it matters now.'

Bishop turned round as Richards brought the car to a halt.

'Nice part of town, this.' He smiled encouragingly at their passenger. 'Quiet. Handy for the shops and the sea.'

'Yes, I know I'm lucky to have this place. It belonged to my parents.'

'Have you been widowed long, love?'

Chance groaned inwardly. Sympathy might bring on the waterworks again. He studied the end-terraced house. A tall side gate and the entrance to a twitten separated Mrs Simmonds's home from the next row of smaller houses where the Dawsons lived.

Victorian houses always seemed gloomy to him. He didn't share Bishop's liking for the past. The Duke of Sussex was an exception.

Downstairs the hem of the net curtain was caught up on a potted geranium in the window. Harold had a porch-full. They stank of cats' whatsit.

Richards' eyes met his in the mirror. Mrs Simmonds was taking a long time to answer.

'Actually I'm not a widow.'

'Sorry.' Bishop looked enquiring. 'I must have got hold of the wrong end of the stick. You said it's hard living alone?'

'My husband and I are living apart. Estranged they call it, don't they?' Mrs Simmonds laughed. The kind you do when life's kicked you in the teeth. 'He up and left me. Ran away with his fancy-woman.'

She looked out at her house. 'Even the thought of getting this place wasn't enough to make him stay. Most people round here think I'm a widow. It's better than feeling humiliated.'

Chance got out of the car. The house opposite had a *To Let* sign in the small front garden. By Mrs Simmonds's low wall there was a bare square of earth in the pavement where a tree had died.

He and Bishop waited while she fumbled for her key and let them in. The stairs were straight ahead and a long passage led to the rear of the house. A man's hat and coat hung on a peg.

'Mr. Freeman's back. Shall I knock on his door?'

As Mrs Simmonds looked at him, a slight cough came from the front room. Brushing past the two detectives, she opened the door instead.

A middle-aged man was sitting in an arm-chair by the gas fire. A handkerchief spread over his knees, he'd been eating an apple sliced into crescents. The core lay on a saucer on the tiled hearth. The peel curled beside the pen-knife was a dead giveaway. False teeth.

'These gentleman are policemen, Mr. Freeman. I've had a terrible shock. They've found Mr. Warrender. He's been murdered.' Mrs Simmonds sagged against the wallpaper by the door.

Her lodger bunched up his handkerchief and dabbed the white cotton at either corner of his mouth before speaking.

'You should have let me accompany you, Mrs Simmonds.' His voice was flat and nasal. A Londoner. They could have been discussing the weather.

'This is Inspector Chance and Sergeant..' She looked apologetically at Bishop.

'Bishop. We'll have a word with Mr. Freeman here and then we'll go through Mr. Warrender's things. No need for you to come, Mrs Simmonds. You must be worn out. You go and have a sit-down. You can leave us to it.'

'Well if you're sure? It's the first on the left as you go up. It isn't locked.'

Bishop steered her from the room.

'Can I have your full name, sir?'

Helping himself to a seat on the settee, Chance dropped his hat on the arm and crossed his legs. The other man had made no attempt to rise.

'Freeman. Arnold Trevor.' He glanced at the door as Bishop returned. 'So Mrs Simmonds finally made up her mind to speak to you?' He tapped a hand on the folded newspaper by his side. 'Someone in the pub let me have a copy of last night's local rag. The body found stabbed on the sea-front, that was him?'

'That's right, sir.' Bishop had taken the other arm-chair and was poised with his pencil.

'You don't seem surprised?' Chance said.

'You are mistaken, Inspector. I am surprised there's been a murder in Tennysham. I shouldn't have thought it the sort of place. Though nowhere's what it was before the war.'

A familiar refrain from everyone except the youth. Chance wondered how old Freeman was. Had to be fifties but which end it was hard to say. Stringy build and tooth-brush moustache, sparse grey hair neatly combed. The sort you'd stand next to at a bus stop and not notice.

'What can you tell us about Leslie Warrender?'

'He was a bad lot.'

Chance raised his eyebrows. 'Care to elaborate, Mr. Freeman?'

'He was a liar. The sort that plays up to women for what they can get, only women never see it.'

'You weren't keen on him then?' Chance said.

'I detest the type, Inspector.'

'Did he say anything about himself?'

'He said he was in insurance when I first arrived. Only because Mrs Simmonds introduced us. I don't flatter myself he'd have given me the time of day otherwise. Wrong sex, unless I could be useful to him.'

It was hard to make out his expression behind the horn-rimmed spectacles. As if to be helpful, Freeman removed them and began polishing the lenses with his handkerchief.

'I asked if he had a street-map he could let me consult. He didn't. I've never known anyone in his line travel without one.'

'You're in stationery aren't you, sir? Mrs Simmonds mentioned.'

'That and other office supplies, Sergeant. I've been staying here regularly for two years now. I always enjoy coming back to the seaside.'

Freeman breathed on his lenses and replaced the frames. Chance watched the cloud on the glass gradually disappear.

'What about breakfast and supper-time? The evenings must hang heavy away from home. Didn't you chat at all, Mr. Freeman?'

Bishop had taken over the questioning.

'I don't think Warrender was inclined to speak to anyone when he rose. He shambled in shortly before I was ready to leave. Muttered a cursory greeting and that was all. Mrs Simmonds came in directly she heard him on the stairs.'

'And after work?'

'I had my daily paper-work which I prefer to do in my room. Warrender didn't have supper here. I've no idea what his arrangements were. On Tuesday evening we met briefly as he was coming out of the bathroom and I noticed there was alcohol on his breath.'

'And Wednesday we know he took your land-lady out.'

Freeman's lips pressed together. 'Mrs Simmonds doesn't always know what's in her best interest. She's a kind-hearted woman.' He spread a hand. 'You can see the homely touches she's provided here. This is a much better billet than some I stay in, I can tell you.'

Chance looked obligingly around the room. Her parents' furniture, good solid stuff, none of the cheap veneer you had these days. Probably a better place to stay than the Belvedere and certainly more welcoming.

He scowled as he thought of his HP payments. *Sign here* Stella had said, leaning over his shoulder. She'd tucked her hair behind her ear in a way he'd found quite sultry long ago when they were courting. That salesman had been an smarmy blighter.

'I saw Warrender on Wednesday as it happens, in the High Street.'

Bishop leant forward. 'What time was this?'

'Mid-morning, getting on for eleven. He didn't see me but I saw him all right.'

'Where was he exactly?'

'Going into the National Provincial. He was with a woman.'

Bishop looked at Chance. 'You're sure it was him?'

'Quite sure.'

'Could you describe his companion?'

Freeman made a regretful face. 'Unfortunately no. I only saw her from the back. Warrender, I caught sight of from the side. Average height, brown hat and coat. Not young.'

'Did you see what colour hair this lady had?'

'I couldn't say. She could have been any age upwards of forty.'

'Well thank you, sir, it all helps.'

'How did they seem?' Chance broke in.

'In what way?'

'Were they talking? Friendly? Arm in arm?'

'Bearing in mind I only saw them briefly, they weren't speaking. They didn't strike me as a couple if that's what you're implying, Inspector.'

'Can you tell us your whereabouts on Thursday evening, Mr. Freeman?' Bishop looked pleasantly at him. 'We have to ask everybody.'

'I'm not offended, Sergeant. On the contrary, I take a keen interest in these matters. I'd have been disappointed if you hadn't.'

Beneath the newspaper a corner of a book protruded. Chance saw Bishop make out the surname on the spine.

'Real murder is rather more than a puzzle, sir. The butler didn't do it.'

Mr. Freeman smiled thinly. 'You cannot chastise the public for taking an interest, Sergeant. After all sensational trials are reported at length in the press and written up afterwards for the serious student of human nature. Murder has a unique fascination for us all. The motive for taking a life, the means of hunting your quarry.. the trail that ends with the hangman.'

Chance looked at the ceiling. It was cracked.

'And Thursday night?'

'I went to the pub, leaving here at precisely ten to eight. A quarter of an hour after Warrender went out. That was intentional. I deliberately gave him a start so I didn't have to walk with him. I sat in The Mafeking Hero and spoke to no one other than a bar-maid. I doubt she'd remember me.'

Bet she would, Chance thought.

'Thank you, sir. What time did you get back here?'

'I returned here at about five and twenty to ten. Mrs Simmonds was in her private sitting-room at the rear of the house. I know this as I saw the electric light under her door. I called good-night to her but she didn't hear. I then retired to my room and read.'

The slices of apple left on the plate had turned brown. One of the sad truths of life was that nothing stayed fresh.

*

'He certainly had his feet under the table,' Bishop said for the second time.

Chance grunted in reply. It was starting to rain again. He stood, hands in his over-coat pockets, looking out at the street. There was a glimpse of the sea between the roof-tops from the first floor.

Richards was flicking through the newspaper Bishop had left him. He looked up as a boy went by on the pavement. The little chap turned round and had a good stare at the car.

He was trundling a knocked-up cart piled with papers. As he watched, the boy turned in a gate further down and disappeared from view behind a hedge. Swapping comics.

'Did you find out who handed in the wallet?'

'An elderly lady. Picked it up in St Luke's churchyard on Friday morning.'

'What time?'

'Early though she didn't bring it in until later.'

'Don't tell me. She was walking her dog.'

Bishop chuckled. 'She was, so Joe said.'

'Is everything in this case going to be found by an old lady? Perhaps I should turn the inquiry over to my mother-in-law. God knows, she could teach me a thing or two about ferreting out information.'

'That goes for all women.'

Outside the light was changing. Not turning dark yet, now it was early March but deepening. You knew you'd reached the fag end of the day. He turned to face the room as Bishop switched on the bedroom light. The weak bulb didn't make a lot of difference. So much for the National Grid he kept reading about.

'Nothing under the mattress. Always worth a try.'

'Between the two of them downstairs they've given us quite an idea of Warrender. Miss Betts implied he was charming.'

Bishop snorted eloquently. 'That type make me sick, battening on vulnerable women.' He picked up a cigarette case on the bedside cupboard.

'Easy prey, I suppose. Sad but it's ever been so.'

'He left this here on Thursday evening. It cost a fair bit. Monogrammed.' Bishop opened the lid. 'Sullivans. Expensive taste to go with it.'

He turned to the top drawer. 'Empty apart from a Bible she's provided.'

'I'm sure Warrender appreciated that for his bedtime reading.'

'What d'you reckon he was up to in Tennysham, Eddie?'

Chance detached himself from the window-sill and wandered over to the single bed. Puffing, Bishop had pulled out a small brown case and dumped it on the bedspread. He clicked the locks and threw back the lid.

'Not selling insurance. Where's his paper-work? We know he was lying about working other towns in the area. How many pubs recognised his photograph?'

'Three. The Ship, The Smugglers and The Marquis Of Granby. He was here every dinner-time. Drinking alone unfortunately. He must have liked The Ship as that's where he took Mrs Simmonds.'

'He had tea in Grove's on Tuesday, as well as Monday before he came here, morning coffee twice in Queen Anne's and once on the pier. I think he was hanging round town waiting for someone or something.'

He hadn't bothered to unpack. Bishop prodded the folded clothes and emptied the case. Underwear, hose, shirts and collars. Inadequate for a week away. As anonymous as the boarding-house bedroom with as little to tell.

'There's nowhere else apart from the bathroom.' Bishop looked round again. The wardrobe doors were open. A chest of drawers contained only lining paper and a lavender bag.

'The clothes are an odd mixture,' he said.

'How do you mean?'

'The hose and underpants look brand new, same as the ones he was wearing on the night he died. His shoes were new too, soles hardly rubbed. His over-coat was decent quality but worn and so are these shirts.'

Chance shrugged. 'So he decided he needed some new underwear.'

'What man goes and gets all new at once?'

'A wife might, I suppose.'

'No,' Bishop shook his head. 'Wives look over clothes and see what needs replacing. They don't go and get all new. See this shirt? That button's been sewn on in a faintly different colour cotton.'

Chance grinned. 'I'd no idea you were so domesticated.'

'A woman replaced that button. It's too neatly sewn for a man to have cobbled it. And thinking back to your theory, a man might need all new underwear if he'd worn out his old things in jug. Shoes and all. The rest could be hand-me-downs.'

'We should hear tomorrow if he had a record. I'll be glad to get the week-end out of the way.'

'We're not doing too badly, Eddie. Post-mortem's done and we have another name.'

'And now a suspect. We know Warrender met a woman in Tennysham. Though how the heck we're meant to find her?'

'Something'll turn up.' Bishop stretched his arms and rubbed the back of his neck.

'Plus the weapon hasn't been found and no pub land-lord remembers seeing him on Thursday night. That's the crucial time.'

'Early days.'

'As long as Superintendent Hayes takes the same attitude.'

'I'll just get Mrs S. to point out anything he left across the landing. Then we can get back to our nearest and dearest.'

'You took Mr. Freeman's details?'

'Home and place of work, both in Croydon. He's off in the morning. Comes here every three months he said.'

Chance frowned. 'I'd have thought that rather often to get repeat business and why stay Sunday?'

'Wouldn't know. He strikes me as a fussy sort of cove. Won't be a minute.'

Left alone, Chance gravitated to the window once more. Richards must have finished his paper. He was leaning against the car door, arms folded, looking gloomy.

Cherchez la femme. Chance knew how he felt.

*

When he was finally dropped off, a scruffy boy was swinging his gate slowly back and forth.

'Has Gran gone?' Chance said.

The tow-coloured head nodded sadly. A foot kicked half-heartedly at the wood.

'What's up then?'

'I've got a sore throat, Dad.' In an unconvincing whisper.

'Done your homework?'

Another nod followed by a strangulated cough.

'You'll have to do better than that, old son,' Chance said as he passed him.

'I've got a temperature. And a rotten stomach-ache.' Vic grimaced horribly.

'That's Mum's department. Coming in?'

The door opened and a welcoming light spilled over the step.

'Vic's not too well, he tells me.'

The boy turned towards the woman standing in the hall.

'It sounds as though he's going down with a cold and a bilious attack for good measure. They've come on all of a sudden.'

Stella half-smiled at her boy. 'It must run in the family. Your father used to be exactly the same on a Sunday night. Bath-time, Vic.'

'What makes you think I'm not still?' Chance said.

'You'll both be sorry if I collapse at school. It could be my appendix.'

Stella beckoned Vic to her and placed a hand on his brow.

'Off you go. You can read in bed afterwards. And don't tell lies.'

With a despondent groan he gave in, his feet stamping up the stairs.

'The coast's clear. You're safe to come in.'

She looked quizzically at him, hands on hips as he hung up his hat and coat. 'You know I think Mum's right. You are putting on weight.'

Chance knew the annoying quality of silence. He looked over at the gramophone as he wandered in the front room. Fat chance.

His wife pulled the new curtains with unnecessary force.

'I didn't arrange to get called back. A murder inquiry doesn't stop at week-ends.'

He sighed as he climbed the stairs. A dreary Sunday evening. And the question was, had he done his homework?

Eight

Wilf Bishop stuck his head out of the window to see what the commotion was. A rag and bone cart had shed its load and a house removal van had mounted the pavement in an attempt to get by. The street was blocked and a big Tourer was trying to back up, despite an Austin waiting behind.

The drivers were in mid-altercation and the row had brought Joe Lelliott out from behind the desk. Get a man behind a wheel and he was sure to lose his temper. Abolishing the speed limit was just pandering to them.

He enjoyed being in the thick of town. There was talk of building a new police station. *To meet the needs of an efficient twentieth century force*, according to the Chief Constable. He hoped it wouldn't happen in his time.

Frederic Street was freezing cold in winter, it was true. The draughts were wicked, especially when his lumbago was playing up. The end window in the C.I.D. room had to be wedged with the back of a fag packet to stop it rattling. None of that mattered.

It had a bit of history. He was fond of the building where he'd spent almost all his working life. The knapped flint walls that gleamed black in the rain were framed in bands of sooty Victorian brick. He liked to see the date *1854* carved in the lintel and the big archway to the yard where the garage had been converted from stables.

All his memories of starting out as a bobby were held in the stale air of the boot room, damp leather, polish and tobacco. Not to mention the disinfectant in the cell block.

The whinnying horse and the rumble of wheels were getting drowned in a tooting horn and rattling engines. There was too much change for his liking. Life has to move on, Chance would say. There was a man with no feeling for history. He'd still come back home to his own though.

Phyllis stuck her head round the door.

'The Yard are on the telephone, Sarge.' She'd tried saying it with a casual air. They grinned at one another.

'Mustn't keep our betters waiting then.'

The voice at the other end had the hard edge he heard in the streets when they visited Helen at Crystal Palace. His son-in-law sounded the same. Their nipper would too when he was old enough. His London counterpart's manner was chirpy as he read out the file and he brought good news of a sort.

Chance would be glad of it before he went in to the Super. On the other hand some poor woman along the coast was going to get the visit every copper dreads.

*

Eddie Chance was feeling frustrated. Leaning against the railings he faced the sea, indifferent to the view. Curse all bank managers. It was particularly awkward that the chubby individual he'd just seen knew the ins and outs of his own account. Mostly outs. He didn't enjoy feeling like a school-boy outside the headmaster's study.

You'd think he'd been demanding to see a customer's account. He'd only wanted to show the clerks a snapshot of the victim and see if anyone remembered dealing with him and his companion. Naturally none of them had.

Eventually he'd winkled out the grudging admission that neither a Leslie Warrender nor an R. Lynch held an account there. He'd cut short a pompous lecture on how busy they were. As if the police were just passing the time.

To a nosy parker he might seem to be idling now. Whereas he was in fact snatching a few minutes' peace to mull over the case. Working out anything he'd left undone before the Super jumped on him.

Old Yeates the manager had seemed surprised he'd come in person. Chance hoped he wouldn't bend Superintendent Hayes's ear. They were bound to be in the Rotary together.

Though he was always happy to delegate the paperwork, he enjoyed getting out of the office and talking to people. To get a handle on things it helped to see for yourself. As long as it wasn't raining.

It was a fresh morning. Quite cheerful with the sun dodging in and out. A couple of old boys were fishing from the side of the pier, the breeze ruffling their lines. In a way he was doing much the same thing. So far he hadn't had a bite.

Chance looked along the promenade towards the shelter at the far end. He wondered how long people would remember. That's after they'd stopped going especially to see. For a while the council could probably sell tickets.

How were they going to find the mystery woman entering the bank? Mr. Freeman's description had been vague and useless. Chance considered the women he definitely knew had met Warrender, leaving aside Mrs Simmonds. There were two, three if you counted the Belvedere's cook.

A woman of average height, not young. That did apply to Mrs Simmonds of course. Was there any chance that Freeman, who wore thick spectacles, hadn't recognised her from the back?

Taking a last drag, Chance threw his cigarette-end down on the pebbles and strode back into the town.

*

You wouldn't know it was almost spring. Easing the front door closed, Ethel Lynch shivered in her cardigan. The garden had never looked anything in the three years they'd lived there. The soil was stony and the hedges on the new estate had never thrived in the salt air.

A solitary splash of colour came from a clump of crocus near the path. The orange-tinged yellow of egg yolk, they were the only cheerful thing in sight.

She wondered when she'd started thinking like that. When they'd first moved in, the green front door with its long sun-rays had welcomed her every time she came home. A newly-built house with a bedroom each for Peggy and Vera, a smart bathroom and the small box-room for Ronald's study.

He was sitting in there now even though he was supposed to be poorly. At least she hoped he was at his desk. Ronald had bitten her head off when she suggested getting a doctor. It wasn't as if they couldn't afford it. If he went to the lavvy and looked out of the landing window he'd see her.

The wind was cruel, rolling up the Channel and she was glad to sit in the car. Without Ronald at her side it felt like forbidden territory. Her heart thumped as she inhaled the smell of leather and tried to calm down. She had her story ready. She'd lost a brooch with a weak catch and thought it had come off in the car.

You know, the silvery one with a rose on trellis-work that her Mum had given her on her seventeenth birthday. It wasn't real silver but it was pretty and she'd always liked it. That way he wouldn't care. Wouldn't tell her off for being careless and losing something valuable he'd bought her. Must remember to find it so she could wear it again.

It was a long time since Ronald had given her jewellery. It had taken her years to realise that he wanted his wife to look well turned out because of what it said about him. She dreaded going to his firm's annual dinner and letting him down.

She slid to the edge of the seat and stared at the dashboard. It was too awkward to wriggle behind the steering wheel and she didn't want to risk catching her stockings. When she tried to add up the numbers in her head, the figure she'd memorised kept slipping away until she didn't know anything for sure.

Another hopeless idea. He was right about her. Besides she already had proof with what she really had found in the car several weeks ago. A neighbour walked by and it seemed to Ethel that the woman looked curiously at her. When the street was empty again, she climbed out, thankful that the box-room was at the back of the house.

As she reached the porch, they called it that though it was only a canopy, the door opened. She jumped back, flustered. Her foot turned over, wrenching her ankle. Ronald was wearing his over-coat and dangling his car key.

'I'm off. What on earth are you doing out here in your slippers?' He didn't wait for her to answer.

'I thought you still felt sick? Are you going in to the office?' She heard her voice sound nervous.

'Someone has to pay for all this.'

'What time shall I expect you home, Ronald?'

He shrugged and wiped the windscreen. 'Couldn't say. I'll be in the office all afternoon then I've a contact to see. Keep mine hot if I'm not back.'

She was still framing her next sentence as he raised a perfunctory hand and reversed smartly across the pavement. Making her way to the open gates, she watched the car disappear. A moment later even the sound of the engine moving towards the main road had gone.

Ethel tried to tell herself it was the stinging of her ankle and the bitter wind making her eyes water. Ronald had reversed a tyre over the crocus.

Every last one was crushed.

*

'Is the inspector back, Sarge?'

Chance grinned at Bishop from the doorway. Like most burly men he could move silently when he chose.

'Your wish is my command, Constable.'

Godwin spun on a sixpence, his face crimson.

'Sorry, sir. Didn't hear you come in. The lab have just been on the blower with the results of the blood tests.'

'Let's have them then.'

Waving him further down the C.I.D. room, Chance perched on Richards's desk. The latter shut the folder he'd been reading and looked expectantly at Godwin.

'Warrender wasn't drunk, sir.'

Chance raised his eyebrows. 'Well, well, I'll go to the foot of our stairs as my mother used to say. Give us the details.'

Godwin glanced at his note-book and looked up. His eyes sparkled with enthusiasm.

'I jotted down the science, sir, but you want the gist?' Receiving confirmation he hurried on. 'To start with, the alcohol in his blood wasn't brandy. It was the volume percentage of beer or cider. The estimate is no more than two drinks. A pint at most. Or he could have had two halves or a couple of small bottles of ale.'

Bishop looked up from filling his pipe. 'So someone sprinkled brandy over his coat? Not something your average party carts round with him.'

'Not on a copper's wages.'

Chance turned to glare at Richards. 'I'm sorry we don't pay you enough. What do you make of this?'

Richards sat up straight. 'Like you said, sir. Make the corpse look like a tramp sleeping it off. Keep people away and confuse the time of death?'

Chance nodded. 'Perhaps our murderer reads detective stories.'

'Fred does.' Godwin murmured.

'In that case you can give us some tips, Richards. I've a feeling we'll need them.'

Chance picked up his hat. 'No go at the bank,' he said to Bishop as they moved towards his office.

'Ah well, you lose some..'

'What? That's your rabbit out of the hat expression.'

'That's not the only 'phone call we've had. The Yard's been on the line. I thought you'd want to hear about it first. They're sending us a record. They've matched the corpse's fingerprints with a felon.'

'That's more like it. So what was his real name?'

'He was Leslie Warrender. Middle name Ernest.'

'What was he in for?'

'He was a rent collector for a well-heeled widow in the Smoke. Only he was paying himself a nice bonus on what he collected.'

'Any next of kin?'

'There is. Name of Lynch.'

Nine

Superintendent Hayes had done all right for himself. His office had a working fireplace with coals laid. Everyone else's was boarded up with a gas fire. And he'd had his own desk brought in. A regular home from home. Chance wondered if he had a private income.

'Take a seat, Edgar. Ah, you prefer Eddie, don't you? Be with you in a moment.'

Not a fool. Hayes hadn't missed his expression. Chance relaxed as much as he could on a hard chair and continued looking about him. It was always the same when you gave someone a spot of power. The old make you wait while I pretend to be studying something important routine. Just so you know the difference between us.

The Superintendent's manner had been friendly enough. Chance's conscience gave him a nudge. He'd done it himself with constables. It had been the same in the army. Waiting on the step of a dug-out while some patronising toff kept up standards. They all stank the same out there, pips or not.

The photograph on the wall behind the balding head was of a young man in uniform. He recognised the badge of the East Surreys. The closing of a drawer returned him to the matter in hand.

'Paper-work multiplies ever more. As you're no doubt finding yourself at present.' Hayes smiled but there was a hint of challenge in his eyes. 'Perhaps you'd care to bring me up to date?'

It wasn't a question.

'We've had a breakthrough this morning, sir.' Chance filled him in on the call from the Yard and the results of the blood test.

Hayes fiddled with a propelling pencil as he listened. He rolled it away as Chance finished, giving a satisfied nod.

'Good. We both know the first days are the ones that matter. Strike while the iron's hot. Memories are fresh and the murderer still feels jittery. Agreed?'

'Yes, sir.' Any fool knew that if weeks went by, a murderer would start to feel safer. Even distanced from the event as though it had never happened. 'Now the victim's identity's been established, the investigation should be straightforward.'

Tread cautiously. He hadn't had that much to do with Superintendent Hayes so far. No point in holding out your own rope for the hangman.

'Quite. So he was released from prison in late November and turned up in Tennysham soon after, using a false name. Obviously up to no good. Contacting another member of the criminal fraternity?'

'It's possible, sir.'

'He must have turned up here about the same time as you, Eddie.'

Chance smiled dutifully. 'Apparently Warrender was born in Sussex and his sister, who is down as next of kin, still lives in the county. Hopefully she'll be able to tell us what he was doing since he got out.'

'A revenge attack could be a possibility. A gang member he fell out with?' Hayes's face hardened. 'I won't tolerate murder on my watch. This is a peaceful town and that's how it's going to stay. We leave that sort of thing to other places.'

Like Brighton hovered in the air. Chance wondered if he was going to be damned by association, just because he'd been transferred there when he'd made sergeant.

'I couldn't agree more, sir.'

Hayes nodded. 'Of course. You're bringing up children here. Settled back in their home town, I trust?'

'Yes, thank you, sir. Though my son doesn't really remember living here.'

'How about Mrs Chance? Making friends and so forth?'

Please don't ask us to dinner. 'She's kept in touch with old friends and she has family here.'

'Good, good.'

'Regarding the victim, sir, according to his record he was convicted of fraud. There was no known involvement with the criminal fraternity.'

'It sounds to me as if he was going straight back to his old ways. How many assumed names did he have?'

'Only one that we know of. Warrender's identity is certain now. We have a fingerprint match and the body has a scar on the left knee which is noted on his prison record.'

'War injury?'

Chance shook his head. 'No, Dr. Wheeler thought it was some minor childhood injury. Nothing unusual.'

'Did he in fact serve in the war?'

'Yes, sir. No details given but I've contacted the War Office to request his service record.'

Hayes frowned. 'At least he did his duty. Go on.'

'When Warrender stayed at The Belvedere Hotel in early December he registered as R. Lynch. His sister is a Mrs Ethel Lynch. Last week when he stayed at the boarding-house in Pearl-street, he used his real name.'

'So why use an assumed name the first time?'

Chance risked a faint shrug. 'Ronald Lynch turns out to be the name of his brother-in-law. I got on to the local station to inform Mrs Lynch. She and her husband are driving over from Marting. Sergeant Bishop and I are meeting them at the mortuary late this afternoon.'

'You seem to have everything covered. Just in time for the inquest. This Mrs Lynch understands she'll be called, I take it?'

'The local men explained, sir. Apparently she and her husband are staying here overnight.'

'Quite a shock for the poor woman. No doubt when she rose this morning she expected an ordinary Monday. Wash-day in fact.'

Chance nodded sagely. *Eh? Wash-day?*

'Pity the weapon hasn't been found.'

'It may still be in the murderer's possession, sir.'

'Possibly. Now we all want to solve this case ourselves. We don't need Scotland Yard here showing us how it's done. Agreed?'

'Agreed, sir.' He was at it now. It was catching.

Superintendent Hayes stood up, his gaze straying to the wall clock. He was short for a policeman and his highly polished shoes were on the small side. They squeaked as he escorted Chance to the door.

'Keep me in the know, Eddie. I haven't forgotten this is your first time leading a murder investigation. I shall inform the Chief Constable of your progress. Unfortunately he's had this wretched 'flu that's doing the rounds or he'd have seen you himself.'

Chance assumed a solicitous expression. 'I had heard, sir. I've two constables down with it.'

'Colonel Vesey will be holding a watching brief and he may decide we need outside help. So bear in mind that the clock is ticking.'

And that old chum is a warning shot, Chance thought as he shoved open the canteen door.

He'd better not find those idle beggars Richards and Godwin in there.

*

You didn't get to be a good detective without determination. That's what Phyllis kept telling herself as she shivered. An empty bus passed the end of the street. She could hear the gears grind as it turned into the Southdown depot.

'Been stood up, love? 'e's not worth it.'

Pretending she hadn't heard, she crossed to the other pavement. She'd seen the man come out of a kitchen door and stack some empty wooden crates. Then he'd stood by the open gate lighting a cigarette, cupping his hand around the match.

The tall buildings with iron fire escapes and blank sash windows had a dispirited air. A gull was drinking from a puddle along the gutter and a whiff of boiled greens hung about the back yards. Greyish tea cloths shifted in the breeze on a sagging line. The dingy street behind the smart facades along the sea-front was one the holiday-makers rarely saw.

Thrusting her hands in her coat pockets, she paced a few yards towards the corner, halting by the rear of the end building. She was regretting wasting her afternoon off when a girl's voice called cheerio, a dustbin lid clanged and rapid footsteps came towards her. When the gate opened, Ivy Betts stepped out at last.

'Hullo Phyl.'

She didn't seem surprised to see her. Phyllis remembered her as a dreamy kid, small for her age.

'Hullo, Ivy. Haven't seen you for ages.'

'I saw you from the window. You've been there a while.'

'I thought you got off at half-past three. I was beginning to think I'd missed you.'

Ivy swung the end of her scarf over one shoulder. 'Depends what job I'm given. I often don't get to finish on time.'

'That's not right, you know.'

Ivy shrugged. 'They all like to get their last ha'penny.'

'Fancy a cup of tea? I thought you might want someone to talk to. You know, after Friday?'

'Don't mind. Where shall we go?'

'Queen Anne's?'

'All right.'

'My treat.'

Ivy fell in step with Phyllis and they set off towards the shops. The Queen Anne Tea-Rooms was where you went in Tennysham if you could only afford Grove's on special occasions. According to Sergeant Bishop it was named after Henry VIII's fourth wife, the one Henry had called the Flanders mare .

She must have done something right, he'd said. Instead of getting her head chopped off, she'd survived to live quietly away from court and Henry had given her some land thereabouts. There was no evidence she'd ever visited Sussex apparently. In any case it was the iced buns people went for.

The tea-room was fairly quiet on a Monday and Phyllis chose a table in the corner. She sat with her back to the wall so she could survey the other customers.

'Why don't we go mad and have cream horns?'

'Well, if you're sure, Phyl? Let me go halves.'

'No, it's on me. I insist.'

'Ta very much, then.'

The waitress winced as she took their order. The leather of her patent shoes was strained over a bunion on both feet.

'How's Vi getting on these days?'

'She's having a high old time. Not that she gets round to writing often. She works in a factory making irons. Funny 'cause she never liked using one. Our Uncle Reggie got her in there. It's good money for a woman. She says she goes dancing every Saturday night. Suits her down to the ground. You remember what she's like?' They smiled at one another.

'She was always fun. It's a shame you lose touch when you leave school.' Vi had thought she was daft when she'd announced she was applying to join the county force. 'Your aunt and uncle didn't have kids, did they?'

'That's right. They always made a fuss of Vi. Dad says she's very like Auntie Lorna, she's his sister. That makes Ma start on about how Vi's heading for trouble. I can't see her coming back here.' Ivy broke off to remove her things from the table as the waitress returned.

'She always said Tennysham was too quiet.'

'Vi says I should do what she's doing. She said at Christmas, she'll never skivvy for a living. Might as well be in service. I wouldn't mind service though. You have to earn a living somehow. Ma says no one'll marry me for my looks.'

'Tuck in.'

'Thanks awfully.' Ivy grinned and helped herself from the proffered cake-stand.

When Phyllis had poured, she sat back with her tea cup, wondering how to bring the conversation round to Leslie Warrender. She didn't even know what she wanted to ask and it was only fair to let Ivy enjoy her cake.

At the table in the window, two women were getting up to leave. The fortyish one in a rather nice hat looked faintly familiar. The brim swept becomingly low to frame her face. The older lady wore a Queen Mary toque which resembled a crushed velvet tea cosy.

Phyllis had decided they were mother and daughter when it came to her. She was Mrs Chance. She'd left a message at the front desk for the inspector soon after they moved in.

'This is lovely. Wish I'd known. Something to look forward to when I was scrubbing the kitchen floor.'

Phyllis felt guilty. Ivy's hands were as red as her hat and scarf set. She looked cheerful as she licked a blob of cream from her finger. As soon as the inspector's wife was through the door, she glanced round the room. No one was paying them any attention.

'How about you, Ivy? Only you had an awful time of it on Friday. I thought I'd come and check how you are.'

'That's real kind of you, Phyl. I remember you always stuck by Vi. It was more than she deserved at times.'

Feeling an absolute heel, Phyllis lowered her voice. 'I wondered how you got on afterwards. If you were shaken up when you went home? Did you have Saturday off?'

Ivy screwed up her nose comically. 'Not likely. Your boss asked Miss Aldridge if she'd given me a brandy. Should have seen her face.' She mimicked a dry, refined voice. *'I shall expect you in as usual, Ivy. Work's the best cure for brooding'.* Her parting shot was *'Have an early night, dear with a hot water bottle. You'll be right as rain by morning.'*

Phyllis smiled in sympathy. 'I expect your mum looked after you.'

'Made me another cup of tea and wanted to know all the gory details.'

Ouch. 'Look, the last thing I want to do is force you to go over it. I thought it might help to talk to someone.. another girl.'

'I thought I might have nightmares but not so far. Have you ever seen a dead person?'

Wiping her fingers on her serviette, Phyllis shook her head. 'Never.'

'I'd seen my gran. Vi wouldn't look but I helped to make things decent. It isn't as bad as you think it will be, even when you love the person. Not if they died peacefully like.' Ivy picked up the strainer. 'Refill? They give you plenty of hot water here.'

'Please.'

'I remember my Ma saying *Put your hand on your Gran's forehead and you'll never be frightened of seeing a dead body again.* She said Gran made her do it when her father died. Her forehead was icy. Ma was right though, Phyl. Gran wasn't there. It was no more than looking at a pile of empty clothes at the jumble.'

'I think you were very brave,' Phyllis said.

'I've been thinking about it all weekend. Why would anyone want to kill Mr. Lynch?'

Phyllis looked round again. The other ladies were deep in character shredding. 'That wasn't his real name. I'm not supposed to discuss the case but you'll hear that much at the inquest. His name was Warrender. They don't say a lot in front of me, anyway,' honesty compelled her to add.

'I've to go to the inquest Tuesday morning. I'm dreading it. Will you be there?'

'Sorry, Ivy. I wouldn't be allowed. I wish I could go with you. What about your mum?'

'She won't be able to get time off from the shop. I'll be all right when the time comes. It's having something hanging over you that's horrid. Miss Aldridge said she'll come with me.' Ivy wrinkled her nose. 'Don't know how much comfort that'll be. It's kind of the old stick though. She didn't even like the poor man.'

Phyllis set down her cup abruptly, her heart thudding. She'd typed up the interview notes for Sid. Miss Aldridge had claimed not to remember Leslie Warrender.

'What makes you say that?' Her voice was casual though it was an effort.

'I heard him in Miss Aldridge's office when he stayed with us. They were having words one morning. She calls it her office but it's more like a cubby hole really.'

'Did you hear what they said?'

Ivy shook her head, her bobbed hair moving like a curtain. 'I was in the downstairs linen cupboard which is next door. I heard Miss Aldridge raise her voice but couldn't make out what she was saying. I didn't know who was in there with her but someone was copping it. Anyway she dropped her voice again at once. You know how people speak when they're angry but don't want to be overheard? All deliberate? It sounded like that.'

'How did you find out who was with her?'

'Well I didn't fancy being found in there and have Miss Aldridge know I'd heard them, so I nipped off. I hung around the front desk in the hall though. Reception she calls it.'

She collected some stray flakes of pastry with her finger and popped them in her mouth.

'The door opened and Mr. Lynch came out. He didn't shut it behind him neither but she did. He looked proper pleased with himself. Gave me a lovely smile and do you know what, Phyl? I swear he winked at me.'

This was better than she'd hoped. 'You didn't tell this to the inspector and sergeant?'

'Not with Miss A. sitting there. She'd get rid of me and I'd have no reference.'

Phyllis nodded. 'I'm worried they'll lay my dad off.' It was the first time she'd admitted it to herself.

Ivy looked sympathetic. 'I suppose firms cut back on advertising when they're feeling the pinch.'

'That's what I think. Dad says Denison's won't go under but I'm not so sure. Something's up with him. I hear it in his voice when I ask about work.' She hadn't realised until she said that. Phyllis stored the thought away to chew over later.

'Denison's has been going for donkeys' years. Try not to worry, Phyl.'

'You're right. It probably won't come to that and we've got my money coming in.' They were lucky. It was a question of what it would do to her dad.

'Funny, isn't it? Vi reckons there's plenty of work around St Albans. They're building new factories.'

'We're not badly off down here. It said in the *Chronicle* there are whole firms being laid off in the North and the places still going have *No hands wanted* on the gate.'

'Maybe Vi's got the right idea but I wouldn't want to leave Tennysham.'

'Nor me. Unless I got promotion and was transferred.'

'Will you tell your boss what I said? I don't want to get into trouble.'

'I'll have to report it but he'll understand about your job. Miss Aldridge sounds a right old dragon.'

Finishing the last of her tea before she answered, Ivy looked thoughtful.

'She is but she doesn't have any family. I don't think the Belvedere can be doing that well. It's half-empty in the winter and last month she let the other chamber-maid go. Miss Aldridge said Meg's work wasn't up to standard but she did all right. She hasn't replaced her.'

'That's hard on you. Can you remember what Mr. Warrender did after you saw him in the hall?'

'He went straight out, whistling. I didn't see Miss Aldridge until she came in the residents' lounge later. I do remember though she was in a terrible mood the rest of that day. Talk about fault-finding.'

'Did you see anything else of Mr. Warrender?'

'Don't remember any more. I never do evenings, thank goodness.' Ivy lifted the lid of the tea-pot. 'Shame to leave any. It's nice to sit down.'

'Let me.'

She wondered what Ivy looked forward to.

'Ta, that's smashing. I remember Miss A. had words with Mrs Thompson. Now Cook generally takes everything in her stride but when I went in the kitchen later that day, she wasn't herself at all. She said it was the onions but they don't affect her like they do me. I swear she'd been crying.'

*

'I can't stand waiting for people.' Chance prodded a cigarette-end out of the way with the toe of his shoe. 'Not when it's like this. I don't mind in a pub.'

'Can't be helped.' Bishop said. 'At least we're not standing in a dole queue.'

'Not yet. Give it a couple of weeks and I might be.'

Bishop cast a sidelong look at him. 'You said Hayes wasn't rough on you?'

'Kid gloves for the moment. Asking after the family. But he's determined to keep the Yard out so he wants results. A murderer in the cells within the week will do nicely.'

An ambulance came up the drive and disappeared round the side of the building as they watched. From their stance outside the main entrance to the hospital they could see the clock on the old Infirmary adjoining the workhouse. Chance compared its hands with his wrist-watch.

'How many times is that? They shouldn't be long now.'

Chance sighed. The workhouse had been built right on the edge of the town. As though the people of Tennysham wanted to distance themselves from the destitute. Nobody liked a reminder that it could be them.

Out of sight, out of mind. He looked over to the forbidding building where his grandfather had died. Before he was born, though the story and the shame had been handed down in his family. He didn't feel it but their Ma had.

She'd always been at pains to tell them as kids that their grandparents had had a roof over their heads. They hadn't been forced into the workhouse. His grandfather had been taken into the Infirmary wing with pneumonia. It was all a long time ago.

He'd suggested they meet at the main entrance. The Lynchs would have trouble finding their way to the mortuary sited discreetly behind the hospital. It looked like a Victorian lodge and dated from the building of the workhouse.

Dr. Wheeler had told him it was reputed to be haunted. Load of tripe, and that the nurses referred to it as Lily Cottage in front of the patients.

A dig on the elbow recalled him to the present.

'I said this must be them.'

Chance removed his hands from his pockets. An Austin Seven had drawn up and a smartly-dressed couple were getting out. The man had a high colour above his muffler and looked older than the woman. He placed his hand beneath her elbow and steered her towards them. Chance had the impression it was more to hurry things along than to assist her.

'I take it you're the police?' He addressed Bishop.

'That's right, sir. Mr. and Mrs Lynch? Good afternoon, madam. This is Detective-Inspector Chance, the officer in charge of the inquiry and I'm Detective-Sergeant Bishop. Did you find your way all right?'

'I drive all over the county. Let's get this over and done with.'

Ignoring him, Chance addressed the wife. 'We're sorry to have to put you through this, Mrs Lynch. I regret there's no other way.'

'Thank you.' The skin beneath her eyes was heavy with watery indigo smudges as she faced him. 'You really do believe it's my brother?'

'I'm afraid so. If you'd come this way. It won't take long and your husband can be with you.'

He wondered if that was any comfort. You never knew with other people's marriages.

'Have you found somewhere to stay, sir?' Bishop asked as they followed behind.

'I've booked us in at the Channel View. Seems decent enough. How long is this going to take if it is him?'

'Ronald, please.' His wife spun round, her voice pleading.

'I told you, Ethel. You might as well face facts. The police wouldn't drag us half-way across the county for nothing.' He gave Chance what could have been a warning look. 'The body's bound to be your brother. Causing maximum inconvenience is always his style.'

Mrs Lynch glanced up at Chance, her face shielded by her close-fitting hat. She looked younger than he'd expected. Her husband was about his own age and doing rather better if his over-coat was anything to go by.

Once in the mortuary corridor Chance felt like apologising to her for the stench. That throat-tickling hospital cleanliness smelt as unpleasant as whatever it hid.

Mrs Lynch coughed as though she agreed with him. 'Sorry.'

'Over-powering, isn't it?'

She returned his smile. It was the sympathetic, lips together one he brought out for victims and the bereaved. Didn't mean he didn't feel sorry for them. On these occasions he felt rather like an undertaker. It was generally a task he managed to dodge.

'Are you going in with Mrs Lynch, sir?' Bishop said.

The husband tapped his wife on the shoulder. 'Do you want me in there with you?' His tone was brusque.

'Will you be with me, Inspector?'

'Yes, Mrs Lynch and the medical attendant will be present.'

'Is there.. I mean to say, will there be any..?'

'Not at all.' Chance said instantly. 'He looks peaceful.' He sounded such a fool. He'd be showing them coffin handles next.

As if on cue the door opened and Jacobs appeared. Chance nodded to him as they trooped past into the ante-room.

Ethel Lynch turned to her husband. 'You needn't come in, Ronald. I'll manage.'

He sat on one of the chairs and fiddled with his expensive driving-gloves. At close quarters Chance noticed his right earlobe was torn.

'This way when you're ready, madam.'

Jacobs took them into the inner room where the body lay. Grasping her hand-bag like a shield, Mrs Lynch was perfectly still. Chance stood near enough to grab her if she looked like fainting. Jacobs whipped back the sheet covering the head with what was very nearly a magician's flourish.

The woman stared, her lips moved. He could see a sort of resemblance in colouring and about the jawline. What was soft in Ethel Lynch would have been weak in the face of the dead man.

She turned her head away. 'That's my brother. That is Leslie Ernest Warrender.' She moved towards the door. 'Can I go now?'

'By all means.'

Chance stepped between her and the corpse. She sounded like a little girl asking if she might get down from the table. 'I'm very sorry, Mrs Lynch.'

Her husband got to his feet as they returned. 'Well?'

'It was Leslie. Oh Ronald..'

She halted a few inches from him. After a moment he patted her shoulder.

'Bear up old thing. You knew the police wouldn't have sent for you for nothing. Think of the children.'

Bishop exchanged glances with Chance. 'Please accept our condolences, Mrs Lynch.'

'Thank you, Sergeant. I don't know what to do now.'

'Don't you worry, madam. The best thing is for Mr Lynch to take you back to your hotel. I'm afraid we do need to ask you a few questions tonight. So we'll meet you both there in.. two hours?'

'We'll keep it brief,' Chance said. 'We can have a longer talk tomorrow morning before the inquest.'

'I understand.' She looked worn down.

'You go and sit down and have a pot of tea.' Bishop said kindly.

'Dash it all, a stiff Scotch is what I need. Six fifteen then, if we must.' Lynch nodded curtly at them and replaced his hat. 'Come on, Ethel.'

'We'll see you to your car.'

When they'd watched the couple drive off, they returned to where Richards was waiting. He stifled a yawn as he held the door.

'Did Mrs Lynch identify him, sir?'

'She did. Back to Frederic Street, Richards.' Chance sat down heavily. They moved off, the tyres scattering gravel. 'We're interviewing the pair of them at their hotel later. I can't say I took to him, did you?'

'Not much,' Bishop said. I don't think his missus is going to get a lot of sympathy there.'

'No. Nice woman. She didn't seem the sort to have a brother in jug.'

Bishop shook his head. 'It looks as though he was the bad lot in a respectable family. She looked very shaken up.'

'Held herself together though. Probably knows she'd have annoyed her old man if she'd broken down. She'll save it for when she's alone.'

'He looked jolly annoyed as it was. The miserable so-and-so. The wife's brother's been murdered and he was put out to drive her here.' Bishop sat back in disgust.

'You'll be home late again.'

'That's all right. Glad will keep something warm.'

'I'll grab something in the canteen after.'

'They stop doing hot food at five o'clock, sir.' Richards's voice was gloomy.

'Just concentrate on the road, Constable and watch your speed.'

'Yes, sir.'

Bishop grinned to himself. 'You off home after this, Richards?'

'Finish at five, Sarge.'

'You can get an early night in that case,' Chance said. 'Perhaps in the morning you wouldn't mind typing up Sergeant Bishop's notes?'

'Sir.'

'As long as you feel up to it.'

Richards drove the rest of the way in cautious silence. Chance yawned several times.

*

Chance cast a disparaging eye over the chrome bar stools and leatherette seating. Downcast wall-lights tried to make the large room look inviting and the place lived up to its name view-wise but the cocktail bar of Tennysham's best hotel wasn't for him. He made a mental note to run it down if Stella asked.

When Bishop returned, Chance was leaning on the deserted bar, looking dubiously at a bowl of olives.

'There you are. Take a look at these. I swear they're dusty. They've probably been coughed over for a fortnight.'

'Pipe down or you'll get us thrown out. The manager's found us a private room and the Lynchs are on their way down.' Bishop peered at the offending bowl. 'Can't say I fancy one. Thank God Glad doesn't go in for cocktails. I don't mind asking for a port and lemon. Long as no one thinks I drink it.'

Stella's tipple is gin and pep. Disgusting stuff. She thinks it's sophisticated'.

Chance wandered over to the window. He stood, hands in pockets, watching a few passers-by.

'A lot's happened since this morning.'

The wind had dropped and the light was slipping into the sea. The lamps were coming on along the sea-front and the evening was the soft grey smudge of a fingerprint.

'It's starting to get dark later,' Bishop said.

Someone bent down, releasing their dog from its leash. The animal streaked across the beach.

'I wonder if the Dawsons will still walk their dog past the shelter?' Bishop pulled out his pipe, thought about it then stuffed it back in his coat pocket.

'Doubt it. Besides Mrs Dawson said she preferred the park.'

A barman came out of the door behind the counter. His oiled-back hair matched his bow tie.

'Evening, gentlemen. Sorry to keep you waiting. May I get you anything?'

'Doubt it.' Chance said. 'And not at these prices.'

'Come on. It's along here.'

Bishop led the way to a small room with comfortable seating and a writing desk.

Chance fingered the note-paper on offer before reflecting that he rarely corresponded with anyone. He left that sort of thing to his wife.

The Lynchs were followed by a young waiter carrying their drinks. There was silence while he unloaded the tray, his eyes darting over their faces.

Chance, generally down to earth, felt as though Leslie Warrender took the empty chair.

Pale and composed, Mrs Lynch sat opposite them with a sweet sherry untouched. Her husband immediately drained the top couple of inches from his pint and wiped his moustache. A whisky chaser stood by his glass.

'Look here, Inspector. Having to take time off is dashed awkward for me. I'd rather not have stayed over only it isn't worth motoring back and forth. We'll be leaving straight after the inquest.'

'That's perfectly all right, sir.'

'There's not much I can tell you so it would suit me if you get all your questions done with now.'

'That I can't promise, Mr. Lynch. We'll keep this short as Mrs Lynch has had a distressing day.' Chance turned to her. 'I thought we could have a longer talk first thing in the morning?'

She nodded. 'Thank you. That's very considerate.'

'We realise this must be very difficult for you. But we have to catch whoever killed your brother and the longer we delay, the harder that will be.'

'I understand.'

Chance switched his attention to her husband. 'What line of work are you in, Mr. Lynch?'

'Insurance.'

'Does that mean you're tied to an office or do you go door to door, sir?'

Mr. Lynch relaxed, his arm along the back of the sofa. 'Neither. I've a string of agents under me who call door to door, as you put it. I'm based at our area office in Chichester but I get out and about, checking up on our chaps from time to time.'

'You often have to see people in the evenings, don't you, Ronald?'

'Yes, all right, Ethel. The police don't want a blow by blow account.'

'Please, Inspector, when can we arrange the funeral?'

'What usually happens is that the inquest will be adjourned and the coroner will release your brother's body to you as next of kin. As far as the police are concerned you'll be able to make your arrangements then.'

'I see.'

'You mustn't worry about tomorrow. The coroner will simply ask you a couple of questions. He'll be as speedy as possible.' Chance avoided Bishop's eye.

Desmond Ridley was known for ripping through cases brought before him in the magistrate's court with the speed of an auctioneer.

'Thank you. I'd like my brother to be buried near our parents.' She sounded tentative.

Her husband shifted his arm. 'That's morbid. Much better have him cremated.'

'No, Ronald. I know it's cheaper but I want somewhere to take flowers.'

'Hang the expense. That's nothing to do with it. I'm thinking of you. It's no good dwelling on what's over and done with.'

'It would mean a lot to me.'

'Be reasonable, Ethel. Your parents are buried miles away. It's not as if you drive. I don't have time to run you over there every five minutes.'

'Perhaps you could discuss this later?' Chance said.

'You'll see sense when you've slept on it.'

Chance took a slow breath. 'I take it you are next of kin, Mrs Lynch? Or was your brother married?'

She shook her head. 'No, he never found the right girl.'

'Do you have other relatives he might have been in touch with?'

'No, both our parents were only children. There was just the two of us.'

'Do you know if your brother made a will?'

'I'm sure he didn't.' She smiled sadly at the past.

Her husband made great play of consulting his showy wrist-watch. 'They'll start serving dinner soon. What else do you want to know, Inspector?'

Out of the corner of his eye Chance saw Bishop's fingers tighten on his pencil.

'To begin with, do either of you know of anyone with a motive to harm Mrs Lynch's brother?'

'No, of course not. Surely Leslie was robbed? The policemen who came to the house said he was found stabbed on the sea-front.' Mrs Lynch turned to her husband. 'We thought he'd been set upon.'

'We don't believe it was a random attack, Mrs Lynch.'

'Deliberate murder? That's a turn-up. Wonder what old Leslie had got himself into?' Mr. Lynch sounded interested for the first time.

'Ronald, how could you? He was my brother and the girls' uncle. We loved him if you didn't.'

'Come off it, Ethel. What man loves their brother-in-law? And the girls hardly knew him. Drink up.' He followed his own advice.

'You didn't even like him.' Mrs Lynch's voice shook as she reached for her glass.

'I'm no hypocrite, old girl. We didn't exactly have anything in common. I let him stay with us, didn't I? Against my better judgement.'

Chance raised his eyebrows at Bishop. You could learn a lot from sitting back and watching witnesses fall out. Had to watch you didn't lose the thread though.

'Do you know why your brother was staying in Tennysham, Mrs Lynch?'

'I didn't even know he was here. He used to say he'd never go back.'

'You lived here years ago?'

'Not me, Inspector but Leslie did at one time. We grew up at Nanstead. I expect you know it?'

Chance nodded. The village was about nine miles inland. 'I need you to fill me in about your brother's background but it will keep until tomorrow.'

'Gladly. I don't know anything that can help but it's all I can do for him. That and see him decently laid to rest.' She shot a stubborn look at her husband.

'When did you last see your brother?

'He stayed with us when he..' She broke off, chewing her lip. 'I suppose you know about..?'

'Of course they know he was in quod,' Mr. Lynch said.

'When Leslie was released from Maidstone, he came straight to us. We're.. I'm all he had.'

'This was the last week of November?'

'Told you.' Mr. Lynch drank some more.

'That's right.'

'I suppose you can't have a snifter on duty?'

'That's right, sir,' Chance said evenly. He gave Bishop the slightest glance that meant fire away. After three months they were as smooth as a variety act.

'Why did Mr. Warrender visit Tennysham briefly in early December?'

'He said he wanted to look up an old friend who might be able to help him. I assumed he meant with work.'

'What he actually said was look up the friend of a friend,' Mr. Lynch said. 'He told me he had a debt to collect. Money owed from way back.'

'When was this?' Mrs Lynch looked at him.

He shrugged. 'Search me. One night after you'd turned in. Soon after he arrived. He was full of himself. On about how he wouldn't be troubling us long. Some rubbish about how he fancied the south of France. I mean to say..'

His wife's face softened. 'He always liked the sun.'

'He didn't tell you the name of this person?' Bishop said. They both shook their heads.

Chance watched their faces. The woman's was regretful, the man indifferent.

'How long did your brother spend with you, Mrs Lynch?'

'A darn sight too long. No use protesting, Ethel, you know he did. It was only ever meant to be for Christmas. Which incidentally guests don't usually turn up for in November. We finally turfed him out on the second of January. My wife persuaded me to let him stay 'til then.'

Mr. Lynch sat back with the air of someone too compassionate for his own good.

'He told me not to worry,' Mrs Lynch said. 'He was going to look up an old friend in London he could stay with. A woman.'

'He could have gone there in the first place.'

Bishop ignored her husband. 'Could you give me the address please, madam?

'I don't have it. Leslie wasn't very good about keeping in touch. He'd get cross if you tried to pin him down. I know where she works if that's any help? And her first name's Sadie.'

'It is, Mrs Lynch. That should be enough to find her.' Bishop smiled encouragingly.

'He told me The Black Cat Club and it's in Soho.'

'Thank you, madam. That's very helpful.'

Her husband snorted. There was a small pause.

'I think we can leave it at that for this evening.' Bishop glanced at Chance for confirmation. 'Please accept our condolences, Mrs Lynch.'

'Thank you. What time will you want us tomorrow?'

'We'll only need to see you,' Chance said. 'If you can't think of anything else to tell us, Mr. Lynch?'

'I've nothing to add. My brother-in-law didn't confide in me.' He drained his glass.

'Very well. The inquest is at eleven o'clock. It's being held at the magistrates' court which is a short walk from here. How about we see you here at nine-thirty, Mrs Lynch?'

'Certainly, Inspector. I'll wait for you at Reception.'

Chance stood, his hat in one hand. 'Just for the record, can you tell us where you both were on Thursday evening?'

'At home together. That's right, isn't it, Ethel?'

She nodded. 'Ronald never takes me out on a school night.'

Ten

'Quite mild out there. Spring's in the air. Any tea in that?' Without waiting for an answer Bishop jiggled the pot, feeling its side.

'It's not long made.' Chance didn't look up from his scrutiny of the *Daily Sketch*. 'I thought I'd snatch a quiet breather before seeing Mrs Lynch.' They'd decided that she might be more forthcoming with one of them.

'Anything you want seeing to while you're out?'

'You could get on to your new pal at the Yard. Get someone to check Somerset House in case Warrender did marry and never told his sister.'

'Consider it done.'

'After that great downpour on Friday, d'you reckon the going will be soft at Plumpton?'

'Shouldn't be surprised. If you do have a minute, our Phyllis is keen to have a word.'

Chance frowned and dropped his paper on the desk. He hadn't slept well. 'What does she want?'

'Says she has some information about the case and she'd rather tell us both together.'

Chance rubbed his eyes. 'It strikes me Bob Forrest doesn't give her enough to do. I suppose she's been reading Godwin's notes again.'

Bishop sipped his tea appreciatively. 'Go on, Eddie, it'll only take a mo. You used to show initiative. Let someone else do the same.'

The folded racing page was swept in a drawer. 'If I must. Thanks for the back-handed compliment.'

'I'll send her in.' Bishop left, balancing his saucer on top of his cup.

When he returned with an eager-faced Phyllis, Chance waved her to a chair.

'Take a pew, Constable, but make it brief.'

'Yes, sir. I've found out something you ought to know at once.' She sat up straight in her spotless uniform.

'Oh yes.' Chance's voice was ominously neutral.

'I've had a chat with Ivy Betts, sir. She says she overheard Leslie Warrender rowing with her boss in December. They were in the hotel office. She couldn't tell what they said but they were definitely having words.'

Pausing for a response which didn't come, she went on in a rush. 'That's it in a nutshell, sir. Ivy felt she couldn't say anything when you and Sergeant Bishop interviewed her. Not in front of Miss Aldridge in case she lost her job. She didn't want to mislead you.'

There was silence while Chance poured himself the last of the tea and added two sugars.

'When did you have this conversation?' Nursing his tea cup, he eyed her thoughtfully.

'Yesterday afternoon, sir.'

'You did right to report it. We'll need an amended statement from Miss Betts.'

'You won't call at the Belvedere, sir? And it would make things very awkward for Ivy if you go round her house. Her mother's liable to kick up a fuss.'

Chance sighed. 'We aren't running this investigation to suit Miss Betts. Sergeant Bishop will speak to her later this morning. So you know each other?'

'Yes, sir. I was pals with Ivy's sister when we were at school. Ivy's two years younger than us.'

'How did you come to question her?'

Phyllis looked uncomfortable as Chance drank his tea, keeping his eyes on her. She looked at Sergeant Bishop.

'I bumped into her yesterday, sir and we went for tea.'

'You didn't seek her out deliberately?'

'Well, I thought if I spoke to her, sir, it might be helpful.'

'It is useful information,' Bishop said.

'So you just happened to be passing the Belvedere when Miss Betts finished work? And conducted her to the Queen Anne Tea-rooms, I suppose?'

'Yes, sir.'

'Don't look so surprised. I haven't been following you. It's what we in C.I.D. call a likely bet. It's where you'd take a young person to butter them up.'

'Did Mrs Chance recognise me, sir?'

'What?' Chance looked confused. 'I'm beginning to wish we'd never started this conversation. What the devil does my wife have to do with it?'

'Sorry, sir. Mrs Chance was having tea. She called at the front desk once. I thought she might have remembered my face and mentioned seeing me.'

'I see.' Chance's face cleared. 'No, she didn't. That proves my point. Everyone goes there.'

Phyllis waited in silence. He knew he'd ruined her day and he wasn't about to make it better.

'Look, Constable, I know you want to assist us but you aren't a detective. The information is useful as Sergeant Bishop says but this is as far as it goes. No more sleuthing behind our backs. Far from helping, you could jeopardise the inquiry. Leave things to us from now on.'

'Sir.' Her voice drooped with her shoulders.

'This isn't a game. We aren't following some treasure-hunt with prizes for the biggest clues. A man has been murdered. Real blood and guts. Snooping around could be dangerous.'

Phyllis's head jerked up. She opened her mouth to protest.

Chance flapped an impatient hand. 'Oh I don't mean I think Ivy Betts is a murderer but someone is and their life is at stake. They're facing the rope if they're caught. *When* they're caught. Do I make myself clear?'

'Perfectly, sir.'

'Sergeant Lelliott was asking for you, love,' Bishop said.

'Take the tray with you.'

'You were a bit hard on her,' Bishop said when they were alone. 'Poor kid looks like she's found a tanner and lost ten bob.'

'It's for her own good,' Chance said. 'I should have seen the Betts girl without Miss Aldridge hovering over her. I missed a trick there.'

'Where do we go now?'

'Will you have a discreet word? Get her to come in.'

'Righto. Miss Aldridge would fit Mr. Freeman's description of the woman going in the bank.'

Chance pocketed his lighter. 'Before we tackle her, let's try and find out how she and Warrender knew one another.'

Bishop grinned. 'Maybe he was complaining about his pillows.'

'If we ask her straight she'll only lie again. Suddenly remember he was trying to cash a cheque or whatever. Then we shan't get anything out of her. You know what barristers always say?'

'Only ask a question if you already know the answer.'

'If there's a prior connection between them, there must be a trace somewhere.' Chance folded his coat over his arm. 'I'll ask Mrs Lynch about Warrender's work history. Maybe he knew Miss Aldridge when he lived here?'

'I'll enquire about the nightclub and find this Sadie,' Bishop said. 'Looks like a trip to London's on the cards. That's if you want me with you?'

'Of course but afterwards I don't see why you can't slope off for a couple of hours. You came in on Sunday. See your Helen and the infant.'

Bishop brightened. 'I wouldn't say no but what would you do?'

'I'll think of something. See you later.'

Chance whistled a few bars of his current favourite jazz recording as he strode along the corridor.

*

There were distinct signs that Tennysham was waking up after the drab, wet winter. Unusually fanciful, Chance thought the streets had an air of purpose about them. Like that crackling moment when the wireless was warming up. There was a feeling of shutters being taken down and housewives scrubbing steps. What's more the ruddy birds had started waking him.

A workman's tent had appeared on the road leading to the sea-front. A man with a fag behind his ear was peering suspiciously down a drain. Not the one that had blocked on Friday naturally. Ladders had appeared outside more than one hotel and someone was cleaning the windows of the kiosk that sold wooden buckets and spades.

Outside the Channel View an old chap was filling flower boxes with soil. Ethel Lynch was sitting in the glass conservatory alongside the entrance. She smiled as she caught sight of him and stood. Chance put up a hand.

'Oy, watch where you're treading, mate.'

He looked down to where his foot had caught a tray of something or other. 'No harm done.'

'You wouldn't say that if you'd just been stood on by great heavy size twelves.'

Nine as it happens. Gardeners could be very nasty types. Always puffing nicotine over poor unsuspecting insects and buying ground up bones.

He obviously didn't look like a guest. Sometimes it didn't matter how tailored your suit was. Somewhere along the line *Copper* became written through you like a stick of rock. It hadn't happened to young Godwin yet. It would.

As he left the revolving door, Chance noticed Ronald Lynch using the telephone-booth. Lynch gave him the briefest acknowledgement and turned his back.

Two old ladies were drinking coffee in the conservatory. It was a pleasant sun-trap with round marble tables and green lacquered basket-chairs. It was strange how many hidden worlds there were within your home town. His Tennysham was a different place from the one the holiday-makers saw.

'Good morning, Mrs Lynch.'

'Hullo, Inspector.' The old ladies looked at them with interest. 'Would you mind very much if we go outside? Unless you want tea, that is?'

'I've just had one. I don't mind at all. Wherever you feel most comfortable.'

'I fancy some fresh air. I feel cooped up in the hotel. Perhaps we could take a turn on the pier?'

Chance studied his companion as they crossed the road. Wearing the same navy-blue coat and skirt and her eyes were puffy. Warrender was mourned by someone which surely meant his life hadn't been worthless, however shady he'd been.

'There goes your husband.'

They watched him walk along the opposite pavement without a glance in their direction.

'Ronald's going to get the motor-car. He thought he might as well use up the time by going for a drive. Of course he'll be back to take me to the inquest.' She sounded anxious to put him in a good light. 'I'm afraid he couldn't think of anything else that might assist your inquiries.'

'I'm hoping you'll be able to help us a good deal.'

'I'll try of course. What else do you want to know, Inspector?'

'Tell me about your brother. I'd like to get a picture of him in my mind. Shall we?' Chance gestured towards the turn-stile and stood back for her to pass through. He followed her over to the railings.

'I'm wondering where to start.'

'How about with your family? I know your brother was born in Sussex.'

Mrs Lynch gazed along the coast. 'Leslie was six years older than me. We lived at Horsham. When our father died, our mother managed to find a position as matron in a prep school near Eastbourne. It can't have been easy to get a live-in job where they'd take us. We attended the village school. Is this the sort of thing?'

He smiled at her. 'Carry on.'

'Leslie felt it was unfair on him. It didn't make any difference to me of course.'

'Children can never understand why they're treated differently,' Chance said. 'They think adults have a choice.'

'It wasn't one of the first-rate schools.' Mrs Lynch turned to look at him. 'Or even second-rate. It was an ugly Victorian house that had once been a convent so it had a chapel and grounds. Our flat was in one of the attics. Leslie always minded that we weren't well-off.'

'Was he clever?'

'Yes.' She looked pleased. 'He found it difficult to buckle down to things. He was easily bored. Always wanted something more.'

It was a toss-up, Chance thought, whether that was the road to high achievement or ruin.

'What did he do when he left school?'

'He got a start as an office boy in a firm at Eastbourne. He stayed there for a few years, working his way up to be a clerk. I don't think he was happy, in the end he left.' Mrs Lynch looked down at the boards beneath her feet.

The tide was going out and Chance following her gaze could see slivers of seaweed caught on rusted girders. He knew evasiveness when he heard it.

She filled the silence. 'There was some awkwardness about a cheque. He was asked to leave but he wasn't prosecuted. The firm didn't want to make a fuss. It was all a misunderstanding. Leslie said he took the blame for something another man did. He protested his innocence but they didn't believe him. The senior clerk was jealous of him.'

Two women ambled past them, discussing someone in avid voices and throwing them a swift glance. Women missed nothing.

It occurred to Chance to consider what Stella would make of his lounging on the pier with a female witness of thirty-four. She'd say he was leaving Wilf Bishop to do all the work. Mrs Lynch was no femme fatale.

He was a great believer in interviewing people away from the police-station. They'd tell you more when they were doing something or moving about.

'What happened next?'

'He managed to get a place in an office in Hastings and was there until he was conscripted in '17.'

'Can you recall where he worked, Mrs Lynch? Or any friends your brother spoke about?'

She shook her head. 'I was at secretarial college and living in Surrey. I used to hear bits and pieces in my mother's letters. It's funny what odd things stick in your memory. I remember her mentioning a fire near his firm and the street being closed but not anything about the business. I don't recall hearing anything about Leslie's friends.'

'Where did your brother serve?'

'He was in France until the end. They put him in the North Gloucesters.'

Chance nodded. At that stage of the war, regiments were desperate for reinforcements. The spurious comfort of pals' battalions like the Southdowns had long gone.

'He was one of the lucky ones. He came back and in one piece.'

'Did he go back to Hastings after the Armistice?'

'No, that's when Leslie came here. He worked as a clerk in the post-office for about a year, I think.'

'He never worked in an hotel?'

'I'm sure he didn't.'

'Why did he move to London?'

'He couldn't settle after the war. I don't know much about what he did there. I'd met my husband by then and was back in Sussex. Leslie was rather vague and he didn't keep in touch often.'

It was looking as though his past would be hard to pin down.

Mrs Lynch looked back at the town. 'I always liked Tennysham. I visited him in his digs a couple of times. I'm glad we don't know what's in store for us. Where exactly was he found, Inspector?'

'That way,' Chance said quietly. He pointed towards Eastcliff. 'The last shelter. He was found by a young woman who works in a hotel over the road. She'd noticed someone sitting there a long time and crossed over to see if he was all right. You'll see her give evidence later.'

'That was kind of her.'

'It won't be pleasant for you to hear the medical evidence but you were told your brother wouldn't have suffered? It would have been quick.'

She nodded and looked for a time towards the end of the town. Pulling off her gloves she slipped them in her hand-bag. 'Could you let me have a cigarette?'

'Of course.' Chance produced his case. Her hand shook slightly as he proffered his lighter.

'Thanks awfully.' She inhaled deeply and gave him a smile that wavered. 'I don't often smoke, only it settles my nerves.'

'Shall we sit?' He led her to a bench sheltered by a wall of the theatre.

'I remember being taken here once when I was a child.' She read the faded poster, still under the glass from the previous summer's minstrel show. 'The pierrots frightened me. They always call it the end of the pier show, don't they? Even though it's half-way along.'

'There's talk of pulling it down and building a new theatre,' Chance said. 'It's seen better days.'

She drew on her cigarette, her fingers splayed awkwardly. 'That's what Leslie wanted. Better days.'

'Mrs Lynch, do you recall your brother's address in Tennysham?'

'No but I can tell you where it was. You know the park? Leslie lived in the first house next to the park-keeper's lodge. He had two rooms at the back. He gave me tea there and we sat by the window with a view of the trees. They were big houses with red tiles on the front.'

'I know where you mean. It's called Fernbank-road.'

'That was it. The house had a name, I think. He lodged with a very pleasant lady, Miss somebody. She was well in her sixties then. She had a lovely garden and she used to do it all herself.'

'So you don't know where your brother was living in London, only that he was a rent-collector?'

She shook her head. 'No, I believe he was doing bar work when he first went. Our mother had died by then and I was married. Leslie came to our wedding but he and Ronald never really hit it off. He sent presents for our girls once or twice but he didn't write apart from an occasional postcard.'

That reminded him. 'When your brother stayed here last December he used your husband's name at the hotel. Why would that be?'

She looked ill at ease. Finishing her cigarette she twisted the lipsticked end beneath her heel.

'It would have been Leslie's idea of a joke. My husband wasn't as welcoming as he should have been. You heard him last night but don't think too harshly of him. He was terrified his boss would find out he had an ex-gaolbird under his roof. He's expecting to be promoted. I was so relieved to have Leslie out of that terrible place. Ronald wouldn't let me visit him.'

'It must have been a shock when your brother was arrested?'

'I was worried sick. We didn't even know he had that job. I still can't bear to think of how he must have suffered. It was the war, you know, Inspector. He wasn't the same afterwards.'

As always when the war came up, Chance felt too weary to comment.

'He was terribly wrong to steal, I know, but he was tempted in a moment's insanity. He worked for a rich widow. I suppose you know all about it. It came out that he hadn't handed over all the money from her rents. He borrowed some and her accountant found out. He swore to me he meant to put it back. No one would ever have known.'

Chance watched his smoke drift toward the railings.

Mrs Lynch looked sideways at him. 'Do you have a brother, Inspector?'

'I did,' he said shortly.

Her forehead pinched together. 'The war?'

He eyed the calm water impassively. 'His ship went down. Three days in.'

'What rotten luck. I'm sorry.'

He shrugged. 'Everyone had someone.' Which was an understatement. A family in their street had lost the father, uncle and both sons. He knew she assumed it was drowning. People always did.

'Ronald didn't go.' Her voice was flat. 'He has a weak heart.'

Chance looked at her in surprise.

'I know. You've noticed his ear.' She looked like a kid telling tales. 'It happened when he was born. He lets people think a bullet scraped him.'

Chance returned to business. 'Can you think of any friends your brother had in Tennysham? Anyone he might have come here to see last week?'

'No, I hadn't even heard from Leslie since he left us. I've no idea what brought him back here. Maybe the woman he was staying with will know.'

'I hope so. Did your brother leave anything with you such as a note-book or letters?'

'No, he owned next to nothing. When he came out of prison I had to buy him some new clothes. Leslie wasn't the type to have keepsakes. He used to say he detested sentimentality.'

Chance wondered if there was anything he'd forgotten to ask. 'You've been very helpful, Mrs Lynch, thank you.'

'Will I be able to have Leslie's things?'

'I'll see his effects are returned to you as soon as possible.'

She hurried along, trying to keep up with his longer stride. 'I don't mean the clothes. I never want to see them again. It's just that I'd like his hip flask returned. It was our father's. I gave it to Leslie at Christmas.'

'Hip flask?' Chance stopped suddenly and she narrowly avoided bumping into him.

'He wasn't sentimental but he did like nice things. Prison was so terrible for him. It was meant to be a sort of symbol, that things were looking up. I filled it with brandy for him.'

'There was no flask on his person or among his things,' Chance said. 'He'd rented a room for the week. The landlady is a decent sort, very respectable. She'll be at the inquest. She liked your brother.'

'Then whoever killed him took it. Doesn't that mean he was robbed? Leslie would have put up a fight, Inspector. He wouldn't have meekly handed over his property.'

'We don't know what happened yet, Mrs Lynch.'

The pier was getting busier. Mild weather was bringing the elderly and the comfortably off out for a stroll. Chance steered his companion out of the path of an old couple.

'I'll need a description of the hip flask.'

He scribbled as she spoke and returned his note-book to his breast pocket. 'Did you give him the cigarette case? That was still in his lodgings.'

She raised her pencilled eyebrows. 'Leslie didn't have one when he was with us. He must have acquired one in London. Perhaps his lady friend? He had no money to speak of.'

They crossed the street together. Chance repeated the directions to the court. On the corner he looked back. Mrs Lynch was standing where he'd left her on the pavement. She began to walk slowly in the direction of the shelter.

*

'You might as well come along', the Inspector had said. 'It'll be good experience for you.'

'And a chance to see all the players,' Sergeant Bishop had added.

It was Sidney Godwin's first inquest. In his opinion it was better than any play. Not that he'd been to many, unless you counted pantomime or the annual Gilbert and Sullivan by the Tennysham Operetta and Players Society. (Playbill caption *We're The TOPS!*)

The goings-on had a feeling of unreality about them. Sergeant Bishop had told him how an inquest was an ancient tradition which pre-dated the Norman conquest. As one after another took the stand it felt as though they were watching the dress rehearsal of *Who Killed Leslie Warrender?*

Inspector Chance, giving his evidence in a clear serious voice made a distinguished older lead. None of the three women came to mind as a pretty young ingénue or glamorous leading lady. Still he drank in every word as Ivy Betts related finding the deceased. The victim's sister confirmed his identity and Mrs Simmonds described his arrival in the town.

Ivy had stumbled over the oath and kept a fixed gaze on the coroner while she fingered her wooden beads. Whereas Mrs Lynch had her eyes all over the place. They flitted between the coroner and the public gallery where a thickset man kept glancing down at his wrist-watch.

'That's the husband,' Sergeant Bishop murmured at his side.

He'd already pointed out the other witnesses Godwin hadn't met. There was Arnold Freeman, the lodger. Mrs Simmonds had returned to sit next to him with Miss Aldridge on her other side. Sergeant Bishop was surprised to see him there.

The old couple who'd walked past the shelter on Friday morning were sitting on the end. Mrs Dawson had shaken her head as Ivy answered the coroner's questions. Her husband had squeezed his hand over hers.

Godwin studied Mr. Lynch more closely. He looked bored with his surroundings. He'd scarcely looked up while his wife was being questioned, even though it was obvious she wanted reassurance. He looked like a business-man, double-breasted suit and a gold tie-pin. In a year or two he'd need a larger collar-size.

Inspector Chance hadn't returned to his seat. Craning his neck Godwin saw that he'd taken up position at the rear of the court. He was sitting, arms folded, on the end of a bench by the double doors. His expression suggested he was miles away, though Godwin had reason to know that could be deceptive.

As he returned his attention to the proceedings, Mr. Ridley was thanking the witnesses and the police. The inquest was adjourned for a fortnight while they made further inquiries.

Dr. Wheeler nipped over to the bench and said something to Mr. Ridley as everyone began to file out. He'd performed like the detective in the last scene of a stage play, explaining the medical evidence as if they were all dim-witted. Talk about playing to the gallery.

Godwin looked around the emptying room, wondering if the murderer of Leslie Warrender had been present. Members of the public had filled three rows but they'd mostly been nosy old ladies, surreptitiously passing round the cough sweets. You'd think they'd been at a matinee.

'Come on lad. Give over day-dreaming.'

Opening his mouth to protest, he shut it again in frustration. He couldn't explain that he'd been thinking about the suspects without sounding a right chump.

Clutching his coat and hat, he followed Sergeant Bishop to where Inspector Chance now stood leaning against the wall. He definitely looked bored. Mrs Simmonds had cornered him. She'd seemed more visibly upset than Ethel Lynch when she was questioned.

'I didn't think you'd still be with us, sir.' Chance addressed the lodger, in a grey mac, despite the decent day.

'Mr. Freeman's been very kind. He insisted on coming with me. I told him I'm used to managing on my own.' Mrs Simmonds gave him a little smile then looked down at her shoes. Godwin found himself doing that when Phyllis was talking to him.

He'd noticed more than one woman his mother's age take a shine to the inspector. Dot, who presided over the canteen, always made a point of serving him herself and was unusually lavish with the custard.

'I've been able to rearrange my commitments and stop on for a few days. Mrs Simmonds is uncomfortable being alone in the house in the circumstances and fortunately I have some annual leave owing.' He smiled at her. 'After all this good lady's kindness to me it was the least I could do.'

Godwin had seen that look before when Inspector Chance was exasperated.

'There's really no need to worry, Mrs Simmonds.' His expression sharpened. 'Have you remembered anything else since Sunday?'

She looked regretful. 'I wish I could, Inspector. Will it be all right to let the room again?'

'Go ahead. We've finished with it.'

'I've no one booked in before next week. I can't say it isn't nice to have some company.'

'If you do think of anything else about last week, please get in touch right away.'

'I'll do that but what if it's something and nothing? I wouldn't want to waste your time.'

'It doesn't matter how insignificant it seems. Anything out of the ordinary or something else Mr. Warrender said and I'd like to know. That goes for you too, sir. Did you happen to recognise the woman you saw going into the bank last week?'

'Here you mean?' Mr. Freeman shook his head. 'I only caught a glimpse of her. She could have been any of the ladies leaving here. All I can say with certainty is that she wasn't one of those in the witness box. If that's all, we'll bid you good day, Inspector.'

Chance raised his eyebrows at Sergeant Bishop when they'd left. 'Not one to miss an opportunity.'

'I'd say it won't do him any good.'

'Did you manage to have a quiet word with Miss Betts?'

Sergeant Bishop nodded. 'The young lady's going to call in on her way home.'

Chance turned to him as they came out in the sunshine. 'I imagine you're good with old ladies, Godwin. I've a nice little job for you this afternoon.' He paused on the wide steps.

The three of them watched as Ethel Lynch said something to her husband and they went up to Mrs Simmonds. They shook hands and the two women were at once engaged in earnest conversation. Ronald Lynch waited, his shoulders stiff with impatience. Nearby Mr. Freeman hovered in the background, no one paying him any attention. He was listening to the two women and keeping an eye on them.

'Yes, sir?'

Chance halted again on the pavement. 'I want you to go to a house in Fernbank-road and find out if an old lady still lives there. Got your note-book handy?'

'Right here, sir.' Godwin felt for his pencil and turned to a clean page.

'I don't know which side the numbers go but it's the house next door to the park-keeper's lodge so you can't miss it. The old lady in question rented rooms to Leslie Warrender right after the war. Mrs Lynch couldn't remember her name. She could be dead by now or moved away but she might still be there if we're lucky. Enquire at the neighbours if you don't get a reply.'

'What do I say if I find her, sir?'

'Fix a time for us to call. Not tomorrow, Sergeant Bishop and I are off to London.'

'Shall I go right away, sir?'

He wished they'd spell things out more. When was he supposed to make an appointment for? He looked at Sergeant Bishop who was lighting his pipe.

'Get yourself something to eat first, lad.'

'Unless..' Inspector Chance turned back. 'If the old lady wants to ask you in for tea and tell you everything she remembers, fill your boots.'

He hesitated. 'Yes, sir.'

'Use your initiative, Constable. We'll leave it up to you.'

'You can rely on me, sir.'

The pleasant scent of tobacco was retreating up the street as the two older men walked off.

Eleven

'Godwin looks quite chuffed,' Bishop said.

Chance yawned. 'At least he'll be thorough. It wouldn't occur to him to slope off to a caff.'

'I thought you'd never ask. I suppose it'll have to be the canteen though.'

'We're entitled to a break. It's well after mid-day even at old Desmond's speed.'

'Richards can hold the fort a bit longer then.'

'He can go round the pawnbrokers this afternoon with a description of the hip flask.'

'You reckon it was flung away like the wallet?'

'I'm starting to think I don't know anything.' Chance rubbed a hand through his hair. 'I'm trying to cover all angles. If I miss something Hayes won't be slow in pointing it out.'

'We'll get there,' Bishop said comfortably.

They turned towards a street just off the sea-front and entered their usual café.

Back in the first months of the war Tennysham, like many south coast resorts, had accommodated its share of Belgian refugees. According to Bishop their sad figures, dressed in donated clothes, had become a familiar sight, drifting about the streets like blown leaves. When the wind was gusting across the Channel they could stand on The Esplanade and hear the guns in France. After the war a few had settled in the town.

Henry's was the business started by one couple who'd escaped with their young son. The proprietor Henri had long adapted his name and cuisine to Sussex taste, having given up the struggle to convert the locals. Eventually he'd learned to fry bacon and squirt H.P. sauce in the English way and rarely looked back.

'Two teas to start, Henry. How's tricks?' Bishop tapped his florin on the counter while he waited.

'Cannot complain, Mr. Bishop. Always a little quiet out of season but we have our loyal customers and the sun is shining.'

Only a trace of elongated vowels and a faintly formal turn of phrase revealed the origin of the proprietor's son.

'Easter's early this year. That'll bring the families down.'

The only other occupant of the room was an old fellow in the corner. An empty plate with a smear of mustard at his elbow, he was busily working a fingernail between his back teeth. Folding his newspaper he stood up and nodded to them as he left.

Chance had sat down at a table by the window. He'd propped the menu against the salt cellar even though he knew it by heart.

'Penny for them,' Bishop said. He placed a cup and saucer in front of him.

'Ta. I don't know whether to go for the ham and egg or the bacon. How about you?'

'I fancy sausages.'

Chance gave their order and sat back. 'I've been thinking about why our friend came here twice in four months. Surely to meet someone?'

'I should think so. How about a woman?'

'It's possible but she'd have to be an old flame. I wonder if anyone was writing to him when he was inside?'

Bishop arranged his cutlery on the oilcloth. 'I'm expecting to hear back from the Yard by knocking-off time.'

'Good. That should rule out a wife in the background.'

'I suppose he could have come here for some reason in December, met a woman and returned last week to see her. He didn't seem to hang about if Mrs S. is anything to go by.'

Chance frowned. 'She's lonely and susceptible. I think meeting someone who could help him is more likely. After all he was with a woman in London.'

'We'll know all about her this time tomorrow with any luck. When you say help him, you mean with money?'

'Yes.' Chance glanced at the counter. Henry was busy talking to his mother through the back. Their food was in the pan.

'He's come out of Maidstone penniless with no prospects. There's no help to be had from family. His sister would do anything for him I think but handing over a few quid she'd saved from the house-keeping would be all she could manage.'

'I doubt he wanted to settle for a humdrum job anyway, even if he could get one.' Bishop drank his tea. 'Not going by what she told you this morning.'

'So what did he think he could get out of coming here?'

'Money. It had to be. Maybe he wanted to set up a job with a dodgy pal?'

'That's the sort of line Hayes is thinking on. But what was it Ronald Lynch said? Warrender told him he had a debt to collect. Something about money owed from way back.'

'All right. So if that was true, he couldn't get the money the first time and came back to lean on someone?'

'Or did he collect the first time and return for another bite? Remember Mrs Simmonds said he had plenty of cash on him on Wednesday.'

Bishop stared at Chance. 'Blackmail?'

Chance shrugged. 'You tell me. It fits.'

*

It was years since he'd walked down Fernbank-road. He sometimes went to the tennis club which was near the park but their premises were right over the far side.

Sidney Godwin had loved Jubilee Park when he and Doreen had been kids. It was captured in all the seasons in their old family album. The red mock crocodile one with the gold tassel that was kept in the sideboard and came out when distant relatives visited.

The avenue of conker trees was there and the pond where he'd sailed his model yacht. The two of them in matching winter coats and pixie hoods on the bandstand and Doreen posing with her new Fairy scooter in the rose garden. He stopped to gaze through the elaborate iron gates that led to his childhood.

The park-keeper's lodge was on the left-hand side, a tiny place with tall chimneys that looked top heavy on the red-tiled roof. The houses in Fernbank-road were prosperous detached villas behind thick hedges. Number Two, next to the lodge, was called Rowanbrae. It had a conservatory at the side and a sundial in the front lawn. Godwin noticed that the flower-bed was choked with weeds.

His stomach tightened in anticipation as he lifted the knocker. His opening words had been rehearsed several times on the way. The trouble was people didn't always give you the chance to say them. They would butt in which threw you completely.

The door opened and an older lady stood there, an enquiring look on her face. He opened his mouth to speak.

'There is a notice.'

He shut it again and inwardly clung to his first line. 'Good...'

'If people would only trouble to read it. The knocker makes a terrible reverberating sound right through the house.' She looked him up and down. 'Well don't stand there like a gaping fish, young man.' Her voice was brisk rather than angry.

He followed her pointing finger to the notice in the small inset window. *No hawkers. Tradesmen to use side gate and knock on back door.*

'I'm sorry, madam. I didn't see it.' Godwin knew he was blushing. It was the curse of being ginger.

'It does keep falling down, I admit but it's there at the moment. Are you from the council?'

'Er no, madam, not exactly.' Why did he say that?

'Only I can see now you're not selling door-to-door. You don't have a suit-case. Those poor men with their afflictions. It's not that I don't feel sorry for them but one can't keep taking a purse to the door for things one doesn't really need. Where will it all end? Frankly the workmanship's usually shoddy.'

She gave a great sigh. Godwin tried not to notice her bosom lift and fall. It was like a bolster being shaken. 'I know you have to make allowances but still.. What *do* you want? Speak up.'

'I'm a policeman, madam.'

Her expression sharpened. 'Oh no you're not, young man.'

He was beginning to feel desperate then understanding dawned. 'I'm in the plain clothes branch, madam, a Detective-Constable. This is my identification.'

She leant forward, screwing up her eyes. 'It looks official enough though I've never seen one in my life before. You look very young.'

Godwin smiled doggedly. His script was long gone. 'There's nothing to be alarmed about, madam. I've making routine enquiries in the area.' He took out his note-book. That always made him feel more comfortable. 'Would you mind telling me how long you've lived at this address?'

'Nearly four years. I can give you the exact date if you wish. It was the day before what would have been my dear father's birthday.'

'That's not necessary, thank you. Do you by any chance know the name of the previous occupant?'

The door widened and he thought she was about to ask him in. Instead the lady stepped forward, making him retreat suddenly, and pulled the door almost shut behind her.

'Let me think a moment.' She looked skywards. 'It will come to me in time. It's no good asking auntie, although it's the sort of thing she might remember actually. If it's important, young man, can't you look through the rate-payers? I daresay the council keep old lists.'

Everyone thinks they're a detective. Suddenly he remembered hearing Chance complain to Inspector Forrest. He felt better.

'I'm enquiring about a lady who was living here straight after the war. She let a couple of rooms.'

Her face cleared. 'Well, you want auntie then. Why on earth didn't you say so instead of going all round the houses?'

'May I have your aunt's name please and her present whereabouts?'

The lady cackled, her large yellow teeth reminded him of a friendly horse. 'Miss Frances Howe. Whereabouts upstairs. She's having a nice lie-down. She's best off asleep, poor dear. That's why I didn't want the door knocker disturbing her. It's hard for her to get off again if she wakes suddenly. She's inclined to be fretful if that happens.'

'I see.' He didn't but it was what you said. There was nothing for it but to keep trying. 'I need to arrange for a detective-inspector to call and interview your aunt, Mrs er...'

'Tully,' she said promptly. 'And it's Miss.. Miss Gwendolyn Tully. What does a policeman want with my aunt?'

Firmer ground at last. 'It's nothing to be concerned about, Miss Tully. We're interested in learning more about a tenant who lived here about twelve years ago.'

'That all sounds very mysterious. I can't help you. I was living in Kent then. I shouldn't think auntie will be able to recall anything.'

'Even so the inspector will need to speak to her. It won't take long.'

'You don't understand, young man. My aunt would enjoy having visitors. There was a time when she'd talk to you 'til the cows came home.' Miss Tully stepped out of the porch, lowering her voice. 'She isn't quite the thing if you take my meaning.'

The dismay must have shown on his face. 'Would it be possible to ask her a few questions?'

'Her mind wanders, poor dear. Docile as a lamb but she has fancies.' She gave a braying laugh. 'Some days she seems as normal as you or I. You could strike lucky. See her by all means but you won't be able to rely on a word she says.'

*

'She's what?' Inspector Chance said over his shoulder.

Godwin repeated his explanation.

'Pity.' Sergeant Bishop finished sharpening his pencil over the waste-paper basket and blew on his pen-knife.

Chance stared thoughtfully at the constable for a few seconds. 'Don't look so worried, Godwin. I'm not about to shoot the messenger. There was a message for you from the lab by the way. That partial print you found at the Acacia Avenue break-in was a goer. It's been matched to a known villain. Well done.'

'Thank you, sir. I still made you an appointment to see the old lady, in the interests of thoroughness. I hope that's all right. Miss Howe did say her aunt's perfectly lucid much of the time. Then she'll say something doolally all of a sudden.'

'I take it that's a rough translation? Yes, you did right.' When is it?'

'Day after tomorrow, sir, at ten. I didn't forget you're off to London. Apparently the old lady's at her best in the morning.'

'Wish I could say the same,' Chance murmured. 'Tell you what, you can come with me.'

'Really, sir?'

'You've met the niece and I shouldn't think you'll alarm the old lady.' He winced. 'Terrible what the years can do.'

'It's best not to know what lies ahead for any of us.' Sergeant Bishop looked unusually fierce. 'Why people go to these so called mediums is beyond me. There's a woman in our street keeps trying to get Glad to go with her. Thank God she's got more sense.' He stopped speaking abruptly.

'There's no such thing as an after-life.' Richards's voice was scornful. 'If you could contact the dead, we could ask Leslie Warrender who done him in. Is it right they can't have séances in Brighton, sir?'

Chance gave him a sharp look. 'Their public meetings get banned under the Witchcraft Act. That doesn't stop it going on in private homes.'

'They're filthy charlatans, the lot of them. Making money out of people's grief.' Bishop snatched up a folder and left the C.I.D. room.

Richards looked after him. 'It's not like Sergeant Bishop to get shirty.'

No one answered.

'What did you find out about Miss Aldridge?' Chance said. 'Stop looming over me, Godwin. You're making the place look untidy.'

Richards reached for his notes. 'Not much, sir. Her father Douglas Aldridge purchased the hotel towards the end of the war. He had it on the cheap side as it wasn't a going concern. It had been turned over to a convalescent home. He built it back up from scratch, medium end of the business, commercials, families. Some residential, a few old parties who get a cut-rate in the off-season.'

'It's sad having to stay with strangers all winter,' Godwin said.

'Come off it, they don't see it that way,' Richards said. 'I grant you Tennysham's a dump but it's cheaper than keeping a house going and they get waited on hand and foot. Beats working for a living if you ask me.'

'We didn't, Constable,' Chance said. 'You're wasted here. You should try your hand at writing tour-guides.'

'When did the father die?' Godwin said.

'1926. Miss Aldridge was an only child. The mother went in the Spanish 'flu.'

'Anything else?'

'Not really, sir. Sergeant Bishop said Miss Aldridge is active in the Hoteliers' Association. She's in the Rotary Club as well. Far as I can tell she's a pillar of respectability. Shame we can't ask the banks.'

Chance grunted. 'They have to be dead for that.' He was still smarting about the bank manager. 'W.P.C. Marden might be able to help. She's friendly with the chamber-maid who found the body. Ask her if she's had anything to say about her employer.'

'Will do, sir.'

'Right, we know the hip flask hasn't been pawned in town. Our murderer could be hanging on to it or it was dumped somewhere and no one's found it. The beat coppers are keeping an eye out.'

'If it had been pawned, it wouldn't have led us to the murderer,' Richards said.

'No, but we'd know where someone had found it. It's like doing a jigsaw, any extra pieces will help us see the picture. We've no idea what Warrender was doing between the time he left Mrs Simmonds's house and his death. So tomorrow, Richards you can try to find out.' Chance enjoyed his disgruntled expression.

'Every pub's been visited, sir.'

'Then use your imagination. Who might have seen him? Where did he buy the pie he ate? Talk to the cabbies, try the station buffet. He wasn't the invisible man.'

If this is a jigsaw, Chance thought when he was left alone, all we're finding is pieces of sky.

Twelve

Tennysham was just that bit too far from London for many commuters. There were a few. The upper civil servants who didn't have to be at their Whitehall desk too early. The type who lived in the big pre-war houses by the golf club and liked to brag about the benefits of sea air.

He'd shaved hurriedly, batting his way between the stockings hanging in the bathroom. Bolted some toast and arrived on the platform before Bishop. When he rolled up there was a damp stain on his tie. Chance reckoned if tested, it would reveal a trace of yolk.

By tacit agreement they smoked silently behind the *Sketch* and the *Chronicle* favoured by Bishop. At Haywards Heath when plenty of lowly commuters and some early shoppers joined the train, they shuffled up in their corner seats and swopped newspapers. There was no chance of discussing the case in privacy.

'How much longer?'

'Patience is a virtue.' Bishop said.

Some misguided optimists had started gathering their things when they passed Clapham Junction but now frustratingly near Victoria, they were stationary between blackened brick walls and railings. Tall, sooty terraces with grimy net curtains loomed far above them.

Chance stuck his head out of the window but could see nothing informative in the blown-back smoke.

'We'll be there any time now.' Bishop reached for his parcel and sat down again, tugging the string bow.

'What is that?'

'A story-book. Present for the nipper. Helen's meeting me in St James's Park so I don't have to go all the way out to Crystal Palace. You'll be able to amuse yourself all right?'

'I'll be fine. We can meet back at Victoria. Under the clock like lovers.'

'Get on with you. Got your commissions from Mrs C.?'

'Something like that.'

He was off the hook, having told Stella they wouldn't have a minute to spare for shopping. Fortunately she didn't hobnob with Glad Bishop.

The carriage shuddered and they moved off again.

Chance disliked descending to the underground but kept it to himself. The shiny white tiles and long echoing passages put him in mind of the subterranean conveniences at Brighton Station. They seemed the length of a catacomb. The tube was probably a safer place to linger.

He was glad to climb up to the small booking-hall and walk out into the wet, grey street. It was raining half-heartedly. The only bright colours in sight were on a flower stall.

The people hurrying along in blacks, browns and navy-blue were vanishing. Umbrellas were going up, heads were down against the weather. A woman scurried past with a clutch bag held against her hat. Cabs were being hailed, shop doorways filling like lifts and others darted down the entrance they had just left.

It seemed to Chance that all the faces were blank. Preoccupied, resigned, the most fleeting eye contact stared through them or veered away. They might have been two ghosts passing unseen through the crowd of Londoners.

Opposite their destination a news-seller was pulling sacking down over his wares. One side of his face was scored and uneven, a relief map of tiny craters. Raindrops spattered on the greasy pavement.

'We're to ask for a Sergeant Niven,' Bishop said.

When he came forward, hand outstretched, he immediately drove them back in the street, suggesting they went to a café first.

'I'm sure you gentlemen could do with a cup of something before you start and it'll be quieter there. We've no canteen to offer you and my shared office has been commandeered. Ah, I see it's started to rain. Still it's only a step.'

'No canteen, eh? I suppose the powers that be reckon you don't need one with all this round you.'

Bishop gestured vaguely at the shop-fronts. They were on the edge of Soho and several of the windows had displays of foreign food. Spaghetti in long packets, the shade of gentian violet, flanked odd-shaped loaves. They walked through the aroma of bitter coffee.

Chance made a face at the mouldy cheese. It reminded him of varicose veins and probably stank like a public baths.

'We're a wee bit cramped where we are. We're due to have a new station by next year. They're intending to call it West End Central.'

'They keep threatening to do the same to us. Personally I'm happy as we are.'

'Nothing stays the same these days.' The two sergeants stepped into the street to avoid a section of scaffolding.

'What are they up to in there?'

'They're converting the picture-house into a theatre. As if we didn't have enough entertainment. We'll turn in here. It doesn't look much but it's clean.'

Following them in, Chance checked the sign on the corner. 'Great Windmill St. The club's in the next street, isn't it?'

'That's right, sir. Down the end and turn right. Not that there's much to see on the outside.'

When they were seated, Sergeant Niven resumed. 'The woman you want to see's expecting a visit. She only lives five minutes away.'

'It's good of you to arrange it,' Bishop said. He generally did the pleasantries.

'She hasn't been told why we want to talk to her?'

'She has not as per your instructions, sir.'

Chance grunted and wiped a clear patch on the steamed-up window. He was quite happy to let Bishop do the niceties while he sipped his tea. The chap who'd served them was frying bacon out the back. His stomach grumbled wistfully.

Three workmen were chatting behind them. Some lingo he couldn't guess, their high cheekbones Slavic. A cosy sort of place. The tea-urn hissed companionably.

'It's a lot quieter round here than I expected,' Bishop said.

Niven's eyes were shrewd. 'You're wondering what all the fuss is about? Things don't get going 'til a lot later in the day. Soho's a wee village. Though it's more like the League of Nations than Dalmally. That's where I hail from.'

'What brought you down to the Smoke?'

Niven spread his hands open. 'Why does any Scot leave home? The need for work drove my parents down south. Subsistence and a better life for the bairns. I was ten and I've stayed put here ever since.' His face stiffened. 'To my regret.'

Bishop shot him a look. 'You mean during the war? I was the same. Still feel bad about it.' He jerked his head. 'The Inspector here was in France from early on.'

Chance frowned. 'We've been through this so many times. There was no point fighting the Hun and letting law and order break down at home.'

'Doesn't make it any easier. I was carrying on in safety when other men were dying.'

Chance knew he was thinking of one young man in particular. Time to change the subject.

He looked at Sergeant Niven. 'I daresay your workload's a lot tougher than ours?'

'It has its moments.'

'If this is like a village does that mean you know everyone who lives here?'

'In a word, no, sir We reckon to know every ponce and the regular street-walkers, by sight if not by name. Then there's the local shopkeepers and so forth but there are always new faces.' Niven shrugged. 'Some stay, others drift through.'

'How about where we're going?'

'Aye, I know Sadie. She's been here for years. Will you be wanting me to stay with you?'

Chance shook his head. 'We can manage, thanks.'

'As I thought. In that case I'll take you to her and leave you both to it.'

'We appreciate your help,' Bishop said.

'You'd do the same for us.'

'Had you come across our victim, do you think?'

'I don't believe so, sir. The name you gave wasn't on our books.'

'So you wouldn't know if this woman had a man staying with her?'

'I would not. There are several flats where she lives. A male guest wouldn't stand out if you take my meaning.'

'What's the club like?' Bishop said.

Niven made a face. 'It doesn't give us any trouble. Over-priced drinks or so I'm told. I'm no drinker myself.'

'I thought all Scotsmen liked a dram?'

He gave Chance a strained smile. 'You shouldn't believe all you hear, sir. I don't care for shortbread either.'

Chance nodded. 'Point taken.'

'These clubs are all much the same. They cater for the low-life and the lonely. The sad husbands who think they're missing out. Sometimes it's love they want as much as the other.'

Helping himself to a sugar lump, Chance drew a face on the window.

Niven addressed himself to Bishop. 'They drink too much, talk too much to a bored lassie who needs the money. She's too busy thinking about her rent or her aching pins to pay much attention. She's heard it all too many times.'

Bishop breathed out forcefully. 'They're all somebody's daughter. I'm seeing mine later. It makes you think.'

'It does that.'

The sound of crunching ended the small silence.

'Anyway there's a tenth-rate band and tables crammed round a dance-floor the size of a biscuit tin. The room's full of smoke and so dark they can't see the short measures.'

'Do they have a vocalist?' Chance asked with interest.

'I wouldn't know. The customers are *encouraged* to spend if they want to keep a hostess at their table. Not just the drinking. They've to buy their smokes and a box of sweeties for their company, a rose mebbe.'

Bishop slurped the last of his tea. 'We've nothing like that in Tennysham. I'd know if we had.' He spoke with complete assurance.

Chance laughed.

'What I mean is I know what's going on in my patch.'

'Why d'you stay here if it bothers you?'

Niven looked up at Chance. 'It's a rat-run, even so there are some good-hearted people.' He shrugged. 'It's a living. Why do men shovel the sewers or dig up the roads in the rain?'

'Talking of which, it's stopped,' Bishop said. 'Shall we make tracks?'

In the next street a dark-eyed girl was leaving one of the food shops. She called *chow* to someone inside as they drew near. Giving them an appraising glance, she walked quickly ahead. Her folded umbrella scattered drops as it swung from her hand.

'Lot of Italians here,' Bishop said. He peered in the shops as they passed.

'We don't want for ices in the summer.' Niven's expression tightened. 'Some of them are Maltese in fact.'

They crossed the end of a narrow street lined with market stalls. Trade looked slow. Chance stopped dead as a throbbing riff that could only be from a saxophone, rippled from an upstairs window and down his spine. The liquid sound cut off abruptly as they looked up. A sash frame slammed down.

'We get enough of that too. Gives me the ghoulies. There's your Black Kat Club.' The sergeant pointed at a doorway two steps down. The sign was not unlike a child's drawing.

The terraced buildings were four storeys high, in narrow Georgian bricks. Chance looked up at the blank windows, wondering to what purpose the rooms were put.

'Do you know who the owner is?' Probably just store rooms.

A shake of the head. 'It's all done through companies. The manager's an inoffensive chap in his manner. Not what you'd expect. He looks like a bank clerk...' Niven paused for effect. 'Except you wouldn't find a bank clerk carrying a razor.'

Chance remained unimpressed. He'd seen it all in Brighton. Not for nothing was it known as London-on-sea where this lot went for their day out. They didn't come for a paddle.

'Down here.'

An alley with a gas lamp high on the corner and a row of overflowing dustbins that stank in the damp. A plump tortoiseshell moggy appeared and rubbed against Chance's trousers. He bent down to stroke him as Sergeant Niven rapped on the shabby blue door.

'Ooh hullo, Mr. Niven. You've got me ever so worried, you know. What's this about?'

The words didn't match the face. The woman who answered the door looked as though she saw life brightly. Her eyes sparkled as she looked beyond the sergeant to the waiting men.

'These are the gentlemen who've come up from Sussex to speak to you, Sadie.' Niven gave their names and ranks. 'I'll let them explain why they're here.'

'You'd better come up.' She led the way up the flight of stairs, turning round half-way. 'Mind this loose stair-rod. The landlord's a miserable old sod, if you'll pardon my French. Won't pay for repairs.' She looked appealingly at Bishop.

'We'll be careful, madam.'

Chance averted his gaze from the cotton frock over a broad though not unshapely behind. The material was too thin for the time of year.

'Well this is it. Excuse the mess.'

She stood aside as they entered straight into a sitting-room. A curtain looped back revealed a kitchenette. Through an open door they could see the end of a bed and wardrobe.

'Sit where you like.'

Glancing at the low sofa draped with a gaudy silk shawl, Chance took the arm-chair. Bishop lowered himself gingerly.

'I'm sorry it's not more comfy. The springs are going. You'll be all right, Sergeant if you don't move about.'

Bishop smiled weakly. 'Not to worry, I've sat in far worse places.'

'Oh I'm sure you have,' she giggled coquettishly.

It was beginning to feel like being trapped in a seaside postcard, Chance thought. Someone had to dampen the mood.

'Can I get you tea or coffee, either of you?'

'Not for us, thanks love. We've just had a cuppa.'

'Mrs Price,' Chance said abruptly. 'Do you know a man called Leslie Warrender?'

'Leslie? I should say. Is that why you're here? What's he been up to? The naughty boy.'

She was standing by the mantelpiece. One hand fiddled idly, straightening the ornaments. Among them were a pair of tiny Turkish shoes made of copper and brass, a cigarette-sized groove on the rim. Ash-trays from Gallipoli lined up with A Present From Mablethorpe china dog.

'You'd better sit down, Mrs Price.'

She sank on to the arm of the sofa furthest from Bishop. 'That only means one thing when a copper says it. He's dead, isn't he?' Her shoulders drooped like a marionette with the strings cut. Powder drifts stood out against her resigned face.

'I'm afraid so.'

Mrs Price sighed. 'That's another one left the party too soon. When did he die?'

'On Thursday night. I regret to have to tell you he was murdered.'

'What?' She jumped up. 'I need a drink. The sun must be over the yard-arm somewhere in the world. 'scuse me, I won't be a minute.' She popped her head back from the kitchenette. 'I don't suppose you gents will keep me company?'

'Not on duty, madam.' Bishop nodded sympathetically at her. 'You go ahead.'

They listened to a cupboard door being opened and banged shut, the tap running.

'Just a drop won't hurt. It's good for shock.' Going to the stand in the corner, she poured herself a generous gin. 'I hate drinking alone. Gin and It's my tipple really, only I'm out of It.'

She managed to make everything she said sound flirtatious. It was now a reflex action without meaning. Returning to her perch she took a swig. Her eyes searched the room. She'd already shaken an empty packet of Player's by the bottles.

'I would be flat out of ciggies as well.'

'Have one of mine.' Chance offered his case.

'Oh thanks ever so.' He lit it for her as she held his hand steady.

'You don't seem surprised,' he said when he was safely back in his chair.

Retrieving her glass from the worn carpet, Mrs Price sighed again and crossed her legs. 'I'm not really. He was a lovely boy but there was always the possibility he'd get himself in serious bother one day. He hadn't been out five minutes. I expect you know all about that.'

'We do, yes,' Bishop said.

'What do you mean by serious bother?'

'I don't mean anything specific but you never know who you're going to upset, do you Inspector? Chance, that's a nice name. Like fate.' She contemplated the bars of the electric fire.

'Let's start from the beginning, shall we? When did you and Mr. Warrender meet?'

'Now you're asking, Leslie and I went back years.'

Cigarette in one hand, glass in the other, Chance could see her wriggling happily on a bar stool. She would be sympathetic and call them dear. She'd get the men who wanted to talk.

She turned to include Bishop in the conversation. Not one to leave any gentleman out in the cold. 'After the war when he came to work at the club. Have you been to the Kat?' They shook their heads. 'He came from Sussex. Is that where he died?'

'That's right,' Bishop said, his voice kind.

'You haven't told me how?'

'He was stabbed at night on the sea-front.'

She screwed up her face like a hanky. 'Knifed? I thought Tennysham was a select sort of place. Was it a gang?'

'We don't think so. The evidence points to him being murdered by a single person. Someone he was meeting.'

Mrs Price gazed at Bishop then drained her glass. 'That poor boy. He couldn't bear the sight of blood. He went white if he cut himself shaving.'

'The doctor was sure it was quick. It didn't look like he knew it was coming. Truly.'

'It's decent of you to say that. There's plenty of your lot wouldn't.' Mrs Price leant towards Bishop and patted his hand. 'I can tell you're a kind man. Your wife's very lucky.'

He looked relieved as she stood up and freshened her glass.

'We had some good times together.'

'Mrs Price, did Mr. Warrender stay with you before he came to Tennysham?'

'That's right, Inspector. He turned up here the day after New Year. He'd been staying with his sis and her husband turfed him out. Mean, I call it after all he'd been through. *I've turned up like a bad penny, Sadie.* That's what he said when he walked in the Kat. He looked in on the off-chance, hoping I was still there. I'm part of the furniture, me. Where else would I go?' She smiled to herself. 'He was a card.'

'How long did he stay?'

'Couple of months. He left last week on the Monday. I was glad of the company but then that miserable old cow across the landing complained to the landlord. I told him it's not sub-letting if you have a friend to stay. They think they own you body and soul when you rent. I know for a fact he's not above letting himself in when I'm not here. And once when I was. It's a wonder you can go for a you know what in peace.'

Mrs Price set down her glass. Chance who was quite happy to sit by a brimming ash-tray, found the scarlet impression of her lip unpleasant. He looked meaningfully at Bishop.

'How did he manage for money? Did you have to sub him, love?'

'I didn't as it happens for a while. Leslie was very flush when he turned up. He took me out to dinner a few times and insisted on buying me a new frock. We went to the dogs but it slipped through his fingers like water. He put Gawd knows what on the gee-gees. Leslie always liked a gamble. His last couple of weeks he was running up a slate and I found him going through my hand-bag.' She laughed without rancour. 'Tried to make out he was after a ciggy. He always had an answer. I didn't mind but I'm always short myself.'

'Did he say where he found the cash he came here with?'

'Well you don't like to ask. He did say something one night. What was it now? He'd had a bit of luck while he was at his relations. That's it, he'd seen an advertisement. Something to do with a man he'd worked for once. Leslie had helped him out or something like that. He said the family could return the favour.'

'With a loan or promise of work? Can you remember any more?'

'I'm sorry, Sergeant, you could never pin Leslie down.'

'He didn't seem to treat himself to any new clothes with his money. His sister said he liked to be smart?'

Chance could hear the bite in Bishop's voice. *Fancied himself*.

'He was waiting until he went away. He used to say it didn't matter what a man wore so much. It was all in the voice. That and how you held yourself. It was one of his hobby-horses.'

'How do you mean?'

'He said in the war when a chap was so plastered in mud you could only see the whites of his eyes, you knew it was an officer by his natural air of authority. Leslie had a beautiful voice. Of course he went to a public school.'

Bishop winced as he shifted position. 'Did Mr. Warrender buy himself a silver cigarette-case while he was here?' He liked to tie up loose ends.

Mrs Price looked coy. She wound a finger through one of her dull brass curls. 'I don't suppose it matters now. He picked it up in the Kat one night.'

'You mean someone left it lying around? It's hallmarked and monogramed.'

'Look I don't know the ins and outs. Leslie acquired it somehow. It had his initials on, L. W. anyway. His middle name was Ernest but he never used it.'

'Didn't the owner report it stolen?' Bishop held up his hand. 'It's immaterial now. I'm just interested.'

She looked aimlessly at the slipper dangling on her foot. 'People don't complain in clubs. They cut their losses. Maybe someone gave it to him. There was no harm in Leslie. He wouldn't hurt a fly but he couldn't help being light-fingered. You know, like a jackdaw. Or do I mean a magpie?'

Chance looked away from the stockinged foot with its varnished toes. A hanger over the wardrobe door held a blue georgette frock. Pointed, patent shoes stood beneath. It was the ghost of Mrs Price by night.

'What about a hip flask his sister gave him? Did you see it?'

'Yes, he showed it to me. It was his old man's.'

'Did he have it when he left here? He didn't hock it if he was hard up?'

'He kept it, Sergeant. I saw him pack it. I had to let him have the train-fare to Sussex though and a few bob on top.'

'Do you think this man Mr. Warrender contacted lives in Tennysham?'

'I should think so. I don't know if he was the same one who came here.'

'Who was that?' Chance took over.

'I haven't the foggiest. Leslie didn't say. Some man was leaving when I came home from shopping one day. He just pushed past, didn't crack his face. He couldn't get out fast enough.'

'Warrender didn't tell you anything about him?'

'I don't remember what he said. It can't have been much. He changed the subject I think.'

Mrs Price crossed the room and waved the bottle of gin. 'Sure? Might as well finish this, it's that sort of day. Bottoms up as they say in the Navy. Here's to Leslie.' She raised a glass to the dead.

'When was this?'

'January. Don't ask me the date.'

'Can you describe him?'

'Shorter than you, thick-set. Just like any man on any night in the Kat. Oh tell you what though, he had a funny ear.' The two men exchanged glances.

'Did Warrender leave anything with you for safe-keeping? A note-book perhaps?' Chance said.

She shook her head. 'He used to like making lists. Is that what you're getting at? He said he worked things out better on paper. He had big plans. Talked about getting out of this country. He fancied some sun, he said, after being locked up. Everyone has their pipe dreams, don't they? Even policemen.'

'Did he leave any lists here?'

'No, you're barking up the wrong tree there, Inspector. He burnt some paper in the sink, not long before he left.'

Chance looked at Bishop as he picked up his hat. 'When did you expect to hear from him again?'

Mrs Price's lipstick was smeared as though she'd been smacked in the mouth. 'He said he'd be down on the coast for a week. After that he hadn't made his mind up. I knew he'd be in touch.'

'There's nothing else you can recall that might help us?'

'Not a thing, dear. They will hang whoever did it?'

'That's up to the judge, Mrs Price, but we'll get them.'

'Just for the record,' Bishop said. 'Were you at the club on Thursday evening?'

'Thursday, that was the night I had off. I had a bilious attack come on in the morning. The night before I had cockles so it serves me right. It only takes one gone off and you can't tell when you eat them.'

'Was anyone with you?'

She shook her head. 'My friend upstairs saw me take the milk in and I told her I felt rotten. She would have stayed with me but she works nights. She needed her kip. She offered to tell them at the Kat I wouldn't be in. That old bitch across the landing wouldn't help me if I was at death's door.'

'What do you do at the club, love?' Bishop said. He got to his feet with some effort.

Mrs Price giggled. You could see the girl she'd once been, Chance thought. 'Officially I look after the cloakroom but I always say I'm like a mother hen to those girls. Everyone's shoulder, that's me.'

'You will be careful?'

'Didn't I say you were a lovely man?'

She insisted on following them down to the street door, still holding her glass of gin.

*

It occurred to Phyllis that her father had stopped making things. She hadn't noticed sooner because he still went into his work-shop. Perhaps he sat at his bench, smoked and read the paper. Ever since she could remember, his hobby had been carpentry. As a girl she'd loved chatting to him while he worked.

She'd sit on an old kitchen chair inhaling the scent of wood shavings. Surrounded by shelves of nails and screws in jam-jars and old St Bruno tins. Hearing the rasp of sanding, watching the smooth, measured sweeps of his plane as he listened patiently.

He liked to keep busy, Dad always said.

She was on the early side and she'd cycled, yet he'd still beaten her home. She wheeled her bike through the side gate round to the lean-to without seeing him. The kitchen door was unbolted and his jacket and cap were hanging in the hall though when she called out, the house was empty. Back she went down the garden path. An old sack had been draped behind the work-shop window.

He came out to meet her, pulling the door shut behind him.

'Hullo, Dad. What were you doing in the dark?'

'Nothing, love. I'm storing a few sticks of furniture for Stan while he's moving. It's to keep the sun off.'

'If it's upholstery you'd better see there's no damp got in over winter.'

'I know what I'm doing.'

'Been home long?' She tried not to sound anxious.

'Just got in. We're starting on a big run tomorrow. A new order.'

'That's good.'

It had to be her imagination that the exchange sounded stilted. She even wondered if her father could have been laid off and pretending to go to work every day. Her mind quickly assembled evidence to the contrary. A stained cuff on one of his shirts, a block of type he'd found in his pocket and left on the window-sill. She was being ridiculous.

'You're early yourself, aren't you?'

'A little. I had to take some papers round to the coroner's clerk. The station-sergeant said I might as well go straight home after.' There was probably nothing for her to do.

'What's happening with your big case?'

The local paper had started calling it The Sea-front Murder. It was front page stuff in town. The Hoteliers' Association were worried stiff about the effect on the holiday season.

'Don't ask me, Dad. The station cat would know before I did.' She grinned in spite of her mood. 'If we had one. The cleaners are probably more up on the gossip than me.'

That was a trifle unfair. Inspector Chance didn't leave reports lying around. He always cleared his desk when he left for the night. She'd seen him do it. Upending his in-tray and letting it drop in his deep bottom drawer.

'I thought you seemed fed up last night. The job getting you down, is it?'

She folded her arms, it was still chilly outside. Thinking how to answer she watched her father click the shiny padlock and give it a tug.

'That's new.'

'The old one had rusted through. Can't be too careful with things being pinched out of gardens. You told me yourself.'

'That was clothes from a washing line. Only one that we know about. Let's go in, shall we?'

'You weren't changing the subject?'

Phyllis put a match under the kettle before she turned round. 'Work's the same as usual. I've had my nose put out of joint, that's all.'

'You could always pack it in, love. Get a job in an office.'

It was like being slapped in the face by a stranger. She felt bewildered. 'Dad, how can you say that? You of all people know how much this means to me.'

'Keep your hair on. I'm only trying to help. You don't always come home full of the joys of spring, that's all I'm saying. A girl your age should be carefree. There's no shame in admitting you made a mistake.'

'I didn't.' She took a deep breath. 'I don't get it, Dad. You've always backed me.'

He looked uncomfortable. 'Of course I'll always back you but I had my doubts at the time. You were so keen to apply.' He avoided her eyes as he leant against the cupboard. 'The police-force is a man's world. I did think you might have done better being a nurse.'

'You never said.'

'Maybe not. There was no talking you out of it. But your aunt liked it and I know you got the idea of a career from her in the first place. That was the war, mind. Things were different then.'

'It was thirteen years ago,' she said tartly. 'Things are meant to be different now.'

'Everything's different these days.' He sounded bitter.

Phyllis stood in the doorway to the hall. 'All jobs have their ups and downs. I don't want to do anything else. I think what Aunt Jo did was tremendous but I didn't fancy scrubbing out bedpans.'

Her father shrugged. 'You'll have to leave when you marry. You'll change your tune quick enough then.'

The whistling of the kettle saved her from having to answer.

*

They were ahead of the first commuters. Victoria was still in its afternoon lull before the evening onslaught of weary men, their years measured in railway lines.

'Did you have a good time?' Chance leant against a pillar, looking rather genial.

'Lovely, ta.'

'That's because you're a lovely man. Your wife's a very lucky woman.'

Bishop grinned sheepishly. 'You can forget all that.'

Yawning, Chance entered an empty compartment. 'How are Helen and your namesake?'

'Flourishing. Freddie's grown since Christmas. We fed the ducks and the squirrels. He loves watching the cheeky blighters. We showed him the guards and meandered through Green Park, taking turns to push him. It was nice to have a real chin-wag, just the two of us.' Bishop sank down opposite with a sigh. 'That's better. We finished up in a Corner House and had a slap-up tea. I appreciate it, Eddie.'

'As long as we've had no more bodies. Then Hayes might want to know why we weren't back sooner.'

'You don't think that's likely, do you? Seriously?'

'Warrender must have died because he was a threat to someone. Let's hope no one else is. It's up to us to find the murderer before anything else happens.'

'We've learnt something. It was worth coming up here.'

'Ronald Lynch has some explaining to do,' Chance said. His voice was grim. 'I don't care to be lied to.'

'He won't like coming all the way back to Tennysham. Look how he complained on Monday.'

'Too bad. He should have told us the truth in the first place. Either he motors over to us or we have to chase half-way across the county. You can put a call through to him at his office in the morning.'

'If he refuses? He lied to us but we don't have enough to hold him on.'

'Explain to him that if we have to waste our valuable time, we'll see him at his office. That should bring him.'

'Sometimes this job can be quite enjoyable.' Bishop hesitated, 'in theory Sadie Price had ample time to get the train down, meet Warrender and get back to town.'

'She didn't strike me as a killer but we'll check with the station. I think I'm going to have forty winks.'

The train lurched off the brakes and Bishop shook open the evening paper. He didn't mind his back to the engine.

'Did you enjoy yourself?'

'Eh?' Chance was examining his trouser legs. The turn-ups were covered in cat hair.

'After we split up?'

'Not bad.' He arranged the large square package protectively between himself and the wall of the compartment.

'Shall I put that up top?'

'Better not, they're fragile.'

Bishop grinned to himself. The engine gave a long hoot as they passed below the tenements where they'd halted that morning.

Chance thought about how much he enjoyed leaving the crowded capital to travel down to the coast at the end of the day.

They chugged through the suburbs and towards the first fields, the long fingers of London finally losing their grip. He slouched back with his hat over his eyes.

'Wake me when we get there.'

It occurred to him as he drifted off that he must look like the sea-front corpse.

Thirteen

Chance sat at his desk in waistcoat and shirt-sleeves. A spiral of smoke rose from the ash-tray. Bars of sunlight slanted across the untidy desk. Richards stood just inside the door holding a buff folder. Chance held out an arm for the report and waved him to a seat. The folder landed on his blotter.

'Give me the gist and I'll read it later.'

'I followed your instructions, sir and tried to work out who might have seen Warrender on Thursday evening. First off I tried the station buffet and questioned the chap who runs the taxis. Then I went round the fish and chip shops. Drew a blank everywhere.'

Chance watched the pale face under the shock of brown hair. Richards was much more assured than Godwin but then he was in his early thirties at a guess.

'Go on.'

'Like you said, sir, he had to have gone somewhere between leaving Mrs Simmonds and being on the prom. I thought it was worth giving the pubs another try. In case we hadn't seen all the staff the first time.'

Chance frowned. 'Wasn't a note made of anyone missed out? Someone was bound to have a day off.'

'Not sure, sir.'

'Good job I'm more easy-going than Inspector Forrest. Do I take it your thoroughness was rewarded?'

'A barmaid at The Bell recognised the photo.' Richards almost looked pleased. 'She was off sick with a cold on Saturday. They thought it was the 'flu but she came back yesterday.'

'What did she have to say?'

'Warrender sat in a corner and she thinks he asked for a bottle of Bass and a pork pie. That fits with the stomach contents, doesn't it, sir? It was him all right.'

Chance nodded, his eyes narrowed against the smoke. 'Was he by himself?'

'No, sir. After he'd been there a while another man sat down at his table and she thinks they were talking.'

'Description?'

Richards grimaced. 'Brown hair, forties, medium height and build.'

'That's half the male population of Sussex. Even so, it's a big step forward. Did she hear anything they said?'

'Afraid not, sir. When I pressed her she couldn't swear they weren't strangers. They might have been passing the time. It was busy that night and she thought Warrender's table had one of the last seats free. He was in the corner tucked behind a pillar.'

Chance looked up at the street map on the wall. The Bell was the town's oldest pub. It stood opposite the parish church in the couple of streets that had been there when Tennysham was a village. The tap-room had stout black beams you could stub your toe against. Wilf Bishop liked the building but he didn't reckon much to the landlord's pumps.

'What about times?'

Richards shook his head. 'She remembered serving him because the church clock struck eight just after. He had a plummy voice apparently but she didn't see him go. The landlord or his wife must have served him the second time. They still don't recall him.'

'Did you ask if they knew the other man?'

'No joy, sir. The landlord laughed and said it fitted half their regulars. None of them saw him leave.'

'So Warrender could have walked to the sea-front with his killer? We have a possible description but he could be an innocent man out for a pint. No way of telling yet. I'd rather not put out some sort of appeal and risk alerting the murderer.'

'Yes, sir. It would take about a quarter of an hour to walk from the Bell to Eastcliff. Dr. Wheeler said Warrender was killed some time after nine. It ties in.'

Chance nodded. 'We'll keep an open mind for now. Did you ask W.P.C. Marden if Miss Betts mentioned anything else?'

'This Ivy told her she thinks Miss Aldridge is feeling the pinch. She dismissed another maid recently and hasn't done anything about replacing her.'

'Miss Betts struck me as an observant girl.'

'How did it go in London, sir?'

'We need to interview Warrender's brother-in-law again.' Chance related what Mrs Price had told them.

'So Ronald Lynch is our main suspect, sir? Family's the most likely, aren't they? I thought Warrender might have had a wife in the background.'

'The Yard have ruled that out. Lynch is certainly a possibility but let's not get carried away. People lie for all sorts of reasons.'

'Do you still need to see this old lady, sir?'

'It doesn't pay to put all your eggs in one basket, Richards. The more we learn about the victim's life the better. D'you see why?'

'Because it's something Warrender did to someone or knew about them. That's why he was murdered?'

'Yes. In what way was Warrender a threat and why was he killed now?'

'Nobody could get at him in prison, sir.'

'True. He was out of harm's way. I think the key lies in his returning to Tennysham. So it is worth speaking to anyone who knew him when he lived here. Although in this case...' Chance checked the time. 'That's enough pearls of wisdom. Godwin and I need to leave.'

Taking the hint, Richards stood. Chance picked up his jacket from the back of the chair.

'Oh and Richards..'

'Sir?' He paused with his hand on the door knob.
'Good work.'

*

There was absolutely no need to be nervous. Waiting by the front desk, Sidney Godwin eased a finger round the inside of his collar. Not for the first time he thought his mother overdid the starch.

'All set, Godwin? Let's go.'

The inspector had come through the door while he was looking the other way. Chance had left off his overcoat. It was that sort of a morning.

He started off a pace behind. The inspector went at a fair lick and he felt like a dog whistled to and trotting obediently at heel. They continued like this for several streets. Inspector Chance had a habit of weaving briskly between pedestrians and suddenly diving across the road. Once with scant regard for an approaching three-wheeler.

The silence lengthened between them like one of the tree shadows reaching between the quiet avenues they were passing. A tentative remark about the fine morning had been acknowledged but that was all. It was like playing tennis with someone who never returned the ball.

Godwin couldn't recall being alone with the inspector until now. Someone else had always been present as a buffer.

'Do you like tennis, sir?'

'No.'

Chance raised his hat to an old lady who said good morning to them. The inspector was safely past when her poodle, straining at the leash tried to wrap himself round his ankles. His owner smiled in a *nothing to do with me* sort of way as he shuffled sideways.

When he'd caught up he tried again, a glutton for punishment.

'What about cricket, sir? Did you play?' He hadn't meant to put it like that. Men the inspector's age did still play on occasion. He could be offended. 'Er, I mean do you, sir?'

His voice sounded desperate. According to his mother, no one ever saw you the way you feared they did. They were too busy thinking about themselves. It went something like that. She often gave him well-meant pep talks.

'Not since school. We aren't on a date, Constable. You aren't building up to ask me to dance, I hope?'

'Sorry, sir.'

Godwin felt Chance flick a sideways look at him. He kept looking at his boots, an eye out for any hole he might climb into.

'Do you like jazz music, Godwin?'

Crikey. 'I haven't really heard much, sir.' He thought quickly. 'There was some on the wireless the other day. My father said it was like a cacophony of monkeys from the jungle.'

'What did you think?'

'I thought it was rather jolly, sir.'

Chance raised his eyebrows. 'There's hope for you yet, Godwin.' He came to a standstill on the corner. 'This is us. If there are any awkward moments I'm relying on you to charm both ladies. Hand round cups and so forth and remember what's said. Notes might not be the thing here.'

'Yes, sir. Um, the lady I saw the other day. The niece.. she does go on a bit. I thought you should know.'

'Women generally do, don't you find?'

He felt curiously flattered at being addressed in such a man to man way.

Chance had replied absently while he was studying the house. It had been noted that he often seemed uninterested or far away. Then he'd make some sharp comment that showed he'd been listening all the time.

'Ever noticed half the houses in this town are called something Scottish? Lord knows why.'

'I'm not sure, sir. Our house is called Polperro.'

'My house has a number and it's staying that way,' Chance said darkly. 'Off we go.'

On this occasion the front door opened as they crunched across the gravel.

'Nice and punctual, young man. Who is this you've brought with you?' Miss Tully flashed her teeth at them as she waited on the step.

'Detective-Inspector Chance, madam. Thank you for arranging for your aunt to see us, Miss Tully.'

'You're welcome, I'm sure, Inspector. I only hope she'll be able to assist you.'

'We'll do our best not to tire her. Constable Godwin explained why we need to speak to Miss Howe?'

'He did in the end. We had a teeny misunderstanding at first.'

Godwin cringed inwardly at her arch expression.

'Auntie's in fine fettle this morning and she enjoys having visitors. I've told her why you're here, though she might have forgotten again by now. You'd like some tea, I expect?'

'If it's no trouble, thank you.'

'No trouble at all. The kettle's just boiled. Come on through.'

They followed her into a large sunlit drawing-room at the back of the house. A tea-table was laid in the window recess where a small elderly lady sat in a large wing-back chair. The heat was stifling.

The white-haired lady turned her head, observing them with benign interest as they crossed the carpet.

'Now then, Auntie. These are the policemen. They're detectives so they're in their ordinary clothes.' Miss Tully emphasised her words with a determined brightness as she addressed her aunt. 'Do sit down anywhere you like.'

Wondering if he should offer to help, Godwin waited to take his cue from the inspector.

'Good morning, Miss Howe.'

Chance spoke perfectly normally to the old lady, taking the arm-chair next to her. He sat opposite them.

'Good morning.' The old lady had a light refined voice. She smiled sweetly at them. 'It's very kind of you both to call again.'

Chance appeared perfectly composed. 'It's good of you to see us. We'd like to ask you about when you were living here just after the war.'

'Just after the war.' She gazed out of the window, seeing something they couldn't. 'It seems like yesterday. When the soldiers came back we used to meet the trains from Folkestone. It was all we could think of to do.'

'I think Auntie's remembering some voluntary work the townswomen did. You knitted for the soldiers all through the war, isn't that right, dear? I'll just fetch the tea and we can all have a nice cup together.'

Godwin watched the inspector turn to the old lady, giving her his full attention.

'They stumbled off the trains like ghosts. Bandaged, crippled, empty-eyed. One felt so helpless. Some of them looked bewildered. As if they couldn't understand they were back at their own railway-station again.'

'That must have been difficult for you.' Chance's voice was quieter than customary.

'There was so little we could do. A hot drink and tobacco, a lift home. We wanted to be *practical.* Do you see? We tried to help the families.' Miss Howe peered earnestly at the inspector's face and then his.

'I do see,' Chance said. 'Action not words.'

'That's what we thought. They didn't want bunting and speeches. Besides they didn't all come at once. The wounded were sent from Netley. We didn't think it right for them to arrive back and feel forgotten. Not everyone had family, you see and some of the wives had jobs and children to mind.'

Miss Howe's fingers fretted with the plaid blanket on her knees. He sat very still.

'Some of them were cheerful but I knew whistling in the dark when I heard it. Some were as young as your nephew here. I can still see them.'

Chance caught his eye and jerked his head towards the door. Hearing a footstep, he jumped up thankfully.

'You mustn't go upsetting yourself, Auntie. This gentleman doesn't want to hear about all that. We've put the war behind us, thank heavens. Thank you, young man. I'll be mother if you'll hand these round for me.'

Wishing he'd never had to come, he handed round the plates, all fingers and thumbs.

'Do try a jam tart, they're Queen Anne's.' Miss Tully laughed, for no reason he could see.

'Thank you,' Chance said. 'I hope you haven't gone to all this trouble on our account?'

'Oh no, Auntie enjoys her treats.' She'd taken the chair between him and the inspector. 'Elderly people always have a sweet tooth. And why not indulge them I say? It's one of the few pleasures they have left.'

Chance glared at her. The old lady stirred her tea too long and took a tiny sip. When they were settled, he spoke again, addressing himself to her.

'A lovely garden you have here.'

He followed the inspector's gaze. To one side of the lawn he could see the weathered posts of a tennis court, long abandoned. Tree-tops in Jubilee Park rose above the boundary hedge.

The old lady smiled at Chance. 'You enjoy gardening yourself?'

'Unfortunately I don't have much time to devote to mine.'

'My knees won't allow me to work outside any more. I still enjoy pottering in the conservatory.'

'We've had a lot of the beds grassed over,' her niece announced. 'It's hard to get a really reliable jobbing gardener.'

Chance cleared his throat. 'Miss Howe, do you remember a tenant you had just after the war? His name was Leslie Warrender.'

Her face lit up. 'I remember Leslie. He used to say what a delightful outlook he had over the garden with the park beyond. His rooms were two floors above us.'

'I'm interested in learning about him in those days. Can you recall any friends who came to visit him?'

'Warrender.' Miss Howe's niece leant forward, clutching her serviette. 'That's why you're here. It was in Tuesday's *Echo*. He was the ...'

'Miss Tully,' Chance interrupted. He held up a warning hand. 'Let us not go into that.'

'Oh, I see. I take your meaning, Inspector. Quite right. Best not to disturb..' Chance waited until she subsided.

He returned to the old lady. 'Visitors who came to see Leslie?'

'It *is* nice to meet someone who knew Leslie. I haven't heard of him in many years but I always knew he'd do well for himself. Do have another tart.'

'Thank you.' Chance helped himself. 'They're very good.'

'What about you, my dear? It's a shame to leave one. Don't be shy.' The old lady smiled at Godwin and gestured at the plate. 'A growing lad needs all the sustenance he can get.'

He mumbled his thanks and took the last tart. Chance had left him the gooseberry one.

'Where were we? Leslie lived very quietly when he was here. I don't think he had many visitors. Of course he'd been very affected by his war. So many young people wanted jollity after the Armistice but they weren't the men who'd fought.'

'Indeed,' Chance murmured.

'He was quite at liberty to entertain friends. I always enjoyed having young people around. He had his own sitting-room.' Miss Howe wrinkled her brow. 'There was a young lady who came to tea with Leslie once or twice. I showed her my herbaceous borders.'

Miss Tully chuckled. 'This chap *was* your boarder, Auntie.'

'A pretty girl, fair. Now what was her name? It began with an E. Edie? No, I don't believe that was it. Evie, Evadne?' She shook her head. 'I'm afraid it's gone.'

'Esme?' Miss Tully said.

'I've lost my thread. Whom are we talking about?' All of a sudden the old lady looked frightened. Her voice quavered.

'Ethel.' Godwin said gently. He wished they were anywhere else.

'That's right, young man. Ethel, she was. They had the same colouring.' The old lady smiled gratefully at him. 'So you knew her too? Of course, you must be about the same age.'

*

Inspector Chance sighed heavily as they reached the park gates. Miss Tully had seen them off from the doorstep and watched them down the short drive. There was a feeling of escape in the air.

'It was worth a try.'

He felt profound sympathy for the old lady, though part of it was fear of course.

Godwin had put on an expression of deferential agreement. Not much the lad could say really. Chance reflected that he pulled that face himself with the Superintendent.

'Very good tarts.'

'Er yes, sir.'

'Take my tip, Godwin. Always head straight for the raspberry. No one really fancies the gooseberry ones. The colour's all wrong.'

Godwin grinned suddenly. 'Like marrow jam, sir?'

'What a disgusting thought. I think you'll find that's more khaki than green.' He should know. Irene had presented them with some when they moved in.

They walked for a time in a silence that was very nearly companionable. When they reached Frederic-street, Godwin looked at him, discreetly gauging his mood.

'Did you want to ask me something, Godwin?'

'I wondered what we do next, sir?'

'A good question. What would you suggest?'

'Maybe follow up on what Phyllis said, sir? W.P.C. Marden I mean.'

'She told you all about it, did she? Yes, I think the time's come for a chat with Miss Aldridge. I wish we knew what was between her and Warrender.'

Bishop was at the front desk, hobnobbing with Sergeant Lelliott. He looked cheerfully at them. Chance shook his head.

'No joy, sir?'

'The old lady was unable to help. I shouldn't have bothered her. Actually she did remember Warrender.' Chance broke off to hold open the inner door for Phyllis. She thanked him without looking up. 'But she was unable to give us anything useful. She said he lived quietly with few callers.'

'She was able to have a conversation with you?'

'Up to a point. She had a vague memory of Mrs Lynch visiting him.' They went through the C.I.D. room to his office. 'She seemed perfectly lucid then all of a sudden she became confused. She thought she knew us and Godwin was my nephew. It was quite unnerving.'

Bishop looked quizzically at him, his head on one side. 'Now you come to mention it, maybe there is a resemblance.'

Chance tossed his hat on the stand and missed. 'Where's Richards?'

'At the railway-station. Asking whether a woman of Sadie Price's description caught the late train to London on Thursday.'

'I think it's time we went through possible suspects.' He threw himself back in his chair. 'I liked Mrs Price.'

'So did I but we can't afford to let that blind us to the facts.' Bishop took out his pipe. 'She knew Warrender from way back. We've only her word for it that they were on friendly terms.'

'He stayed with her for two months. That's rather friendly in a flat that size. We could ask Sergeant Niven to check with the neighbours. See if anyone overheard any rows, that sort of thing.'

'All I'm saying, Eddie, is she could have had a motive we know nothing about. If she spoke to her neighbour when she took the milk in, that must have been early on Thursday morning.'

'Not necessarily,' Chance said. 'She works in a nightclub. She may sleep in late.'

'Even if she did, she had plenty of time to get here in the afternoon. She could have met him and arranged to see him again later. Done the deed and been home in bed by midnight.'

'Chucking the knife from the train?'

'She said she cried off work that night, with a bilious attack. Say no one after the neighbour saw her until what.. Friday evening? Wheeler said a woman could have done it. Warrender was sitting down, not expecting to be attacked.' Bishop waved his match until it went out.

Chance considered. Some more papers had been left in his wooden tray. The one on top received a cursory glance and was slapped back. The typed sheets splayed out like a broken fan.

'If she murdered him it would be hard to prove without knowing the motive. Without a confession we might never find out why.'

'We don't necessarily need one.'

'Juries like it though, especially on a capital charge. Besides I dislike loose ends.'

'Fair enough. Mind you, life's full of them.'

'Mrs Price would have to be a darn good actress, Wilf. Her reaction when I told her Warrender was dead seemed spot on.'

'Some women are good actresses.'

Chance had to agree. Stella saying *This old rag? I've had it for ages* would convince any judge. 'There's the wallet. St Luke's isn't on a direct route to the railway-station.'

'Let's see what Richards comes back with.'

'All right. What other suspects do we have?'

'Miss Aldridge and the brother-in-law,' Bishop said promptly.

'Let's drop in on her tomorrow.'

'It will have to be later. I fixed up for Ronald Lynch to be here in the morning.'

'How did he take it?'

'Grudgingly. He didn't seem keen we called at his place of work though.'

'Miss Aldridge will keep until the afternoon. What about her?'

'I'm not sure,' Bishop frowned. 'Thanks to Phyllis, we know she had words with Warrender and she might be having money troubles. For all we know he did complain about something and that's all there was to it.'

'If so, she didn't admit it. Embarrassed, perhaps? What's up with Phyllis, by the way? She didn't look her usual chirpy self just now.'

'You were quite short with her the other morning, if you don't mind my saying.'

Chance removed his hands from behind his head. 'Perhaps I did over-do it. I was annoyed with her for ferreting around behind our backs. And with myself when she came up with something I missed.' He gave a wry smile. 'She's a bright girl.'

Bishop nodded. 'She'll settle down.'

'Can you see Miss Aldridge as a cold-blooded killer?'

'Not on the face of it. She's a respectable lady. Though she had the best opportunity. The murder took place near her home.'

'It's more likely the murderer wouldn't do the deed on their doorstep.'

'True,' Bishop said. 'Ronald Lynch?'

'Neither of us took to him but you're right. We can't let liking or disliking prejudice our thoughts. We need hard facts.'

'He lied to our faces in the hotel. That's a hard fact. He went to London to visit Warrender in January.'

'Again, why?'

Bishop gestured with his pipe. 'Could be innocent. Might have seemed simpler not to tell us. Let sleeping dogs lie.'

'Maybe.'

'He should be more forthcoming without his wife sitting there.'

'Oh he's going to tell us everything tomorrow.' Chance's voice was grim. 'Warrender was murdered a week ago this evening. I don't feel we've made much headway. Hayes made it clear that the Chief Constable wants us to solve this. But he'll have to call in the Yard if he thinks I can't handle it.'

Bishop looked sympathetic. 'I'm sure it won't come to that. Thinking about Lynch, he was miles away in Marting. His wife gave him an alibi. She would have to be lying too.'

'A wife's alibi isn't worth much. What about Mrs Simmonds as a possibility?'

'She was distraught when we told her Warrender was dead.'

'You were the one who mentioned actresses.'

'So where does all this leave us?'

Chance leant across his desk. 'Warrender wasn't long out of prison. He was tucked up in Marting with the Lynchs until New Year, then in Soho with Sadie Price. He hardly had time to meet anyone new and drive them to murder. His death has to be connected with his old life in Sussex.'

'He made two trips here.'

'We've only Mrs Simmonds's word that she and Warrender were strangers. In theory she could have come forward to put herself in the clear. Everything she told us on Sunday could be concocted.'

Bishop looked sceptical. 'She struck me as genuine. We seem to have more women suspects than men.'

'That's a thought. What d'you reckon to that lodger of hers? Arnold Freeman, he's still hanging around like a bad smell.'

'He claimed to have met Warrender for the first time on Monday evening.'

'He seemed to take quite an interest in murder.'

'It takes all sorts. You spend every Sunday wrapped round the *News Of The World.*'

Chance laughed. 'Point taken. There's the bald man seen in The Bell with Warrender. The murderer or a bystander passing the time with a stranger?'

'We've no way of finding out that I can see.'

'Let's see what the two tomorrow have to say. In the meantime, I'm paying a visit to the lending-library this afternoon. No, that's not why,' he said as Bishop smiled. 'I'm going to go through back copies of the *Observer*. Quicker than going to Hastings.'

'You're thinking of what Sadie Price said? Warrender saw an advertisement when he was staying with his sister. One that reminded him of an old friend? That's clutching at straws, isn't it? You could never pick it out.'

'It's nothing to do with that. We still don't know where Warrender worked during the war. Who did he know who could still be around? Mrs Lynch couldn't recall where but she said there was a big fire opposite and this was around the time he went off to France in '17. That must have been reported. I'll only have to search some of that year.'

'That's good thinking. If you're lucky it made the front page.'

'Depends on the casualties. Then there's Warrender's work-place when he was Miss Howe's tenant in '19. According to Mrs Lynch he was at the post-office. We'd better enquire there also.'

'I'll get someone on to that.'

Chance went over to pick up his hat. 'Somewhere there's the connection we need. I can feel it in my water.'

Fourteen

Tennysham Lending-Library was not somewhere Inspector Chance had frequented since childhood. He remembered being taken there with his elder brother. The whispering staff, the tall bookshelves of cloth spines and the stern notices had all been intimidating.

Books, wood and polish, the high windows with coloured light from their patterned glass had made the Edwardian building seem like a church.

They hadn't been a great family of readers. Though his parents had been determined to do the right thing by their sons. The works of Dickens and *The Diary Of A Nobody* had always been in the glass-fronted cupboard in their front room, dusted but never disturbed.

An impossibly long set of encyclopaedias had been painstakingly purchased for their improvement. The young Eddie Chance had been through Tennysham Grammar School for Boys without often troubling their pages.

Stella and Daphne swopped paper-backed novelettes and Vic had a shelf of adventure stories in his bedroom. He was the one who'd left off books with his cricket bat and card tricks.

Chance shook off the past and climbed the steps. The heavy double doors led him from the town centre bustle into a sanctuary of silence. His shoes echoed on the tiled floor.

The interior was cool and calm. Sunlight came in banners in the bays formed by bookcases. In the middle of the vast space, two dark wooden counters stood back to back. A motherly-looking woman was writing beneath the *Books Out* sign.

Looking up with a smile and murmured word, she passed books to the couple who stood waiting. As they turned to leave, he realised they were the Dawsons.

Heading towards the entrance, Mrs Dawson recognised him and stopped. 'Inspector Chance, this is a surprise.'

'Good afternoon, Mrs Dawson.'

Her husband greeted him, taking the basket from her. 'We saw you at the inquest, Inspector. We were glad not to be called.'

'We'd have gone in any case,' Mrs Dawson said. 'For Lily Simmonds's sake.'

'As it turned out we weren't needed,' her husband said drily.

'She mentioned you know each other.'

'We were friends with her mother. Well I was really more than Herbert. She was very neighbourly when we first moved in. We sort of inherited Lily.'

'Where did you live before?' Chance said politely.

'On the other side of town. We both come from round here. Herbert used to work at the railway-station.'

He picked up on her husband's remark. 'Do you know Mr. Freeman?'

They exchanged glances. 'We've been introduced.' Mr. Dawson's voice was stiff with disapproval. 'I suppose we mustn't ask how your enquiries are faring, Inspector?'

'They're continuing. You'll understand I can't discuss them.'

'Of course. No doubt we'll read all about it when you've taken someone in custody.'

The woman at the desk caught his eye and pointed at the *Silence Please* sign. Chance gave her his warmest smile.

'I believe we're disturbing the peace.' He retreated a few steps back to the entrance lobby. The Dawsons followed. 'Now you know the victim was boarding with Mrs Simmonds, did either of you see him last week?'

They both shook their heads.

'Not knowingly,' Mr. Dawson said. 'We're too far down to see her gate from our windows. There are several lodging-houses further along so a stranger doesn't stand out.'

'It was just a thought.'

'His poor sister. She did look upset.'

'It doesn't do any good to dwell on it, Olive.'

'I should try to put it out of your mind, Mrs Dawson,' Chance said.

'The inspector's quite right.' Mr. Dawson gave him a grateful look. 'Come along, my dear. We're holding him up.'

'So sorry, I didn't think.' Mrs Dawson peered anxiously at him. 'I'm sure you'll catch whoever did it soon.'

'Good day to you, Inspector.'

Chance watched him hold the door for his wife. As they left he heard little Mrs Dawson fussing over where she'd put her ticket.

He walked back in and made his way along the bookcases. Towards the rear of the library a young assistant was replacing volumes from a wooden trolley.

'Excuse me, miss,' he said, putting on a funny voice. She spun round.

'Hullo, Daph.'

The young woman gave an exasperated sigh. 'What are you doing here, Dad? I suppose you're checking up on me?'

Chance grinned and leant against a shelf. 'Do I need to? Found yourself a boy-friend on the staff?'

'Hardly. There's only Mr. Harris and he's...'

'What?'

'Ancient. He must be nearly as old as you.'

'I'm here for the reference library. Think I'll manage to totter up the stairs?'

His daughter grinned back. She'd become pretty, Chance realised. He hadn't noticed. Her shingled hair was dark like his side of the family whereas Vic had Stella's fairness.

'Need any help finding anything?'

'I'm after back copies of the *Observer*.'

'Mr. Harris is up there. He'll show you. I'll introduce you if you like.'

'If you're not ashamed of your elderly papa.'

'Don't call me Daph then. Don't say anything daft and keep your voice down.'

'Yes, miss. Is that your Miss Randall on the desk?'

'No, that's Cath. Miss Randall isn't in today so Mr Harris is in charge.'

Daphne escorted her father back to the entrance and up the imposing staircase.

'Gran and Harold are coming round tonight.'

Her expression was bland. Chance couldn't decide if that was an innocent comment or his daughter was tipping him off.

'I'm not sure what time I'll be back. Tell Mum to expect me late.'

'Are you here in connection with the murder?'

It was on everyone's mind. 'You know I can't talk about work. It's just a routine inquiry.'

'You have constables for that.' She gave him a shrewd look. 'You fancied getting out of the office, Dad.'

'Guilty as charged, m'lud.'

They passed an elderly gent scribbling in a note-book, several volumes at his elbow. He looked up and nodded at Daphne.

Three men were studying the vacancies in the papers. Chance could see at a glance that the young chap was fresh to it. The others hunched over the reading desks, didn't expect anything to come of their daily ritual. The *Silence* sign hung over their heads like a guillotine.

'That's him.'

The man at the desk was several years younger than him, no more than mid-thirties. Studying a sheaf of papers, he looked up at the sound of Daphne's heels.

'This is my father, Mr. Harris. He'd like to look through the newspaper archive.'

'You're the policeman.' He studied Chance with frank interest. 'Sorry, Jack Harris. How d'you do.' His floppy hair falling over his brow, he rose clumsily to his feet.'

Chance shook hands, noting the walking stick by the desk.

'I'll show your father as we're short-handed. Thank you Daphne.'

'I'll get back downstairs then. See you later, Dad.'

He watched her go, thinking how professional she looked in her demure blouse with its neat Peter Pan collar.

'How's my daughter settled in?'

'Fine. I know Miss Randall's more than happy with her work. She'd tell you herself but she's not here today.'

'Good of you to say so.'

'Not at all. Let me show you where you can sit, Inspector. They're in a room over here.'

He followed the other man in a small office where the walls were lined with tall shelves. There was just sufficient space for a table and chair.

'Is it the *Sussex Echo* you want or the *Observer?*'

'The weekly. I don't think I could face wading through the daily.'

Harris nodded. 'I've done a spot of research myself. It's easy to get distracted. All human life is there.' He gestured at the metal shelves and turned away abruptly, a hand to his mouth.

Chance was very good at seeming not to notice things. Jack Harris wasn't the first chap he'd encountered with a nervous tic.

'This side holds the *Observer*. It's self-explanatory, quarterly volumes arranged in date order. They go back to 1902 when we opened and we've a complete run to the end of last year. Will that do you? This year's issues are in a pile in the stock-room.'

'That's ideal.'

'If I can be of further assistance, just give me a shout. Metaphorically speaking.'

'I shouldn't need to but thanks.' He liked the way Harris hadn't shown any curiosity about what he was after. Pity about the game leg. It looked a trial.

Always curious himself, Chance peered out of the small window before setting to work. He could see a narrow slice of the triangular green around which stood the municipal buildings. The wall opposite was the side of the town hall. It always reminded him of an ugly miniature French chateau. By craning his neck he could see the dust-bins of the alley between.

Harris had shut the door. Chance, not over keen on confined spaces opened it slightly. The newspapers had been bound in leather covers, blue for the *Observer.* He selected the first volume for 1917 and settled down to search.

It took a fair time. Mrs Lynch had been unable to recall which month Warrender was conscripted beyond spring or maybe autumn. They were still waiting for his service record.

Predictably it wasn't spring. Chance was starting to think the whole idea had been a waste of time. The pages received a more cursory search. Week after week the headlines were dominated by news from the Front.

Local matters were pushed inside after the yellowing lists of dead and wounded Sussex men. After the sad narrow columns were accounts of fund-raisers, angling matches, church fetes and sports. Now and again a familiar name caught his eye.

Timeless Tennysham life limped on despite the mud and guts across the Channel. He hadn't been present but Stella had with an infant Daphne. Irene was still married to Bill, Stella's father. Bishop was at Frederic-street,

Richards driving an ambulance maybe somewhere near him. Godwin and Phyllis had been school-children.

In an issue from mid-September he finally found what he was searching for. A report on a fire in Hastings. He was after the street name so a directory would give him the names of the businesses there. Mrs Lynch had thought her brother worked over the road from the fire but the lot could be checked if necessary. He'd send someone over to Hastings in the morning to see if anyone remembered Warrender.

Chance scanned the account with a professional eye. The fire had been severe though fortunately no one had been hurt. It had broken out some time in the evening in the premises of a gent's outfitters. The building was badly damaged and the business a write-off. He wondered immediately if that had been the idea.

The leading fireman who attended the incident told the reporter that arson had been ruled out. The cause was surmised to have been a cigarette-end smouldering in a bin. The fire had been made much worse because the shop was about to be redecorated and paint had been stored in the rear of the premises. The fireman warned the public about the danger of storing flammable materials inside.

The owner of the shop, also interviewed was predictably devastated. He blamed himself for permitting employees to smoke in the room where they had their sandwiches. The business and the goodwill he'd painstakingly built up were his lifetime's work. All his records had been lost.

However all that mattered was that no one had been injured. It was a blessing that as they lived in the rooms upstairs, his family had been away visiting while the work was being done. His wife was asthmatic and better away from the odour of fresh paint.

He had been attending a public meeting and arrived back on the corner to see the building ablaze. Luckily neighbours had been able to tell the firemen that the premises were empty and the blaze was contained on either side.

All thoughts of where Leslie Warrender had worked were forgotten. Yet it hadn't been a waste of time after all.

*

Harold agreed with his wife apparently, though Chance didn't see his lips move. His mother-in-law had been telling some yarn for a while and he concentrated on his sandwich. Peeling back the bread his suspicions were confirmed. Stella had skimped on the mustard. He contemplated making do or wandering into the kitchen. When he looked up, the room had gone quiet and Irene was studying him like a cat who'd spotted a mouse. He stood up.

When he returned she resumed staring at him like a hostile barrister. 'What are you doing about this murder? Only my neighbour, Mrs Wright, you know the one with the leg, Stella? She was saying it's a disgrace. People are frightened to walk along the sea-front.'

Chance chewed a mouthful of cold lamb and Colman's while he ignored that.

'She knows my son-in-law's the head of C.I.D. I didn't know what to say to her.'

That was a first.

'You mustn't ask Eddie, Mum. You know he can't tell us.'

'That's all very well but people have a right to know. Wait until someone's murdered in their bed. Someone said the council will have to have that shelter demolished. Who's going to want to sit in it now?'

'I suppose holiday-makers wouldn't know,' Harold said diffidently.

'That's not the point. Everyone who lives here does. There's a killer walking the streets and he doesn't seem concerned. Long as his stomach's all right.'

'That's a bit harsh, Mum. Eddie's been working all hours.'

'Oh I know he's never here for supper with his family.'

Chance smiled sweetly. 'When we make an arrest, Irene, you can read all about it.'

'But are you and your men getting anywhere?'

Harold coughed. 'There's talk of replacing all the shelters anyway. Nothing to do with what happened. There's a scheme of modernising the sea-front after they do up the theatre.'

'There's a sight too much change going on, if you ask me. That's the first I've heard of it.'

'Did I not tell you, dear? Someone in town-planning mentioned it the other day.' He smiled apologetically and subsided.

'I can't wait until we can go to the pictures in town.'

'Nor me.' Stella smiled at her daughter's bent head. 'Not all change is bad, Mum.'

'Don't expect your husband to take you.'

'Did you find what you wanted today, Dad?' Daphne looked up from flicking through her magazine.

'I did actually.'

'What's this?' Irene's eyes narrowed suspiciously.

'Where was your Miss Randall?' Chance ignored his mother-in-law.

'She's off sick.'

'I don't want you going down with the 'flu'.

'It's not that, Mum. She's had toothache.'

'Is that the new woman in charge? I've seen her swanning around the library. On the plump side. She should cut down on the sweets.'

'She's not really, Gran.'

'What's she like?' Chance said idly. Let some other poor devil be in the dock.

Daphne considered. 'She's quite old. Thirty-seven, so Cath said. I like her though.'

Her parents exchanged a rare look of agreement.

'Cath, that's the dowdy one. She wears a wedding ring, always gossiping. She's usually on the desk when I change my books.'

'Lost her husband in the war,' Daphne said indifferently.

'And your Miss Randall lost someone, I shouldn't be surprised. Still she can keep herself.' Irene nodded, satisfied she'd pigeon-holed a woman she'd seen in the distance. 'We must be making a move. I'll go up and say goodnight to Victor. They give that boy far too much homework for his age. He should have been down long since.'

There'd been a strong whiff of glue when he'd gone up to change and put his head round Vic's bedroom door. He'd ended up holding the model S.6 while Vic stuck the floats in place.

Another good deed was required. Chance heaved himself out of his arm-chair. 'No need, I'm going up. I'll root him out.'

Fifteen

Ronald Lynch was sitting at the table in the interview room when the two detectives entered. P.C. Knowles was waiting stolidly by the door. Chance jerked his head to indicate he could go.

He and Sergeant Bishop took the seats opposite. Mr. Lynch watched uneasily as Bishop opened his note-book and began writing the date on a blank page.

'Sorry to keep you waiting, Mr. Lynch. Thank you for coming to see us.' Chance's voice was bland.

'Your sergeant here didn't give me much choice. Look here, Inspector. I told you everything I know after my wife identified the body. It's a bit much to drag me all the way to Tennysham again. I'm a busy man.'

'We're all busy, Mr. Lynch. Sergeant Bishop and I are investigating a murder. If you'd been frank with us in the first place you wouldn't be taking up our time now.'

He looked sulky and didn't answer.

Bishop looked up. 'Why did you visit Mr. Warrender in London?'

'Who says I did?'

'Answer the question please, sir, or you'll keep us all here longer.'

'It was that woman, I suppose? All right, I visited Warrender because I happened to be in London on business. I had occasion to call at my head office in Holborn.'

'That doesn't answer my question, sir. We can play this game all day if need be.'

Mr. Lynch stopped touching his ear and visibly made up his mind. 'I went to tell him he wouldn't be welcome in my home again and to keep away. He upset my wife and I wasn't going to stand for it.'

'Upset Mrs Lynch in what way, sir? She gave us the impression she was very fond of her brother.'

'Asking for money. Getting her worried about what would become of him. That sort of thing. My wife gets worked up to the point of making herself ill. I didn't want Warrender near my daughters either. Dash it, you must have worked out by now that he was a bad lot. A man in my position can't afford to be associated with a gaol-bird.' He sat back in an *I've said my piece* sort of way.

'What position is that?' Chance intervened.

'On the way up, since you ask.'

Bishop scribbled something. 'So you knew where Mr. Warrender was to be found all along?'

'Not for sure, it was an educated guess. He'd stayed with that Price woman years ago. They worked together in a club. After I'd given him his marching orders, I overheard him tell Ethel he'd look up a woman friend in London. I assumed she'd be the one.'

'Really? That isn't what you told us on Monday.' Bishop waited, his pencil poised. 'As I recall when we asked where your brother-in-law went after leaving your home, you kept very quiet. How did you know where Mrs Price lived?'

'Warrender wrote to my wife a few years ago. I opened the letter and happened to keep the address.'

'Did Mrs Lynch ever receive her letter?' Chance asked.

'No she didn't. You needn't look at me like that, Inspector. A man has a right to protect his wife. He wrote asking for money. Not for the first time. I sent him a curt refusal and he didn't try again.'

'Why didn't you tell us you'd seen Mr. Warrender in January?'

Mr. Lynch sighed in exasperation. 'Because I didn't want my wife to know. We'd got rid of him. Why stir it up again?'

I walked into that, Chance thought. Try again. 'That won't wash, Mr. Lynch. Why stir things up by visiting your brother-in-law after he'd left you?'

There was a short pause. He fancied a cup of tea but it would have to wait. He had no intention of offering hospitality.

'I can do without all this.' Lynch flicked his hand at his surroundings, his expression sullen. 'Look, I'll tell you the whole story and then I trust I can go.'

Chance glanced at Bishop with the hint of a smile.

'It's always wise to tell us everything, sir,' Bishop said. 'In your own time.'

'First, let me make it clear I had absolutely nothing to do with my brother-in-law's death. Nor do I know who killed him. Got that?'

'We're listening, sir.'

'The truth is, I didn't tell you I'd seen him in London because by the merest chance I was a few miles from here on the evening he was killed. I didn't want you getting the wrong idea. Surely you can see that?'

Bishop shook his head sadly. 'Perhaps now you can see that lying in the first instance only makes you look suspicious, sir?'

'I didn't lie to you. I didn't tell you everything. There's a difference. It's just one of those damnable coincidences life throws up.'

'Can you be more specific, Mr. Lynch? Where were you on the evening of Thursday the fifth?'

'I had a sandwich in a pub on the coast road just outside Bexhill. I told you I have a team of insurance agents under me. Purely by chance I was in Bexhill that day, sorting out a new recruit. The fellow's still on trial, I had to check on his work, accompany him on calls and so forth. We had lunch and I went over his paper-work with him.'

'So this can all be verified by your employee?'

'Yes, if you wish. Though I don't see why you're interested in the day. I thought Warrender was killed at night?'

Bishop ignored him. 'We'll need this man's details.'

'I can let you have them. My secretary can show you my office diary. These dates are worked out weeks ahead. Months sometimes.'

'And the details of where you had supper? What time was that, sir?'

'I'll have to think.' Lynch folded his arms. 'Around seven, quarter-past.'

'Did you eat with this employee again?'

'No. Look I've dozens of witnesses to where I was that evening. I stood by while he called on people, collecting premiums. They have to make some calls in early evening when men are home from work. That's how I started.' A note of satisfaction crept in.

'Presumably the staff at the pub will remember you. Did you get chatting to anyone there, sir?'

'Not that I recall. I read the evening paper. I hope one of the staff will remember serving me but it means nothing if they don't. They'll have had plenty of customers since me.'

'I shouldn't worry about that, sir. We'll find someone.'

Chance was amused that Bishop's quiet voice sounded like a threat.

'What was the name of the pub?'

Lynch shrugged. 'It might have been The Plough or was it The Seven Stars? I didn't really notice. There are a couple along that stretch. It was a big place, quite new with a car-park.'

'And what time did you leave?'

'About an hour later, fifty minutes. I didn't clock-watch.'

Chance calculated rapidly. Lynch would have been on the coast road behind Tennysham at the right sort of time to meet Warrender and kill him.

'It's a long drive home to Marting.'

Lynch glared at him. 'I've told you. My job takes me all over the county and into Hampshire and Surrey for that matter.'

'What time did you get home?'

'About ten, quarter past? My wife will remember.'

Chance studied him. 'Your wife didn't remember you were out at all that night.'

Now Lynch was fingering his ear again. It would have been his *tell* if the three of them were playing poker. And in a sense they were.

'Don't blame Ethel. I told her to say I was in that evening.'

"It's possible we may need to speak to her again,' Chance said. 'It depends on whether you've told us the whole truth this time.'

Bishop looked a query at him. He nodded.

'I'll take your employee's details if you please.'

Voices sounded in the corridor and footsteps went past. Someone let a door slam. The small patch of sky visible was the colour of wadding. They'd had their quota of sunshine. Chance listened to Lynch give the address, noting he had it off-pat.

'I've been very frank with you. Can I go now?'

It was Bishop who'd told him in his first year to beware the suspect who says *frank. Honestly* was another dead giveaway. So was the release of tension he'd just seen in Lynch's eyes.

'One moment, Mr Lynch.'

'What now, Inspector? There's nothing more I can tell you.'

'You still haven't explained why you really visited Mr. Warrender in London.'

Lynch who was on the point of lifting himself off the hard chair, sank back down again. He sighed. 'All right. Cards on the table.'

'I think we've already done this,' Chance said pleasantly. 'These will be the ones up your sleeve.'

'I had business at our head office in town. That's absolutely true. As I was in London I decided to find

Warrender and settle with him for once and for all.' The detectives said nothing while he swallowed and continued, speaking rapidly. 'Warrender had got hold of the wrong end of the stick about something and he was holding it over me.'

Chance suppressed the picture that conjured up.

'I determined to have it out with him.'

'Go on.'

'While that unspeakable swine was staying with us and he made the most of my hospitality, I can tell you...' Lynch collected himself and continued, his face darkening. 'He wanted a lift into Chichester one day. That's where my office is. Said he wanted to get Christmas presents for my daughters. At lunch-time as I later found out, he lay in wait outside my place of business and followed me. His twisted mind saw something perfectly innocent and put the worst connotation on it.'

Chance managed not to grin. He signalled Bishop to take over.

'What was that, sir?'

'I had a bite to eat with a lady colleague. A most respectable lady. We had work matters to discuss. Warrender spied on me and later on he had the confounded cheek to threaten to tell Ethel.'

'Couldn't you have told Mrs Lynch yourself, sir? If it was all perfectly above board?'

'You don't know my wife, Sergeant. She can be totally unreasonable. She was in tears last night about a lipstick she claimed she'd found in my car. I tell you the woman's a neurotic. My secretary must have dropped it. I ran her home a while back when she was unwell.'

'Your wife has suffered a recent loss, sir.' Bishop eyed him with distaste. 'What was the outcome with your brother-in-law?'

'That was the worst of it. I had to put up with some insolent taunting but he didn't want money. Not right away, said he had another source of funds. Warrender said he'd keep my secret for now as he didn't want his little sister hurt. He'd have a think about what he was going to do.'

'In that case weren't you taking rather a risk when you told him to leave at New Year?'

Lynch's face had an unhealthy-looking mottling. 'My temper got the better of me. As it was, he laughed. He made sure to tell my wife I was throwing him out so as to stir up trouble. The truth was it suited him to go. He'd had enough of playing the doting uncle and Ethel fussing round him. Marting was a sight too quiet for him.'

Bishop looked up from his scribbled line. 'Please continue.'

'I went to see him in Soho as I'd had enough of waiting for him to make a move. I'm in line for a big promotion and he could have ruined me there.'

'What passed between you at this meeting?'

'He admitted he enjoyed making me sweat. There was no point appealing to his better nature. First he said I could relax, he'd be going abroad. Then he laughed and said he'd drop Ethel a post-card. I was only there ten minutes. It's my bad luck his woman friend saw me as I was leaving. That's the last I saw of him. Can I be off now, Inspector?'

'In a while, Mr. Lynch. After you've signed an amended statement.'

'I'll say this much,' Lynch sat forward. 'Warrender turned on the charm with women when it suited him but he enjoyed getting men's backs up. I've no idea who did for him but I'd gladly shake them by the hand. That's the honest truth.'

This time Chance believed him.

*

There was a cup and saucer on the Superintendent's desk. Not any old regulation china, the thin stuff with a pattern. The privileges of rank, eh? Personally he didn't care if he drank out of a tin mug.

'I'll be seeing Colonel Vesey this evening at his home. What do you suggest I tell him?'

'That we're making steady progress, sir. Sergeant Bishop and I interviewed the victim's brother-in-law this morning.' Chance outlined what was said while Hayes listened with his fingers pressed together like a vicar.

'So you have both motive and opportunity. And you still find that insufficient to charge him?'

'I do, sir. I'm not convinced Ronald Lynch is a murderer. He's all bluster. I don't see him as ruthless or calculating.'

'That's for a jury to decide. Your job is to build a case on the evidence. Don't dismiss a suspect out of hand, based on what may be a flawed character assessment.'

'I'll bear that in mind, sir.' *Jolly grateful for the tip.*

'The decision not to charge a suspect is a heavy responsibility, Chance.'

'The evidence against Lynch is circumstantial, sir. We'd need a sighting in the town. We appealed for witnesses. No one's come forward to say they were near the sea-front at the relevant time. Residents of all the buildings opposite were questioned.'

'Make sure you leave no stone unturned. Facts are what's required.'

Superintendent Hayes uncapped his fountain pen and made a note. Chance had been reading upside down since his schooldays. Hayes contrived to shield his writing with his hand like the class swot.

'The sister now has no alibi of course.'

'No, sir. She had no transport though. We're a long way from Marting and they have children. I don't believe she's a likely prospect.' He couldn't resist. 'The facts suggest otherwise.'

'As far as you're aware. Someone else could have looked after the children. She could have borrowed a car. Does she in fact drive?'

'I don't believe so, sir.'

'Keep Mrs Lynch in mind. Agreed?'

'Certainly.' Chance scowled at the photograph of the King hanging over the fireplace.

'Mrs Price in London is a possibility. What are your thoughts there?'

'The station staff have been questioned and no woman travelling alone caught a late evening train, sir.'

'A woman could attach herself to a man at the station. Did you consider that?'

'It did occur to me. There were three couples after nine o'clock. All purchased local tickets. One couple were known to the booking clerk and neither of the other women fitted Mrs Price's description.' *And don't suggest she was in disguise.*

Hayes shifted his leather gloves along the polished surface. There was no ash-tray, no ink on the blotter. He lined up his paper-knife. Never trust a man who was that precise. You expected it of women.

'It's a great pity you haven't been able to find the weapon.'

He made it sound like a personal failing on Chance's part.

'It's often the way, sir. As you know.' He wasn't about to get discomfited. 'Every possible search has been made. Inspector Forrest has been very helpful.' Might as well put in a good word. He liked Bob.

'Excellent.' The superintendent brightened. 'Cooperation yields maximum efficiency. Incidentally Chance, you have my authority to borrow W.P.C. Marden for routine enquiries. A woman's way of looking at things could be useful.'

'Thank you, sir.' Like a music hall he always saved the best 'til last. 'Actually, we do have a further promising line of inquiry.'

He explained what he'd found in the library.

Sixteen

They didn't make a habit of going to the Duke Of Sussex at dinner-time. Bishop often went home for his meal when they were quiet. After a session with the Super, Chance had declared his need to be shot of the place before they tackled Miss Aldridge. He'd suggested a swift half to cheer him up.

'Feeling better?'

Chance looked up from staring into his glass. 'D'you ever wish you were back on the beat, Wilf?'

'Once a year maybe when it's a glorious summer's day and the lads are getting on my wick.'

'That little?'

'I'm a realist. I haven't forgotten getting home dog-tired and soaking my feet in a bowl. Getting soaked night after night an' all. No, it's all right for young coppers. I like to be in the dry.' He reached for his shandy. 'I'll even say the work's more satisfying.'

Chance grunted. 'I hope something comes of this afternoon. Only I feel I'm on borrowed time. There was a definite frost in the air. No more calling me Eddie or asking after the family.'

'I suppose Hayes is under pressure too. I hear he's been summoned to see the Chief Constable this evening.'

'Apparently the old boy's been down with the 'flu.'

'I bet Hayes isn't dining with the family. Colonel Vesey's old money. He'll be seeing him in his study beforehand. Probably won't even get offered a drink.'

'I remember his father, regular old buffer. He nearly caught me trespassing on his estate once. I only fancied a look in his woods and didn't see why I shouldn't. That was on a hot summer's day. They looked inviting, all the more for being forbidden.'

'Your career was nearly over before it started then.'

'I'd have had a thrashing from his keeper anyway.'

Chance loosened his tie. Bishop glancing at his face, thought he was recovering his spirits.

'What else did the Super say?'

'He pointed out we've a little over a week until the inquest is resumed. He's still keen we solve this ourselves naturally but implied it won't look good if we've nothing fresh for the coroner. The Chief Constable backs the county force, it would be a feather in his cap after all. But his nibs thinks if we don't get a break soon, we may have to admit defeat and hand over to the Yard.'

'I daresay he's thinking of the reaction in the town and the holiday season. So Hayes fancies Ethel Lynch as a suspect?'

'Don't you think it implausible that she could leave her daughters somewhere, manage to borrow a car and motor forty miles to murder her brother?'

'Put like that, I do.' Bishop drained his glass. 'Did she know her husband was going to be back late that evening? If not, where could she say she'd been?'

'And what motive was she supposed to have? No, Hayes didn't see her. I had a long talk with her. Besides she can't drive. When we were at the hotel Lynch said something about having to take her to see her mother's grave.'

'That's right. Was that all Hayes had to say?'

'He wasn't happy that we haven't turned up the weapon.'

'That's the way it goes. It's not for want of searching.'

Chance frowned. 'It's a funny thing. I keep getting the feeling I've seen a knife somewhere. The sort that would do.'

'That's the trouble, isn't it? The right sort can be found everywhere. All we know for sure is that it wasn't large like a carving knife.'

'It's no good. I've racked my brains, such as they are. Somewhere I've been.'

'How about the library?'

Chance considered. 'Don't think so. Mr. Harris had a letter-opener of the right size on his desk but that doesn't satisfy my nagging feeling.'

'It'll come to you if it's important.' He eyed the level of Chance's glass.

'Actually Hayes was fiddling with a paper-knife. A dainty thing for a man, with a bone handle.'

'There you are then. He did it. Drink up.'

'Thanks.' Chance looked at his wrist-watch. 'No point calling on Miss Aldridge when she's busy with meals.'

The saloon was half-full with regulars. On his way to the bar he nodded to his neighbour who kept the fishmonger's. He was scraping at a stub of pencil over the ash-tray. A paper at his elbow was folded at the crossword. You couldn't open a daily without one.

Bishop watched him fold his pen-knife and stick it in his pocket. There was a knife for a start. They were found in everyone's possession.

He waited to be served, catching the eye of the pot-man drawing a pint. Those in the know considered he kept the best cellar in town, under the watchful eye of the land-lady.

'Be right with you, Wilf.'

Bishop nodded. 'No rush, Bill.'

The pot-man had skin the colour of leather and his rolled-up shirt sleeves revealed a dark tattoo on each forearm. As blurred as old bruises, he'd once explained they were seagulls done in some foreign port when he'd been a bally young fool.

'I'll see to Mr. Bishop. Same again is it, Wilf?'

'Please, Beattie.'

He wouldn't swop his Glad for anyone though the land-lady of the Duke was a fine figure of a woman. All her curves were in the right places, even if the proportions were remarkably generous. He'd heard her described as well-upholstered but that didn't do her corset-maker justice.

Her upswept hair, big earrings and hint of cleavage made her look like she was off to the theatre. Not presiding over the bar in a back-street pub. Beattie had dignity and a look that could quell a drunk across the room. If she liked you, there was a sparkle in her eye and you felt the better for talking to her.

'I've been waiting for you and Mr. Chance to come in.'

He looked enquiring. 'Anything we can help you with? Just say the word.'

'That's very kind of you.' She concentrated on her task. He watched appreciatively as she held up the glass to the light, her rounded bare arm lifting gracefully from its bell sleeve. 'I heard something that might interest you both.'

'Oh, yes?'

Beattie motioned him discreetly to the far end of the bar. She lowered her voice. 'I wouldn't want my gentlemen to think I eavesdrop. Am I right in thinking you're interested in anything a little bit odd at the moment?'

'Thanks, love, have one yourself.' He passed over the money. 'If there's something you think I should know, I'm all ears.'

'Thanking you. I'll take mine later.' She unscrewed a lemonade bottle and added the top to their drinks. Her movements were swift yet unhurried from long practice. A man could be hypnotised watching her.

Her voice was a sonorous murmur. 'On Monday evening I was at a meeting of the victuallers' association. I overheard a conversation between the landlord of The Mafeking and a few others. He was saying they've had an unexpected windfall in their blind box.'

Bishop took a sip. 'Where's this leading exactly?'

She looked beyond him, her eyes roaming the tables. Satisfied all was well, she leant towards him, resting her bosom on her folded arms. He kept his gaze on the shelf behind her head.

'Apparently he went to empty the collection box that same day. He only checks it every quarter, then he takes it to the bank and sends a cheque to the society for the blind. By the by, Jim always counts it in the presence of someone else. It's all above board.'

'I don't doubt it.'

'Usually they only get a few coppers at a time, no pun intended. The odd florin at most but it all adds up. This time a pile of fivers had been pushed in on top of the coins. He couldn't believe his eyes apparently. He counted out ninety-six pounds, folded in four wads.' Beattie straightened up.

Bishop breathed out. 'That *is* interesting, Beattie. I appreciate your passing it on.'

The landlady inclined her head. 'I have an eye for the curious. Enjoy your drinks.'

She sailed further down the bar, her head held high. Well you had to in those earrings. He had plenty to think about as he carried their glasses back to the snug.

Chance's eyebrows rose as he listened. 'Too late for fingerprints. You're right though. It could be the contents of Warrender's wallet.'

*

The afternoon had grown overcast while they were in the pub. As they left the High Street, Chance noticed that the new cinema building had risen higher behind the hoardings. The word was it would be open by autumn. A crane swung at the dull sky and a workman yelled across the site.

'This time last week we'd just got back from Henry's. We were soaked and things were ticking over nicely. We both had the week-end off.'

'At least it's not raining,' Bishop said.

Chance was in philosophical mood. 'We'd never heard the name Leslie Warrender nor Miss Dorothy Aldridge.'

'I said I'd vaguely seen her name in the local paper. I think she was one of the fund-raisers for the mayor's charity.'

'I was thinking about where Warrender's wallet was found. She might attend St Luke's. She strikes me as the type who'd go to church.'

'She'd go to All Saints. Bit nearer.'

He'd had to go inside once for a funeral. A dingy Victorian pile with a half-hearted spire and hardly any churchyard.

Just as in London the east end was the Cinderella quarter of Tennysham, where the bus and charabanc depot was situated. The dairy and the laundry were on that side of town, further back from the sea-front. Douglas Aldridge had never had sufficient capital to take on a hotel nearer the pier.

Bishop paused on the kerb. 'I've seen the box for the blind at The Mafeking. It's in the passage on a table on the right as you go in, opposite the saloon door.'

'Where someone could pinch it.'

'No, it's one of those big ones shaped like a dog. You couldn't run off with that under your arm. Anyone could shove notes in it without being seen though, if they picked their time.'

On the far pavement Chance stepped out of the way of a woman pushing a pram. She smiled at him.

'They could go inside for a drink or disappear. No one would know they'd been there. Mind you, they had to know the box was there.'

'The outer door's always back during opening hours,' Bishop said. 'Anyone could look in.'

'So we're no further forward?'

'What foxes me is why they dumped the money at all? I can see they took the wallet to prevent or at least delay our identifying the body. But why not keep the cash?'

Chance thrust his hands back in his pockets. 'Because that wasn't what the killing was about? They aren't by nature a thief?'

'So all we have to do is find a murderer with scruples.'

'They took Warrender's hip flask but that wasn't found in the churchyard.'

'Maybe the murderer hung on to the flask and the weapon.'

They cut down the short street that led to The Belvedere Hotel. Its unattractive bulk came into view on the right. A black iron fire escape disfigured the rear above a patchily rendered wall. On the side of the building was a blank door with small windows above. Their mean size suggested landing or bathroom.

At the end of the street the tide was out. A lone figure was digging for bait. When you thought about it, all life was spent searching for something or other.

'Meant to say,' Bishop said, 'I told Richards to cut along to the main post-office this afternoon. See if anyone there remembers Warrender.'

Chance nodded. He looked across the road at the empty shelter. Nothing to say what had happened there. Possibly there'd been a little fingerprint powder on a window ledge but the breeze would have dispersed it by now.

In any case it resembled fag ash.

He glanced at Bishop. His face was tired. 'You've worked solidly for over a week. Glad will be forgetting what you look like.'

'She understands.'

'Lucky you. Take tomorrow off at least. You deserve it.'

'Ta.'

'One of those idle blighters ought to be back at work by Monday, if not both.'

'The 'flu can be very nasty. Those who can afford it go to a convalescent home somewhere like here.'

'They can get their recuperative sea air while they're working. Shall we go in?'

A large gull was perched on one of the Belvedere chimney pots as though he owned the place. His expression checked them over for fish and chips and found them wanting. As they rounded the corner to the entrance he took off, screeching in a great mourning sweep of discordant notes. Chance spared a thought for the new recordings he'd found in London and not had time to hear.

Bix Beiderbecke it wasn't.

The desk in the reception area was deserted. Bishop pressed the brass bell. Impatient, Chance had an urge to pound the gong. After a moment hurried footsteps came from the door at the rear.

Ivy Betts appeared, hastily straightening her cuffs. Her white apron was spotted with damp. Her face was apprehensive as she recognised them.

'Hullo, Inspector, Sergeant Bishop. Did you want me?'

'Afternoon, Miss Betts. We've come to see Miss Aldridge. Is she in?'

'Yes, she's in the office.' She gestured at the door. 'Through there. I'll take you to her.'

'Just a moment, young lady. How are you bearing up?' Bishop said.

'All right, thank you. I was glad to get the inquest over and done with. Though the coroner was very nice to me, like you said he would be.'

'You spoke up well. Anything you'd like to say to Inspector Chance?'

Ivy stepped nearer. 'Look, about what I told Phyl Marden.' She lowered her voice. 'She said she'd explain to you. I'm sorry I didn't let on. It was all a bit awkward.' She pulled a face, making herself look even younger than she was.

'We get the picture, love. We're not ogres.'

'You won't drop me in it, please? We need my money at home.'

Bishop winked. 'We'll keep you out of it.'

'There's nothing else you didn't like to tell us?' Chance fixed her with a stern expression.

She shook her head. 'No, sir.'

'Off you go then. Show us in and you can get back to the dishes.'

'Yes, sir. Thanks ever so much. It's this way.'

They followed her into a short passage and hung back as Ivy knocked on a door and entered. The runner along the lino was marked and worn. They were decidedly behind the scenes.

'Miss Aldridge, the police are here again.'

A chair leg scraped on the floor and a voice mumbled.

'The same two as last time.'

Ivy's voice was cheerful. Chance could hear the relief. Without waiting to be asked, he pushed the door further open and Bishop followed him in.

Miss Aldridge was sitting at an open roll-top desk against the wall. She'd turned round to speak to Ivy and stood as they came in.

'Inspector Chance,' she looked worried. 'Take those away, Ivy and that will be all.'

'Yes, miss.'

Lifting the tea-tray from a small table, Miss Betts gave Bishop a final grin as he held the door for her.

'Good afternoon, Miss Aldridge.'

'What brings you here?'

'We believe you can assist us further with our inquiries.'

Sounding like a stage policeman. He was wondering how to avoid revealing that Ivy had overheard her and Warrender. You could only play things by ear.

'I don't see how but I can spare you a few minutes if you insist.'

He glanced around the small room. There was no window and the space felt cramped with the three of them standing. 'May we sit down?'

Miss Aldridge nodded. 'We could speak in the dining-room if you prefer?'

'This will do.'

She sat down reluctantly and waited as they arranged themselves. The few items of furniture were cast-offs from other rooms. Chance took the old kitchen chair drawn up to the folding table and Bishop had to make do with a stool. It was obviously somewhere guests were never expected to see.

'Would you and your sergeant care for tea or coffee?'

'We won't, thanks.'

Miss Aldridge looked distastefully at Bishop's note-book. 'I can't tell you any more about the man who died. I assume that's why you're here?'

'His real name was Leslie Warrender.' He kept his manner neutral.

'So I understand from the inquest. I thought it my duty to accompany Ivy. Her parents were unable to take time off work easily.' She was still holding her fountain-pen.

Chance studied her. 'I should tell you that we've spoken to someone who knew Mr. Warrender. That person was able to tell us why he came here last December.'

'What has that to do with me, pray?'

He felt sorry for her. The fingers clenched on her pen belied her neutral tone.

'Let's not waste time, Miss Aldridge.' A Sussex calendar hung on the wall behind her. March was a gay poster of Rye. Chance didn't set much store by beauty spots. 'We know about your father.'

'Be good enough to ask your questions and leave me in peace.' This time there was a faint tremor in her voice.

Chance hesitated. He didn't fancy himself as someone who bullied women. It had been a long week and he'd had enough of verbal fencing. 'Leslie Warrender came here in December to blackmail you. We can understand why you chose to conceal this but we need to know everything that took place between you.'

Miss Aldridge sniffed. He was relieved to see that she wasn't trying not to weep. It was resentment.

'I didn't kill him and I've no idea who did. I suppose my word is unlikely to satisfy you, Inspector?'

'We can't leave it at that, Miss Aldridge. We must have chapter and verse, I'm afraid.'

'Am I to understand I'm a suspect?'

'We're investigating a murder. By withholding information you've delayed us and made things harder for yourself.'

She closed her heavy eyelids for a second, as though in pain.

Bishop coughed. 'Would *you* like some tea, Miss Aldridge, or a glass of water?'

'No, thank you. If I answer your questions, will that be an end to it? You won't come here again?'

'If you're completely straight with us, we shouldn't need to.'

'I must insist this conversation is confidential. I don't care to have my misfortunes the talk of the town.'

Chance sighed. 'Miss Aldridge, the police are used to being discreet. I can't make any promises about a court case, you must see that. But if what you tell us has no bearing on the murder, I can guarantee it won't be made public.'

'Can you vouch for your men? One person's misery is the stuff of gossip to others.'

Bishop snapped shut his note-book and tucked it in his inner pocket. 'We've kept a fair few secrets, madam. Blackmail isn't unknown to the police. You can trust us.'

'Very well. I have no choice other than to accept your assurance.'

'Thank you, madam. Please tell us what happened in your own time.' Bishop smiled reassuringly at her.

She began to speak in a dull monotone that distanced herself from the account. 'You already know that Leslie Warrender stayed here briefly in December, under an assumed name. He sought a private interview with me in this room where he attempted to blackmail me. Is this what you wish to hear?'

'Please go on.'

'I should say rather, that he was successful. He told me some facts about my father of which I was unaware. They were a terrible shock but I was unable to dismiss what he said. To my shame, I paid him a hundred pounds to keep quiet.'

Chance breathed out. They were going to get the whole story. All the *Observer* had said was that the owner of the fire-damaged premises was called Douglas Aldridge.

'Did Warrender contact you again last week, Miss Aldridge?'

'Yes he did, Inspector. After he swore I'd never hear from him again. I was foolish to believe him but three months went by and I was starting to put it behind me.'

'They always say that,' Bishop said. 'Then they always come back for more.'

Miss Aldridge glared at him. 'He came here last Tuesday morning. I would prefer not to relive this.'

'Can't be helped, Miss Aldridge. You'll feel better afterwards.'

'I very much doubt that. He wanted another hundred pounds. He had the impudence to claim he had no wish to harm me. He said it was a simple business transaction. I told him I couldn't afford to give him any more.'

'What did Warrender say to that?' Chance knew he'd made a mistake in speaking gently when she threw him a look of pure dislike.

'He threatened me a second time with the loss of my good name and that of my father. He said all he had to do was drop a word in the right ear. He was right, of course. Rumour would be enough to destroy my reputation.'

'What precisely did Warrender say he had on your father?'

Miss Aldridge stared at him. He felt like Ivy caught sweeping dirt under the carpet. That or something she'd trodden in. 'You said you know, Inspector?'

Her lips pressed tight. She was a sharp one. Good job he could guess.

'Fourteen years ago, your late father paid Leslie Warrender to commit arson. An insurance fiddle.'

She bowed her head. 'Who did Warrender tell?'

'I can't discuss how we come by information but I promise you've nothing to worry about.'

'If you could take us through what happened, madam, then we can be out of your way,' Bishop said. 'From when you first met Warrender.'

'You know he stayed for two nights in December. On the first morning after breakfast, he requested a private interview with me. I brought him in here, thinking he had some sort of complaint.' Another sniff.

Bishop smiled sympathetically, managing to convey *surely not?*

Miss Aldridge responded to his expression. 'You wouldn't believe how demanding guests can be, quite unreasonable. To my surprise he began by saying he'd lived in Hastings during the war. That was where I spent my childhood and indeed my whole life until we moved here late in 'seventeen. He said he'd seen an advertisement I'd placed and wondered about my surname so he made inquiries.'

She was telling Bishop now, ignoring him. Chance sat back, quite satisfied. He willed his sergeant to keep her talking.

'He seemed pleasant when he arrived. Naturally I didn't know his name was assumed. So when his manner suddenly changed, it was such a shock. He said he'd done some work for my father and at first I thought he'd been an assistant in the shop. I couldn't understand what was happening. He kept smiling while he was saying terrible things.'

'It must have been very frightening, madam.'

'Yes, it was. A lesser woman would have fainted but I'm made of sterner stuff. Warrender said he'd been a ledger-clerk at the furniture business across the road from where we lived. As you evidently know, my father owned a gentlemen's outfitters. We lived, my parents and I on the upper floors.'

'Had you met Mr. Warrender in those days?'

Miss Aldridge shook her head. 'I'm certain not. We didn't know anyone of that sort socially.'

'Please carry on.'

'My father did not have a good head for business. It wasn't his fault. He was a gentleman. He was struggling to stay afloat with the war and rising prices. He had a certain weakness.. for drink. Of course my mother shielded me. Warrender claimed he made my father's acquaintance in the public-house on the corner. I don't doubt he was the one who made the proposition. A way to end all my father's troubles was how he put it. Left to himself my father would never have thought of such a desperate measure.'

'He offered to burn down the premises for a cut of the insurance money?'

Miss Aldridge looked as though she'd aged since they'd been there. 'Yes'.

'It isn't the first time we've heard something of the sort.'

'I take no comfort from that, Sergeant. My father was an upright member of society. He was lured to break the law when he wasn't himself. He was confused and sick with worry.'

'He won't be the last. And this scheme was set up for when you and your mother were absent?'

'My father insisted on my mother taking a short holiday. The shop was to be redecorated and she suffered from asthma. The paint fumes would have been difficult for her. I accompanied her of course.'

'Did it seem strange at the time that money was found to do up the premises?' Chance said.

'My mother and I didn't know how bad things were financially. We knew only that the shop was going through a difficult time. Many business-people were in the same fix. We accepted what my father told us without question.'

'Did Warrender say he had any proof?'

'He claimed he'd kept a note in my father's hand. It supposedly gave a night when the yard gate would be unbolted and the premises left unlocked.'

Some handy dust-sheets, paint would go up like an inferno and no questions asked. Just as well the firemen had got there in time to stop it spreading. Privately Chance doubted her father would have been so foolish as to write something incriminating. Then again, people were stupid or the police would be out of a job.

'Did he let you see this note?'

'No. He said it was safely lodged with a friend. I am not naïve, Inspector. I did suspect that it might not exist. It made no difference.'

He looked at Bishop. They both knew she was right. It seemed horribly apposite to think *no smoke without fire.*

'So you paid up in December?'

'Yes. I had to sell some jewellery to raise the amount. He called back on the afternoon after he'd checked out to collect it.'

Chance gazed at the safe in the corner. A small model, he wondered what was left inside. The Belvedere wasn't the sort of establishment that was asked to store guests' valuables.

'Last week,' Bishop said. 'He turned up out of the blue on Tuesday and repeated his demands?'

'Yes, I was in the dining-room. Breakfast was over and fortunately I was alone when he walked in. I was forced to hear him out, in case he made a scene. Then I told him I couldn't pay any more. The hotel hasn't been doing well. I hadn't been able to put back the money he took from me previously.'

Bishop eyed her kindly. 'A nasty fix to be in.'

Miss Aldridge looked away. Chance recognised she found sympathy harder to take than hostility.

'Particularly as I do not accept that his extortion was based on anything more than wicked lies.'

'What was the upshot, Miss Aldridge?'

She was silent for a moment. 'Once again I had no choice but to capitulate. I told him I had little cash here.' An involuntary glance at the safe. 'He took what I gave him and made some vile remarks about my father not paying him adequately for what he'd done. He had the insolence to say my family owed him. Then one of the guests appeared. Warrender said he'd be back at the end of the week, on Friday when I'd had time to think about it and he left.'

Friday morning. Assuming Miss Aldridge didn't murder Warrender, whoever did had done her a favour, Chance thought.

'Was that all he said?'

'He didn't make small talk. But he did say I'd never hear from him again. He was going away.'

'Can you think of anything else to tell us?'

She sighed heavily. 'No, I've told you everything he said, Inspector. I don't know why but I believed him.'

'You didn't accompany him to a bank on Wednesday morning?'

'Certainly not. I never saw him again.'

Miss Aldridge removed her pince-nez, revealing a sore red mark on either side of her nose. She looked tired. 'I've no wish to help you catch the person who killed him. They probably suffered as I have. It won't return what was stolen from me, let alone my peace of mind.'

'One thing more and we'll be on our way,' Bishop said. 'Where were you on the evening of Thursday the fifth, Miss Aldridge?'

She stiffened on her chair. 'I've told you everything, humiliating though it's been. Are you implying you believe I killed him?'

'Purely routine, madam. We're asking everyone who encountered the deceased.'

'In that case are you questioning my chamber-maid and the boot-boy?'

Chance fidgeted. 'They don't live in. Answer the question please, Miss Aldridge.'

'I was here all evening, supervising the guests' dinner. This is my home, I'm their hostess.'

Chance gave Bishop an exasperated look.

'Were you busy with the hotel guests all the time, ma'am?'

'I was either in the dining-room or in the kitchen with Cook, that is Mrs Hilda Thompson, until about eight. Then I made up a fourth at bridge with three of my guests. After that I went upstairs to my private quarters where I had a bath before retiring.

'What time would that have been?'

'I wasn't staring at the clock, Sergeant but I'd say we broke up around five and twenty to ten.'

'Did anyone see you later that evening?'

'Yes, Cook did. After my bath I went down to make myself a cup of cocoa and check we were properly locked up. Guests have their own key but they tend not to keep late hours. I passed Cook on the back stairs and the hall clock was striking the quarter after ten.'

'Would Mrs Thompson be in your kitchen now, Miss Aldridge?'

'She is. Question her if you must.'

'Like I said, routine, ma'am. It's the same for everyone. It's just the two of you live in, you said?'

'Yes, Sergeant. You went through this last week.'

'Just checking I had it right, ma'am. I'll pop out and have a word.' Bishop jerked his head at Chance as he left, meaning he'd wait out the front.

'Did you look out of the window at any time, Miss Aldridge?' Chance managed to stifle a yawn.

'Not as far as I recall.'

'Pity. You might have seen the whole show.'

'I consider that remark in very poor taste.'

'People often look out at the sea, Miss Aldridge.'

'You asked us a week ago if we'd seen anything.'

'So I did. People sometimes remember things later. I imagine you were having an extremely unpleasant evening?'

'What do you mean?' She looked suspiciously at him.

'You were expecting to see Leslie Warrender here in the morning and hand over more money. That would guarantee most people a sleepless night.'

Miss Aldridge coloured. Good job looks couldn't kill. Not like that Greek woman what's her name?

'Had you managed to get the money together?'

She nodded. 'I had no choice.'

'What did you think when Warrender didn't turn up the next morning?'

'I didn't know what to think.'

'When Miss Betts came running back and told you she'd found a man's body, did it cross your mind it could be him?'

'Of course not. Why should I expect him to be sitting on the promenade? I assumed the corpse was a vagrant.'

Chance sighed. 'It would have saved a lot of time if you'd been frank with us last week. Thank you, Miss Aldridge. We'll see ourselves out.'

He picked up his hat from the cluttered table. It held a portable typewriter, some envelopes, a pile of menus and a heap of napkin rings. Chance had been surprised on entering to see the small office was disordered. He would have had Miss Aldridge down as someone fussy.

His gaze roamed over the desk as he stood. Some of the pigeon holes held correspondence. Pens, pencils, a wooden ruler lay jumbled. A spike held what looked like bills, the uppermost one in red ink. There was an old-fashioned stamp box and a string-holder.

It reminded him of that parlour-game, twenty objects on a tray and you had to remember them all. He prided himself on his memory. But he had an uneasy feeling there was more than one thing he'd noticed in recent days. Connections he should have made. Things drift through the mind, as insubstantial as cigarette smoke.

Seventeen

It made a change to feel useful. The time passed quickly and she felt a rare sense of satisfaction on her return to Frederic-street. An ordinary member of the county force, not a special case. That was all she asked. If she stuck it out, she'd end up part of the furniture.

Sid was a good listener and she would tell it all again to Dad over their high-tea. Perched on a desk, Phyllis felt a flicker of unease as she thought about him. Things hadn't been quite right between them since he'd mentioned her leaving the force. Cheerful enough on the surface but awkward underneath. Like a roughly made bed with the counterpane smoothed over a rucked bottom sheet.

She was still baffled. Dad had always understood her. Encouraged her to be independent ever since she was eight years old. When they'd stood side by side in the churchyard on a bitter winter's day and listened to an elderly retired vicar stumble over her mum's name. He knew how much having a real job meant to her.

'Sorry, Sid. Something popped in my mind.'

'Did you have to explain it to the kids?' Godwin repeated.

'They were too young to know what was going on. It's funny, I thought I'd be out of my depth, not having had any brothers or sisters but it was fine. They were hungry so I washed their hands and cut them some bread and jam. There wasn't much in. I made a pot of tea and looked after them until the neighbour collected them.'

'Sergeant Bishop says there's talk of widening the coast road, then there'll be more accidents. He doesn't reckon this highway code will make any difference.'

'The main thing is the father wasn't killed.'

'It'll be tough for them without his wage while he's in hospital.'

Sid was a decent sort. 'The mother will cope,' Phyllis said. 'Women always do.' If only men would realise that.

She became aware that Sid was watching her with what she thought of as his goofy expression. It seemed prudent to move away and busy herself with what she'd come in for, emptying the out-trays.

Too late. There was a strangled sort of cough as he cleared his throat.

'Not long 'til Easter now. The tennis club will be getting going again.'

Keeping her back turned, she made a preoccupied sound.

'You play don't you, Phyl?'

He knew perfectly well she did, having seen her there the previous summer. The club-house with its bar and terrace overlooking the courts was the most popular meeting place for the young crowd. You could get a good tea after the game and they held regular Saturday night dances throughout the season.

It wasn't just the youth of Tennysham who joined the tennis club. Their parents' generation were all members, even if they never had so much as a knock-about or possessed tennis whites. It was an alternative to the golf club and much easier to get in to.

Rumour had it that Inspector Chance had been spotted in the bar at the big do held before Christmas. Which meant he'd been someone's guest or more likely that the family had joined.

At all costs avoid a direct question. Time to make a tactical retreat.

'Used to. I doubt I'll have much time this summer.'

Men were exasperating. She was no good at hurting people, why couldn't he take a hint? It was like that sign you see in grocers'. *Please don't ask for tick as a refusal may offend.*

'I was wondering whether you'd...

Sid went quiet as the door opened. Never had she been so pleased to see Richards.

'While the cat's away eh?'

'We're working actually.' She made her voice frosty and her expression colder. If she and Sid became an item of gossip, life would be a misery.

'They not back yet?'

'Haven't seen them. No one's in the office.'

She made that a few degrees warmer. The last thing she wanted was to get on the wrong side of anyone at work. There was a fine line between making a point and an enemy.

Richards collapsed in his chair. 'I've just spent a boring hour in the post-office for nothing. They've had a good clear-out there, I can tell you. None of the staff date from Warrender's day except for one old boy. He'd forgotten all about him. I spent ages jogging his memory and he never knew anything in the first place. The post-master back then has turned up his toes. Just my luck.'

'It's twelve years ago,' Godwin said. 'You can't win them all, Fred.'

Richards yawned. 'It's been a waste of shoe-leather. I only like interviewing when it pays off.'

'They should be back by now.' Godwin moved over to the window. 'Wonder how they're getting on?'

'Where are they?' Phyllis said.

'The Belvedere, seeing the owner.'

She shouldn't have asked. Inspector Chance had made it very clear she was to keep out of their business. There was no justice. It was her blooming tip-off that had taken them there.

'Get us a cuppa, Phyllis.'

She was about to be livid when she spotted the glint in Richards's eye. There was no harm in him really. He only meant to get a rise.

'You know where the canteen is.'

'Don't feel like moving.' Removing his shoe, Richards rubbed the underneath of his foot. 'I suppose I'll be back on the beat soon. It's wrecked my feet. I'm sure I'm getting a blister.'

'Well we don't want to see it.'

'Here they come,' Godwin said. 'They're crossing over.'

'Blimey, that was quick.'

'No, they've been gone a long while.' Godwin turned round as the door closed.

'Nah, not them,' Richards said. 'Phyllis has done a disappearing act.'

*

Bishop was sitting by the window in the corner of the canteen. He was getting round-shouldered. Chance sometimes thought that life was measured not in seasons and anniversaries but in fresh pots of tea and empty cups. He unloaded his sticky bun and abandoned his tray on the next table.

'What kept you?'

'Got collared by Hayes on the way up. Wanted to know how we got on with Miss Aldridge.'

'You told him we're satisfied?' Bishop said.

'Yes, Miss Aldridge could hardly get a married couple and an elderly lady to cover for her. Besides Mrs Thompson brought them drinks while they were playing and saw her later, straight out of the bathroom.'

'Nice woman, a bit like the missus. Seemed to get on well with young Ivy. Rolled her eyes a bit about Miss A. Said she has 'one of her heads' when it suits her. She felt poorly on Friday morning apparently. That ties in with her expecting to face Warrender.' Bishop poured Chance a cup of tea as he spoke and placed it before him.

'Ta, so that's two dead ends today.'

'I never did think a respectable middle-aged lady could suddenly take a knife to someone.'

Chance stirred his tea slowly. 'You never know what people can do. My mother was the kindest woman imaginable. She'd take in stray kittens, sit up all night nursing a sick dog. Yet she'd think nothing of pouring a kettle of boiling water over an ant's nest. When I was a boy that used to bother me. I couldn't watch.'

Bishop shrugged. 'Everyone does it if they're coming in. Can't have them racing all round your larder.'

'Ah well, you grow up and you can watch a post-mortem without it meaning much.' Chance gazed out of the window at the grimy building across the street. 'Where do we go from here, Wilf?'

'We've found out why two witnesses lied and we know Warrender was a blackmailer. They usually acquire more than one secret. He was probably killed by another victim. Maybe we need to start again from scratch?'

'Who with? We've worked our socks off for a week. We've learnt a lot about Warrender and his unsavoury ways but we're no nearer finding out who killed him. We haven't found the weapon and we can't identify the woman with him in the bank. Maybe the Chief Constable should call in the Yard.'

'You don't mean that, Eddie. You're tired, eat your bun.'

'Through my gritted teeth?'

'A good night's sleep and you'll see things differently. The day's almost over. Go home and spend some time with your family.'

'That goes for you too.'

Bishop was looking frayed round the edges. He started the week sent out by Glad with his clothes pressed and his shoulders brushed. By Friday he was crumpled. His hair needed a wash. The mousy brushed-back wave became more corrugated with Julysia cream as the days went by.

The row of pens and pencils lengthened across his sagging breast-pocket.

Chance reached for his plate. 'Did Richards come up with anything useful?'

'He says not. He's reverted to being grumpy 'cause he reckons he wasted his time. I told him most police work leads to dead ends. They still have to be followed. Forget flashes of inspiration. It comes down to elimination and cross-checking. Hard spade-work.'

'Did no one there recall Warrender?' He spoke through a mouthful of bun.

'There's only one chap left who worked with him. According to Richards you couldn't shut him up about the old days but he wasn't pally with Warrender. Too much age difference. He'd forgotten all about him until his memory was jogged.'

'Half the time those garrulous old boys make things up. Tell you what you want to hear to keep the conversation going.'

'Apparently the post-master from those days is dead. One young woman died in an accident, another married and moved away. The men tended to be older of course. The young counter-clerks went off to fight and didn't come back. The old ones are long retired.'

'Another dead end then.'

'Well no one can say we aren't being thorough.'

'It's fish and chip night for us then Stella's going round a friend's. I'll have a good think about the case without distractions. I'm glad Fryer Tuck's is still going.'

'Best chip shop in town. I might see you in there.'

Chance shook his head. 'We send Vic or Daphne down for ours on their bikes.'

'I don't mind coming in on my day off, you know.'

'Wouldn't hear of it. I'll be at my desk early if not bright. I'll catch up with some routine stuff and clear the decks for Monday. Nothing's likely to happen over the week-end.

*

Lily Simmonds regretted that none of the others were walking her way. She didn't even know why she'd agreed in a weak moment to help with the church fund-raising. She might as well not have been there. In the end the other women had decided on a bring and buy as they often did. Except she did know why. The vicar's wife had approached her weeks ago and she wasn't very good at saying no to people.

There was another reason if she was honest with herself. Even sitting uncomfortably at a trestle table, ignored and clutching a cup of urn tea with dried milk globules floating on the surface was preferable to being alone.

They'd been supposed to finish by seven but the church clock was chiming the half-hour as she stood indecisively. It seemed to her that the streets took on an unfriendly feeling at night. Pulling her coat closer about herself, she felt reluctant to set off back to her empty house.

The others had finished calling good-night and cheerio and vanished in different directions. No one else seemed to be alone. St Luke's looked dark and forbidding, the weather-vane silhouetted against the faint moonlight. A street-lamp cast a feeble pool across the headstones nearest the wall.

At the end of the street The Bell was a haven of warmth and distraction. Red velvet curtains pulled against the night. If only she could go inside and have a conversation with someone who'd buy her a sherry, make her laugh and see her home. Some hope. Lightning didn't strike twice.

The lych-gate seemed sinister after dark, its pitched roof flanked by clipped yews. She could almost convince herself that a man stood motionless in the deepest shadows.

Just then someone did come out of the pub. He stood lighting a cigarette, turned her way. She watched the flare of the match and the tiny glow as he inhaled. Too far away to see his face, she still had the uneasy feeling he looked her up and down.

The light in the church hall went out. The man standing under the inn-sign began to move towards her. Suddenly she wanted to be safely indoors. Grasping her hand-bag she crossed the road and began the walk back to Pearl-street.

Nobody else was about. They would be enjoying themselves in the town's many pubs or at home with their families. For an instant she wondered what her husband and his fancy woman were doing.

In the summer there would be holiday-makers strolling about and a variety show on at the pier. A repertory company would have the summer season at the Alexandra theatre, she still thought of it as the Kursaal. In the run-up to Christmas they held concerts. These were the dead weeks in Tennysham. The panto was long over and the spring run of amateur dramatics and occasional talks not begun.

The dead weeks. In a few days she'd met someone, felt a spark between them and he'd gone. It was as though fate had held out a hand and shown her something lovely. Beckoned and smiled like a conjuror she'd seen last summer. The cloaked magician had held a ring he'd borrowed from a woman in the audience. He'd closed his hand and when he opened it again, it was empty.

In one of the gardens she was passing, a cat yowled, making her nearly jump out of her skin. The low vibrating became a high-pitched shriek. It was only two moggies fighting or something else. Though it sounded like someone being murdered.

The man was still behind her on the opposite pavement. She could hear his hollow footsteps as she neared the end of the High Street. It was Friday the thirteenth.

She mustn't be so daft. It wasn't as if it was late at night. These were the same streets so familiar in the morning when people were about their business. Roads lively with delivery boys, milkmen and postmen. Lads like the one from the baker's, who looked too small to hold up his heavy black bicycle with its basket of loaves.

Someone would be sweeping their path or doing a spot of gardening in their front. She gave a few bob to a chap in the next street to do hers. That was more expense because she couldn't say no. Other women would be cleaning their windows or scrubbing their step. When you lived alone it was comforting to think of the people in their homes all around you.

When she lay awake at night she quite liked to hear the small sounds made by her boarders. The snores coming from across the landing, a tread creaking along the passage, even the cistern gurgling in the small hours. They were all signs of another presence in the house. Even Mr. Freeman was better than nobody. She couldn't bring herself to think of him as Arnold, as he'd suggested.

Much as she wanted company, it had been a relief to see him leave. She didn't want to think too closely about why he'd stayed on. But at least he'd given her work to do and kept her from feeling scared. She'd never become accustomed to being alone and that was before there was a murderer on the streets.

That was why when Mum died, she'd decided to let some of the rooms she didn't need. It seemed an easier way to make a living than going out to work. She was a failure at that as well. No one was booked in before Monday. Other landladies were turning them away. Her money was only coming in fits and starts. She couldn't manage like this indefinitely.

The High Street was dim and shadowed. Some of the shops had shutters down and there was a grille across the jeweller's. The mannequins in Grove's windows would be creepy with their wigs and empty eyes. Further down was Frederic-street and the police-station. The windows would be lit and burly reassuring men inside.

The inspector had asked her to tell him if anything else came to mind about Leslie and last week. She had remembered something odd but it was really too trivial to tell. It can't have been the sort of thing he meant. But he had fixed his rather attractive hazel eyes on her and stressed *anything at all, no matter how small.*

That young police-woman had been pally. She'd had a capable manner and praised her for helping them. It would be nice if one of them came round for a cup of tea and a chat. Easier to mention something that might be daft in her own home.

Maybe they'd tell her something not in the papers, that they were about to arrest the murderer. She didn't believe it was anyone she'd met but she'd sleep easier when they had him. There was something the sergeant had said, about being careful when she let strangers into her home. That had made her nervous.

The street-lamp shone on the notice-board of the Methodist church, *Prepare To Meet Thy God.* All this time the man was still somewhere behind her. His footsteps kept following and he'd lessened the gap between them. She walked faster, wishing she hadn't worn heels.

The bare trees along the streets cast spindly shadows and every house had their curtains tightly drawn. A wind was getting up and a paper bag shifted along the gutter. If anything should happen, there was no one about to help her. The thought or the uneven brick pavement made her almost stumble, giving her ankle a nasty wrench.

A sliver of moon reappeared between the clouds and she risked a look behind. Her heart thudded. The pavements were empty. It had only been someone on his way home like her. He must have turned in his gate.

She was being very foolish. Nevertheless she moved away from the hedges and hobbled as fast as she could down the edge of the road. Nearly there now.

Again, she could have sworn she heard the scrape of a heel somewhere behind her. Then she rounded the corner and could see her house at last. She couldn't turn round again.

Opening her hand-bag she scrabbled for her latch-key. Her fingers fumbled at the lock, her insides somersaulted with relief as the door swung open.

Still in her hat and coat she toured the house switching on lights and drawing curtains. Upstairs she resisted an urge to look under the beds like a little girl. Then while she washed her face, she made up her mind.

Ten minutes later she wondered why she'd been so daft. She'd taken her tablets rather than risk lying awake half the night. It would soon be morning and Inspector Chance had been ever so sympathetic on Sunday.

She switched the fire on in her living-room. March was still a chilly month, especially in the evenings. Even when she had nobody in, she didn't care to sit in the lounge. It was kept ready for her guests and the front room still seemed the province of her mother. The breakfast-room had been repapered and turned into her cosy hidey-hole.

She was thinking of making a cup of tea when someone knocked on the door. As Lily Simmonds went in the hall she saw a blurred figure through the two dimpled glass panels. She licked her lips, conscious that they were now bare of colour. Her heart was beating faster but the chain was on. She was feeling much stronger now as she opened the door.

She relaxed as she recognised her caller.

'Hullo. This is a nice surprise.'

'I hope it isn't too late to call?'

'No, of course not. I'm glad of the company.'

'You're all alone tonight?'

'Yes, I've no one booked for a couple of days. Do come in out of the cold. I'll put the kettle on.'

Some unexpected company was just what the doctor ordered. Lily Simmonds smiled cheerfully as she slipped off the chain.

Eighteen

Red sky in morning, shepherd's warning, that was the old saying. Phyllis thought the sky looked ominous. She'd been lying awake since dawn and now she was leaning on her window-sill in her dressing-gown. The work-shop roof was below her and the privet screening the door of the outside toilet. The grass was soaked with dew and the old redcurrant bush heavy with pendulous pink buds. They seemed to have appeared almost overnight. She'd been missing a lot of things lately.

Dad had gone downstairs and she heard the sounds of him coughing as he filled the kettle. He liked the early morning quiet with a first cigarette as he sat finishing last night's paper. By the time she'd washed and joined him, he had a fresh pot of tea made and felt ready to begin the day.

People talked about a sinking heart. Hers felt like a stone in her chest as she reached the bottom of the stairs. At work, she knew she wouldn't be afraid of confrontation. She felt she could arrest the murderer without flinching, if needs be. This was harder.

They sat munching toast in an uncompanionable silence. If she left it too long, her father would finish and put his crumbs out for the robin. He was a good man. The bird-table he'd made was in view of the window, a half of coconut shell still hanging from Christmas.

'You're quiet this morning, love. Sleep well?'

It had to be now. Speak up or pretend she hadn't worked it out. She could say nothing. Her father would fetch his packet of corned beef sandwiches and say cheerio. She would change into her uniform and wheel her bike through the gate. They could both have an ordinary morning.

Phyllis put down her toast. The bread might as well be saw-dust. Her throat was contracting when she tried to swallow.

'Not really.' Deep breath. 'Dad.. what's in the shed?'

Silence while she watched a glistening blob of marmalade slide off his knife. The tap dripped and her father scraped back his chair.

'You know what's in there, I told you. Some stuff I'm storing for Stan.'

'While he's moving, you said. So has he moved yet? What's the problem?'

'Why all the questions? You're not at work now. Stan asked me to look after some things for him while he gets his new flat straight. He's had to find somewhere smaller. That's all there is to it.' Her dad remained with his back to her. 'That dratted thing. Needs a new washer.' He wrenched at the tap.

'What things, Dad?' There was no answer. She tried again. All she wanted now was reassurance. She felt like a child. 'Is it furniture, boxes?'

Frank Marden swung round. 'You've changed, you know? You really are a copper, poking your nose into everything.' His voice had a bitterness she'd never heard directed at her. 'They say they'd shop their own grandmother. Why can't you let things be? Isn't a man entitled to a bit of privacy in his own home?'

'Dad, please don't ..'

He spoke across her. 'It's a few boxes, all right? What do you want me to say?'

'Oh, Dad.' She pushed away her plate and took a mouthful of cooling tea. 'What have you done?'

'Nothing.' His voice was defeated now. That was worse. 'Next to nothing.'

'I want to believe you.'

Their eyes met. Her dad sighed and sank into his chair. 'Don't take on, love, please. I don't know exactly what's inside or want to. Electrical stuff, it's nothing dreadful. A mate of Stan's in London sold him some at a knock-down price. I don't know where he had them from. Stan asked if I'd like to make a few quid storing them for him. He's going to sell them on. That's all there is to it.'

Phyllis thought frantically. However much she'd moaned to herself about work, she couldn't bear to lose her job. Was it really going to be snatched away by the person she loved most in the world? It was so bloody unfair. She never swore aloud but this came close.

'Don't look so sad, love. I'm sorry if I've what d'you call it.. compromised you. You were never meant to know.'

She felt very tired. 'This is why you wanted me to leave the force. Would that make it right if I did?'

Her dad shook his head. 'No.' His hand struck the table, catching the edge of his plate. Making her flinch. 'Sorry. It's just frustration. I swear to you, Phyl, I've never done anything like this in my life before. Never so much as taken a sheet of paper from work. You know that.'

She nodded. 'I know, Dad. So why have you gone along with this now?'

'You're the detective.'

That bitter note again. He spread his hands in a helpless gesture. She'd never seen him look so low since her mum died. Leaning across the table, she put her hand over his.

'You're worried about work? Money?'

'Arthur's saying we might have to go on a short week if things don't pick up.'

'You said you had a big order?'

He grimaced. 'Not that big, I exaggerated. There's nothing else on the books except piffling jobs. I didn't want to turn down a lump of cash. I'm sorry, love. I've been that worried, I suppose I wasn't thinking straight. There didn't seem any harm in it. No one's said the stuff's fallen off the back of a lorry.'

Out of the back door of a factory more likely. 'We both know it must be.'

'What are you going to do?'

'What can I do? Nothing.'

She knew she should tell Inspector Forrest. That was her duty. That would also wave good-bye to her career. Anyway it was unthinkable that she report her dad.

'Get rid of it, Dad. It has to be out of here today.'

'I'll see to it, Phyl. Stan can take the lot away.'

'But Dad, please, he mustn't know it's anything to do with me. No one must ever know but us. I can't lose my job.'

'I'll tell him I'm worried you'll find out. He said it was only for a few days. That was..'

'Please, Dad, don't tell me anything. I've never seen the stuff so we can forget we ever had this conversation.' She gave him a worn-out smile.

'I've let you down.'

Phyllis summoned up the energy to refute his words. 'I hate to think of you being worried and bottling it up. I wish you'd talked to me.'

'It's not easy to talk about. You expect to provide for your children not go whining to them.'

'I've had the key of the door, Dad.'

He gave her a quick smile. Bit shaky. 'Sometimes I forget.'

'The important thing is to get this mess cleared up today.' She caught sight of the kitchen clock. 'Is that the time? We're both going to be late if we don't watch it.'

'The work-shop'll be empty by the time you get home. That's a promise. In fact I might as well take the whole damn thing down at the week-end. It's not as if I ever use it anymore.'

She couldn't be bothered to argue.

Her dad left soon after. As she quickly washed up and changed, Phyllis forced herself not to think. She felt numb.

Then she cycled steadily through the streets, exchanging good mornings to neighbours and the milkman. Sparrows were flitting in and out of hedges. There were hop-scotch squares chalked along the pavement and the sun was trying to come out. An ordinary morning except the only job she wanted would always feel tarnished now.

*

Feeling unusually virtuous, Eddie Chance scrawled his initials, tossed the last folder in his tray and dropped his pen on the desk. Yawning, he stretched his arms behind his head and fancied a change of scene. He'd cleared his backlog and been at his desk all morning, apart from wandering in Bob Forrest's office to check a query.

He hadn't so much as been to the canteen. One of his constables, newly back on duty and looking wan, had been dispatched to fetch him a sandwich. It hadn't been a great hardship to duck out of Stella's plans and he seemed to get a lot more done without Bishop to distract him. The truth was he'd half-expected the Chief Constable to appear at some point and didn't intend to be caught napping.

Someone knocked on the door. A not unwelcome diversion. He told them to come in.

'What is it, Constable?'

It was Phyllis holding a scrap of paper.

'Excuse me, sir. Sergeant Lelliott asked me to give you this message with his apologies.'

She was looking decidedly glum. In some ways she reminded him of his daughter. Though if Phyllis was sulking about his ticking-off, she didn't sound resentful.

'Why's that?'

'Mrs Simmonds telephoned last night, sir, just after eight o'clock. She wanted to speak to you if you were on duty or..' She hesitated, 'apparently she asked if I was here.

She must prefer to talk to someone she's met. She asked if you'd call round to see her today.'

He frowned. 'Has she remembered something? Why wasn't I told last night?' His voice was deliberately pleasant. It was obviously nothing to do with her. He knew he had a clipped manner, modelled on his superiors when he'd been starting out. Couldn't pull rank or collar villains without an air of authority.

'I couldn't say, sir. The note's only just been found. Someone took down the message and unfortunately it must have been swept off the desk.'

'Give it here.'

He scanned the paper. 'Says she'll be in all day. We'll give her a call. Don't go away.' Glancing at the digits he began to dial. 'Did you find it?'

Phyllis blushed. 'Yes, sir. It was on the floor under the counter.'

'Well spotted.' He listened to the tone. Funny how you get a feeling that it's ringing in an empty house. 'No answer. Maybe she's in the garden.'

He considered Phyllis, standing stiffly before the desk. Her face was pale, no sign of her usual good humour. Perhaps she was going down with the 'flu? Naylor had better not have come back flinging his germs around.

'Not going off duty, are you?'

'No, sir. I'm here all afternoon.'

'Tell you what, we'll see Mrs Simmonds together. She obviously took to you and you look as though you could do with some fresh air.'

Phyllis looked surprised. 'Thank you, sir.'

'Dig us out a car, will you? And better ask Sergeant Lelliott if he can spare you. I'll meet you in the yard.'

Chance sauntered outside a few minutes later. He hoped this would prove a breakthrough. The scrawled message indicated she had remembered something. The thought crossed his mind that she might intend to spin them a yarn just to get attention. No, he was doing her an injustice. Glancing at his wrist-watch he found it was gone two.

'Let's hope she hasn't given up on us and gone out,' he remarked to Phyllis. 'Hop in.'

'I'm sure she'll wait, sir. She could have been taking her washing in or talking to a neighbour.'

'Pearl-street, Naylor.' He sat back and thought of Superintendent Hayes wittering about wash-day. His waist-band was pressing against his middle. Outside the afternoon was soft and grey. The sky looked as though it might brighten in a while.

'Whereabouts shall I stop, sir?'

'You can drop us at the end of the terrace. We'll make our own way back.'

'Okey dokey, sir.'

'Quite well now, are you?'

'On the mend, thank you, sir.'

Chance grunted. 'Nice quiet week in bed, being waited on. We've all had to buzz about like the proverbial bluebottles.'

Naylor wisely said nothing. A placid detective-constable in his forties, he'd given them a smooth ride. Unlike Richards who still seemed to think he was bouncing an ambulance over the ruts to a field-station.

They stood outside Mrs Simmonds's house. The sign in the window said there were vacancies. Phyllis stood back for him to open the gate and go first. Chance tapped the door knocker and glanced over his shoulder.

'You can take notes if it's anything worthwhile.'

'Yes, sir.'

'We should get a cup of tea, I'm gasping.'

There were no sounds of anyone coming. He rapped again, louder.

'Women,' he muttered. 'Always keep you waiting.'

Phyllis waited at the bottom of the step. Turning round he saw a tired ghost of a smile. Something was definitely up there. Stooping, he rattled the letter-box. Nothing to see but the empty hall. No spare key on a string. He looked at the shallow porch. No flower pot. Two pints of milk standing by the wall. Not good.

'Let's try round the back,' he said casually. He led the way round to the side gate. It was bolted. 'We'll try the twitten.'

The narrow alley led between Mrs Simmonds's wall and the next end terrace. It met a path behind all the houses on that side and the gardens of properties in the next street.

Chance tried the first gate. It didn't shift. Something had to be done. 'Mind out. I'll take a look.'

Cursing inwardly, he scrambled up the wall. Breathing heavily, he straddled the top and gazed at the house. All the rear windows were shut and their curtains drawn.

He was out of condition. Maybe Stella was right. Still he didn't appreciate her saying it. It occurred to him that if he'd brought Godwin or any of the others, he'd have told them to climb over and his shoes would have remained unscuffed.

'Hang on, I'll let you in.'

Descent was easier with a dustbin nearby. He unbolted the gate. Phyllis looked round with interest. They were in a small, neat garden with a lawn and clothes-line. The only border was dug over and mounded like a grave. The only flowers were the creeping purple bells that seemed to cling in every crack in Sussex.

'It doesn't look good, does it, sir?'

'No, it doesn't.' He strode down the path with Phyllis just behind. No gaps in the curtains.

'Could she have been called away suddenly?'

'It's possible but unlikely I'd have thought.'

The house had all the appearance of being locked up and its owner gone. Stepping forward he tried the back door, then tested the give. It didn't. Too solid. No point in dislocating his shoulder. Especially not with an audience.

'One of the neighbours could have a spare key.' Phyllis said carefully.

'They could but I'd rather not involve them unless we have to.'

Chance went to the door of the coal-shed which did open, then the adjacent lav. No sign of her gardening tools nor any handy brick lying around. Sighing he removed his jacket and wrapped some of the material clumsily round his fist.

'Step well back.' He waited then smashed his fist through the window nearest the back door. 'Let's hope that doesn't bring the neighbours running.'

'Are you all right, sir?'

'Fine.' His hand hurt despite the padding but needs must. 'If Mrs Simmonds is lying down, I'll have some explaining to do.' Knocking out some jagged shards, he put his hand through to lift the catch.

He climbed through the window, flapping the curtain out of his way. An empty teapot on the draining-board made him freeze. Mrs Simmonds had breakfasted. Had he over-reacted and was about to face the most embarrassing moment of his career?

No one came. If she'd gone out at least he could explain without being caught in an undignified position. The house felt empty and something more than that. Conscious of Phyllis watching, he moved again. The glass in the sink crunched beneath his shoe and he banged his knee clambering to the floor.

An instant later Chance opened the back door. 'Stay here while I take a look around.'

She looked as though she'd like to protest then nodded.

As soon as he opened the other door, Chance saw an envelope against the skirting-board by the mat. The ominous feeling he'd had since he saw the drawn curtains enclosed him. The other doors were shut. Coming to a decision he hurried up the stairs. Knowing as he did so, it was too late to hurry.

Seven doors in all. Three were wide open, presumably to air. He knew the first was a letting bedroom, the one used by Leslie Warrender. A glance confirmed that the next two were also for paying guests and empty. So was the bathroom and second toilet.

Mrs Simmonds's room had the door left ajar. That was where he'd half-expected to find her. It was almost a shock to see only a nightdress-case lying on the bed. The final door turned out to be a linen cupboard. As he turned to descend, Phyllis called out.

'Inspector Chance..'

A strained note distorted her voice. He ran downstairs. She was standing by the open door of the room next to the kitchen.

'In there, sir. She's in there.' Her colour was wiped away.

'I told you to stay where you were.'

Chance stepped inside and halted. The room was dim with the curtains pulled. Mrs Simmonds was lying on a sofa. Turned slightly towards the fireplace, a cushion beneath her head, eyes shut and one arm hanging stiff towards the carpet. Her stillness was absolute.

He had no doubt she was dead.

Skirting the sofa, Chance moved to the window and flung back the curtains. He took in the scene from that angle, Mrs Simmonds's body looking as though she'd rolled towards him in her sleep. A cup and saucer on the low table, her slippers on the carpet. No sign of violence.

A tiny sound made him look up. A swallow of breath. Phyllis was in the doorway staring at the prone body.

'Don't touch anything,' he said automatically.

Chance moved over to the body and felt the arm. Not breakfast then. The limb was as solid as a gate-post. A small bottle, nearly empty stood by the cup and saucer.

He recognised the label. 'Veronal.'

'The poor woman.' Phyllis had stepped nearer, her hands behind her back. 'Why do you think she did it, sir?' She looked at him, biting her lip.

'Don't you find it queer? She wanted to see us and then this.' He gestured at the corpse.

'Maybe..' Her voice trailed away. Averting her eyes from the body she looked around the room.

'Go on, Constable, think. How does this strike you?'

'Well, it looks straightforward, sir. Mrs Simmonds took an overdose. Maybe she made up the message to get us round here to find her body?'

He considered the young woman. Her hair was disarranged where she'd dragged her fingers through it and there was a run in her stocking. Not her usual immaculate self, she looked badly shaken. No tears or hysterics though and trying to piece together what had happened. He admired her pluck. He wouldn't like his daughter to do this for a living.

'Doesn't hold water. If I'd been on duty I would have come round here directly she telephoned. She couldn't have been sure she'd be dead.' He wondered if he should send her back when the others came. 'There's a 'phone in the hall. Get on to the station and summon assistance. Tell the desk-sergeant it's a suspicious death. I want Godwin here with his kit.'

Her eyes widened. 'Not suicide, sir?'

'Suspicious death,' he said firmly.

While part of him was aware of Phyllis's low voice in the passage, Chance stood on the square of carpet thinking furiously. The room would soon be filled with activity. He wanted to muster his impressions before they were lost under trampling feet and Dr. Wheeler's gallows humour.

In other circumstances the room would have been cosy. The sofa sideways on to the gas fire with an arm-chair opposite. A small table with magazines and a wireless where she obviously sat, a standard lamp behind her head.

An old-fashioned cabinet displayed glass and china. They had a never disturbed look about them. He recalled her saying she'd inherited the house from her mother. A jug of spring flowers stood on a drop-leaf table by the window. They were horribly cheerful.

Chance glared at his reflection in the fan-shaped mirror over the fireplace. Bleary-eyed and fed up. He should have prevented this. No envelope on the mantelpiece. A favourite spot to leave a suicide note.

He tried the small bureau in the corner. Aware as he did so, he was acting out a part. Wasting time though it had to be done. The room put him in mind of a stage set. Like that wretched play Stella had dragged him to last year.

In the bar during the interval, she'd said he was ruining it for her with his fidgeting and exasperated sighs. He'd pointed out it was a right busman's holiday, even if the actor playing the detective hadn't been risible. They'd had words on the bus on their way home.

Using his handkerchief he managed to let down the flap after some fiddling. Women had the nails for these things. No letter addressed to him or the coroner.

Phyllis returned. 'They're on their way, sir. I suppose Mrs Simmonds lived in these two rooms at the back. There can't be any paying guests at the moment or they'd have found her.'

'The bedrooms aren't in use. We'll have to find out when Mr. Freeman left. Switch the vacancies sign, will you? We don't need anyone turning up on the doorstep.'

He stared at the scene round the fire. It wouldn't take long for the others to drive from Frederic-street and Sergeant Lelliott would have no trouble locating Wheeler on a dry Saturday afternoon. A solitary cup and saucer. She'd emptied the teapot. He'd nearly sent it flying as he climbed over the draining-board.

'That's done, sir.' Phyllis came to stand beside him, her back to the body. 'These flowers are new. Still in bud and they don't take long to open in water. Mrs Simmonds must have bought them yesterday. *"It's not easy for a woman on her own*." She said that to me on Sunday.'

'Her husband left her. He'll still be next of kin though.'

'Flowers are so hopeful. She can't have been planning to kill herself when she bought them.'

Chance followed her gaze. Perhaps Inspector Forrest was wrong and there was some merit in a woman's eye on things. He wouldn't have noticed. On the other hand she was young and it was all a bit much for her.

'D'you want to wait in the car when they get here? Or Naylor could drop you home if you like?'

She answered quickly. 'Thank you, sir but I'd rather stay if I can be of any use. If you don't mind. I'm all right, really.'

Chance nodded. 'If you're sure. Trot upstairs and see if there's a note lying around. Mrs Simmonds's bedroom is the one over this.'

At the door Phyllis paused and looked back. 'I see now what you meant on Monday. I didn't understand at the time. This really isn't a game, is it, sir?'

'No, Phyllis,' Chance said quietly. 'It isn't.'

Nineteen

That was the fourth time Wheeler had complained about being called off the golf course. Eddie Chance was contemplating murder himself. Preferably with a mashie niblick. He was counting the minutes until he could walk away when he heard a welcome voice in the hall.

'Joe tipped me off.' Bishop answered his unspoken question. His sergeant's expression hardened as he caught sight of the corpse. 'This is a bad business.'

'Thanks for giving up your day off.' *And stopping me saying something I wouldn't regret.* Chance knew that Bishop had taken in the situation at a glance.

'I've had most of it. Afternoon, Lionel.'

'I'm glad you didn't preface that with *Good.* It was very satisfactory until I was summoned here.'

'Ah well, that's what comes of being our valued police-surgeon,' Bishop said easily. His trilby in his hand, he studied the scene.

Chance watched him note the small bottle, glance at Godwin, concentrating on his camera and fasten on the body. Already she was no longer Mrs Simmonds.

'What have I missed?' Bishop addressed Wheeler.

The doctor straightened up. In his plus fours and hose he made an incongruous figure. 'As you see, obvious overdose. Straightforward enough. Though Chance here begs to differ.'

'I don't beg anyone,' he said. Godwin looked up at the edge in his voice.

Bishop flashed him a warning glance. 'It's quite a coincidence in the circumstances. This is where last week's victim was lodging.'

Dr. Wheeler shrugged. 'Happens from time to time. Silly women get their doses wrong. These patent medicines are nothing but trouble. I understand no note has been found.'

'If it is a suicide, they don't all leave them.'

'Come off it, Wilf. Women like their moment of drama, even if they won't be around to see the coroner read it out. In my experience, which is considerable, women always want to tell you what they think.'

Bishop leant round the doctor to see the bottle. 'Veronal, that's not on prescription, is it?'

'No but chemists warn people to stick to the dosage or they should do. Sold for sleeplessness of course and perfectly safe *but* with prolonged use it takes longer to work. It's not uncommon for sufferers to ignore the instructions. They increase their dose over a period of time and one day.. bingo, they cross the waters of Lethe. That's death to you. The sleep from which none return.'

Godwin came over to him. 'What about dabs, sir?'

Chance considered. A hopeless job in this house of boarders. If there had been someone, they would have taken care what they touched. He pictured a shadowy figure passing through open doors in the wake of Mrs Simmonds.

'Any signs of force used?' Bishop said.

'None. See for yourself, the wrists are unmarked.' Dr. Wheeler pushed up the jumper sleeves. 'No bruising around the mouth and jaw. I can't believe she was forced to take them.'

Bishop looked over at the table. 'What if they were put in her tea?'

'A murderer would have to hang around, wouldn't they? She'd slip into a coma first. Too much risk someone would return and save her.' Wheeler reached for his bag.

'Mr. Freeman had left, had he?'

'I assume so,' Chance said. 'The bedrooms are empty. He'll be one of the first we talk to.'

He resumed his thinking. No sign of a break-in. Well, only his. Yet they couldn't wear gloves all the time, not if she'd offered tea for instance. He realised Godwin was still waiting.

'Come in the kitchen a moment.'

Bishop and Wheeler were still chewing over the possibilities as he walked out.

Chance indicated the teapot. 'Do you think you can get any prints off that? It's dry.'

'I'll try, sir.' Godwin placed his case on a cupboard.

'Right, I'll leave you to it.'

Giving a lingering look at the back door he'd unlocked, Chance reluctantly returned to the other room.

'Is Phyllis still with you?' Bishop said.

'I sent her and Naylor to speak to the next-door neighbours.'

'I've done all I can here,' Wheeler said. 'Hardly worth interrupting my game.'

Chance raised his eyes to the ceiling. 'She was a human being. Not one of your patients, I suppose?'

'Never seen her before the inquest, old chap. Struck me then as a nervy type.'

Bishop nodded. 'Mind you, we only saw her when she was under a strain.'

'Let me see,' Wheeler pursed his lips. 'Tomorrow's Sunday. No great rush this time. I can do her Monday morning after surgery. It'll mean making my rounds late.'

'If that's your best offer,' Chance said. He couldn't push for sooner.

'It is. I'll bid you both good afternoon then, what's left of it.'

Dr. Wheeler stepped towards him. Chance, who happened to be blocking the doorway, stayed put.

'Hang on. What about time of death?'

Wheeler indicated the gas fire. 'Was that off when you arrived?'

'It was.'

'Rigor is well on the way to fully advanced. I don't need to tell you what that means?' He looked from one to the other, like a professor lecturing medical students.

'We're with you so far,' Bishop said obligingly.

He told them anyway. 'Maximum twenty-four hours after death, give or take. Sometime last evening. You can see by her clothes she hadn't retired.'

'Any help gratefully received,' Bishop said. 'We know you'll narrow it down when you've seen the stomach contents. I'll see you out, Lionel.'

'Sir?' Godwin stuck his head round the door and came in. 'Sorry, no can do. The lady washed up her teapot.'

Chance frowned. 'Someone did.'

There was the sound of voices by the front door, then Bishop returned.

'The undertaker's men are outside when you're ready, sir and the others are back.'

'They can take the body away. Can you see to them? Then could you see if you can find an address book or something for next of kin? It looks like she kept her papers in that bureau. Have a hunt for a will while you're at it.'

'Leave it to me. There was a husband, wasn't there? She'll have kept her marriage lines.'

'The kitchen window's bust.'

'I know someone. Consider it seen to.'

'Glad's a lucky woman. I'll take the others in the dining-room. You too, Godwin.'

He'd only had time to glance in there and check it held no more nasty surprises. The room was as immaculate as the rest of the house though of necessity, it looked unlike a private home. There were three small tables and a long modern sideboard. A painting of the sea with an improbably gold sunset hung over the fireplace.

Chance tried to imagine the room with Leslie Warrender at one of the tables. Perhaps the one by the window, overlooking the path along the side of the house? Mr. Freeman over by the wall and a whiff of bacon in the air. Mrs Simmonds bustling in with breakfast, telling them to be careful as the plates were hot. She'd never do that again.

Leaning against the edge of a table, he raised an eyebrow at Naylor. Phyllis stood next to Godwin who gave her a concerned look.

'What have you got?'

'Lady next door here,' Naylor gestured at the wall, 'saw the deceased at approximately five thirty pee em, while she was getting her cat in for his tea. The deceased left her premises and was seen walking in an easterly direction towards Millais Road.'

'All right, Naylor, you aren't in court now. I told you the victim's name.'

'Mrs Simmonds, sir.'

'Well, man. Did they speak?'

'Not on this occasion, er, no, sir. Mrs Simmonds was already just past here on the opposite pavement. She knew where she was off to, though.'

'She's the cat's mother,' Chance muttered. 'So where was Mrs Simmonds going?'

'To a meeting at St Luke's church hall, sir. Mrs Simmonds mentioned it to Mrs Ryan, that's the neighbour, in the week.'

'That's something. Did this Mrs Ryan see her return or anyone else about?'

'No, sir. We asked her husband as well. They drew their curtains at dusk and settled down for the evening.'

'Pity. They didn't hear a caller or anything untoward?'

Naylor shook his head. 'They're solid houses, these.'

'What about the other side?'

'A Mr. Packham, old chap, sir. Didn't see a thing and he's further away.'

Chance pulled a face. There was the width of the twitten and the next terrace was turned at a slight angle. The wretched trees didn't help with obscuring viewpoints even though they weren't leafy. It would have been dark as well.

As if she could follow his thoughts, Phyllis spoke quietly. 'The house right opposite is empty, sir.'

So it was. A useful place for someone to wait in the shadows. Though someone waiting to be sure the street was empty could linger in the entrance to the twitten. You could use them as a back way across many of the older parts of Tennysham. Duck into one of the dirt paths and emerge on the sea-front or several streets away with little risk of being seen.

Heavy footsteps sounded in the passage, followed by Bishop's voice at the front door. They waited in silence as the body was loaded in the plain van and driven off to the mortuary.

*

'Quite a place, sir,' Naylor said as he drew up. 'Do you think it's all right to leave the car here?'

'Why not? I'm not hunting for the tradesmen's entrance. Stay put. I don't expect to be too long.'

As Chance slammed the car door, a flurry of rooks rose cawing into the tall trees of a nearby copse. The house sat at the foot of the downs. Their steep, bare slopes made a rounded back-bone across Sussex, the soft green turf holding the chalk.

He gave a quick assessing glance as he walked to the entrance. He'd been to the Chief Constable's home once before, when his transfer had come through. On his previous visit in autumn the old place had been plastered with crimson leaves.

In March the façade was covered in a skeletal tracing of grey twigs and tiny red knobs. In the early evening it resembled the veins on an old drinker's face. Lamplight glowed from several windows. The door opened silently before he could ring and the colonel's manservant showed him in.

'If you'd like to wait in here, sir, Colonel Vesey will be down directly. He instructed me to offer you a drink.'

'Thanks very much.' He could do with one. Chance inspected the decanters indicated on the butler's tray. He opened his mouth to speak.

'Might I suggest a small Scotch whisky, sir?'

'Fine.' He wondered if Superintendent Hayes had been offered a large one.

The man handed him a meagre glass. His deft movements were like a dumb-show, the firelight reflecting on his smooth pink face.

Left alone, Chance wandered over to the hearth-rug and read an invitation on the mantelpiece. Eyed the stuffed fish in the glass case. They were burning logs, sparking and scented of apples. Very nice if you had a gardener to chop them and cart them indoors.

He sipped and the fiery liquid warmed his mouth. Blended. He didn't rate a decent malt then. Not even at Christmas.

There hadn't been time to pop home. Even if the morning felt like a lifetime ago. Phyllis had taken his jacket and picked the specks of glass off his sleeve. Stella would cluck her tongue behind her teeth when she saw the state of him. He rubbed his scuffed toe-caps on his trousers. That would have to do.

There was a scrabble of noise beyond the door. An excited yapping quelled by a male voice. The door opened and the Chief Constable came in. He was dressed for dinner.

'Good evening, Chance. Sorry to keep you. That infernal din belongs to my wife's Sealyham. Knows we're off out. Been looked after, I trust?'

'Yes, thank you, sir.'

'Good of you to come out here after a long day.'

'That's perfectly all right, sir.' His thoughts exactly.

'Cigarette?' Vesey proffered the box on his desk.

'Thank you.'

'Do sit down.' He gestured to the wing-back chairs on either side of the fire.

Chance inhaled the fine tobacco appreciatively and sat back against the firm leather. Sullivans. That was more like it.

'Pins still a bit dicey,' his host said. 'Prefer not to be going out tonight. Still, needs must, long-standing arrangement. Unfortunately means I can't spare long.'

'I'm glad to hear you're on the mend, Colonel.'

'Dashed inconvenient. Try not to get it, Chance. We don't want you laid up. You're two men short, I hear?'

'One's just returned to duty, sir and I have a constable on loan from Inspector Forrest.'

'What do you make of this new death?'

'Dr. Wheeler thinks it likely that Mrs Simmonds took an accidental overdose.'

'But you disagree?'

Chance blinked in surprise. A pair of faded blue eyes, red-rimmed, regarded him shrewdly.

'Too much the coincidence, what?' The Chief Constable waved his cigarette in emphasis.

'My feelings exactly, sir.'

'Your nose says it doesn't smell right, eh? A useful attribute in your business.'

Chance tried to look modest.

'For instance, Superintendent Hayes tells me you're reluctant to charge the victim's brother-in-law?'

'I don't believe he's our man, sir.'

'I've cast an eye over the statements. One could build a case but all hypothetical. You're thinking it's a house of cards?'

'At the moment, sir. I haven't written off Ronald Lynch entirely but..'

'D'you fish, Chance?' Vesey interrupted suddenly.

'I don't, no.'

'Pity. If you did, you'd say you're casting about for a more likely prospect?'

'Yes, that's it, Colonel.'

The Chief Constable snorted and produced a handkerchief. Chance tactfully looked away as he cleared his throat. His surroundings were pleasantly masculine. The only way he'd ever get a study was if the pools came up and he'd been doing them since they started. He imagined that rooms in a decent London club were something like this.

'That's better. Shouldn't really have these things.' The handkerchief was stuffed away. Vesey took a last drag and threw his half-smoked fag in the fire.

'When's the post-mortem?'

'First thing Monday, sir and the inquest's the day after.'

'We shall soon see if you're right. Next of kin been informed?'

'In hand, sir. The lady was separated from her husband. He's living in Eastbourne. Sergeant Bishop tracked him down and the local chaps are contacting him.'

'Good man, Bishop. N.C.O.s are the most valuable chaps in the army.'

'He's a first-class detective. I'm lucky to have him.'

The Chief Constable nodded approvingly. 'I like to see loyalty. Always look after your men. Brings me neatly to my next point. Reason I brought you out here is to be sure you're coping, Chance. First time in charge and all that. We've every faith in you. Wouldn't have been appointed otherwise but it seems a devil of a case. I expect you to say if it's time to send for outside help. Speak up, man.'

Chance set down his empty glass. He'd been pretending to sip, not wanting to look like a lush.

'This is a tough case. You'll know if you've seen the reports that we've had no obvious suspect. But with respect, I don't believe we need to call in the Yard, sir. We should await the result of the post-mortem at least.'

Vesey watched his face as he spoke. Brushed an invisible speck off his crossed leg. He was a distinguished-looking old cove, Chance thought. Well over six foot, receding hair immaculately barbered.

'I agree. It seems to me you and your men have conducted a thorough investigation. Not your fault if it's a tricky one. You don't feel the need of a fresh eye and so forth?'

'Not yet, sir. My team have worked hard. I think we're perfectly capable of solving this case in Sussex.'

'We'd all like that. I sometimes think county forces are too quick to admit defeat and invite Scotland Yard in. However..' Vesey held up a hand to forestall any comment. 'Reluctantly it might come to that. There are other matters to be taken into account. The local press are making noises, they may stir up the nationals. We're only three weeks away from Easter. Concerns have already been raised about the effect on the tourist season, you get my drift?'

'I do, sir.'

'Nil desperandum, Chance. I understand you don't want your first command snatched away. You've done all the spade work, don't want some johnnys from London taking all the glory? I feel the same. Remind me, when is the inquest reconvened?'

'The twenty-third, sir. Tuesday week.'

'Until then, don't you think? Or rather the day before. If we're no further forward, you'll inform the coroner we've requested assistance from the Yard.'

Chance agreed that he would.

'Splendid. I've every confidence it won't come to that.'

It felt like a stay of execution.

Twenty

He'd lived all his life by the sea, Chance thought idly, yet he couldn't swim. It was said many sailors couldn't. Certainly that had been true in his brother's case. In the end it wouldn't have made any difference. The tide was on the turn. He gazed beyond the dirty line of seaweed and washed-up gash thrown overboard from ships in the Channel.

People walked along the prom all year round at Tennysham. Dog walkers like the Dawsons, they were just off to see. Young couples seeking a bit more freedom than the streets, old couples well wrapped up, families and loners.

A family were down on the shore. Three generations, parents swinging a little kid between their hands, the grandmother walking gingerly backwards, beaming encouragement. Behind him a woman plodded, pushing an old chap in a wheeled chair. In the distance a boy was flying a red kite.

'Sorry about that.'

Bishop was at his elbow. After a cup of tea at Henry's, they'd stopped at the tobacconist where Bishop had been waylaid by a pal of his. Chance had wandered over to the sea-front to wait. The word 'rate-payers' had been enough to make him disappear smartly.

'I was looking at the people. D'you think the shelter will always be avoided by courting couples and old folk?'

Bishop grunted sarcastically. 'You should know better of people. Locals might not fancy it for a while but holiday-makers will be queuing up to see where it happened. Posing for snapshots I shouldn't wonder. Anyway,' he gestured with his pipe, 'you said they're supposed to be tarting up the prom.'

Chance looked back at the rusting ironwork. It was typical of Tennysham that much of the best sand was under the pier. He examined a cigarette card. 'I smoke too much.'

'I know that,' Bishop said.

Church bells were ringing through the town as they made their way to Pearl-street.

'I wonder if Mrs Simmonds made a will?' Chance said.

'I didn't come across one. She kept everything very neat in her bureau.'

'It's a big windfall for the husband if she didn't. And he's free to remarry.'

'If there has been any funny business, at least we know he's in the clear.'

'An ankle in plaster is a good alibi, I grant you. Almost too good. I suppose he isn't faking it?'

Bishop smiled. 'You've a suspicious nature. He gave the Eastbourne lads chapter and verse. Slipped on a patch of oil at work apparently. Came down an iron staircase. Easy enough to check with the hospital. His fancy-piece swears he hasn't left the house in four days.'

'I'll be glad to hear what the post-mortem says. It feels like we're in limbo 'til tomorrow. The Dawsons live along here.'

There was no reply to their knock and Chance felt an unpleasant sense of *déjà vu*.

'We'll have to call back.' He followed Bishop out of the gate and glanced along the street before turning away. 'Hold on, there they are.'

The granddaughter was in front with the small white dog panting on the leash. Herbert Dawson and his wife followed behind, a newspaper under his arm. Chance watched as they recognised him and exchanged a word. Mrs Dawson looked apprehensive. They caught up with their granddaughter and greeted him soberly. Bishop raised his hat as Chance introduced him.

'We've heard, Inspector,' Dawson said quietly.

'That didn't take long.' Chance felt no surprise.

'Mr. Packham knocked and told us last night. I don't know what the world's coming to. It's one shock after another lately.'

'Won't you both come in?' Mrs Dawson said.

'No, thanks. We only want a quick word.'

'Joan, take Tessie in for a drink, will you?'

Stooping, the girl unclipped the leash. The dog sniffed Bishop's fingers and gave her tail a perfunctory wag before ambling through the gate.

'She's tired out,' Joan said. She hesitated, looking at them both. 'Is it about Mrs Simmonds? I spoke to her on Wednesday.'

'You never said?' Mrs Dawson sounded fretful.

Chance wondered if the poor kid had any life.

'I mentioned it to Granddad. She stopped me in the street on my way home.'

'We mustn't keep the gentlemen. They don't want to hear this.'

'I would like to,' Chance said.

The young girl tugged her plait over her shoulder. 'She asked the sort of thing all adults say. How I was getting on at school and how old Tessie is now. She said you could set your watch by Granddad when he takes her for a walk and she talked about the weather. That's all really.'

'I see.' Chance gave her a friendly nod.

'Run along now, dear.'

'All right, Gran. In we go, Tess.' Joan gently ushered the dog over the doorstep.

'How old's the young lady?' Bishop said when she'd gone.

'Twelve,' Mrs Dawson turned to him. 'She has a vivid imagination. I don't want her having nightmares.'

Mr. Dawson glanced impatiently at his wife. 'What did you want to ask us, Inspector?'

'Did either of you see Mrs Simmonds since I saw you on Thursday?'

He shook his head. 'No, the last time we saw her was at the inquest.'

'So you wouldn't happen to know when Mr. Freeman left?'

Mrs Dawson looked up at him. 'Friday morning. At least he went past here carrying a suitcase. I assumed he was off back to where he came from.'

'What time was this?'

'Not long after nine. I was going shopping. He crossed over and went down Battle-road.'

Chance and Bishop exchanged glances. Battle-road was the main thoroughfare that led from the railway station to the sea-front.

'Did you speak at all?'

'No, I was some yards behind him.'

'Did you walk your dog past Mrs Simmonds's house on Friday night, Mr. Dawson?'

'Yes, we always wander down that way.'

'What time was that?'

'Half-past eight, same as usual. We don't stay out long.'

'Did you see anyone about?'

Mr. Dawson shook his head. 'No one. It's very quiet round here. I sometimes see a fellow dog-walker.'

'Thank you. We won't take up any more of your time.' He was already turning away when she spoke urgently.

'Inspector Chance, please will you tell us what happened? We don't know how Lily died.'

'What did your neighbour tell you?'

'That the policeman said she'd been found dead indoors. That's all he knew.'

'All right, Olive.' Mr. Dawson touched his wife's arm. 'Inspector Chance may not wish to discuss it.' He looked half-apologetically at him.

'There's little I can add. We don't yet know the cause. I found Mrs Simmonds's body. She was lying on her sofa as if she'd fallen asleep.'

Mrs Dawson was too pale. 'What a relief. She wasn't attacked like the man we saw?'

Chance didn't answer.

'Best not to go dwelling on it,' Bishop said. 'She looked peaceful, love.'

'She was forty-eight. That's all.'

'It's no age, very sad.' Bishop exuded grave sympathy like an undertaker. 'Would you know if Mrs Simmonds ever took something to help her sleep?'

Mrs Dawson gasped. 'She did, ever since she lost her mother. She often complained of trouble getting off, especially when she was alone in the house.'

'She lived on her nerves,' Mr. Dawson said. His eyes met Chance's. 'Let's get you inside, Olive.' He began to lead his wife in much the same way as Joan had encouraged Tessie. 'Thank you for telling us, Inspector. Sergeant.'

'Cheerio, sir. Mind how you go, Mrs Dawson.' Bishop shut their gate after them as they went inside.

They set off down the street. A motorcycle-combination broke the silence with a great din.

'They seem a decent sort.'

Chance grunted. 'Over-protective. It's hard lines on the girl, their being so much older.'

'It must have been a lot to take on in their fifties. Hardly surprising to lose a son-in-law, what with the war but a daughter too. That was bad luck. Do you think the kid was posthumous?'

'Possibly. They had a photograph on the mantelpiece of the father in uniform.' Chance had spoken without thinking. He glanced sideways at Bishop as they stopped outside Mrs Simmonds's house.

'We've got one of these.' Bishop picked at a dead leaf on the bush beside the gate, his voice neutral. 'Syringa, strong scent. Shouldn't have been put there, they get quite a size. Ours is out the back.' He looked up, tight-faced. 'Don't you think there's something bloody awful about a person dying and everything going on just the same?' He waved an arm at the bush as he followed Chance inside. 'I mean, that will still come out but Lily Simmonds won't ever see it again. I bet she stopped to smell it umpteen times every summer.'

'Suppose so,' Chance muttered uncomfortably. He thought to himself that she might have loathed it for all they knew.

'The food she'd planned to eat today will be sitting in the larder. The clocks don't even need winding yet.'

'It's the way things are, Wilf.'

Bishop sighed. 'I know, I know. But it makes you wonder what it's all *for*?'

He trudged after Chance who opened the door of the room where Mrs Simmonds died.

'What are we doing back here anyway?'

'Just looking,' Chance said vaguely. He swung round and smiled at Bishop. 'I'm hoping I'll know what for when I see it.'

'You're still convinced she was done in, aren't you?'

'I'd like to know why she 'phoned Frederic Street.'

'Wheeler's sure it was accidental but I did wonder if she'd taken too many on purpose? It could have been coming on for a long while, then Warrender dying makes her feel like giving up? Husband walked out on her, she's lonely, sleeps badly, finds life a struggle. We don't know anything about her, like who did she lose in the war? She might have been grieving ever since.'

Chance shook his head. 'She struck me more as the soldiering-on type when she came to us. Phyllis thought so too. See these flowers? She reckoned they'd been bought on Friday. The question is did Mrs Simmonds buy them?'

Bishop rubbed his jaw. 'You think she was murdered and whoever did it brought the flowers? What, as an excuse for calling?'

'I don't know. I'd have missed them but for Phyllis.'

'I know you can barely tell a rose from a pansy. It is a dirty great coincidence, first the lodger's killed, then the land-lady dies.'

'I don't believe in 'em, Wilf. Two women wearing the same party frock is a coincidence. Not something like this.'

Chance watched Bishop as he produced his battered leather tobacco pouch.

'Why not have that outside? I'll only be a few minutes poking about, then we can get back.'

'Suit yourself.' The gingery tweed of Bishop's jacket matched the mixture he was running through his fingers.

He didn't know what he was looking for.

For the second time in two days Chance stood in the middle of the room and concentrated. Mrs Simmonds had come home from her meeting at the church hall. Easy enough to check she'd been there and when it had finished. They had the time logged when she rang the station.

She made a pot of tea and afterwards she washed up the teapot. Why do that but leave the cup in the sitting-room? If she was like his wife, Stella fussed about missing anything when she washed up. Not all women were the same but you only had to look around to see Mrs Simmonds was the house-proud sort. Her home was her livelihood.

Scenarios chased round Chance's head. All right, if she did take her own life, she wouldn't have been worrying about housework. In that case why wash up the teapot? Could have been habit or instinct to leave everything tidy?

Having played devil's advocate, he allowed himself to consider what was left. Had someone else been there with her and emptied the pot to hide their presence?

Removing his hands from his pockets, Chance went in the kitchen. The pong of fresh putty lingered round the newly glazed window. You'd never know he'd been there. Had anyone else left any trace behind?

He had some hazy notion that the amount of tea leaves would have been a give-away. *A spoonful per person and one for the pot*. Hardly something you could put before a jury though. He imagined a procession of witnesses all swearing that Mrs Simmonds liked a strong cuppa.

The kettle sat on the hob. His eyes ranged over the things on the cupboard nearest the stove. An enamel bread-bin, a sugar bowl on a tea-tray. A box of matches in a wooden holder, a twee souvenir from the Isle of Wight. You could see the island from further along the Sussex coast. Tennysham was too far east.

Using his pencil he prised open the cupboard door. Breakfast things, several jars to suit varying tastes. She'd looked after her guests. Marmalade of course, a jar getting low with a new one next to it. A couple of jams, all with hand-written labels, no sign of gooseberry. Honey provided as well, mustard, salt and pepper.

The china he was looking for was in the next cupboard. Cups were stacked on their side, in threes on their saucers. At the end of the row one cup was sideways on its saucer. In front a single pair were placed with the cup upright. Did that mean anything? He might as well be playing the children's game, *getting colder* not warmer. *Do you give up?* Blowed if he would.

Chance straightened up abruptly. There was a teaspoon in the sugar bowl. His mother-in-law's querulous voice last Sunday came back to him. Irene had been complaining to Stella about the many shortcomings of his sex. Probably his in particular as she'd moaned about him taking more sugar with his wet teaspoon. *Would it hurt him to use the sugar spoon?* Of course when you went round Lady Muck's, she had sugar lumps and tongs.

Later that same afternoon they'd met Mrs Simmonds. Bishop had handed her a cup of sweet tea for shock and she'd made a face when she sipped it. He could picture her cup when she'd left, still nearly full. But when he'd arrived, her cup was empty. She'd placed her clean spoon on the tray. She didn't take sugar.

He went outside. Bishop was at the end of the garden. He gestured at the gate as Chance joined him.

'This was definitely bolted and the door secured when you broke in?'

'Yes, she'd locked up for the night.'

'So if there was someone else, they left by the front door.'

'There was someone here.' Chance told him what he'd found. 'I'm sure of it. I want Godwin back to fingerprint the cupboard door handles.'

'It would be demolished in court,' Bishop said. 'Defence counsel would say Mrs Simmonds always kept a spoon in the bowl or it was left from when Mr. Freeman was here.'

'What about the cup? I tell you she had a dozen. Nine stacked on their side in threes on three saucers. One set next to them, sideways on its saucer like the others. Mrs Simmonds was using a cup and saucer. And the last one right at the front sitting up.

'You can't build a case on a teaspoon and an upright cup.'

'I know,' Chance said impatiently, 'but they're indications. People always leave a trace of their presence if you can find it.' He pointed to the two spent matches near Bishop's feet.

They went inside in silence. In the hall Bishop leafed through the visitor's book on the telephone table.

'Phyllis has been through it. No customers since Warrender. A name's pencilled in for Tuesday with a question mark. No way of getting in touch.'

'There you are,' Bishop said. 'Trade was slack. I see Freeman didn't leave an entry. I suppose by the time he left he reckoned he was a family friend.'

Chance entered the guest lounge. He didn't know why he was still reluctant to leave. The air already seemed stale. In the window the geranium smelt musty and there was a dead fly. Arnold Freeman had been sitting in that chair a week ago when they'd walked in.

And suddenly Chance remembered.

Twenty-one

'Ah, I was about to telephone you. Give me one moment then I've something to show you.'

Dr. Wheeler's voice was positively pleasant. Chance raised an eyebrow as he stepped further into the mortuary. The remnants of what had, before the weekend, been a living seaside land-lady lay on the table beneath a green sheet. The body of Mrs Simmonds was draped in much the same way as a dust-sheet over furniture in a shut-up house.

Her face looked shrunken and the outline beneath the covering appeared slight. He'd noticed before that the dead seemed deflated. Letting the air out had the same effect as on a rubber tyre. Even without Wheeler and his assistant removing God knows what.

The dead feet sticking out held the shape of pointed shoes. Her huddled toes curled under and one of them had a dried corn. If you'd ever seen trench foot they were perfect.

Jacobs, after glancing at him, had carried on holding out a kidney-shaped bowl of something unmentionable. He was like a waiter proffering a vegetable dish for the customer's approval. The doctor was probing the contents with tweezers. It had started out as a meal. Chance's own stomach didn't flinch.

'I was passing so I thought I'd stick my head in,' he lied.

Wheeler gave him a look over his half-moon spectacles but let it go. 'It seems I've done you an injustice,' he said.

'Oh yes?'

'Take it away.' The mortuary assistant was dismissed without looking. 'You can finish up in a minute.'

Trot off back to the kitchen, Chance thought, as Jacobs wheeled his trolley through the swing doors. So there's no audience. He waited while Wheeler unpeeled his surgical gloves, clearly in no hurry to continue.

'She was murdered, Eddie.'

He knew it.

Eddie eh? All pally colleagues together. He was prepared to be magnanimous in the circumstances.

'Was she, by Jove? Go on,' he paused, 'Lionel.'

'It appears the victim was suffocated. No way of telling from a quick look at the scene.'

'Of course not.' Mustn't forget, Chance sobered inwardly as Wheeler shifted and he caught sight of the face again. A woman lay dead.

'What did you find?'

'Come over here.'

Chance followed Wheeler to the long counter above the line of cupboards. On the other side of the wall Jacobs could be heard running a tap.

'Take a look at this.' The doctor gestured with the side of his stained finger-nail.

He peered in the small dish. A tiny thread of powder-blue. Chance straightened up. 'Where did it come from?'

'I'll show you.' Wheeler returned to the dissection table. Switching on an angle lamp, he directed it across the face. He opened the mouth.

'It was caught between these two. I had to tease it out with tweezers. Same stuff as the cushion beneath her head.' He studied the wall. 'You were right all along.'

'Just a hunch.' Professional satisfaction sat uneasily with a woman's murder.

Wheeler closed the mouth. 'No bruising to be seen, see? I looked at the scene. That indicates the victim didn't struggle. Probably didn't have time. The cushion would have been held against the whole face, even pressure. No finger-marks. It would have been over very quickly.'

'What about the veronal? Did she even take it herself, I wonder? Assuming she took some as soon as she came home, would it have taken effect, d'you think?'

The little doctor pursed his lips. 'We won't know the amount until I get the results back. I'll see they get priority now. If she ingested a large dose, she would have felt sleepy soon after. Were you attending when I explained all this to Bishop?'

Chance nodded. 'People up their dose to make it work faster.'

'It wouldn't have mattered if she was taken by surprise. Someone wanted her dead.'

'Would it have taken much strength?'

Wheeler shrugged. 'Not if the killer stood over her. A woman could have done it as easily as a man.'

'Regarding the first victim, I hope to have a knife for you soon. Identical to the one used. It's a paper-knife about so long.' Chance held out his hands and described the knife Arnold Freeman had been using to peel his apple.

*

Bishop was replacing a file when he entered his office. Sunlight was streaming through the window. Outside in the Monday morning streets it was a good day to be alive. Chance lobbed his hat at the stand and missed.

'Morning. I've been up at the hospital.' Perching on his desk, he brought his sergeant up to date.

'Suffocated?' Bishop's voice rose in the air.

'I knew it, Wilf, when Godwin said there were no prints on the cupboard handles.'

'So we've a second murder on our hands.'

'I've never seen Wheeler so polite. I could have been one of his paying patients. Presumably he does lay off the point-scoring with them.'

'Lionel's all right underneath. Let's get down to business. We need the time of death. Stomach contents?'

'Had a private view of those. Good job I didn't bring Godwin. Digested three to four hours before death. An egg sandwich or egg on toast, sort of thing.'

Bishop leant against the cabinet. 'The neighbour saw her leave about half-past five. She has a high tea, finished say half an hour before, give her time to clear away. Around half past four?'

'Sounds right. Something to fortify herself for the meeting. Then she 'phoned the station just gone eight. That gives us, from what Wheeler said, dead by half-past eight, quarter to nine-ish.'

'Then the murderer had to get back to where they came from. Anyone with an alibi from about eight o'clock to ten is in the clear.'

Chance sighed. 'Which means everyone we've spoken to will have been alone.'

'We'll see. I haven't been idle myself. We're interviewing Mr. Freeman late this afternoon at his home.'

'You managed to get hold of him? Well done.'

'I rang his place of business and fortunately he was in the office. First morning back, he could have been off on the road again. That would have been the devil of a job to track him down if his firm don't know where he stays. He's leaving work early to see us. His manager didn't seem pleased at the prospect of giving him more time off.'

'That's his problem.' Angling his head, Chance glanced at some papers newly appeared in his in-tray. They looked deadly dull. 'You didn't tell him why we want to see him?'

'He asked of course but I fobbed him off.'

Chance scribbled his initials and slapped the figures back in the other basket. 'Good. Let's see his face when we tell him. What about the paper-knives?'

Bishop grimaced. 'They hand them out to their customers as a free gift come advertising gimmick. So in theory lots of people could get hold of one.'

'It's quite likely Mr. Freeman presented Mrs Simmonds with one. I do think one of those was the weapon.'

'They're sending us a sample. The manager's horrified. Naturally I didn't go into detail but he reads the papers. I emphasised he should keep it to himself. He passed me to his secretary for a complete list of firms they supply. Luckily they're all in the south-east.'

'We're only interested in anyone who's come up in connection with Warrender. I suppose we can rule out the club where Sadie Price works? Shouldn't think they need stationery.'

'It's all firms and stationers'. There is one interesting name.'

'Let's have it.'

'Nugent's supply the company Ronald Lynch works for.'

'Do they indeed? You dealt with his local station. Can you get someone to see him and check where he was on Friday night?'

'Will do.' Bishop jotted it down. 'He'll most likely say he was indoors with his missus.' He raised his eyes. 'Which will leave us nowhere.'

Chance grunted. They both knew a wife's evidence was worse than useless. 'How are we getting to.. where was it Mr. Freeman lives?'

'Croydon. Train or motor?'

'In view of our work-load I think we can justify going straight there.'

'Any preference as to driver?'

Chance patted his pockets. 'Richards, although I may live to regret it. Naylor can ease himself back. Which reminds me, any news of McInnes, or is he planning to make a month of it?'

'There is as a matter of fact. Godwin tells me he went round to see him yesterday. He's on the mend but he's planning to hand in his notice, move back north of the border. His father died a few months ago. He had time off for the funeral not long before you came back. Wants to be nearer his mother apparently.'

'In that case we'll sort out his successor when this case is over. I had a word with Bob on the way in. Superintendent Hayes has said he can lend us some extra hands just for today.'

'That's helpful. I've gone through the rest of the papers from Mrs Simmonds's bureau. No sign of a will though there's a copy of her mother's. That suggests she didn't make one as she kept her things orderly. There's a letter from the solicitor she seems to have used, it's Crowther's. Like me to make an appointment?'

'Please. It'll have to be tomorrow.' Chance consulted his wrist-watch. 'Shall we rally the troops we do have?'

Bishop led the way into the outer office.

*

'Inspector Forrest said you wanted a word, sir.'

'Eh?' Eddie Chance looked up from studying Godwin's photographs. The only clear prints on the veronal bottle belonged to Mrs Simmonds. 'Oh, it's you, Knowles, I thought it was my elevenses. Yes I do, I expect you can guess what about?'

P.C Knowles looked politely blank. 'Not really, sir.'

Chance sighed theatrically. 'You may be pounding pavements all day, getting some much-needed exercise but I take it you have heard there's been another murder? Surely it's all round the station by now?'

'Sir.' Knowles shot him a reproachful look.

'Well? I'm conducting a little post-mortem of my own. You took the message from the victim. Friday evening. She asked to speak to me.'

The fleshy face cleared. 'Yes, sir, that's right. I told the lady you'd gone home and she asked if Constable Marden was on duty.'

'I want you to tell me exactly what Mrs Simmonds said to you. Every word.'

'I'm not sure I can recall the actual words she used.'

'If you'd written it down verbatim at the time I wouldn't need to be wasting my time now.' Chance glared at him. 'Oh, sit down, man, if it'll help.' He waved at the other chair.

'Thank you, sir. The lady didn't ask for W.P.C. Marden by name. She asked if the young lady she'd met was available. Course there was only one person that could be. I told her that you and Phyllis had gone home.'

'You noted the time, I'll say that for you. What did Mrs Simmonds say when you told her neither of us were here?'

Knowles looked around the C.I.D. room for inspiration.

'Concentrate. It was only last Friday.'

'I've got it. She said she'd seen something in er.. Leslie's room. Leslie, she didn't say a last name. It didn't matter or it wasn't important.'

Chance sat up straight. 'Don't stop, this *is* important.'

'It didn't seem important but you told her to tell you anything, sir. So she was telephoning.' Knowles finished with a triumphant air. 'I'm certain that's the lot.'

There was silence while Chance finished scribbling. 'Why the devil couldn't you have taken this down? Next time make sure you do. It could be vital.'

'I was only out the front for a minute, sir. While the night-sarge went for a ..'

'Cut out the excuses,' Chance interrupted. 'And for Pete's sake, when you take a message, stick it somewhere it won't get missed. Don't plant your size twelves on it.'

He flapped Knowles from the room as though he were a wasp at a picnic.

Twenty-two

Sid Godwin spotted a familiar figure on a bench in the sea-front gardens. Her coat hiding her uniform, an open packet of sandwiches on her lap, Phyllis was facing the wishing-well. She didn't seem hungry.

'Hullo, Sid.'

She'd noticed him approach. Women always seemed to have eyes in the back of their head, if his mum and sister were anything to go by. You could say the same for Sergeant Bishop.

'Hullo, Phyl. Mind if I join you?'

'Be my guest.' She moved her hand-bag without enthusiasm.

'Penny for them?'

'What?' Phyllis looked at him properly, her face clouded. 'Why do you say that?'

'Dunno. I thought you looked a bit sad. Were you thinking about Saturday?'

'Not really.' She looked down at her lunch. 'I spoke to Mrs Simmonds, you know, that Sunday she came in?'

He nodded to his toecaps.

'You make sure you find whoever killed her. She was a nice woman.'

'We will.' He said it firmly.

'How's it going? I know Inspector Forrest is short-handed.'

'They've been calling at every house in Pearl-street. Inspector Chance is off to Croydon this afternoon to interview the lodger. I haven't been back to hear if there's any news.'

She shook her head. 'I think they drew a blank. It's not like it was summer-time.'

He stretched his long legs more comfortably and thought about his own street on long summer evenings. There'd be the sounds of children playing, shears clipping hedges, the hollow back and fro rasp of lawn-mowers and the green scent of grass.

The tennis courts at the club were in use until nine and along where they were now, the tourists promenaded in their new clothes. On the pier the theatre doors were hooked back and if you were nearby, you'd hear snatches of drum-rolls and laughter rising like waves.

Phyllis was restful to be with. She seemed down in the dumps but it was no wonder.

'Who do you think killed them, Sid?'

He looked at the dark, weathered groynes descending into the sea. The water was the pale milky blue of a spring day on the south coast. 'I don't know.' That sounded lame, he reached for something better. 'I think Mrs Simmonds died because she found out who killed Leslie Warrender and let the murderer see she knew.'

Phyllis nodded slowly. 'It must be something like that. The question is did she know all along or work it out?'

'They believed her when she came to report her lodger missing, didn't they?'

'Yes, I'm sure they did. I didn't feel she was hiding anything when we spoke in the ladies'. You're right, Mrs Simmonds must have realised later.'

He felt gratified he was holding his own. 'So she telephoned the inspector to tell him.'

'But she was murdered so soon after that. Inspector Chance could have been round her house in quarter of an hour. Who knew she'd made that call and had the time to silence her?'

'That's what we're up against.' It wasn't much of a remark but she didn't seem to mind.

'What have you been up to this morning?'

'I've just come from St Luke's. Sergeant Bishop sent me to find the vicar's wife 'cause she saw Mrs Simmonds that evening.'

'What did she say?'

'Nothing helpful.' She'd told him he looked too young to be a detective-constable and asked if his mother had any clothes he'd grown out of. 'Mrs Simmonds did go to the church meeting but didn't say anything about seeing anyone later. The vicar's wife said she was quiet. Didn't contribute much.' He'd half-promised to bring his family to the bring and buy before she'd let him go.

'Perhaps she was working out what to tell the inspector.'

'He has a theory about the knife used in the first murder.'

'Go on, Sid. Murderers are supposed to favour the same method. That could mean Mrs Simmonds's death was unpremeditated.' Phyllis listened attentively as he repeated everything Sergeant Bishop had told them.

'I'll tell you all about Mr. Freeman's interview when I hear. I know you're interested.'

'You won't need to. I'll probably find myself typing it.' Phyllis looked at her lunch and held out the paper wrapping. 'Fancy these? I'm not hungry.'

He peered at them, not wanting to appear too keen.

'Ham and pickle, fresh made this morning.'

'If you're sure? Don't mind if I do. Thanks, Phyl.' He tucked in. 'I always think food tastes better outside.'

She didn't answer. When he was on the last half, he tried again. 'These are great, thanks.'

'You're welcome. I was going to leave them for the gulls.'

'How was your day off? I hope it wasn't ruined.'

'What? Oh, you mean finding the body? Not too bad. I turned out some cupboards. My dad was busy in the garden all day.'

'My mum's on about spring-cleaning.'

'It wasn't too dreadful on Saturday. A nasty shock but it could have been a lot worse. Inspector Chance was very decent.' He'd been matter-of-fact but she'd felt safe. If he'd been unusually kind, she'd have burst into tears.

Somehow, she dimly thought, he knew that. 'You have to take these things in your stride in our job.'

When he'd finished she took the paper bag from him, shaking out the crumbs and folding it into a square.

'No thanks.' He shook his head at the proffered packet.

'Sorry, I forgot you don't.'

'I didn't know you did.'

'Once in a while.' Her brown eyes regarded him behind a drifting wisp of smoke.

It made her look sophisticated. Mysterious even. There was a lot he didn't know about her. 'What made you join the force?'

'My Aunt Josephine, my Dad's sister. She was a V.A.D. and I always looked up to her.' Her face relaxed. 'She was great fun, plucky and full of high spirits.'

He wanted to know what had happened to her. Couldn't ask just in case.

'She married an American soldier she nursed. She writes but it isn't the same.'

'She moved over there?'

'A little town right by the Canadian border. Watertown it's called because they're near Niagara Falls. I wanted a proper job like her. Something where you help people but I didn't fancy rolling bandages and emptying bed-pans, not in peace-time.'

He noticed the past tense. 'It can't be easy for you.'

'I do object to feeling like a novelty act. Anyway, what about you?'

'It's a good steady career,' he said, echoing his father. 'With prospects.' He hesitated, feeling round his collar. 'This'll probably sound stupid.'

'Go on. I'm not going to laugh.'

'The way I see it, life's tough enough for ordinary working people without being robbed or cheated or harmed by types who couldn't care less about anyone. It makes me so angry. Someone has to stand up for them.'

It was hard to put how he felt into words. He hurried on to cover his embarrassment. 'I'm not being a prig. It could be my family or yours.'

Phyllis smiled sadly. 'It doesn't sound stupid at all.'

*

Bishop had been commenting on the scenery and complaining about new development since they'd left Tennysham. Chance had contributed the occasional grunt. He didn't believe in preparing much for interviews and his thoughts were stuck in the front bedroom in Mrs Simmonds's house.

'There's another one going up.' Bishop jerked his elbow. 'Blooming awful tiles. Like a public urinal.'

Chance sensed Richards grin as his head turned. They both glanced at the shiny buff road-house surrounded by raw earth.

'Flat roofs are no use in this country, not with our weather.'

'We didn't miss anything in Leslie Warrender's room, did we?'

'Don't see how. Not in or behind the furniture.' Bishop's voice was confident. 'I checked behind the bedside cupboard and the chest of drawers, even the wardrobe. And nothing was caught between the drawers or fallen down the back. You watched me look under the mattress.'

'I didn't think we did.' He was conscious that he'd spent most of the time looking out of the window. Bishop was so reliable he tended to let him get on with things.

'We did everything but take the carpet up. I reckon Mrs Simmonds saw something Warrender had. He removed it before he was killed so there was nothing for us to find.'

'Maybe.' Chance lapsed back into silence.

The clouds had been darkening for some time and as chain-fencing replaced hedgerow, they ran into rain.

'Fancy a joy-ride?' Bishop nodded at the window.

'Not madly. Vic's desperate to go up.'

They were passing the flat fields of the aerodrome. The sky was like a tarpaulin pulled low over the line of hangars, a flat-roofed control tower jutted into the distance. Chance saw a flag drooping above the cream terminal building, glistening wet tarmac, no sign of life.

They drove through the suburbs, street after street, mostly of semis with rounded bay windows, much like his own.

'D'you know where we're going, Richards?'

'I think so, sir. I looked it up. We turn off along here.'

They were approaching a wide junction beneath an ugly railway bridge. A parade of small shops, the stragglers of any town, where awnings were being rolled and the stalls outside taken in. The houses were older as Richards jerked them around another corner, tall, sad pairs with basements.

An overgrown garden lay to one side of Mr. Freeman's address. As Chance and Bishop hurried up the exposed steps they heard the rumble of a passing train. A whiff of burning coal met the damp air. They exchanged an expressive glance. You wouldn't want to live there.

The front door was open. In the hall a woman in a wrap-over apron stood by an open doorway. A weak light showed stairs leading down. A bicycle was leant against the wall.

'Who is it you want?' Her face was framed by greying hair flattened viciously to her head.

Bishop removed his hat and opened his mouth to reply as Chance caught a darker shape on the dim landing.

'Good afternoon.' Bishop's smile was thrown away.

'These gentlemen are my visitors, Mrs Doyle.' Mr. Freeman stood watching them.

She looked them up and down. 'This is a respectable house. There's plenty of people wanting rooms that don't bring the police to the door.'

Chance ignored her, taking a step towards the stairs.

'Please come up,' Mr. Freeman said. The basement door banged. 'I'm sorry about your reception.'

'We've had worse,' Chance said. The smell of disinfectant clashed with last night's onions as they reached the first floor.

'You're a little earlier than I expected.' Mr. Freeman stood aside and politely showed them through a door at the back.

'I hope we haven't inconvenienced you, sir.' Bishop's tone was affable. 'We made good time from the coast.'

'By no means. I confess to being curious. Please be seated, gentlemen. I realise this must be important to bring you here in the middle of a murder inquiry.' Mr. Freeman waited until Chance had taken the arm-chair and Bishop the hard chair placed alongside.

His eyes gleaming, he seated himself on the edge of a battered bentwood chair. Chance wondered if he'd removed it from a shared bathroom.

'Can I offer you a cup of coffee or tea?'

'We won't, thanks all the same,' Bishop said.

Chance followed his sympathetic glance at the milk jug and bottle of Camp by the gas ring.

Mr. Freeman cleared his throat. 'In fact I can guess why you're here. It wasn't hard to put two and two together.' He looked at them both. 'You've requested a sample of our paper-knife. You obviously suspect one was used to kill Leslie Warrender. But I assure you, you're barking up the wrong tree if you think I murdered him.'

'No one's saying that, Mr. Freeman.'

'What about you, Inspector? You surely haven't come all this way merely to question me about my knife?'

'Could we see your own paper-knife, sir?' Chance preferred not to answer questions from male witnesses on principle. Women received slightly more leeway. He had a soft spot for old ladies.

'Certainly.' Reaching behind his chair, Mr. Freeman opened the top drawer in his narrow desk. It was the one stick of furniture that looked worth something. The wooden chair he'd given Bishop didn't match. 'As you can see, its main purpose is an advertisement for the company. Nevertheless they're well-made and a useful item.'

Chance weighed the paper-knife in his hand. *Nugent's Office Supplies* was inscribed along the handle in a clear lettering. The blade was Sheffield steel. The right length. Sturdy enough. He touched the edge.

'Careful. They're very sharp.'

He handed back the knife. Too ruddy late.

Mr. Freeman wriggled on his chair. 'You can understand my interest? Was one of our knives the murder weapon?'

'We're exploring possibilities, sir.' Chance resisted the instinct to examine his finger-tip.

'So you still haven't found the weapon? I've been attempting to follow the case while I was in Tennysham but there's been nothing fresh in the nationals.' He sounded hard done by.

'When did you leave Tennysham, Mr. Freeman?'

'On Friday. Mrs Simmonds was concerned about my using up my annual holiday. In fact I had to return to work today, though I was all for staying until yesterday. I'm off on my travels again shortly.'

Chance barely nodded at Bishop.

'Can you tell us about who you give the paper-knives to, sir?'

'It's perfectly straightforward, Sergeant. We commercial travellers give them out to customers who place firm orders, particularly if it's the first time. For instance I wouldn't hand one to someone who took a catalogue and was only considering using Nugent's.'

'You wouldn't give one to a private individual then?'

Mr. Freeman shook his head. 'Not as a rule but I did make an exception for Mrs Simmonds. She was pleased to have one for her desk.' He hesitated, 'I gave her a box of stationery. That was for her private use. It wasn't headed for her little business. There wouldn't be the need.'

'I see. Did you give a paper-knife to any other friend?'

'No.'

The answer came a little too quickly. The only thing he was hiding, Chance thought, was that the poor beggar had no friends.

'Would you have given out many of these knives in Tennysham, do you recall, sir?'

'Hard to say. We've been offering them as a gimmick for a couple of years now so firms would have had them a while ago. On this latest trip I only made two new orders. Times are hard.'

'So I've heard, Mr. Freeman,' Chance said. 'Which lucky person gets the paper-knife?'

'I'm not with you?'

'Do you give it to the owner of the firm?'

'I see what you mean. If it's a small business I may deal with the owner. It's more likely with a larger company I'll be shown in to a manager or whoever runs the office, perhaps a secretary. I'd hand it to that person when we fill out the order form. A token of our thanks and a reminder of our name for when they come to re-order. Of course it's intended for their office not for someone's personal use but there's nothing to stop someone appropriating one.'

Bishop consulted Chance with a look as Mr. Freeman spoke again.

'I must say this is quite an insight into the way the police conduct an investigation. I'd be most interested to know what put you on to our paper-knives?'

Ask away, old chum. He was hardly going to admit it suddenly came to him.

'We don't like to leave any stone unturned, sir. It pays to be thorough,' Bishop said.

'I telephoned Mrs Simmonds from the office after I'd spoken to you, Sergeant. She wasn't in. I thought she might know more about why you wanted to see me.'

The sound of a train became apparent, steadily building like a kettle coming to the boil. The sash window rattled. Carriages strung past at the bottom of the garden. A house two streets back from the sea would seem very desirable.

'I regret to say we have some bad news, Mr. Freeman.'

The words everyone dreaded.

Chance watched the recipient run the tip of his tongue round his dry lips.

'Something's happened to Mrs Simmonds, hasn't it? Tell me.'

'She was found dead at her home on Saturday. Are you all right, sir?'

Mr. Freeman got to his feet. You couldn't say sprung. He moved like an old man. A spot of red stood out on his pale cheeks. 'You should have told me at once. Not sat here playing games. You mean she was murdered, don't you?'

'I'm afraid so,' Bishop said.

'Not stabbed like the other one? It's too horrible to contemplate.'

'No.. no. Mrs Simmonds was suffocated. It would have been very quick. She'd taken sleeping tablets and might have been semi-conscious.'

Mr. Freeman stood still. His hands hung at his sides. They were trembling.

'Excuse me.' Moving unsteadily to the sink, he picked up a tumbler and filled it to the brim. When he'd downed a good half of the water, he took the few paces back to stand before them. 'I should have been there to protect her.'

'Come and sit down, sir. You've had a nasty shock.'

Ignoring Bishop, Mr. Freeman held the glass against his forehead. The edge touched the frame of his spectacles. He resumed his seat, placing the glass on the rubbed carpet.

'You're here to question me about an alibi.' A resigned statement.

'Is there anyone here we can fetch for you? A neighbour?'

Chance knew Freeman would detest the concern in Bishop's voice. In his experience people came in two sorts. Those who were grateful for a spot of kindness and those who resented it.

'No, thank you. I'm quite all right.' Mr. Freeman eased the knot of his tie fractionally away from his collar. 'The theory that I would harm a hair of that dear lady's head could not be more misplaced. For that matter I'm a peaceable man. I abhor violence.' His eyes shifted to Chance.

Bishop had unobtrusively placed his note-book on his knee. He waited patiently. Mr. Freeman passed a finger over his neat moustache and briefly touched both corners of his lips.

'I was giving serious consideration to making Mrs Simmonds my wife.'

'I'm sorry, sir.'

An incline of the head. 'Thank you, Sergeant.'

As Freeman began to describe his movements on Friday morning, Chance thought the London accent more pronounced in his nasal voice. Other people's capacity for self-deception baffled him.

'So I arrived back here mid-morning. The train gets in at eleven fourteen and the station is five minutes' away. I stopped to purchase some food. The stall-holders may remember me. Then I stowed my suit-case, made myself a cup of coffee and went straight out again.'

Bishop looked up encouragingly. As far as Chance could see he'd only jotted down the train time.

A handkerchief appeared and Mr. Freeman polished his spectacles as he spoke. 'I took a bus up to town and spent the afternoon in Charing Cross-road. Where there's a proliferation of book-sellers. I rarely find myself with free time in the week and I felt a small treat was in order.' His mouth tightened.

'Buy anything nice, sir?'

'No, plans never seem to turn out as envisaged. Allow me to save you both some time. I spoke to no one and I'm well aware I cut an anonymous figure among crowded streets. I returned here and spent the evening in this room. However at approximately twenty to seven the young woman who lives across the landing knocked, in search of change for her meter. She usually returns from work in half an hour should you wish to check my story.'

'Thank you very much, Mr. Freeman.' Bishop looked at Chance. 'I don't think that will be necessary just now.'

'Did Mrs Simmonds say anything last week about the murder?' Chance said. 'Or anything that seemed a bit odd? Was something on her mind?'

'I regret I can think of nothing to help you, Inspector. She didn't wish to discuss Warrender's murder and she discouraged me from speculating.'

Chance regarded him thoughtfully. 'Can you cast your mind back to the woman you saw with him?'

'I'll try.'

'You said she was about average height?'

Screwing up his eyes, Mr. Freeman nodded. 'Yes, her hat was about level with his shoulder I think.'

'Were there people between you? Wednesdays are usually busy in Tennysham, the day before early-closing.'

'Yes, there were. I only noticed Warrender because they were on the steps to the entrance of the bank.'

'That's what I wondered.' Chance looked satisfied. 'Thanks.'

*

The rain was only spitting as they descended the steps. A man on a bicycle gave them a curious glance as he went by.

'What was all that about, if you don't mind my asking?' Bishop paused in the gateway.

'Only that the mystery woman might have been on the small side. If Freeman saw them on the bank steps and his view was partly blocked by passers-by, his impression of height is meaningless.'

'I get it. Clever. Anyway, this one's crossed off, poor devil.'

'Shall I get you a pillow, Richards?' Chance scowled through the open car window.

'Sorry, sir.' Sitting up straight, the constable rubbed his eyes.

'Did you see his bookcase?' Chance sank in his usual corner behind the driver's seat. 'Edwardian Trials, a biography of Marshall Hall, Archbold even. Fellow's a fantasist. Perhaps he won't be so keen now the real thing's hit home.'

'He wasn't in Tennysham on Friday evening,' Bishop said. 'He wouldn't lie about speaking to his neighbour, knowing we could ask her.'

'It has to be checked, I suppose, but I don't intend hanging around any later.'

'I'll get on to the local station when we're back.'

'The morning will do.'

'Is this Freeman out of the running, Sarge?' Richards spoke over his shoulder.

'He is, Fred. We'll have to look closer to home.'

'Was it a waste of time coming up here?'

'Nothing's ever wasted, Richards,' Chance said loftily.

'That's not too draughty for you, is it, sir?'

'I'll let you know.' He turned to Bishop. 'I wish now we'd stopped at Nugent's and collected a paper-knife. It looked right to me and I can personally testify the wretched thing's sharp enough.'

'I noticed.' Bishop's face remained deadpan. 'It'll be with us in the morning. If it arrives after you've left, I'll send it straight over to the court.'

'Good, the sooner Dr. Wheeler sees one the better. You're certain there wasn't one in the house?'

'Positive. Richards here helped me search. Isn't that right?'

'Yes, Sarge. Definitely no knife like the one you described, sir, only cutlery.'

Chance remained thoughtful, breaking his silence only to tell Richards to watch out when he braked abruptly.

The traffic had increased as they drove through the older streets into the newer residential sprawl. On the outskirts near the aerodrome, the gates of a modern factory were open. A stream of men on bicycles waited to join the main road. Others in caps and mackintoshes were on foot, a knot of women beneath umbrellas.

Bishop wiped his window. 'Must be rush-hour.'

Chance grinned to himself. He had a habit of stating the obvious. Funny how someone could be irritating, however much you liked them. Bishop probably felt the same about him.

In touch sporadically during the years he'd been in Brighton – barely more than Christmas cards written by the wives – they'd quickly settled into a comfortable double act. Bishop had never been ambitious. He was a born sergeant, good at sorting out paper-work and men.

Chance wondered if he'd ever been as idealistic as young Godwin. He doubted it. Though it was hard to recall the way they were before 'fourteen. He thought about Phyllis. There was no rewarding future for her in the county force. Should have been a nurse or a school-teacher. She spent so much time hanging round the C.I.D. room, he tended to forget she was Bob Forrest's problem, not his.

*

When he parted from Bishop in the yard, the first person Chance saw was Phyllis wheeling her bike.

'All set for tomorrow, Constable?'

'I think so, sir.'

'You can do a job for me afterwards. It's all right with Inspector Hayes.'

'Sir?'

She gave him a look of polite enquiry. He wondered if he and recent events had demolished her enthusiasm for good.

'See if you can find out where Mrs Simmonds's bunch of flowers came from.'

'If she bought them herself, sir?'

'Yes. I suppose dozens of the things have been sold but if the sellers remember anyone, you might jot down anything significant that occurs to you.'

'There aren't many places that sell cut flowers, sir. I'll report back to you as soon as possible.'

He wished her goodnight.

Tuesday inquests were becoming a habit. Superintendent Hayes had informed him that the Chief Constable would be attending. That meant a more active interest. Time was running out.

Instead of heading up the hill home, Chance intended to go through every report again while there were no distractions. In the empty C.I.D. room he gathered a sheaf of folders and took them to his desk. Occasionally he broke off from reading to scrawl a note of something to be followed up.

Eventually Chance stood up, stretched and rubbed the back of his neck. The reports were shoved in his bottom drawer. Someone would shortly be along to empty the waste-paper baskets and ash-trays. Dinner would be between two plates over a simmering saucepan. He'd better make himself scarce.

It had stayed dry in Tennysham and the evenings were noticeably drawing out. Soon Easter would be upon them, then daylight saving and Whitsun. The town would throng with trippers. One way or another the case would be over.

As he strode through the quiet streets he couldn't stop thinking about the idea that had come to him on the way to Croydon. He tested his theory again, pulling cautiously, the way you would on a rope.

It was beginning to hold.

Twenty-three

Bishop tapped a few bars with his pencil as he decided what to do next. He'd restored the filing cabinet to his satisfaction and the C.I.D. room was ticking over nicely, just as he liked it.

The package from Nugent's lay open on his desk. Phyllis had brought it in to them, dealt with the string and whatnot. He'd had a word about what to expect with it being her first time on the stand. That young woman hadn't been the same since she'd found the body.

Still she knew the coroner, by sight at least. Everyone knew of the family and their rambling premises. The maroon and cream pantechnicon with Ridley & Sons Auctioneers in gold lettering was a familiar sight in Tennysham.

Richards was still on the 'phone at the other end of the room, listening as he scribbled. Naylor had driven Chance and Godwin had his head down over his typing. A sheet of paper fluttered on the floor as the door opened.

'Morning, Wilf. Thought I'd turn the tables and drop in on you for a change.' Ignoring the others the dapper police-surgeon came sweeping in.

'Your timing couldn't be better, Lionel. I was just fancying a cup of tea and I've something here for you.' He caught Godwin's eye. 'See to it, will you, Sid?' Grabbing the cardboard box, Bishop ushered Wheeler in the office.

'Chance not about?' Wheeler deposited his bag on the floor and took the other chair.

'He's had to nip to Hastings. Nothing to do with the Warrender case. They arrested an old lag last night and we think he might have burgled a house here. He's going straight to the inquest if you want to see him.'

'You'll do. It's the results of the Simmonds woman's blood test.' Wheeler paused deliberately to extract his cigarette-case from his jacket. 'Have one of mine and save us from that bonfire you light up.'

Bishop refused as expected. It was all part of the show. 'Go on, I'm all ears.'

'I'll skip the measurements, shall I? Very well then. The deceased had helped herself to a foolishly generous dose of veronal. One and three-quarter times the recommended amount. Patients on the whole are an extremely stupid bunch and this tinkering is all too common as I explained. In other words nothing significant in that.'

'I remember. So Mrs Simmonds didn't want to do herself harm. She was looking for a good night's kip?'

'Undoubtedly. I find a clear conscience does the trick myself.'

'How long would it have taken to make her drowsy?'

'You know better than to ask questions like that, Wilf. How long is a piece of string? Her reactions would have been slower within fifteen minutes or so. Then again would it have made any difference? Someone was determined to finish her off that night.'

The door opened and Godwin appeared with a tea-tray.

Bishop moved the package. 'That was prompt. Shove it down there, lad.'

'I suppose Darjeeling is too much to hope for?' Wheeler made a tight face as he watched his cup filled.

'Go to Grove's if you want that malarkey. They'll do you a nice china plate of sponge fingers to go with it.' Bishop smiled benignly at him. 'Squashed fly biscuit?' He bit into his with a satisfying snap.

'If I must.' Wheeler held a biscuit up to the light and examined both sides.

'Relax. It's just a name. A dead currant won't hurt you.'

'Is that what you want me to see?' Wheeler indicated the box with his teaspoon.

'That's the one. Could you take it back with you and see if it's a possibility?'

'Even if it is, I take it you don't have the purported murder weapon?'

'No, but we now know Mrs Simmonds had one of these and it's gone missing.'

'It *is* a possibility. I can tell you that much by looking. May I?'

'Sure.' Bishop swallowed his tea and watched as Wheeler gave the paper-knife the same attention he'd given his biscuit.

'You can tell Eddie it appears to be the right length. One of these would have sufficient power but I can't be definite until I've checked the measurements.'

'Tell him yourself. He'll be chuffed. You'll see him before I do.'

'I shan't have time to stand around chatting afterwards. I've a lot on. You can tell him to do something about these bodies piling up. My live patients are feeling neglected.'

'I'll pass it on. You'll ring me today?'

'I doubt I'll be free to telephone before late afternoon. I'll have my round to do.' Wheeler sipped his tea and shuddered.

After a few insights into where Eddie Chance was going wrong, the police-surgeon announced he couldn't be delayed any longer and Bishop showed him out.

When he turned back to the main office Godwin was waving his carbon and cursing as he wiped his smeared fingers.

'We're all up to date, Sarge. Blast this thing.'

Bishop shook his head. 'No point in getting exasperated over trifles. I've learned that much.' He switched his attention to Richards who was hovering. 'Any joy at Marting?'

'They interviewed Mrs Ethel Lynch yesterday and went back to see her husband when he got home from work. He went to his local on Friday night. There from about half-past seven, plenty of witnesses.' Richards rapidly scanned the sheet he was holding. Bishop noticed his lank hair was nudging his collar. 'They've spoken to the land-lord. He's well known.'

'Ronald Lynch wasn't over here then.'

'His wife was in with their children and she answered the door to their pools collector.'

'Thanks, Fred. Get yourself off to the barber's. Sooner rather than later.' Bishop grinned at his expression. 'Inspector Forrest might not have said anything but Colonel Vesey's liable to drop in.'

'Can I go in work time, Sarge?'

'Not if I catch you. You want to take a leaf out of the D.I.'s book. He keeps his like he's still in the army.'

Bishop chuckled to himself as he went out to the front desk. Chance kept his dark hair severely short. Left to its own devices, it had a tendency to wave, which he detested. These days the first grey hairs were noticeable but he recalled a young Chance being ticked off for the same offence.

*

They'd arranged to meet at Henry's though most of the tables were busy and they couldn't talk shop. Afterwards they strolled over to the sea-front, pacing a few yards away from the pier in the direction of Eastcliff.

'Phyllis was fine in the witness box. About as emotional as a waitress reciting a tea order.'

'One way and another she's been getting quite an education lately.'

Chance shrugged affably. 'Perhaps now she'll be glad to get back to typing and wiping kids' noses. That's the inquest adjourned. How did you get on at the solicitor's?'

Bishop glanced across the road at a Daimler drawn up outside the Channel View. A uniformed chauffeur was ferrying luggage. 'Mrs Simmonds dealt with old Mr.

Crowther himself. He'd looked after her mother's affairs. Not that he'd had any business from her since her mother died. Mrs S. didn't make a will. He'd had a go at persuading her but you know what some people are like. They feel it's tempting fate. She was definitely alone in the world. He's a decent old stick. Said he'd like to attend the funeral. Suppose that'll be down to the husband who beggared off.'

'I've never thought for a minute that her murder was unconnected with Warrender's,' Chance said. 'But I can tell the Chief Constable we've looked at everything. I had a good read through the reports after we got back yesterday.'

'I saw you'd had them out.'

'I've told Richards to call at The Bell and have another word with the bar-maid. We need to find the man at Warrender's table. Not a regular, she said, but he may have been in since.'

Bishop nodded. 'He said. So what else are we left with?'

Chance took a deep breath of the salty air. A cargo ship was passing in the distance with puffs of dirty smoke smudging the powder-blue sky. 'It all hinges on why Mrs Simmonds had to die. I've been giving it a lot of thought. You know I could make out a very good case for Arnold Freeman murdering Leslie Warrender.'

'For queering his pitch?'

'Exactly. Freeman had a nice thing going, or rather so he thought. You and I both know Mrs Simmonds was never going to fall into his arms,' Chance grinned cynically, 'but hope springs eternal and all that. Our Mr. Freeman couldn't see it. Suddenly along comes friend Warrender and dazzles her. Takes her out Wednesday night. Mr. Freeman could have had a murderous hatred of him. Follows him to the pub on Thursday. Maybe suggests a turn along the sea-front, rather like us. One quick thrust. Rival out of the way.'

'That's all very well but he'd never have killed Mrs Simmonds.'

'No,' Chance sounded reluctant. 'Mind you, I could even see that if he discovered she wasn't a widow. But I accept he was tucked up in Croydon at the relevant time.'

Bishop wandered to a halt and leant on the railings with his back to the sea. 'What's all this leading up to?'

'Mrs Simmonds's message for me on the night she died. I questioned Knowles about her actual words. Then I had a thought in the car yesterday. *I saw something in Leslie's room*. That's what Mrs Simmonds was supposed to have said on the telephone. We all thought she meant an object. I don't know... a snapshot, a letter, pile of banknotes? But what if she meant she saw something through the window? What then, Wilf?'

'It's possible.' Bishop's voice was cautious. He lifted his hat automatically as a friend of Glad's acknowledged him.

'Don't you see, it's instinctive to look out of a window? I stood watching the street when we were in there. You did all the work, sorry about that.' Chance gave him a quick smile.

'So what d'you reckon she saw?'

'*Who* she saw. Not something but someone.'

'Why was she in there, I wonder? With Warrender?'

Chance shook his head impatiently. 'No, my betting is, she was in there for some reason when it was empty. Taking him a towel, turning his bed down, something like that. Having a snoop? She saw someone in the street – it had to be the night of the murder - and only realised the significance days later. A week ago after the first inquest I asked her if she could think of anything else to tell us and she couldn't.'

Bishop was silent while he digested this. Chance gazed at the cliffs rising beyond the end of the town. The clear solid white chalk they seemed in the distance was deceptive. When you neared them the cliffs were stained a grubby yellowy cream, crumbling dangerously to the pebble beach. Rusted warning signs kept people away.

'You think she saw someone follow Warrender when he went out that night?'

Chance hesitated, 'Possibly but that would mean she rushed up to his room the moment he left.'

'In which case the murderer saw Mrs Simmonds looking?'

'It's more likely she saw someone later. Look, I think I'm starting to see but I don't have all of it.'

Bishop stared at him. 'You know who it was?'

'Let's say I have a suspect. Though I'm not sure why Leslie Warrender was murdered. I've a vague idea what it was to do with but I need information.'

'When are you going to tell the rest of us?'

'I'll tell you later today if I can get confirmation. I need to do some digging first.' Chance threw his cigarette-end over the railing. 'Shall we start back?'

Twenty-four

There was no sign of Daphne. Chance looked in all the bays of the lending-library before climbing the stairs to the reference section. Sunlight behind the huge stained glass window on the landing cast rose and yellow wavering lights across the wall.

Three haughty, under-dressed nymphs stared down at him. The scene put him in mind of a tableau Stella had taken part in the previous summer. The one waving a harp looked like her mother.

His daughter didn't appear to be upstairs. He wondered if she was having a tea-break or sorting out books in some stock-room.

This time no one was sitting behind the desk though a knitted cardigan was draped over the chair. To his annoyance voices were coming from the small room containing the newspaper archive. Through the half-open door he could see a man's tweed back, moving as he leant forward.

'Thank you, Miss Randall. These are sufficient to be going on with.'

'You're welcome, Mr. Jenner. I'll fetch you the glass.'

The woman speaking was wiping her hands on a handkerchief as Chance filled the doorway. She looked up, her expression friendly. 'Good afternoon. Did you need some assistance?'

He stepped back, enabling her to come out. 'I was wondering if I might go through some back numbers of the *Observer*?'

She glanced behind her at the other man. His spectacles were perched on his pink head. He looked alarmed, his arms protectively stretched over the pile of leather folders before him.

'Certainly. I'll be with you in a second.' Slipping past him she fetched a magnifying glass on her desk. 'That should help, Mr. Jenner. I'll be back to collect some folders for this other gentleman then you won't be disturbed.'

There was a testy murmur. Chance waited by the desk as the woman returned.

'That gentleman's writing a history of the bowls club. I don't believe we've seen you in here before?'

'I don't get much free time.'

She studied him, her brow furrowed.

Chance wondered if she was going to give him fifty lines for non-attendance. She broke into a sudden grin, knocking a few years off. Hadn't Daph said she was thirty-five or thereabouts?

'You wouldn't be Detective-Inspector Chance?'

Chance agreed that he was. There'd been a column about his appointment in the local rag when he returned to Tennysham. To his disgust they had insisted on a photograph.

'You must be Miss Randall.' They shook hands.

'Jack Harris said you called in. I can see the resemblance to Daphne. She's gone to the post-office but she won't be long.'

'No matter. I hope she's pulling her weight?'

'Indeed she is. We're very lucky to have her. I haven't been here a lot longer myself so we've more or less settled in together.'

'Your predecessor had a reputation as something of a dragon.'

'I shall aim to keep up her high standards.' Miss Randall's face was now perfectly serious. Her eyes said something else. 'Now what issues would you like to consult, Inspector Chance?'

'1919 and 1920.' He thought quickly, 'possibly '18 but those will do to start.'

'That's a lot to go through. I hope you can narrow your search.'

Chance pulled a face. 'Unfortunately it has to be done.'

'And can't be given to a constable?' Miss Randall murmured. 'It must be important.' She gave him a quick smile. 'Sorry. Incorrigibly nosy. It comes with the job. I'll get them for you.'

'If you can prise them away,' Chance said.

'I should think you rather pull rank.'

She returned swiftly with two bulky folders bound in blue leather. Chance took them from her.

'They're frightfully dusty. Look, if you'd like to be more private, Inspector, you could use my office.' A loop of brown hair was coming adrift. Twisting it back, she transferred a smudge of grey to her cheek.

He glanced back at the tables. They were all occupied by at least one reader. 'Thanks, Miss Randall. If you're sure that won't keep you out, it would be helpful.'

'Not at all, I'm working out here. This way.'

Chance followed her through a door marked *Private* to a panelled corridor. They did themselves all right before the war. The first door had *Librarian* on a slotted sign with *Miss M. Randall* underneath.

'Make yourself at home.' She swept some papers off the desk, dumping them on a cupboard. 'Shut that if it's draughty.' She nodded at the sash window open a few inches at the bottom. Looked around and shifted a heavy glass ash-tray out of his way. 'Do smoke in here if you wish.'

'This is very good of you.' He sat in her chair, giving it a half-swing.

'Stay as long as you like.'

Airily dismissing his thanks and saying she shouldn't be away from the desk, the librarian was gone.

He was looking for the report of a drowning. Whether it was a lone tragedy or part of some boating disaster, he had no idea. He'd worked out the likely years from Joan Dawson's age. Mrs Simmonds had mentioned that Joan's mother had died when she was a baby. On Sunday Bishop had helpfully asked Mrs Dawson how old their granddaughter was.

Surely a drowning would have been reported in the weekly press? Too much to face hunting through the evening *Echo*. He didn't even know quite why he was looking except you learnt to follow a hunch. He had to start somewhere.

His eyes were sore and his throat raw with tobacco when Daphne turned up.

'Hullo, Dad, back again? Miss Randall thought you might like one.' She placed a cup and saucer at his elbow.

Chance took an immediate mouthful. 'I needed that. Do thank her.'

'I will. She and Mr. Harris drink Earl Grey but I made you the ordinary tea.' His daughter bent over his shoulder. 'What are you doing?'

'Trying to work.' He waved absently at a folder. 'You can take that one away with you.'

'I can take a hint. I'd better get back.'

Cradling the folder, Daphne paused to look in the small mirror by the hat-stand. Checked her lipstick with a satisfied air.

Chance spoke without looking up. 'Miss Randall seems very.. jolly.'

'I told you she's all right. She thinks I have brains.'

'Does she indeed?'

'It isn't *quite* as boring here as I thought.'

'Work is meant to be boring,' Chance said.

'I don't suppose yours is.'

He stared blankly at the page before him.

'No men of course,' Daphne turned slightly, admiring her shiny waves. 'Mum says I'll soon get into the swing of things now the winter's over. I thought I might join the Players.'

'Good idea, all the men are over fifty,' Chance said nastily. He turned over a page with a snap. 'You know they only act to meet young women?'

Daphne giggled. 'There's the tennis club. They get going after Easter.'

'Be off with you. I need to concentrate.'

'See you later, Dad.'

As Chance drank his ordinary tea he wondered what the M. stood for.

*

The late afternoon sun had moved around the old building, leaving the office in shadow. Second-hand pipe smoke hung in the fraught atmosphere. A full waste-paper basket had fallen over and its contents spilt by Chance's shoe. He kicked a ball of crumpled paper further away.

'Well, say something. You think I'm off my head, don't you?'

'I didn't say that,' Bishop said. 'Don't put words in my mouth. You think the murderer is one of the Dawsons?'

'It's him. Herbert Dawson.' Chance was emphatic. 'It did cross my mind yesterday that his wife was the woman going in the bank with Warrender. But on reflection I don't believe Olive Dawson is capable of killing or being an accessory. You've seen how dithery she is. I wouldn't be letting her in on plotting a murder.'

For a wonder, he wasn't smoking. Instead he fiddled with a pencil as he watched his sergeant's face, intent on convincing him.

'In that case who was going in the bank?'

'Probably no one, just someone going in at the same time as Warrender. Freeman only caught a glimpse.'

'You believe Warrender was Joan Dawson's father? I don't want to pour cold water but where's the evidence?'

'We can get proof,' Chance said, 'now we know what we're looking for. We'll get sight of Joan's birth certificate. Think about it. Warrender could have ruined the Dawsons' lives. Would you want someone like that in your precious granddaughter's life? Especially if you'd always lied to her and said her father was dead. They'd never have been safe if they'd paid him off.'

Bishop looked at him, his expression concerned. 'You know, you're under a lot of pressure, Eddie. Why not sleep on it before you go rushing to Colonel Vesey?'

'Thanks for backing me up.'

'I don't want you to dig yourself a hole and jump in. Once you've reported this higher, you can't unsay it. It all gets written down on your record.'

'What does? Unsound judgement. Promoted above his capability?' Chance threw himself back in his chair. 'I could be right. Ever consider that?'

'Best keep your voice down.' Bishop nodded towards the office door. 'That lot won't need a glass on the wall.'

Chance grinned suddenly, his temper collapsed. 'It doesn't really work. I've tried it. At best you get the odd word.'

Bishop gestured with his pipe. 'No point in getting cross. You've been chewing it over. I need to let it sink in. You haven't explained what put you on to it?'

'Working out that Mrs Simmonds saw someone from the window on the night Warrender was murdered and that's what she wanted to tell me.'

'Go on.'

'If I'm right, she could have seen Ronald Lynch or Sadie Price or even Ethel Lynch. But the most likely person was Herbert Dawson because he lives further down the street.'

'We haven't even considered him. There's been no hint of a motive.'

‘At the time Mrs Simmonds would have hardly registered a friend and neighbour passing by or maybe hanging around.’

‘So it wouldn’t have occurred to her to mention seeing him when we interviewed her?’

‘That’s right. Her attention was on him being killed on the sea-front. She might have noticed a stranger walking past if they’d been behaving suspiciously. People you expect to see fade into the background, you don’t register them.’

‘She can’t have seen them together when Warrender left. She would have told us that when she came in to report his disappearance.’

Chance nodded. ‘I agree. What makes sense is she saw Dawson some time later. She didn’t know Warrender hadn’t come in until Friday morning. She wasn’t worried about him. Nothing about the Thursday evening would have seemed significant at the time.’

‘So what did she see, according to you?’

‘I’ve been thinking about this from all angles and eventually it hit me. Remember what young Joan said to us on Sunday?’

‘Something about Mrs Simmonds stopping her in the street and asking how she was getting on at school. What was it now? Saying she could set her clock by the time Mr. Dawson walked their dog.’ Bishop’s expression sharpened as he planted his elbows on Chance’s desk. ‘I begin to see what you’re getting at.’

‘According to Joan, Mrs Simmonds asked if the dog had been poorly. Why would she think that? At first they sound like the sort of banal remarks adults always say to children. What do you ask the little blighters apart from how do you like school?’

‘What do they want to be when they’re grown up?’ Bishop said immediately.

'If you look a little deeper, I think she was fishing. Mrs Simmonds wanted to know why she saw Mr. Dawson walking past her house at a different time in the evening. He told us himself he always takes the mutt out at half-past eight and they only go the length of the street. So did she see him pass her house much later? Did he even have the dog with him?'

'What about Mrs Dawson? When you first met them she never said *you were out later than usual on Thursday night, dear*.'

'Why should she? She wouldn't think for a second her husband had murdered the man in the shelter. He'd have fobbed her off or maybe she goes to bed early and didn't even know. Joan would be tucked up by then.'

'If you are right, she'd have recognised the name once Warrender was identified.'

'Yes and then Mr. Dawson would have easily convinced her to keep quiet. Think about it, Wilf. If Warrender fathered their daughter's child out of wedlock, they'd hush it up for all they're worth. Their dead daughter's reputation and Joan's legitimacy were at stake.'

Bishop nodded, his expression grave. 'No one likes having the finger pointed. Look how worried Miss Aldridge was about her good name. Not unless you're in the Fort Belvedere set of course. That lot do as they please and never mind decent behaviour.'

Chance smiled to himself at the sneer implicit in the voice. Unlike Stella, Bishop wasn't among the Prince of Wales's many admirers.

'I did notice Mrs Dawson seemed very distressed during the inquest,' Bishop added. 'Her husband had to comfort her. I put it down to finding the body.'

'I've been wondering about the weapon. I admit if Dawson saw Warrender, he didn't have much time to call at Mrs Simmonds's place and pinch her paper-knife. In any case with Warrender on the scene I imagine he'd have kept away.'

'Bound to have done if you're right.'

'Perhaps Mrs Simmonds didn't want the knife Mr. Freeman presented to her and passed it on to one of the Dawsons ages ago. Would a woman want a memento of him and his fishy eyes?'

Bishop shrugged. 'It's still speculation. We can't prove Mr. Dawson knew Warrender was staying with Mrs Simmonds.'

Chance gave an exasperated sigh. 'You have to assume something as a starting point. They were in the same street. Wait until you hear the rest before picking holes.'

'That's a sergeant's job. Do you really think Herbert Dawson could have killed Warrender?'

'Yes.' The pencil was slapped on the blotter. 'He's only in his sixties. You can see he's fit. His wife looks like a puff of wind would blow her over but Dawson's powerfully built. Warrender didn't see it coming.'

'The knife would be easy to conceal in a sleeve, I grant you.'

'When I met the Dawsons, she said she'd wanted them to walk the dog in the park on the Friday morning. Her husband had insisted they go along the sea-front even though the weather looked dodgy. Remember all that rain was on the way? He wanted to see if the corpse had been found. You know what they say about murderers revisiting the scene of the crime?'

'It's a tiny point. Nothing you could use in court.'

'Mrs Dawson sounded sad when she talked about the sea. I wondered why at the time. I found the daughter's death in the *Observer*. The end of October 1920. Copied out the whole column. Took me long enough to find it but it's all here.' Chance tapped his note-book.

'Their daughter killed herself?'

'It was an open verdict but yes. You know coroners are decent if there's any leeway, for the sake of the family. She drowned off Spit Rocks.'

Bishop frowned. 'No one would swim near there. It's notorious.'

'No local certainly and there is a warning sign. Although they know that's where she went in. Her shoes were left on the beach. Her father bore the brunt of the inquest. According to the paper Mrs Dawson was too ill to be in court.'

'I don't recall it.'

'Not ours, it was right on the border. The body came under Bexhill's jurisdiction.'

'And you'd been transferred by then. Any witnesses?' Bishop asked the first question of any policeman.

'None. A doctor's report was rather glossed over but reading between the lines.. you hear of women who have nervous trouble after giving birth. The mother's on the twitchy side.'

'That's terribly sad. If she was unmarried they might well have held the father morally responsible.'

'Interestingly enough the daughter was named as Mrs Evelyn Dawson, a widow.'

'That could be if she married a cousin on her father's side. People do, Glad's sister married one of their cousins. It's not that uncommon.'

'The parents were covering. Evelyn was unmarried. I'll put my shirt on it.'

'You haven't said what makes you think Warrender was the father?'

Chance rubbed his temples. 'Once I worked out Mrs Simmonds may have seen Mr. Dawson, naturally I wondered about motive. She told us that the Dawsons were bringing up their granddaughter because her mother drowned. I needed to find out more about them and the death was bound to have been in the weekly rag so I had a look.'

'Where would you have started if you didn't know about the daughter?'

'Looked into where Mr. Dawson worked. See if his path ever crossed Warrender's.' Chance scowled at the door. 'Where's our tea got to? Naylor could have milked a cow by now. When I visited their house, Mrs Dawson showed me a photograph of their daughter and said Joan was getting very like her mother. Suppose Warrender saw her in the street with her grandfather? What we can't know is which of them spotted the other. Did Warrender see Mr. Dawson and blackmail him?'

'Did they mention the girl's father?'

'No, I told you they had a photograph of a young man in uniform, next to Evelyn's. At the time I assumed he'd died of wounds or whatever.'

Bishop looked thoughtful. 'Unusual really that they didn't fill you in. Most people trot out where their relative fell or received their injuries.'

Chance knew he must be thinking of his own son. Bishop never spoke of him but Glad liked to talk about their Harry when he wasn't in hearing.

'Not a word was said. If I'm right the photograph is a fake. It would have to be someone Joan would never meet.'

Stretching, Bishop stood and wandered over to the window. He glanced down at the street, quiet at that time of day. 'It sounds plausible but we need proof.'

'Give me some credit. That's why I've been out all afternoon.' Chance sounded impatient again. 'When I saw the daughter's name, it came to me, Evelyn Dawson. You weren't there when Godwin and I met Miss Howe. She described a girl who visited Warrender a few times. A fair-haired girl whose name began with 'E.' We assumed she was talking about his sister. Ethel Lynch is blonde after all and Warrender was fair.'

'Anyone would,' Bishop said.

'Miss Howe couldn't recall her name. She reeled off two or three and luckily Godwin, who's no slacker, recalled every word she said. I read his report again last night. One of the names was Evie.'

'Evie for Evelyn,' Bishop said. 'Miss Howe might recognise a photograph of her but we can't put a senile old lady in the witness box.' He turned to look at Chance. 'There's more though, I can tell.'

'It was something tiny a witness said to Richards yesterday. When he was at the post-office.'

'Which was?'

'There was one old boy who remembered Warrender. He gave Richards a run-down on what happened to the others who'd worked there at the same time.'

'You're not saying..?'

'Yes. He said one woman had an accident and died. I called in there after the library. Nice old boy, his name's Norman Teague. I couldn't stop him talking but the gist is the young woman was called Evelyn Dawson and she was sweet on Leslie Warrender. They were walking out together. He left suddenly and not long after, so did she. He thought she moved away.'

Bishop whistled through his false set. 'That's more like it. What do we do next?'

'Have Dawson in for questioning. I think he'll confess. He isn't one of life's hardened murderers. I could find it in me to feel sorry for him if it weren't for Mrs Simmonds.'

'That was a dreadful business.'

'Who better placed to pop around without being seen? We know Mrs Simmonds welcomed her killer in for a pot of tea.'

'He wouldn't have needed much of an excuse to call.'

'At first I wondered about the flowers,' Chance said. 'When Phyllis pointed them out I thought the murderer might have brought them. Mrs Simmonds bought them herself by the way, from her usual green-grocer. I saw Phyllis on the way in. Anyway when we were back there on Sunday, I noticed an unopened jar of marmalade in the kitchen cupboard. Hand-written label.'

'What of it?'

'Mrs Simmonds did a lot to point us in the right direction, poor woman. When we drove her home she said she bought her marmalade from Mrs Dawson.'

'I didn't think you were listening.'

'Long practice. I generally switch off when women start nattering but it sinks in. Mr. Dawson might have dropped round with a jar, knowing she'd invite him in.'

'Perhaps he'll tell us himself.'

'I'm glad you think I'm right.'

'I didn't quite say that. You've proved a connection between Warrender and Evelyn Dawson. We know Warrender was a blackmailer and it's likely he did see the Dawsons and Joan, staying as he was in the same street. Quite by chance because the Dawsons had moved there since he knew them. Although he didn't necessarily know them because he courted their daughter. All right,' Bishop held up his hand. 'I can see your face. It's probable he called for Evelyn Dawson at home at some time.'

Chance groaned. 'Get off the fence. Do you think Herbert Dawson did it?'

'All right, yes. You've come up with too much to explain away.' Bishop moved back to the desk and tapped his pipe in the ash-tray. 'He must have realised Mrs Simmonds saw him on the night of the murder. Come to think of it, Joan did say she told her Grandad about Mrs Simmonds speaking to her.'

'Dawson can't have known she was going to telephone me on Friday evening. From his point of view he got to her just in time. Something she said last week alerted him.'

'Her questions to Joan,' Bishop said.

Chance looked pensive. 'She can't have thought he was the murderer or she wouldn't have let him in. If I hadn't asked her to have another think, she might still be here..' He broke off as someone knocked on the door and told them to come in.

'About time. Too exhausting for Naylor was it? I didn't say go to India to pick the leaves.'

Richards looked unabashed. 'Sorry, sir. There's a telephone call for you, Sarge.'

'On my way.' Bishop left the room.

'I'll pour if that's why you're waiting.'

'I've something to report, sir. I've been back to The Bell and I've got a sort of a lead.'

'Let's hear it then,' Chance said, rather more pleasantly.

'I talked to the same bar-maid, Ginny her name is. The one who served Leslie Warrender.'

'And?'

'I asked if she'd seen that man again. You know, sir, the one who shared a table with him the night he died?'

'I am managing to keep up, Richards. Stop spinning it out. I take it the punchline is, she had?'

'Yes, sir.'

'Don't sound so deflated.' Producing a large handkerchief, Chance mopped up the tea he'd splashed. 'Blast this spout. Who is he?'

'She doesn't know. He hasn't been in again.'

Chance raised his eyes to the ceiling and studied the yellow stain over the desk. Courtesy of his predecessor.

'But she saw him on Saturday night. He was queueing for fish and chips with a chap she does know. Not personally, he's one of their regulars. She said they were definitely together chatting, like.'

'Did she tell him we'd like to talk to him?'

'No, sir. She was across the road at the bus stop.'

Stirring his tea, Chance eyed him thoughtfully. The constable's collar was frayed. He wondered if Richards lived alone. Bishop would know. So it was Ernie's Plaice, eh? Their batter's soggy, if you ask me. Did you get this regular's details?'

'Enough to find him, sir. His name's Hector..'

'Poor devil.'

Richards smirked briefly. 'He works at the StayFresh Laundry.'

'Get yourself round there.' Chance glanced at the clock. 'Tomorrow will do. Leave it until the afternoon. You might be needed to bring someone in before then.'

Raising his eyebrows, Richards looked about to speak when Sergeant Bishop came in. He held the door wide for the constable to leave.

'Richards has a line on the chap at Warrender's table in The Bell. I'd like it followed up in case they did know each other. Best leave no loose ends.'

Bishop scribbled a note. 'Before we go any …' He subsided as Chance resumed speaking at the same time.

'We'd better get someone round the town hall to the registrar's first thing. Get a copy of Joan's birth certificate and check there are no marriage lines for Evelyn.'

'I'll see to it.' Bishop looked increasingly unhappy. 'That was Lionel on the 'phone.'

'Not before time.' Chance sat up expectantly. 'I suppose he strung it out deliberately. What does he have to say?'

'Not what you wanted to hear. He's now certain a Nugent's paper-knife wasn't the murder weapon. Sorry, Eddie. The measurements don't fit.'

Twenty-five

With a pained expression, Phyllis Marden marched an apple-core at arm's length over to the waste-paper basket. She couldn't leave the desk so there was nowhere to tip the dregs of cold tea left in a tin mug. It looked unprofessional on the counter so she put it on the shelf behind her.

The memos were stacked in date order and the notice-board tidied. Satisfied, she surveyed her temporary kingdom. Sergeant Lelliott had told her to man the front desk for half an hour. All it lacked now was members of the public.

Despite having a headache, her natural cheerfulness was returning. Spring did that to you. Best foot forward. Finding a dead body -especially of someone she'd spoken to – would shake anyone up but her common sense hadn't deserted her. She hadn't screamed and made a fool of herself in front of the head of C.I.D. Some women would have done, she didn't doubt.

Relations with Dad were back to normal on the surface. If they were tip-toeing around one another, neither of them were going to talk about it. Their careful conversations about the weather and the neighbours lasted through meal-times. Awkward subjects, his work and hers, the garden and work-shop might not have existed.

Dad had been as good as his word. When she finally reached home on Saturday, tired out and her head throbbing, the work-shop had been swept bare. She hadn't felt like talking about poor Mrs Simmonds but she'd had to tell him briefly. He couldn't do enough for her and the misery on his face only made things worse.

She'd waited until she finally heard him snoring that night before having a good cry. Afterwards she couldn't work out which of the three of them she was crying for.

She looked up expectantly as the door swung open but it was only Sid.

'You're looking pleased with yourself.' He was bare-headed, his hair darkened by damp. 'What have you been up to?'

'A job for Inspector Chance.' Sid tapped the side of his nose mysteriously.

'Oh?' She wasn't going to give him the satisfaction but her curiosity was piqued. 'Where've you been?'

'The town hall.'

She wouldn't ask even though it meant biting her tongue.

'Heard the latest?' Sid leant confidentially on the counter, his elbow across the ledger.

'I've been up to my eyes in work.' Her voice was lofty.

'We may be bringing in another suspect later.'

'Oh, that.' She yawned. 'D'you mind? You're making the page damp.'

'Sorry.' Sid straightened up. 'If you like.. if you aren't doing anything tonight, I could take you for a drink and tell you all about it.'

It had to be faced some time.

Only hadn't she had her share of facing up to things lately? She looked at Sid's face which managed to be hopeful and nervous all at the same time. His eyes were roaming around the reception area and back to her.

'I can't, I'm washing my hair.' The first remark that came to her but she didn't have to be so crass.

Sid gave her a grin that wavered away. 'It always looks great.'

Phyllis felt as though she'd rubbed a puppy's nose in it. Her hands smoothed the pages unnecessarily. 'It's very kind of you, Sid, but it isn't a good idea to see too much of each other socially. Not with us being colleagues. You understand, I'm sure. That sort of thing's frowned on.

Inspector Forrest wouldn't like it. And..' her mind searched desperately, 'this job's hard enough for me as it is.'

His face cleared. 'Of course, the last thing I'd want is to make things difficult for you, Phyl.'

'Thanks. After all, we'll run into each other at the tennis club. We can chat then. We're bound to fix up a doubles some time.'

He nodded. 'Bound to. I'd better get back to the inspector.' His neck as he turned away had a crimson haze like a port-wine stain.

She didn't watch him go.

*

As they drove around to Pearl-street, Richards was keeping up his usual bored expression. It didn't ring true. Bishop could feel the tension coming off him. If all went well, an arrest was imminent.

Glad had burnt his bacon that morning, an unheard of occurrence. A moment's inattention, the dripping caught and you could sole shoes with his rashers. The woman opposite had knocked. Low voices on the door-step. On the cadge he suspected, with the tallyman due. His missus was a soft touch and half the neighbourhood knew it.

They were past the Ides of March but it seemed a bad omen all the same.

A little kid was rolling a rubber ball across the street as they approached. Richards drew up short with brakes worthy of cornering at Brooklands. They turned to each other and exchanged weak grins. The little lad disappeared down a twitten before he could cop an earful.

The weather was quite different from the day before, in that English way of turn and turnabout. Bishop got out, feeling reluctant. His arm brushed against wet leaves as he opened the gate. He never usually minded bringing someone in. Tapping the knocker, his thoughts wandered to how many collars he'd felt over the years. He waited, shoulders hunched against the drizzle.

The door was opened by the man they'd come to collect. Herbert Dawson stood there waiting for him to speak. Bishop caught the spark of fear in his eyes, quickly fading to resignation. It looked as though Chance was right.

'Come in, Sergeant.' Mr. Dawson looked beyond him at the car. 'Is Inspector Chance not with you?'

'Thank you, sir.' Bishop wiped his feet on the mat. 'The inspector's back at the police-station.' He was feeling his way to continue when Dawson spoke suddenly.

'I've been half-expecting you. I suppose it was only a matter of time.' His Adam's apple bobbed against the knot of his tie as he swallowed.

Dawson had shut the front door behind him and there was little room for the two of them at the foot of the stairs. The pong of polish tickled Bishop's sinuses. The house smelt like a church.

'We have some questions to put to you, Mr. Dawson. We've reason to believe you haven't been entirely frank with us.'

'No.' That sounded like an apology. 'Will you come through, Sergeant? It will be a relief to get this over, man to man.'

Bishop found himself stepping behind the usual jargon. 'That isn't what I meant, sir. The inspector sent me to bring you to the station for questioning.'

'I see, of course. Forgive me, I don't know the form.' Mr. Dawson reached for the mackintosh hanging by Bishop. He stared at the gabardine over his arm as though he'd never seen it before. 'I'm ready to tell you everything you want to know. Only may I leave a note for my wife? I'll be quick. She's gone shopping and she'll worry..'

Bishop agreed that he could. He watched patiently while Mr. Dawson darted between pen and paper in the middle room and dashed off a line. The paper was placed in front of the clock on the mantelpiece. He noted the studio photographs of a young woman and the soldier.

'Thank you, Sergeant.' Holding his cap, he followed Bishop outside.

The short return journey was in silence. Richards kept eyeing their passenger in the mirror. His mac folded over his knees, Mr. Dawson gazed out of the side window with a blank expression.

*

'We left him in the interview room.'

'Good. We'll leave him to kick his heels for a few minutes.'

Frederic Street only had the one. A small window overlooked the yard though it was too high up to show anything but sky. There were narrow bars, presumably to foil any Victorian miscreants who'd fancied climbing out. The atmosphere gave more than a flavour of what lay ahead if you couldn't talk yourself outside.

'How did he seem?' Chance said.

'Almost relieved. Sort of anxious to be helpful.'

'Did he say anything else?'

Bishop hung up his mackintosh. 'Not a word in the car.'

'I'd have read the note.'

'It was only a line to his missus.'

'Not having second thoughts?'

'I didn't say that.' Bishop patted his pockets. 'I was watching when we drove past Mrs Simmonds's house. He didn't react.'

'Godwin drew a blank at the registry. That supports my theory. Evelyn Dawson didn't marry locally and she didn't give birth to Joan round here.'

'It's register office,' Bishop said. 'Everyone says registry but it's wrong.'

'Drink your tea,' Chance said, 'and we'll go and get it over with.'

*

Richards stood stiffly to attention when they walked in. Chance knew perfectly well he'd been leaning against the wall until he heard their footsteps. They all did.

Mr. Dawson, facing them at the table, made as though to get up and sank down. Chance raised his eyebrows at Richards who shook his head to indicate the suspect had said nothing. He left as they took the two chairs. Bishop cracked open a fresh page in his note-book and looked expectant.

'Good morning, Inspector.' Dawson cleared his throat, his voice tentative. 'May I enquire if I'm to be arrested?'

'At the moment you're helping us with our enquiries, Mr. Dawson.' Chance was deliberately stern. 'What happens after that depends on your answers. Sergeant Bishop may caution you at any time and you are at liberty to telephone for your solicitor now, should you wish to do so.'

'Thank you but that won't be necessary.'

Chance sat back and considered where to begin. The other man's shoulders were rigid, his hands linked. Clearly nervous, yet his eyes met Chance's gaze steadily. He didn't look like a murderer.

'I'll do my best to answer any questions you wish to put to me, Inspector.'

Something was wrong. His attitude was decidedly rum. 'In that case Mr. Dawson, perhaps you'd care to tell us the true nature of your connection with Leslie Warrender?'

'We had a slight acquaintance for a few months after the war.'

It was evidently going to be inch by inch. 'How did you meet?'

'He was a friend of my daughter Evelyn. She introduced him.'

Chance said nothing, giving the hanging light-bulb a long suffering look. It seemed to do the trick.

'If you want the truth, I loathed him.'

The words were like a hand of cards face upwards.

'Getting at the truth is why we're all here, Mr. Dawson. When you found the body, why didn't you tell us you recognised who it was?'

For a moment it seemed he was going to remain silent. 'This isn't easy for me, Inspector. You've found out what he did to my daughter or I wouldn't be here. I knew it was only a matter of time. I suppose you want every last detail?'

'Go ahead.' Chance folded his arms.

'Leslie Warrender seduced my daughter and walked away when he'd had what he wanted. He never had any intention of marrying her. Shortly after he left Tennysham, Evelyn found she was carrying a child. You've met my granddaughter, both of you.'

Bishop nodded, his expression sympathetic.

'She had no way of getting in touch with him. Her mother and I had to cope as best we could. Evelyn never heard from him again. Though that was a bloody good thing.' His voice quivered, the Sussex burr more pronounced. 'I'm sorry but if either of you have daughters, you'll understand.'

Chance had been about to signal *told you so* at Bishop. Only the triumph had unaccountably vanished. They did both have a daughter.

He put his question as much to forestall an embarrassing scene as to get to the point. 'Mr. Dawson, did you kill Leslie Warrender?'

'No, Inspector. I did not. Twelve years ago I wanted to kill him with my bare hands. You know I had good cause, I can see it in your faces but he'd vanished. I enquired at his place of work. Someone there thought he'd gone to London so that was that. I wanted to ask his land-lady if he'd left a forwarding address but Evelyn begged me not to. By then she'd realised he wouldn't make an honest woman of her, even if we found him.' He shrugged helplessly. 'I told myself I'd thrash him if I ever caught up with him. When it came to it, I couldn't even do that.'

Bishop made a brief note. He looked up when he'd done, his face now impassive.

Chance thought furiously. 'Did you meet Leslie Warrender here last November?'

'No.' His eyes were startled. 'I'd no idea he was here then. Was he after me?'

'Why would you think that, Mr. Dawson?'

'If he'd found out about Joan. Not that he'd be interested in her but if there was money to be made..'

'Do you have reason to suppose Mr. Warrender was a blackmailer?'

'I wouldn't put it past him. I knew a remittance man when I saw one. If only my wife and daughter had seen through him from the start.'

'What was he like?' Chance said with interest.

'Full of hot air. He'd been to public school. Came from a good family who'd lost their money, according to Evelyn. He must have been the black sheep. I knew he was amusing himself. He'd had an easy war, you know. Held out 'til he was conscripted then wangled his way in the cycle corps. Came back without a scratch.'

'The Cyclist Corps hardly had it easy, Mr. Dawson,' Chance said dryly. 'When did you meet Leslie Warrender again?'

'I didn't meet him first or last. I saw him in the street on the Monday of the week he died. It was an almighty shock, though I always feared he'd walk back into our lives one day. I never quite felt safe though it got easier over the years.'

'Where did you see him?'

He looked up at the window, smeared with rain. 'In the High Street. He was going into Grove's. I thought I recognised him from the way he walked, even though he was carrying a small case. I had to be sure.'

Chance nodded. A walk was more distinctive than most people realised. 'What happened next?'

'I followed him. I had to know what he was up to, in order to protect my family.'

'Go on.'

'He went up to the tea-room. I hung around watching the stairs and followed him when he came down. It wasn't difficult. When the passers-by thinned out, I dropped further back but he didn't turn around. It looked as though he was making for my house but to my relief he slowed and I realised he was picking out lodgings.'

'And?'

'He knocked on Mrs Simmonds's door and I saw him go in. I was horrified.'

Chance shifted position on his chair. 'This is obviously difficult for you, Mr. Dawson, but we need to know everything you can tell us about the last few days of Leslie Warrender's life. You say you didn't kill him, so help us find whoever did. Remember that person almost certainly murdered Mrs Simmonds as well.'

Mr. Dawson hesitated, 'I know nothing about her death, Inspector. She was a good woman and didn't deserve to have her life taken away. But I don't care who did for Warrender. That swine as good as killed my daughter.'

'You'd better explain what you mean by that.' Chance sounded uncharacteristically gentle.

'My Evelyn was a good girl. She couldn't cope with the shame. She was only eighteen. We did our best to cover things up, once the shock had sunk in. We've family in Wales so Evelyn went there until the baby was born. We gave out that she was marrying a distant cousin. Then once she had Joan, we brought her home and said she was newly widowed. We've always kept ourselves to ourselves but in a way that made it worse. There was talk, of course. People like to see someone taken down a peg.'

'Gossips can be cruel without meaning to be,' Bishop said. He'd put down his pen and was listening intently.

'Yes, Sergeant, they can.' Dawson sighed. 'Evelyn meant everything to us. She came along when we'd given up hope of having children. She and Joan had a home with us but she couldn't put what happened behind her. She wouldn't take an interest in the baby. My wife did everything. We had to watch Evelyn fading away from us. In the end she took her own life. Drowned herself. They said it was an accident. It was kindly meant. Olive and I knew what she'd done and who was to blame.'

'Thank you for being frank with us, sir,' Bishop said. 'I'm afraid privacy is the first thing to go in a murder inquiry.'

'I understand you have your job to do,' Mr. Dawson said. 'Perhaps you'll understand my attitude now.' He turned back to Chance. 'You want to know everything I did, Inspector? After Warrender had gone in, I didn't go straight home. I needed time to compose myself and think what to do so I turned back and walked along the sea-front. I decided not to tell my wife I'd seen him. She would only have been frightened.'

'What else did you decide?'

'To do nothing. Isn't that what men like me usually do? Wait and see. I met Joan from school.'

'Did Mrs Dawson find out Warrender was here that week?'

Mr. Dawson shook his head. 'No, I kept it to myself. She didn't know anything when you called to see us on the Saturday. When you'd gone I had to tell her I'd recognised the body.'

'She didn't recognise the dead man herself?'

'No, Olive only glanced in the shelter for a second. All that part was quite true. His trilby was partly over his face.'

The two detectives looked at each other. Chance sat up straight.

'Then which part is lies, Mr. Dawson?'

His face drained of colour like a plug being pulled.

'We can sit here all day if needs be. You'll have to come clean in the end.'

Mr. Dawson passed his tongue over his lips. 'I didn't murder Warrender, Inspector Chance. All this has shown me I couldn't kill anyone. I admit I haven't told you everything. I can't think straight.'

'Just tell us, Mr. Dawson,' Chance said wearily. 'Whatever it is you're hiding.'

'I saw his dead body on the Thursday night.'

'What?' Chance looked confounded. He glanced at Bishop. 'What the devil do you mean?'

'I found him dead,' Dawson repeated. 'I was there on the sea-front. Oh, I didn't see who killed him but I must have just missed the murderer.'

Chance stared at him in disbelief. 'You never thought you should tell us this?'

'I'm sorry. Think of the position I was in. If I reported finding the body while I happened to be along the promenade at night, you'd want to know why I was there. You'd be bound to suspect me. Once you looked into my background you'd discover I'd known Warrender.'

Chance breathed out audibly. 'Which is exactly what has happened. If what you say is true, you've made yourself look more suspicious. If you'd told us this in the first place, you'd have saved us a lot of time.'

Mr. Dawson bowed his head. 'I can only repeat I'm sorry, Inspector.'

'If you were so keen to avoid notice, why look at the body with your wife the next morning?'

'I needed to know if he'd been found. I shouldn't have done that to Olive but I wasn't thinking clearly. I've been a fool.' Chance grunted. 'If I hadn't followed Warrender, the police wouldn't know I exist. Why didn't I let well alone? Only I wasn't to know someone else would do for him.'

With a questioning look at Chance, Bishop took over.

'Right, Mr. Dawson, let's go back from when you saw Leslie Warrender go into Mrs Simmonds's house on the Monday afternoon. What time was that?'

'Some time after three.'

'Tell us what happened next and let's have no more prevaricating. I'm sure you'd like to get home.'

'I didn't set eyes on him again until the Wednesday evening. I didn't sleep much that Monday night. Then I spent all Tuesday worrying and wondering what he was up to. By Wednesday I couldn't stand it any longer. Anything was better than waiting for a knock on the door so I decided to try and find out.'

His voice was becoming hoarse. Bishop poured a glass of water from the jug on the table.

'Thank you.' He swallowed quickly. 'I didn't know if he was still at Mrs Simmonds's or why. If he'd been asking around about me, she'd have put him on to us at once. We moved from the other side of town after we lost Evelyn. Olive couldn't cope with the memories in our old house or the pity in neighbours' eyes. We had to think about Joan growing up.'

'A fresh start.'

Chance was amused to see that his sergeant had Dawson talking more readily. Bishop applied the same no nonsense manner he adopted with old lags, firm but avuncular. Stretching his legs under the table he surreptitiously rubbed the toe of his left shoe hard along his right calf. Blasted cramp.

Dawson drank some more water. 'Warrender wasn't the type to sit in his room all evening and I knew when Mrs Simmonds served supper for her guests so I lay in wait in case he went out.'

'Did your wife ask where you were going?' Chance said. In his experience all women would.

Mr. Dawson looked down at his hands. 'I have an old pal who's had a rough time with the 'flu. Olive thought I was visiting him. I told her I was sitting with him the next night too, when I found the body.'

'We'll come on to that, Mr. Dawson,' Bishop said. 'Finish telling us about Wednesday.'

'I waited at the end of the twitten. It was after dark and no one came by. I didn't have to wait long. Warrender came out all right but Mrs Simmonds was with him. They set off towards the town centre so that was that. All I'd found out was that he was still here.'

'Now we come to the Thursday. The day Warrender was murdered,' Bishop said. 'Keep going, Mr. Dawson.'

Someone knocked on the door. The sound seemed hesitant to Chance as he inclined his head to see who it was. Godwin's face appeared in the gap. Bishop rose and went in the corridor, putting his head round the door almost immediately.

'Could I have a word, sir?'

Chance got up, glad to move his leg. A moment later he and Bishop resumed their seats.

'Please continue, Mr. Dawson.'

'I didn't know what to think, Sergeant. I wanted to ask Mrs Simmonds how long her lodger was staying but I couldn't show my face round there.'

'What happened on the Thursday?'

'I took my wife out because I couldn't stay in the house. I felt safer when Joan was at school and I determined to take them both out all weekend if need be. Warrender had to leave sometime. That evening I tried waiting for him again.'

'Why not carry on keeping your head down?' Chance said.

'I couldn't stand not knowing what he was going to do. I wish to God I had done nothing.'

'Did you take your dog?' Only that's quite a handy cover, isn't it? Hanging around with a dog sniffing the gutter.'

'No, she didn't get her walk that night. I told my wife I'd see to Tess when I got home but as it turned out, I had other things on my mind. It was later than the previous evening by the time I got away. I was thinking of giving up when the door slammed and Warrender appeared. This time he was alone and I followed him to a pub.'

'Which one, sir?'

'The Bell in Church Row. I didn't dare go inside in case he saw me. I loitered in the churchyard and then sat in the lych-gate. There's a good view of the pub entrance from there.'

'So you aren't able to say if Warrender was meeting anyone?' Bishop said.

Dawson shook his head. 'I was feeling more and more angry with myself.. and him. There I was, wasting my time, hanging around in the dark, achieving nothing. Some men went into the pub and he came out. I made up my mind to tackle him, once and for all. I reasoned that he couldn't be in Tennysham to track me down. It came to me in the churchyard that he probably didn't even remember Evelyn.'

'What did you do, Mr. Dawson?'

'I was going to accost him but he set off down the road at a fair lick. Not like a man strolling back from the pub and in any case he was going in the other direction. I admit I was curious so I followed him as far as The Esplanade. He crossed to the sea-front and started walking towards Eastcliff. I guessed he was meeting someone in private, either some dodgy business or a married woman.'

'Did you see anyone else?'

'No one. The small hotels opposite were lit up but the street was deserted. I let him get a fair way ahead. When he reached the last shelter he went inside. I slipped in the nearest one myself.'

'Where exactly, Mr. Dawson?'

'Two shelters along from where he was. I didn't like to get any closer.'

Bishop made a note. 'Were you still intending to accost Mr. Warrender?'

'I don't know. I had some idea that if I knew what he was up to, I might get the upper hand somehow. I was nerving myself to steal nearer when I thought I heard a footstep.'

Chance pictured the scene on the dark promenade. Mr. Dawson shrinking back in the shelter, churning with anger, weakness and fear. Why not march up to Warrender and give him a bloody nose?

'Did you look out?' Bishop said.

'No. I wasn't sure, it could have been the sound of the waves. For all I knew he'd turned along there for a smoke.'

'Tell us exactly what you saw and heard, Mr. Dawson. I'm sure you see how important it is.'

'I'll help you all I can, Sergeant but I saw nothing. I stayed put for a while. Don't ask me how long. Twenty minutes?' Mr. Dawson reached for the glass and drained the remaining water. 'I started to feel trapped and an even bigger fool.'

'D'you know what time it was roughly?'

'I looked at my wrist-watch on the corner, as Warrender crossed to the promenade. It was five past nine. I was thinking my wife would likely be asleep by the time I came home.'

The timing was right but he was no murderer. Chance scowled in frustration. Dawson had been on the spot and seen sweet Fanny Adams. To cap it all he could feel his stomach rumbling.

'What happened next?'

'Eventually I had to move. There was no sign of Warrender and no sounds apart from the sea. I didn't hear him being killed. I edged cautiously up to the shelter, listened and there was nothing. It felt empty so I thought he'd gone without my realising. I looked in and he was sitting there. It made me jump, I can tell you. He was in deep shadow, looking straight at me but he didn't speak or move an inch.'

'Think back,' Bishop said. 'Could you hear anyone? Footsteps on the road or a vehicle?'

'There was nothing.'

'How did you realise Warrender was dead?'

'I knew something was terribly wrong. The moon shifted from behind the clouds and I saw his eyes were open. I took out my electric-torch and shone it on his face. He was gone all right. I held my hand before his mouth to make sure.'

'His hat wasn't over his face?'

Mr. Dawson hesitated, 'No, I did that. It was on the bench next to him.'

Chance stared at him. 'Why did you interfere with a corpse? Let's have the rest of it.'

'There was a wound on his chest. His pullover was ripped and there was a small dark stain. I realised he'd been stabbed. I suppose I panicked.'

'What did you do, Mr. Dawson?' Bishop said quietly. Dawson shook his head and looked away. 'Better make a clean breast of it. We'll know if you hold anything back.'

The other man sank lower in his chair. 'I'm sorry. I've been law-abiding all my life until I saw Warrender again. I was frightened, certain I'd be suspected. Someone could have seen me following him. I went through his pockets for identification. There was nothing but a wallet and a bill from a shop with a London address. I took them and buttoned his overcoat to hide the wound. There was very little blood.'

'Did you by Jove?' Chance murmured. His voice was grim.

Mr. Dawson shot a glance at him and returned to Bishop. 'I did something else. I felt contempt for him but I'm not proud of what I did now.'

'Let's hear it, Mr. Dawson.'

'There was a hip flask next to him with the top off. It smelt of spirits. I sprinkled the contents over his coat. I had some idea he'd be taken for a tramp and it would keep people away. I thought it would make it harder to tell when he died. I put his hat forward on his head so he'd look like someone sleeping it off.'

Within the small room there was silence. Outside the window, rain spilled from a blocked gutter. Chance treated the ceiling to a withering glare.

'What did you do with the things you stole from the corpse?'

'I didn't steal them, Inspector. I've tried to explain how it happened. It was done in an instant. D'you really think I wanted anything of his? I took a quick look at the wallet and the bill and thrust them in my pockets. I was frantic to get away from there. I thought I could burn them when I was safe but I couldn't destroy the flask. I wasn't wearing gloves so I wiped it with my handkerchief and flung it into the sea. Then I took a look around to make sure no one was in sight and hurried across the road.'

'Was there any cash in the wallet?' Chance said.

'Yes, there were a lot of banknotes folded together. You can't think that's why I took it? I didn't want his filthy money but I couldn't bring myself to throw it in the sea and I needed to search the wallet thoroughly in case I'd missed anything with his name on. I thought there was a good chance the police would never find out who he was.'

'Why did you leave the wallet on the churchyard wall?'

Dawson's expression was appalled. 'But I didn't. When I got indoors, I realised I'd dropped it. I was worried sick in case it was found in the street near my home. I even went out again to look. I went back to my daughter's grave. She's buried in St Luke's churchyard. It may sound odd but I wanted to tell her Warrender was dead. The wallet must have fallen from my pocket on the grass. I still had the bill. I burnt it the next morning.'

'What did you do with the cash?' Bishop said.

'I gave it to charity. I wouldn't have kept it for the world. Please believe me.'

'I do believe you, Mr. Dawson.' Bishop sounded tired. 'Just answer the question, if you please.'

'As I was hurrying through the streets, a man came out of The Mafeking. He turned out of sight and as I drew level with the pub door, I glanced in and saw a charity box in the passage. The door into the bar was shut and no one could see me so I stuffed the banknotes in the slit as fast as I could.'

'What time did you get back to your house?' Chance said.

'Just after ten. My wife was in bed reading. I managed to act normally, though inside I was in turmoil.'

'And you still maintain she knows nothing of all this?'

'Not a thing, Inspector. I wanted to protect her and Joan. God knows, I failed to protect my daughter.'

'One thing more, did you walk home past Mrs Simmonds's house?'

'Yes, it's the quickest way.'

'Did you see her at the window?'

'No, I hurried past and didn't look. Did she see me?'

Chance shrugged. 'We'll never know. That's everything, is it?'

'Yes, Inspector Chance. I give you my word I've kept nothing back.'

He watched Herbert Dawson gather what remained of his dignity.

'What will happen to me?'

'That won't be up to me. You'll be informed if charges are to be made.' Chance stood as Bishop capped his pen and pushed back his chair. 'Your wife is here waiting for you.'

'What have you told her?'

Chance looked down at Dawson. 'She turned up worried about you. She's quite safe, drinking tea in my office. A young police-woman is looking after her.'

'Thank you, Inspector.'

Chance followed Bishop and turned around at the door. 'You've led us quite a dance, Mr. Dawson. I suggest you take your wife home and the pair of you stay out of my sight.'

Twenty-six

The rain which had eased during their dinner break, was falling heavily again. A butcher's boy in the High Street idled in the open door. Blood smears streaked either side of his apron. A Southdown 'bus ahead of them was holding up the traffic as passengers clambered down. Richards drummed his fingers on the steering wheel as he waited.

Chance briefly considered telling him off for an impatience he possessed himself in bucket-loads. It had been a long, trying day and it was only ten to two.

'I doubt anything will come of this.' Thinking aloud, he repeated what he'd said in the canteen to Bishop. 'But we can't afford to ignore any lead.' Not when the case against his only suspect had collapsed in front of him.

'No, sir.'

'I thought you might as well come along as you questioned the bar-maid.'

'Thank you, sir.'

'How are you finding life out of uniform, Richards?'

'I think C.I.D. work's more interesting, sir.'

The street was full of umbrellas. A woman outside a draper's was trying to shield a bunch of daffodils inside her coat. A couple were sheltering in a doorway. The woman laughing, the man lighting up, flicking a match in the gutter. They looked familiar.

'Do you now? We'll be one short when McInnes leaves.'

'I heard, sir.' A note of caution in Richards's voice. He flinched as a horn sounded somewhere behind them.

'Don't keep everyone waiting, Constable.' The two from the library. Probably on their way back to work. Daphne cycled home for dinner most days. He wondered how well they knew one another.

They moved off again. Richards glanced sideways at him, gauging his mood.

'Did you mean, sir, that you'd consider me?'

'Do you want to be considered?'

'Yes, I do, sir.'

Chance grunted. 'Could do worse I suppose. If Inspector Forrest feels he can spare you permanently. I won't have any slackers.'

'Understood, sir.'

'I'll see what Sergeant Bishop thinks when this case is over. In the meantime keep your nose clean.' *And your collars.*

The premises of the StayFresh Laundry were dingier than the name would suggest. A brick building with skylights in a dirty zig-zag roof and a single-storey afterthought tacked on the rear. They were sandwiched between a parade of shops put up a few years ago, a few small businesses and the main road that ran behind the town. A new building, black and white timbered above enormous plate-glass windows stood on the corner. A banner advertised the arrival of a motor-car showroom.

Richards parked in the yard outside a door marked *Office*. A van at the far end was being loaded. Steam was coming out of a pipe and vanishing in the rain.

Inside, machinery rumbled quietly. A middle-aged woman rose from her typewriter to fetch the manager. Chance tried not to breathe in the pervading atmosphere of warm soap as they waited.

'Police, you say? What can I do for you?'

A tubby man in a cheap suit bustled further into the room. Chance turned round from his casual reading of dockets pinned on a notice-board.

'It's not one of our vans, is it?' He took them in properly. 'You're not in uniform.'

'This is Detective-Inspector Chance, sir. We're from Tennysham C.I.D.' Richards, having performed his introduction, stood back as Chance took over.

'We're here to speak to one of your men. We're looking for a chap on your books, name of Hector. We don't have his surname. Will you look up your work-force?'

'No need. We only have the one.' The manager frowned, passing a hand over his patch of stiff hair. 'What's he done? I've always found him reliable.'

'Nothing,' Chance said hastily. 'It's in connection with a witness. Is he here now?'

'Yes, he is'.

'Good. What does he do?'

'General maintenance.' As he spoke, the manager threw open the door. 'Eileen. Get hold of Hec and fetch him to the office straight away, will you?' He turned back to them. 'He won't be a minute. Do you need me to stay?'

'That won't be necessary, sir. We won't keep your chap long. What's his surname by the way?'

'Fenton. Well, if you're sure. He isn't in trouble?'

'I said not.'

When they were alone Chance perched on the edge of the untidy desk, hands thrust in his pockets. 'Dogsbody,' he murmured. 'Let's hope we don't get him the sack to go with his broom.'

The office had an inner glass wall overlooking a large space where women in overalls and hairnets were working. As he watched them moving about, there was a tap on the door and a big, red-faced man in a brown overall came in. A screw-driver handle stuck out of his top pocket.

'Hector Fenton?'

'That's me. There's not been an accident?'

'We're not here about anything like that, sir. Nothing to do with you in fact. We're trying to track down someone you know.'

'Right.' The wary expression sank into cheerful folds. 'No one's done anything to interest the police that I know of. What's it all about?'

'Nothing to concern yourself with, Mr. Fenton. We're looking for a man who may be a witness.' Chance jerked his head.

Richards stepped forward. 'If you cast your mind back to last Saturday evening, sir, you were seen chatting to a man in a fish and chip shop in town. Can you give us his name?'

'Who's been following me around then? Can't a fellow go to the chippy now without someone tipping off you lot?'

Richards didn't react. 'If you could tell us, sir? Do you know who he is?'

Fenton scratched his head. 'Of course I do, he's the wife's brother but surely he's not in trouble? He wouldn't say boo to a goose.'

'There's no question of that. All we want is his name and where we can find him. We only need a brief word.'

'In that case you won't have far to go.' Fenton pointed at the window. 'His name's Jim Buckley and he's over there. He were by the van a minute ago. If you come with me, I'll show you the way round.'

They followed him down a corridor through a room which was clearly used for packing. An entrance gave on to an open back where rain was beating steadily on a corrugated iron roof. A laundry basket on wheels was drawn up to the open doors of the van they'd seen. In the dim interior a man was checking hefty brown paper parcels on racks. Tied with sturdy string, each had a cream label hanging to the front.

'I say, Jim, you're wanted. There's two plain-clothes bobbies here for you.'

'You can be off now,' Chance said coldly.

The van creaked as the other man stepped down carefully. In his forties, mousy hair retreating from his temples, he eyed them cautiously.

'Detectives?'

Richards explained who they were once more. Chance didn't believe in repeating himself.

'But why d'you want me?'

'We think you may be able to assist us in an inquiry, Mr. Buckley. Can you think back to the evening of Thursday the fifth of this month? That's two weeks ago tomorrow.'

'I was staying here that day.'

'Don't you live in Tennysham?' Chance leant against a wooden pillar.

'I do now. I moved down from Surrey at the weekend.' The other man set down the clip-board he was holding and stuck his pencil behind his ear. 'My sister and her husband are putting me up until I can find digs. I lost my last job when I ricked my back. Couldn't find anything. He tipped me off there was temporary work going here as a relief driver. First off I had three days then I got given this week. They're short-handed with the 'flu but there's the chance of a permanent job. I don't want to put a foot wrong. What about that night?'

With a look at Chance, Richards explained, finishing with a description of Leslie Warrender. 'So you see, all we need from you is everything you can remember about him.'

'I heard about the murder but never dreamt that was him. Strewth.. you never know when your number's up. He was just an ordinary chap. I didn't take much notice. You don't, do you, in a pub?'

'Never mind all that,' Chance said. 'Just tell us everything you can recall.'

'Well I'd done my three days and thought I'd treat myself to a pint. I reckoned one wouldn't hurt. So I walked along to the Bell. When I went in, it was busy. Most of 'em at the tables were playing dominoes. Still I didn't want to miss out. I bought my drink and there was no room to stay at the bar. Besides I fancied a sit-down so I looked round and saw a place left at a little table in the corner. Only this one chap eating a pie and reading a paper.'

Chance and Richards exchanged looks.

'Do you recall what time it was?' Richards pulled out his note-book.

'Getting on for eight or thereabouts. I can't say any nearer.'

'That's close enough. Now what was said?'

Buckley gazed across the wet yard as he thought. 'Nothing to speak of, I don't think.' He shook his head. 'Sorry, I can't remember.'

'Try,' Chance said. He folded his arms.

'I'm doing my best, sir. I asked him if the seat was taken and he said.. That's right, he said *'free as a bird, old chap'* or something like that. He nodded, quite friendly when I sat down.'

'Did he say anything else?' Richards said. 'You're doing well.'

'That was it, I think. We didn't have a chat. I had the evening paper myself. Had to wait 'til my brother-in-law had finished with it.'

'The bar-maid had the impression you were talking.'

'Only when I came over. Look if you don't mind, I ought to get on.' Reaching over the basket, Buckley heaved out a parcel of laundry. Breathing heavily he swung it on the floor of the van.

Reluctantly, Chance detached himself from the pillar, ready to go.

'These weigh a ton. Sheets and such for the hotels. I've to be careful not to put my back out again. You know, there was something else.'

'What?'

Buckley's face cleared. 'Got it, it's not much. The chap drained his glass and as he stood to be on his way, he caught my eye and said, *'Mustn't keep a lady waiting'.* And he winked.'

Chance stared at him. 'Is that everything he said?'

'Yes. He walked out and I never thought any more about him until now.'

'Thanks for your help.'

Chance strode towards the car. 'Back to the station'.

'Piece of luck, that.' Richards slid behind the wheel. 'What did you make of it, sir?'

'That there's only one person the murderer can be.'

*

Two people were dead.

The thrill of the end in sight that Chance had felt at the laundry had gone. Perhaps later, much later.. there would be a quiet satisfaction that a killer had been brought to justice. For now he felt as though Herbert Dawson had stepped aside and behind him he was seeing clearly at last, the face of the murderer.

A face he had spoken to and briefly pitied.

Bishop was waiting in the office, his expression grave.

'He's agreed, Wilf. We've sufficient grounds for a search warrant.'

'Did you have to persuade him? You were gone a while.'

Chance shook his head. 'No. I had to take him through the whole lot again and he agrees with us. The alibi can be demolished. I didn't get hauled over the coals for swallowing her story. Hayes said it was perfectly reasonable to believe what she told us at the time. He's satisfied we have our man. Or rather, I should say woman.'

'When do we go?'

'Mid-morning, I think. He's getting the warrant signed tonight but he wants the whole show as discreet as possible. I've to see the Chief Constable with him later.' Chance pulled a face. 'Another missed supper. Stella's been complaining I'm only at home to wash and sleep.'

'I'm sure your missus understands. A murder inquiry isn't an everyday occurrence, thankfully.'

Chance shrugged. 'She was keen on my promotion and moving back here. Besides we all have to make a living somehow.' He hesitated, looking away. 'Someone has to do it, I suppose.'

Bishop was no fool, taking a meaning he hadn't put into words. 'We don't make the laws, Eddie. Can't have murderers roaming the streets. Make the case and that's our part done.'

'What if we can't prove it? If the weapon was thrown away? It doesn't look as though Warrender's hip flask will ever turn up.'

'The tide was quite high that night. It probably got swept along the coast. Buck up, if she didn't keep the knife, we'll get a confession. She'll know it's over as soon as we turn up.'

'That's what Superintendent Hayes said. What baffles me is why kill Mrs Simmonds? We still don't know.'

'She had to be a threat in some way. We'll find out tomorrow. Who do you want to take with us?'

'I think Godwin, useful experience and he has a personable way about him. He won't alarm anyone. Richards to drive us but he'd better remain in the car. We don't want to look like a mob.'

'The same four of us as the beginning.'

'It's been quite a fortnight.' Chance gave him a wry smile. 'I had a word with Richards, by the way. Think you can lick him into shape?'

'I've done it before.'

'You get off now. I have to wait around for Hayes.'

'If you're sure?'

After the door closed on Bishop, still shoving his arms in his mackintosh, Chance stood at his open window. The rain had stopped. The wet slates of the roof-tops opposite gleamed. He couldn't see the Channel from where he was.

Though he could catch the sea on the breeze, invigorating as a dose of smelling salts. Smoke left a chimney across the street like fag-ash tapped into the grey sky.

He felt calm and determined as he wondered what the next day would bring.

Twenty-seven

Thursday morning, exactly two weeks since the last day of Leslie Warrender's life. It made sense to clear some routine tasks while he was waiting but he'd read nothing for the last ten minutes. An arrest would be made and the business of living go on.. for those who were left.

The people involved would fade from his mind after the trial. There would be more reports on his desk. More visits from Irene and Harold to look forward to. More perfunctory sparring with Stella and the occasional rapport. More bills. Not enough time to lie back in an arm-chair with a cheap scotch and jazz on the gramophone. Such is life.

The door handle rattled and Bishop's head appeared. 'The car's ready when you are, sir.'

It was time to leave.

The sea was calm as they turned into The Esplanade. Everywhere looked fresh and rain-washed. The air was mild and a weak light behind the clouds suggested a better day in a while.

Chance realised he was holding himself tense. Judging by the back of Godwin's neck, he wasn't the only one. No one spoke in the car.

The youth Eric was sweeping the steps as they drew up outside the Belvedere Hotel. He stopped as they approached, Chance at the rear.

'Morning, son,' Bishop said. 'Is your employer about?'

'She's inside, sir.' He pointed at the lounge windows on the right. 'In there.'

'Good lad.'

Chance had already spotted Miss Aldridge standing between two seated old ladies with their backs to the window. The next instant she was gone. When they entered the reception area, she was behind the desk.

Pince-nez lodged on her prominent nose, heathery jumper and tweed skirt, she looked respectable and dull. One of those faceless spinsters always in the background, stalwart of church committees and afternoon teas. Chance felt a flicker of uncertainty. She appeared so very ordinary.

'Inspector Chance.'

'Miss Aldridge.'

'Do you wish to speak to me?'

He moderated his voice. 'We have a warrant to search your premises. We should like to begin with your private quarters if you'll show us where they are.'

There was a blink while she reacted. Her face went an ugly blotched red and white as she drew herself up. 'What can you possibly mean by this?' Her voice was low and icy. 'How dare you? This is an outrage. I shall ring up the Chief Constable this instant.'

Godwin studied a potted fern as Bishop leant forward. 'It won't make any difference, madam. The Chief Constable has given his approval. Here's the warrant, all correct, signed by a JP. Best to let us get on with it. No one wants to make a floor-show in front of your residents.'

Miss Aldridge stared at him as though he were a slug she'd found in her cabbage. 'You can't mean to invade my guests' rooms?'

'Not unless we have to. But we mean to carry out our duty. We'll be as swift and discreet as we can. I advise you not to attempt to hold us up. Just go about your business and leave us to it, madam.'

'I don't know what you think you'll find.' Miss Aldridge pressed the bell on the counter. 'I suppose I have no choice but you haven't heard the last of this. I am not without influence in this town.' She looked scornfully at Chance.

One of the old ladies appeared in the lounge doorway. Leaning on an ebony stick, she regarded them with unashamed interest and a sweet smile. She moved slowly towards the reception desk.

'I wonder, Miss Aldridge, may I ask you one thing more? I don't mean to push ahead of these gentlemen but it'll only take a moment. For you, that is. Would you be so good as to...' She held up a needle with an apologetic face. 'So clumsy of me. I'm afraid it's come adrift again and I simply can't see well enough unless I hold it very close to my eyes, which doesn't seem sensible.' She turned towards them. 'So foolish. Fortunately I can still embroider if the stitches aren't *too* complicated.'

Bishop raised his hat. 'You go first, ma'am. We can wait.'

Miss Aldridge swung round at her. 'I can't come now, Mrs Hooper.'

Ivy Betts came from the back, her eyes widening as she saw them.

The old lady faltered. 'I'm so sorry to be in the way. If I might say, you don't look well, Miss Aldridge.'

'Ivy will help you,' Miss Aldridge said with an effort. 'I have one of my heads coming on.' She hesitated as they stood waiting. 'No, look... Oh very well.' Reaching under the desk she thrust a bunch of keys at the waiting girl. 'Ivy, take these men upstairs to my sitting-room. I'll see to you now, Mrs Hooper.'

'Don't forget the office,' Chance said neutrally. He smiled at the old lady.

Miss Aldridge spoke rapidly without looking at them. 'Kindly leave things precisely as you find them. You're wasting your time. Come along, Mrs Hooper.'

'Up here, Sergeant.'

As the others followed Ivy, Chance lingered a second to watch the two women go. If he was wrong this time, there would be the devil of a stink. Harassment of a refined, middle-aged spinster wouldn't be forgotten by the Chief Constable. Her hem dipping, Miss Dorothy Aldridge cut rather a sad figure from the rear.

The white-haired old lady almost stumbled as they entered the lounge and Chance watched those large capable hands grip her shoulders. An unremarkable gesture suddenly seemed full of menace. Those hands had held a cushion over Lily Simmonds's face. No, more likely one hand, with the other jerking back her hair.

He knew.

Moving swiftly up the stairs he caught up with Godwin. Ivy led them up to the first floor and along a corridor at the back. She stopped at the end door, which had no number.

'You're honoured,' she turned cheerfully to Bishop. 'Miss A. generally stands over me when I clean in here. What's ..? '

'Thanks, Miss,' Bishop took the keys from her. 'You can leave it to us from here.'

'Righto. Better lock up again when you leave. She's a stickler for her privacy. That one's for the office.' Ivy gave them an appraising look before disappearing down the passage.

'I wonder how long we have?' Chance said dryly.

'Sir?' Godwin looked questioningly at him as he stood back.

'She'll be up here soon enough. We'd better get on with it.'

Bishop rapped his knuckles on the wall by the door as he let them in. 'Hollow.'

A flat had been made by partitioning the end of the passage. A quick glance showed a bedroom, sitting-room and bathroom.

'She must have had this done since her parents' time,' Chance said. 'Take the bathroom, Godwin. Eyes peeled for anything of interest.'

'Yes, sir.'

'I can already feel the egg on my face,' Chance murmured as the door closed. 'She wouldn't keep the knife, Wilf. And she doesn't strike me she's going to crack. No pun intended.'

'The beach and surrounding streets were searched next morning.' Bishop opened a cupboard as he spoke. 'Mr. Dawson would have heard her on the shingle if she'd thrown the knife in the sea. She wouldn't have taken the time. Every instinct would have been to get back here. Where could she have disposed of it? In my experience men discard weapons. Women hide things.'

'She didn't use it again.'

Chance eyed the furniture. The room was considerably neater than the office had been on their first visit. There were few places to hide anything. It seemed ridiculous to feel down the back of an arm-chair or behind the books on their shelf.

'These must be her late father's,' Bishop said. 'Funny hand-shake brigade.' Metal chinked as he went efficiently through a drawer. 'Honestly, the way they get themselves up. Ever been asked to join?'

'No,' Chance said shortly. 'Nor likely to be.'

'Now we've seen the layout, Miss A.'s alibi was safer. If anyone tapped on her door, she could easily say she never heard from the bathroom. I was imagining it straight off a passage.' Bishop paused as Chance didn't answer. 'Anyway who would, short of a fire?' The guests wouldn't bother her up here and they'd been with her all evening. There was only Mrs Thompson and she wouldn't disturb Miss Aldridge in her bath unless they had an emergency. It was a good illusion of an alibi.'

'What?' Chance sounded distracted.

Bishop sighed, his face sympathetic. 'We went through it. You see someone coming out of their rooms in their dressing-gown, going for a last cuppa to take to bed. They'd told you they were having a bath. Well you wouldn't dream they'd run the water, slipped out and murdered someone, would you? The mind sees what it expects to see.'

'Did you notice that flight of stairs we passed, leading down on the right?'

'What about them?'

'They aren't the back stairs. They must lead to the side door on Brunswick-street. The way Dawson went that night.'

Bishop straightened up, surveying the rest of the room. 'Handy if you wanted to slip over the road without going out through the front entrance. I'll see how Godwin's getting on.'

Searching the bedroom was a task Chance didn't relish. A heavy dressing-table in the window cut out much of the light and a great wardrobe dominated the wall opposite the bed. Rifling through someone's personal things, particularly a woman's, was deeply unpleasant but it couldn't be shirked. He started on the drawers.

The wardrobe stank of mothballs. A fur took up one end, beaver he thought. Getting on his knees, he felt around the bed-stead where a knife could in theory be lodged. Nothing. An old tin hat–box under the bed was empty.

'Anything?' Bishop reappeared in the doorway.

'Not a dickey-bird,' Chance said glumly.

'Godwin drew a blank. Shall we try the office?'

'What about the attics or the outbuildings? She could have stowed the knife in a guest-bedroom.'

'Not there, too much risk of being found. Let's not give up yet.'

Godwin glanced at him as they went downstairs, looking like a polite nephew, solicitous about the old buffer. As for Bishop, Chance reflected, he had the manner of a cheery sergeant nannying an incompetent officer through the trenches. The whiff of failure hung about the venture.

The only places in the office where anything could be hidden were the roll-top desk and the safe. There was little room to manoeuvre. Chance leant impassively against the wall with his arms folded while Bishop searched the desk. Godwin stood by the table, looking as though he'd rather be elsewhere.

Turning round, Bishop shook his head very slightly. He held up the keys. 'This one's for the safe, I should think.' They watched him open the heavy door. A bag of coins and a few banknotes, a large envelope and on the shelf above, a slim jeweller's case.

'What's in the envelope?'

Bishop opened the flap and partly pulled out the contents. 'Looks like a copy of her will and a few share certificates.' He replaced them and without being asked, opened the case. Holding it up, he showed them a string of pearls before putting it back.

'So Warrender didn't bleed her quite dry,' Chance said.

'What do we do now, sir?'

He could always resign. Miss Aldridge had given in too easily. She was confident they'd find nothing.

'Take her in for questioning, Godwin.' Moving swiftly, he threw open the door. Ivy Betts was outside.

'What is it, Miss Betts?'

'Miss Aldridge was wondering if you've nearly done, sir?'

'Did she send you to ask us?'

Ivy shook her head vigorously. 'No, she told me to go and have a peek.'

'Where is Miss Aldridge now?'

'In the dining-room, filling up the cruets.' Adjusting a hair-pin on her bandeau, she grinned at him.

'All done here?' Chance raised his eyebrows at Bishop. 'In that case we'll have a word with Miss Aldridge now.'

They followed Ivy back through the hall, where an unappetising smell was starting to taint the air.

'Liver and onions.' She wrinkled her nose, making Godwin smile.

Chance's mouth was set in a hard line as he led the way in the dining-room. Miss Aldridge was facing the door, sitting at the table where he'd interviewed Ivy.

Salt and pepper pots stood about the table like miniature nine-pins. Ignoring them, she continued filling a salt cellar. Her hand shook a little.

'Oh, Miss,' Ivy darted forward. 'You don't want bad luck. Throw a pinch over your shoulder.'

She received a look of such malice that Chance almost expected the girl to flinch.

'My keys.' Miss Aldridge held out her hand to Bishop. He placed the wands in her palm, carefully not touching. Her fingers closed over them. 'I won't ask if you found what you sought. I warn you, Inspector Chance. I intend to lay a formal complaint against you.'

'That's your prerogative, madam.'

'Now perhaps you'll all leave my premises.'

'When we've finished, Miss Aldridge,' Chance said. 'Do you have anywhere else in the hotel where you keep your things? The attics for instance?'

'You're wasting your time and mine. The attics are swept and empty. Ivy here will tell you. See for yourself if you wish.'

Pushing back her chair, she stood. Her indifferent tone convinced him there was no point.

'What about down here? This is a large building. Surely you stow things somewhere to save you constantly running upstairs?'

He was the one running out of things to say. They had to take her in or leave but instinct told him to stay put.

This time she spoke stiff-lipped with barely supressed impatience. 'All my possessions are kept in my private quarters and my office. Both of which you've invaded. I am not in the habit of leaving things lying around. Preparations are underway for the residents' luncheon. My guests will be in. I insist that you leave.' Miss Aldridge directed her last sentence at Bishop.

There was a small stifled sound. 'Yes, Miss Betts?' Chance swung round to Ivy. 'What were you about to say?'

'Nothing really, sir.'

'Don't be shy. You went to say something but thought better of it.' She'd opened her mouth to speak and dried up at a look from her employer.

'It's only that you left your sewing box in the residents' lounge, Miss Aldridge.'

'Kindly stop interfering, Ivy. You shouldn't even be here. Cook will be needing you.'

'Yes, miss.'

Before she could disappear, Chance held up a hand.

'Hold on, Miss Betts.' He hadn't mistaken a flash of fear, quickly gone from the other woman's eyes. 'Show us, will you?'

'In here, sir.'

The three of them followed Ivy Betts across the wide hall and through the open door opposite. Miss Aldridge came last, reluctantly, he was sure.

No sign of the old lady. The lounge was empty though its habitual occupants had staked their claim. While they'd been at the Belvedere, the sun had broken through the clouds. Light fell on *The Times*, folded on the arm of an easy chair by the nearest window. Knitting needles poked in a ball of puce wool were stuffed down the side of a sofa cushion. A used ash-tray shared a side-table with an abandoned game of patience. To Chance the long room seemed as staged as a play when the curtain went up.

Ivy moved behind a sofa and picked up a large wooden sewing box, setting it down before them without comment. She glanced at her employer with the face of someone who knows they're storing up trouble.

'Might as well take a look,' Bishop said breezily. 'Just to be thorough.' The interior swung out, revealing shallow trays of cotton reels and other bits and bobs.

'I must protest at this further invasion of my privacy. This is ludicrous.' Stepping forward, Miss Aldridge clenched her hands. 'I insist you leave my home. You're making utter fools of yourselves.'

'Don't worry on our account, ma'am,' Bishop said, moving a pair of scissors. 'Hullo, this lifts right out, does it? Leaving a hidden compartment.' He moved the bottom tray aside and contemplated in silence the space beneath. 'Sir?'

Chance came to see over his shoulder. Miss Aldridge lunged at Ivy with her hand raised.

'You filthy little guttersnipe…'

'I don't think so.' In a single stride, Chance grasped her wrist.

'What did I do?' White-faced, Ivy stared at them, her mouth gaping.

Colouring, Godwin obeyed Chance's nod and moved close to Miss Aldridge's other side. She stood rigid between them, her breathing shallow. They all watched as Bishop produced a white handkerchief and gingerly picked up an object by its metal handle.

Sunlight illuminated the dust motes moving in the air. Touched the fleck of hissed spittle as Ivy went to wipe her cheek and glinted on the narrow blade.

Twenty-eight

'What are you up to, skulking out here?'

Eddie Chance looked up, his hands full with cigarette, cup and saucer. 'Oh hullo, Bob. Having a quick breather. I didn't feel like the canteen. Needed some air.'

'Not charged your suspect? I thought your lot would be celebrating.'

Chance took a comforting gulp. The colour of brick despite plenty of milk. Hot and sweet, the way he liked it. 'Soon, we're not done yet.'

'How's it going?'

'The doctor's checking her over to be on the safe side. She worked herself up spewing venom and Bishop didn't like the look of her. Thought she was going to have a seizure. She confessed to both murders. Seems to think she was perfectly justified. Refuses a solicitor.'

Inspector Forrest leant against the yard wall, watching a large uniformed backside stuck out from under a bonnet. He grinned as a spanner clanged to the ground. The constable cursed, glancing at them as he sucked his knuckles.

'I gather you found the weapon in the end? My lads did all that searching for nothing?'

'The knife was her father's. His initials were on the handle. She didn't dare throw it away.'

'Is she insane?'

Chance shook his head. 'Who knows? Legally not, I'd say. The murders were premeditated. She's talked us through the first one. Proud as punch of her cleverness.'

'How did she do it?'

'She arranged to meet her blackmailer in the shelter, late in the evening. Ran a bath, slipped over the road in the dark, stabbed him and was back indoors, no one the wiser. Then she waited behind a door until she could hear her cook about to come upstairs. Pulled the plug so the woman could hear the bath emptying and makes sure she's seen in her dressing-gown, ponging of bath salts.'

'Devious. What about the land-lady?'

Chance grimaced. 'We're just getting to that.'

He looked down at a blasted fly, dead in his tea. Never saw it coming. He hoped it had been quick for Mrs Simmonds.

'Marden will be sorry she missed this. Women.. eh? Always in the way when you don't need 'em, never around when they'd be of some use.'

Chance splashed the remains of his cup over the cobbles. 'She's been looking peaky ever since she found the body.'

'They're unreliable.'

'Godwin said she'd gone down with the 'flu.'

Forrest grunted. 'Her neighbour called in with a message. She's not a bad worker for a woman.'

'She knocks spots off most constables.' He must be going soft in his old age.

'Talking of unreliable, you're welcome to keep Richards. I'll put a bow on him if you like.'

'Ta, very much.'

'I must get on. Someone's peddling knocked-off electrical goods round town by the way. I'll see it gets on your desk. You can treat the missus.'

'You're a regular tonic, Bob.'

Chance smiled wearily as he followed him in the door. His opposite number in uniform was a likable chap, if quick to take umbrage.

He spotted Bishop coming along the passage. Pulling faces as he ran his tongue round the edge of his plates.

'The doc says she's fine to go on.'

'I'm glad it wasn't Wheeler.'

'Too busy with his private patients this time of day. They pay more than we do. Ready to hear the rest?'

'If we must. At least we'll get home on time tonight.'

When they were seated opposite Miss Aldridge again, Bishop resumed the questioning. He glanced at a list in his note-book before looking up at her.

'You've described your interview with Leslie Warrender on Tuesday the 3rd, Miss Aldridge. Previously you denied meeting him the next day at the National Provincial Bank in the High Street. Did you in fact do so?'

She sat calmly now, shoulders back, spine rigid. Chance pictured her as an ungainly child being taught deportment with a book on her head.

'Does it matter? I've told you I stabbed him.'

'We like to clear up loose ends.'

'Very well.' Her folded hands tightened. 'He said he'd return the next day when I'd had time to get more money. I was desperate to keep him out of my home. If any of my guests saw him, I didn't know what he'd say. Instead I suggested he met me outside my bank. I said I'd instruct them to sell my remaining shares and they'd let me have the balance the next morning.'

'I see.' Bishop made a tick by his list.

'Had you decided to kill Warrender at that point?' Chance said.

'Of course not. My mind was in utter turmoil. I was frantic with worry. I took my knife with me that night for protection because I was frightened of him. it was an accident, I only meant to threaten him. Make him leave me alone.'

No one likes blackmailers. Chance could see that going down quite well with the jury, except for one thing.

'Tell us about Mrs Lilian Simmonds,' Bishop said abruptly.

Her face shuttered. 'I don't see the point in going over every little detail. I'm very tired.'

'Not much longer, Miss Aldridge. How well did you know Mrs Simmonds?'

'We attended the same congregation, St Luke's.' Bishop looked at Chance. 'She came to meetings of the Hoteliers' Association.' A disdainful sniff. 'Boarding-house keepers shouldn't be members in my opinion. She was a foolish woman.'

'So you knew her well enough to call at her house?'

Miss Aldridge smiled thinly. 'I had never had occasion to do so.'

'Until the night you murdered her.'

Bishop's mildly voiced remark lay on the table between them. Chance watched Miss Aldridge's throat work, though she said nothing.

Bishop waited before he pressed her. 'Tell us about that night.'

'I knew she was on the church committee. She was always putting herself forward, trying to ingratiate herself with people. Men as well.' She cleared her throat. 'I waited until after eight, knowing the vicar's wife is incapable of organising a meeting that doesn't run over.'

'How could you know Mrs Simmonds would be alone?'

'I couldn't be sure no one had turned up but I overheard her speaking to a man at the inquest. I sat next to them. She was encouraging him to go home on Friday morning and assuring him she'd be all right on her own all weekend.'

Bishop finished a sheet of paper and looked up. 'Why did you kill Mrs Simmonds?'

'Because she knew what my father had done, of course. I had no choice. Surely you can see that? I had to protect his reputation and my own good name. I couldn't live with people pointing behind my back. I'd have had to leave here. I couldn't start again at my age.'

Bishop's gaze slid away from her as he listened, up to the small window.

Chance watched them both. He wanted to be out under the sky again. The painted-brick walls felt claustrophobic.

The room was too quiet. Hidden away at the rear of the building, no sounds came through from the offices. He felt irrationally that he'd like to hear someone whistling or a door slam.

'Are you admitting you went to Mrs Simmonds's house with the intention of murdering her?'

'No, Sergeant. I am not. I went with the intention of finding out how much she knew. What happened.. she brought it on herself. She provoked me.'

'She didn't make you press a cushion over her face,' Chance said. 'We know that's what you did.'

Miss Aldridge fastened her gaze on a spot on the wall behind them. 'I was prepared to give her a chance but she was taunting me. The moment she saw me she was all smiles, inviting me in for a cup of tea, saying how pleased she was to see me. Like a cat with a mouse. Do you think I'd seen off one blackmailer to have my life ruined by a second?'

Bishop looked at him, his eyes questioning. Chance shook his head. He didn't know either.

'What made you think Lily Simmonds intended to blackmail you?' Bishop said.

'Because she knew about the arson,' Miss Aldridge said impatiently. 'You've been through this. Warrender told her why he was here. She said to me that night that they were much more than land-lady and boarder. The stupid woman started snivelling. She wanted to die. It was obvious. She told me she'd taken some sleeping pills.'

'A regular dose. It didn't mean anything of the sort. The lady had trouble sleeping.'

'She didn't struggle. Her life had little meaning. I did her a favour.'

A patch of skin either side of Bishop's mouth was white. 'What did you do afterwards?'

'There was very little to do. I placed the cushion under her head and arranged her on the settee. She already had her pill bottle on the table. I washed up my tea cup and rinsed out the pot so nobody would guess she'd had a visitor. I let myself out of the front door. Nobody saw me. If they had, I was taking a stroll to clear a headache.'

Chance leant forward. 'I don't understand, Miss Aldridge. Did Leslie Warrender tell you he'd confided in Mrs Simmonds?'

'He did not.'

'Then who told you Mrs Simmonds knew about your father's fraud and Warrender's part in it?'

Miss Aldridge studied him, a cold glint in her eyes. 'When you came to the Belvedere, you said Leslie Warrender confided in someone about his purpose here. You wouldn't tell me their name but I wasn't fooled. It was someone you'd interviewed. Not his sister. She said at the inquest she hadn't known Warrender was in Sussex. I could tell she was speaking the truth. I knew the Simmonds woman would have thrown herself at him. It had to be her.'

Bishop shifted on his chair. 'You're quite wrong.'

Ignoring him, Miss Aldridge smiled at Chance. 'So the answer to your question is... you did.'

Twenty-nine

Three months later

It wasn't a day for dying.

A summer morning in June. Not yet eight with the sun shimmering on a calm sea, the cliffs looking freshly white-washed and the sky paint-box blue. Deck-chairs stacked ready for the trippers who would tilt in rows along the shingle. Eddie Chance leant against the promenade railings and smoked.

No one else around except a solitary fisherman near the end of the pier. He'd left the house before breakfast. Partly to clear a thick head after an awkward evening spent in the Duke Of Sussex with Bishop.

He'd had the streets to himself, seeing only a milk-cart. Someone was watering the bowling-green as he skirted the park railings. The big marquees were going up for the town's annual flower show.

Ending up on the sea-front was rather like Vic picking a scab on his knee.

Bishop's voice telling him to let it alone. Stella carefully cheerful, concerned glances when she thought he wasn't looking. Not that she knew the half of it. The suggestion of a fry-up on a week-day morning. The tick of the mantelpiece clock sounding unnaturally loud as the hands moved nearer the hour.

He would chalk it up to experience. That was all anyone could do. They'd been to the Duke, the two of them, that evening back in March, when Dorothy Aldridge was finally in the cell.

Superintendent Hayes had congratulated him. The Chief Constable had wanted to see him the next morning for a pat on the back. A hearty handshake and a *Well done, Chance. Never doubted you'd see it through.* As though he'd saved the cricket match for the jolly old school.

You know, this case was all about assumptions, he'd said to Bishop. People assuming things and getting them utterly wrong. Mrs Simmonds thinking that Leslie Warrender was romantically interested in her. Poor old Arnold Freeman thinking she'd ever marry him.

Everyone had their day-dreams or their nightmares. Herbert Dawson took it for granted that Warrender was back to destroy his family. He was no better himself, Chance thought. He'd over-complicated everything. The first dog-walker appeared in the distance.

The beach was different from the way it had looked in March. The ticket booth by the pier entrance would be open for business later on. The summer show posters were new. Clumps of mauve flowers were sprawling among the pebbles as they did every year since he could remember. No idea what they were. The promenade urinals were being mopped out.

He'd picked up the clues to the Dawsons' past, he'd give himself that much. Though he'd been convinced Freeman's knife was the murder weapon. The murderer had made the worst assumption of all.

It wasn't your fault. Forget it, Bishop had said.

The town hall clock struck the hour and began to chime distantly through the streets. You're not responsible for the ideas a madwoman gets in her head. Chance looked at his wrist-watch. The bill-board outside the newsagent, *Tennysham Double Murderer To Hang Today,* was already out of date.

Up on the pier the fisherman surveyed the morning scene. Already the best part of the day was over. The first dog was bounding along the shore, same as usual. Soon there'd be more people about. The peace of having the place to himself all gone.

The man on the sea-front wasn't a regular. He'd taken a last look towards Eastcliff, then he'd tossed his cigarette-end over the railings, tightened his neck-tie and walked off along the promenade. Striding off for another day at work, his jacket over a shoulder. The fisherman envied him as he began to dismantle his rod. They weren't biting though that wasn't really what being there was about.

He'd take an amble along the tide-line before he went home to an empty house. You never knew what might be washed up or lost. Coins fallen out of trouser pockets were commonplace, though further up where the deck-chairs were.

The wife had liked him to bring home shells. A few months back he'd even found a drink flask. Worth a bob or two, not water-stained and still smelling of spirits. He was saving it for winter mornings.

It was surprising what you found on the beach.

About Our Books

We've have published two Inspector Abbs mysteries set in Victorian England, A Seaside Mourning and a novella A Christmas Malice. John is also the author of The Shadow Of William Quest, Deadly Quest, Balmoral Kill, Loxley and Wolfshead.

For more information about our books please visit our blog at www.gaslightcrime.wordpress.com

Printed in Great Britain
by Amazon

60255313R00220